JOURNEY
TO THE
TEMPLE
OF RA

DAVID P. TANGREDI

JOURNEY
TO THE
TEMPLE
OF RA

ISBN: 978-0-9893673-0-1

JANUARY 19, 2017 EDITION

PUBLISHED BY:
A FOOL'S INCLINATION PUBLICATIONS
AFOOLSINCLINATION.COM

PROLOGUE

M y Lord, if I may?" Seth peered into the great room and saw Ra reading from a book with golden pages.

"But of course, Seth. Please come in!"

"My Lord, it is almost time...I...I mean it is almost **Earth** time. The year prophesied is nigh."

"Yes, my son, I am aware."

"But...is...is everything on track?"

"Hmm, how do I explain? There isn't a schedule to these things —at least not precisely, but everything does work out perfectly, so by that measure, yes, everything **is** on track."

"Oh. I wasn't sure."

"Well, my son, sit with me and observe, but observe as I observe and you will see..."

PART I – THE MIDDLE EAST

0 – THE FOOL

A cool breeze tousled the young man's hair as he jumped down from the back of the wagon. He waved to thank the farmer who had brought him this far and strolled down the road towards the village. The Middle Eastern summers had a way of lasting too long, but then a beautiful September morning like this one came along and reassured the boy that his favorite season was indeed just around the corner. He had no inkling of what lay ahead, only an unyielding desire that propelled him away from the place he once called home. A shiver of excitement ran through him as he anticipated newfangled exploration.

The young traveler entered the village and was immediately struck by the vivid colors, aromas, and sounds coming from the shops. Both men and women were dressed in brightly dyed muslins of yellow, orange, and gold; an obvious contrast to his faded tunic, tan pants, and over-worn boots. The rich aromas of anise, coffee, and freshly baked bread tickled his nose. With a deep breath, he took in the pulse of life around him.

The strangely dressed boy approached the corner floral shop, which spilled into the street. He had never seen such intricate orchids, irises of blue, as well as purple, pink, and yellow. There were flowers he could not identify with perfumes that were not only sweet, but also intoxicating. The boy peeked into a crate full of lilies then paused to admire an assortment of roses. He reached out and hesitated before picking up a blush-red rose, gazing at it straight on and then from above. He closed his eyes and brought the flower up to his nose, drinking in its scent with a deep inhale. He then gently rubbed its pedals across his upper lip. He carefully replaced the flower and picked out another, following a similar routine.

The florist noticed the odd behavior through the window and eyed the boy suspiciously. He was actively assisting a customer, but kept the boy keenly within sight.

Employing all of his senses, the boy was aware of everyone around him. Although he had just arrived, he did not feel like a stranger. When someone new passed him by, he looked the stranger in the eye and greeted him or her with a nod, a smile, or a simple, "hello." This too struck the florist as unusual.

A woman, assembling a bouquet, perused a bin near the boy. As she selected blossoms to her liking, her young daughter watched the lad and began imitating his unique floral inspection. He picked up a yellow rose; she picked up a purple daisy. He held his rose out with an extended arm, and she stretched her arm in response. He drew the rose up to his nose with eyes closed, and she drew the daisy up to her nose with her eyes closed. Peeking through a half-closed eye, a smirk appeared across the boy's face, giving away his awareness of her.

In an attempt to entertain the little girl, the boy departed from his typical routine and began a silly dance, inspecting the rose in a most emphatic way. Finally, he tucked the stem behind an ear and began admiring his reflection in the window. He mimed combing his hair, stroking his eyebrows, and straightening an imaginary bow tie. The whole time, he eyed the little girl's reflection. Just as she began to imitate his motions, he quickly, and surprisingly, tossed his face in her direction, and what a face it was!

At first, the little girl was startled by his distorted expression, then yelped out a giggle and quickly covered her mouth. The foolish boy laughed audibly and knelt down to the girl's level and bowed, giving her the most formal of greetings.

The girl's mother had not been paying much attention, but caught the last of boy's performance and discretely giggled as well. She pretended not to notice, not wanting to make either of them self-conscious. In response to the show, she grabbed a white rose and a pink daisy and added them to her purchase, but kept them separate from her bouquet.

As the young man continued entertaining the little girl, he became aware that he had at least two admirers, although he never let on to the woman that he was cognizant of her attention.

The florist waved to the woman, letting her know that the bouquet was ready. The woman paid for it along with the rose and daisy. She tapped her daughter on the shoulder, indicating that it was time to depart. As they made way to leave, the young man greeted the woman with a nod and the woman held out the rose in response; she then handed her daughter the daisy.

The boy graciously accepted the flower and gave it his full attention as he had the others. He blew a kiss to the little girl, winked at her mother, and proudly placed the rose in the buttonhole of his shirt. The woman slowly and gently led her daughter away by the hand as both of them smiled over their shoulders at the silly lad.

Satisfied with his accomplishments, the boy nodded to the florist and continued on his way. He paused as soon as he realized that the clouds had parted from the sun for the first time that day. He held his face up to the warming rays in homage to the daystar.

The breeze shifted, placing the lad downwind from the bakery and in response, he deeply inhaled the delicious aroma. Without glancing left or right, the young man stepped off of the curb and headed directly across the street towards the bakery.

The florist, who continued to spy on the boy, shook his head in disbelief and smiled despite his lingering suspicions. *This boy is like a fool in love! He wanders the streets without a care in the world.*

The boy approached the bakery and smiled at the man who stood in the doorway. Unbeknownst to the young stranger, the baker had been observing him from across the way with a growing fondness. As the boy passed through the doorway, the baker was captivated by the boy's sparkle. His eyes were bright and beamed directly into the baker's. His teeth, which shone through his broad smile, were white and handsome. The baker guessed that the visitor could not be much older than twenty.

"Good morning, sir," the boy began, "what delicious scents you have created on this beautiful morning!"

Although his speech was stilted and his accent was indiscernible, the baker knew the young man was being sincere.

The boy examined the pastry case and continued, "What beautiful croissants, surely you have learned from the best chefs in France to have created such perfect specimens."

The baker blushed and felt silly for having been charmed by the boy so quickly. Still, he smiled appreciatively for the compliment. "Today, we are offering free samples, but to you my charming friend, I offer a whole croissant. Would you like one?"

The boy nodded repeatedly, uttering a, "please," and, "thank you," as the baker placed a croissant in his outstretched hand. He first admired it with his eyes and then his nose. Only after both had sufficiently been satisfied did the boy let his mouth partake. He took a bite and savored each mouthwatering chew.

The baker looked on, pleased, as he watched the boy enjoy his creation with complete satisfaction.

The young man took a second bite, chewed slowly, and then took a third. It wasn't until the fourth bite that he hummed at the pleasure in his taste buds. He turned and complimented the baker...and in perfect French: *"Monsieur Boulanger. Ça croissant, c'est très bien. C'est manifique!"*

The baker was speechless. He had not heard such beautifully spoken words since he had studied in France years ago. The poetry of the boy's words made him feel both nostalgic and proud. He was so impressed with the fine young man that he quickly prepared a bag with additional pastries and his finest bread and gifted them to him in thanks.

The boy smiled again; he was genuinely appreciative of the baker's generosity. He ate a second pastry, offered additional thanks, and then packed the rest in his satchel. He bid the baker farewell and departed. From the bakery he headed toward the center of town to carry on with his unplanned adventure.

Δ ▲ Δ

As enticing as the shops at the entrance of the village were, what greeted the young man as he entered the majestic town square was beyond his imagination. Along the perimeter, merchants had set up booths to sell a variety of goods. The nearest corner, and the busiest, housed a farmer's market where myriad fruits, herbs, and vegetables were sold. The lad joined the throngs and observed the women selecting pungent melons and sampling mint, turmeric, and other fragrant herbs. As the lad meandered, he enjoyed the multitude of colors and smells, and then became overwhelmed by them. He made his way toward the center of the plaza, passing booths of glittering pots and pans, and weavers with shawls of silk and cashmere.

Once the boy passed by the booths, he was able to see the square in its entirety. Directly in the center, a large fountain featured what he guessed to be a statue of Poseidon. The figure was frozen in time—battling a vicious water beast with his mighty trident. Water spewed out from behind and above, causing the muscular figure to glisten in the sunlight. Along the edge of the fountain sat a number of adults with children scurrying around them. Many of the youngsters were fixated on the characters who performed nearby: a juggler, a mime, and an acrobat. A fourth literally towered over the crowd. This performer traipsed about on three-foot stilts, operating a mechanical puppet.

The puppet commanded center stage. It resembled a giant green and purple dragon and gave the illusion that the performer was riding atop its back. It had wings that extended three feet on either side and would occasionally flap, ensuring that no child approach too closely from the periphery. A six-foot tail of green and black scales trailed behind and protected the performer's back. When the performer turned quickly, the dragon's tail would sweep out, occasionally catching one or two children by surprise and sending them off screaming. Extending out in front, and of primary interest to observers, was the long neck and ferocious head of the dragon.

The young man was as entranced by the dragon and puppeteer as the children were. "It's so lifelike," he observed. He was amazed by the way the puppeteer drew the children in and how they reacted. The dragon would sniff the air above the children and then examine one, first from a distance and then close up. Depending on the reaction, the dragon might favor the child and nuzzle the child's neck, or it might find the child a threat and open its mouth with a silent roar. At its worst, the dragon would snap or impishly steal a hat off of a child's head.

At one point, the dragon took up pursuit of a small group of boys only to encounter early signs of bravery. The boys withdrew at first, and then advanced, turning the pursuer into the pursued. The puppeteer soon found himself retreating into the fountain itself, splashing water on his makeshift hunters. Now it was the parents' turn to scream as they fled the spray. Once a path was cleared, the puppeteer leapt from the fountain and galloped out of the square; he quickly rounded a corner and was out of sight.

I – THE MAGICIAN

A fter the crowd dispersed, the young man noticed a solitary table in a distant corner. The rest of the square was busy with shoppers; by comparison, this booth seemed deserted. He wondered for a moment if he was merely imaging the table, since no one else seemed to notice it. He rubbed his eyes, but the image remained. Intrigued, he set off to investigate.

As the boy neared, he examined the robed figure standing behind the shimmering table. Despite the warmth, the man's hood was pulled up over his head. The hooded stranger stood with a wand in one hand, pointed skyward, while the long, crooked finger of his other hand pointed to the ground. The figure stood with his unseen gaze seemingly focused on something far away.

Why is he standing like that?—the boy wondered.

Like a fish on the end of a line, the young man found himself drawn toward the table; and once there, he notice various items arranged in a pattern. His eye was drawn to a hand-written sign in a simple script that read: Magician/Fortune Teller.

I've seen magicians before. The boy remembered a man in a wagon who had come to his village when he was a child. The man performed tricks with playing cards and made caged birds disappear and reappear. The figure before him bore no resemblance to the trickster in the wagon. *Tricks and slight of hand are for children, but fortune-telling? I certainly would like to know more about that*—the boy considered.

"Sir, I have no money, but I was wondering if you would share with me a bit of your knowledge in exchange for a portion of bread and some pastries. I am curious how you see into the future."

"I would be happy to share my knowledge with you, young man. We shall make a feast of your offering and I will supply drink." With that, the Magician pulled out two simple mugs from a trunk under the table and filled them with water from a metal pitcher. The boy reached into his satchel and pulled out the bag the baker had given him. He broke out a piece of bread for each of them and placed the pastries on the table.

Although the boy was anxious to ask questions, he sensed it was not the right time. He was intrigued with the man before him as they ate in silence.

The Magician remained focused on his food, hovering his hands over each piece before eating it. Only after completing the meal, did he look up into the boy's eyes and commence conversation. "Thank you, my friend. The pastries were divine. Did you enjoy them as well?"

"Yes, very much," replied the boy. "This whole day has been full of wonder. I have enjoyed every minute of it."

"Yes. It has been a gift indeed," the Magician said. "May I ask your name?"

"I am John. Pleased to meet you."

"I am happy to make your acquaintance, John. I see you have an innate understanding of the bliss of presence."

"Thank you, sir. May I ask you some questions now?"

The Magician nodded.

"I noticed what you were doing with your hands before taking a bite. Why do you eat that way?"

"First, allow me to ask **you** a question. When you receive a gift from someone, what is your response?"

"'Thank you.'"

"Exactly. Appreciation is a powerful response. However, it is even more powerful to be thankful **in advance**."

"In advance?" the boy echoed.

"Anticipation is a high form of prayer and manifestation. So, before eating, I thank the Universe for the deliciousness."

"But how do you know it will be delicious? Sometimes food doesn't taste as good as it looks."

The Magician sat up in his chair. "John, there is much to learn about the workings of the Universe."

John considered the statement. "If there's a lot to learn, where does one start?"

The Magician looked at John. He looked beyond the youth's innocent gaze and into his soul. "The success of any endeavor begins in the present."

"The present? But I feel disadvantaged. I've been on my own for a long time, so I haven't had as much schooling as most."

"It doesn't matter where you've been, only where you are and where you want to be. Mindfulness and presences will show you the way. This is an astute way to live. By emulating the Fool, we allow the abundance of life to be presented to us moment-by-moment. We develop trust that we will always be taken care of because we permit the Universe to choose what experiences to give us and when. This leads to everything we desire."

Everything?—the boy wondered.

"Yes, even when it fails to appear that way."

Surprised that the Magician had read his mind, John asked, "Even when things go wrong?"

"Even then. Most men do not reach that level of understanding. But you, Master John, you have the capacity."

John smiled at the compliment. "Do you really think so?"

"Yes. But first, let's consider the **other** ways men live. Look around. See those merchants over there? They live in what I will call the first realm of creation. They create with their hands. They work hard: they till the soil, plant seeds, and tend to their crops. They harvest their bounty and haul it to markets like these in order to earn a living. The farmers **believe** they can support themselves in this manner and therefore they do. They are hopeful that the weather will cooperate and are thankful when things turn out well."

"I come from a farm community and know many farmers," John offered.

"Then you know that when storms or pests lessen their yield, or when the markets devalue their crops, they often become angry and bitter. They may believe that their hard work was wasted, so they feel cheated. This first realm of creation is straightforward and most men believe that given enough effort, anything can be accomplished, but they also believe those efforts can be thwarted by misfortune."

John's face grew somber. "I've seen a lot of misfortune."

The Magician waved his hand over the table to distract the boy and went on, "Now, look here. You see how I have laid out these items? Each represents one of the four basic elements of the Universe. The cup, for example, holds **water**. Living things are primarily comprised of water and water covers most of the planet. Next to the cup is a wand, which can be fashioned into a torch for carrying **fire**. Fire is the most active element of the Universe. Here we have a sword, which slashes through the **air**. When an object is cut in half by the sword, air is placed in between the two remaining parts. Air surrounds and connects all of the other elements." He picked up a forth item. "And, finally, this is what is called a pentacle, a coin of currency. It represents the element of **earth**."

John ran his fingers through the dirt on the ground in front of him.

The Magician could see the young man was trying to sort out what he was hearing. "The coin is a symbol of physical **things** because we often exchange coins for them. Earth is the most stable of the elements."

The Magician reached into the flowerbed and grabbed a clump of dirt. He placed it on the table and, like John, swirled his fingers in it as he continued, "When one creates in the first realm, one is primarily working with earth. Since it is the most stable element, one must apply the greatest force to change it. That is why physical work is so strenuous. In the first realm, one is seemingly creating earth from earth, but we must also understand that the workings of the other elements are always at play. Wind and water erode the earth, and fire transforms it." The Magician then blew all of the dirt off of the table.

John nodded. "So how do we use the other elements?" he asked.

"First, we must understand that each element has a deeper meaning. Water characterizes **feelings**—such as love, hate, joy, and sorrow. Notice that when someone **expresses** their feelings, they cry tears of joy or tears of pain."

"And air?"

"Air corresponds to thought and communication. When we speak to each other like this, our words travel through the air. Most don't realize this, but even our thoughts travel through the air, leaving our minds after we think them."

"So earth represents everything that is physical. What does fire represent?" John asked.

"Fire, which is simply energy, is hidden within **everything**. When an object is burned, the energy hidden within it is released as more fire—namely light and heat. No matter what form an object takes, it is really only energy inside. Examine objects close enough, and you will never find matter, only movement and vibration. Fire also symbolizes spirit, the non-physical part of us that lives beyond the physical realm. Vibration **is** spirit. Spirit **is** energy. And energy **is** action. In ultimate reality, fire is all there is."

John was appreciative of the Magician's knowledge, but was eager to learn about his fortune. "So am I destined to live, as my forbearers, in the first realm?" he asked.

The Magician continued as if he had not heard the question. "Now, in the **third** realm, one creates without **trying**. Through trust in the divine, the Universe is allowed to bring what is most appropriate for our highest learning and our fastest evolution. This contrasts greatly to the first realm, where life can be strenuous, repetitive, and evolves slowly. However, the level of trust needed to live in the third realm is not easily attained or maintained. Luckily, there is another option."

"The realm in between the others?"

"Exactly! The second realm of creation is the realm of conscious, intentional manifestation. It is in this realm that one creates using all four elements together. Through discipline, thought (air) can be focused and directed toward that which is desired."

John raised an eyebrow in question.

"For example," the Magician said, "if I want to acquire a piece of furniture, I can visualize it. I can imagine using it, or picture it in my home. I can do this to attract events and experiences just the same. If I desire the pleasure of dancing with a beautiful woman, I can fantasize about it in my mind."

John frowned with skepticism, "I've pictured things that never happened."

The Magician cut in before John's frustration expanded. "Yes, and the journey is not over. As you have experienced, air alone is not sufficient to complete the manifestation; it is only the beginning. It **is** good to consistently direct one's mind toward what is desired over what is feared, but to create…one must also **feel**. Emotions provide the power of attraction needed for manifestation. For example, feelings of gratitude **in advance** of a desired experience are significant and powerful. Gratitude is, of course, only one of many positive emotions that work in this regard."

"So I need to **feel** it before I experience it?" John asked.

"Allow me to explain. What I feel when I imagine an experience is what will be most easily felt when the experience actually manifests. And remember, this works in both directions. If you feel strong fear, fixated on something dreaded, that emotion draws the unfortunate experience into your life. That is why discipline of mind is so important. But do not worry. Fear is not as powerful as joy. And of course, there is also the element of fire. Passion is beyond watery feeling; it is a demonstration of **intent.**"

"I have wanted many things, but I don't think I've ever felt passion," John admitted.

"Passion is more than mere desire. Passion originates from the soul," The Magician explained, "…and inspired action is a spark that ignites creation."

"I can tell you are a very passionate man," John said.

The Magician smiled at the boy's observation. He could tell the young man really wanted to comprehend what he was hearing. "Fire can also burn away inappropriate beliefs. At times, we lack faith in our situation, or ourselves. Spirit can help us overcome these obstacles. Belief in God, deities, the higher self, or guides and angels (all of which are pieces of God) can transform our denser vibrations, thus paving the way to our desired manifestations."

John did not consider himself a religious person. He understood the Magician's explanation of passion, but comprehending this aspect of fire would require more pondering on his part. He was relieved that the Magician was willing to share his knowledge without any expectation of comprehension or response.

"And lastly," the Magician said, "there is earth. Everything that we see is wrapped in earth and therefore we must always acknowledge its part. It is through our physical interactions that we demonstrate willingness, which is necessary to keep things moving. When our faith is great, effort is not needed. However, some interaction **is** required, even if it is merely to reach out and accept that which is given."

"So do you use the elements to create your magic?" John asked.

"My **magic** is not really magic at all. I merely recognize the workings of the Universe and thus have learned to create my part of it more consciously."

"What about the fortune-telling?"

"That, my boy, is nothing more than careful observation paired with a developed intuition. When I look at someone, I examine their expression and emotion to see what they are attracting. A wise teacher once said: 'To know about your past, look to your present. To know about your future, look to your present.'"

The boy furrowed his brow.

"Your past created your present, so all that you have in the present came from your past thoughts, feelings, and actions. In the same way, looking at what you are thinking, feeling, and doing in your present will reveal what lies ahead."

It was obvious to the Magician that the boy was still uncertain of this claim. "I will use you as an example. Observing your charming, candid, and whimsical nature, I am guessing that you have received a few gifts along the way here this morning." As the Magician said this, he brushed the rose in John's lapel with the back of his finger.

John nodded his consent.

"Therefore, you see, from your present, I can see your past. As for your future? Witnessing your thirst for knowledge, your attention on the present, and your ability to ask for what you seek without hesitation, tells me that you are commencing a journey that will bring you to many places; introduce you to new friends and teachers; and reward you with much love, joy, and wisdom. I sense that the Universe has brought you to me because it is now expanding your awareness and preparing you for that journey."

All the uncertainty left John's being. He suddenly felt confident. And while he had felt content throughout the day as he interacted with others, he now felt an additional emotion...excitement. "I assure you, Mr. Magician, I am ready for whatever the Universe has in store for me."

The Magician looked at the horizon and the sun not too far above it. He began gathering the items from the table and placing them in the trunk. "In that case, John, would you like to partake in a full moon ceremony this evening? We are gathering at my home and it would please me to have you as my guest. Are you interested?"

"I am honored by your invitation. This will be a new experience for me."

"Then you are in for a treat!"

John helped the Magician dismantle his booth and then followed the man across the square and back to the road where he had earlier in the day met the florist and the baker. All the shops were now closed except for one. John followed the Magician inside where the elder purchased candles and incense. After thanking the shopkeeper, they were back on the road, walking in silence. Considering the abundant conversation in the square, John was a little surprised that they hardly spoke during the walk, but was not disappointed. He was used to being by himself. As they walked, he silently enjoyed the scenery they passed.

When they reached the Magician's home, John observed that others were already busily preparing a feast. The Magician decided to forestall introductions until dinnertime.

The smells emanating from the kitchen were intoxicating to John. His only sustenance all day was the bread and pastries from the baker. Not only was he looking forward to a good meal, and curious about the ritual, he also anticipated a comfortable night's sleep on a **real** bed.

As if reading his mind, for a second time, the Magician directed him to the guest room and suggested that John rest up while he helped the others finish with the preparations. He offered John a towel and use of the washroom.

John bathed, changed into fresh clothes, and settled in for a brief rest. He tried to sleep, but his mind could not stop reflecting on his extraordinary day.

II – THE HIGH PRIESTESS

T he Magician peered in through the doorway and saw that John was awake.

"You look refreshed. Did you sleep?"

"I don't think so. But I do feel rested."

"Are you hungry?"

"Yes sir!"

"Good. The meal is ready. We've been blessed with a gorgeous evening. It is ideal since we will be dinning outside, awaiting the imminent rising of the moon. Come with me."

John followed the Magician through the house and out the back door where four others were gathered at a long table. Before sitting, the Magician introduced John to them: a man and three women, but offered no additional information about them. It took a bit of conversation for John to learn about each.

"Are you a magician too?" John asked the man.

"We are all magicians of our own lives," the man replied.

Based on the conversation John had overheard between the man and the Magician, it was obvious that the man was well versed in the concepts of the three realms.

"Well, then, are you a teacher like the Magician?" John asked

"We are all teachers," the man replied. He smiled and put down his drink. "But I am not a teacher like the Magician. I have learned to apply spiritual wisdoms to my work as a builder. I am blessed to be a successful businessman. I guess you can say that I am a teacher by example."

The women were more forthcoming about their work. Each in turn described and then demonstrated to John their specialty. The youngest, an intuitive who worked with crystals and flowers, went first. She splayed out an array of stones on the table and arranged a single row of vials behind them. Then she instructed: "John, select a stone that appeals to you."

John hesitated, mesmerized by their brilliance.

"Go ahead, touch them, pick them up, **feel** their energy."

Following her prodding, John fingered the gems. Some were beautiful to look at, while others were soft to the touch. For a moment, he felt self-conscious at having to choose while the others watched. But then he found a simple looking black stone that was smooth and felt good in his hand.

The young woman motioned for John to place it in her hand.

He obeyed.

She closed her eyes for a moment and then shared her message. "The consciousness of crystals is difficult for us to understand. They seem lifeless and yet live far longer lives than we do. They witness eons of time and have an understanding of the cosmos beyond what we can even imagine."

John followed her lead and closed his eyes.

She continued, "This piece of Obsidian **sees** what lies just ahead for you. He has chosen to be your travel companion, but only for a season. He will leave when his work with you is done, just as he is leaving me now that his work with me is done. He invites you to hold him in your hand whenever you feel trepidation." She folded his palm around the stone.

John opened his eyes, as did the woman.

She looked into his soul. "He is a grounding stone and will help you feel more surefooted as you walk the earth. Spiritual work is important, but so is keeping one's feet firmly on the ground."

Then the young woman closed her eyes and allowed a particular flower to come to mind. When she reopened them, she scanned her collection until she found the appropriate vial. "This is the essence of Fawn Lily, here specifically to help spiritual people deal with the often-harsh aspects of life in physical form. If you ever feel the need to retreat from the outer world, but are unable to do so, place a few drops under your tongue twice each day until you feel centered. The Fawn Lily and Black Obsidian work well together."

John accepted the vial and the stone. However, before he had a chance to respond, the woman, older than the youngest, but younger than the oldest, began to speak. She was an herbalist and, as with the younger woman, she intuited an appropriate gift for John, explaining, "It is not uncommon for spiritual quests, as the one you are about to embark on, to be physically straining. In stretching your awareness, you'll be stressing your body, too. If at any time you feel your strength waning, you can stave off sickness with this Goldenseal. Take it each morning and evening until you feel rejuvenated."

Finally, it was time for the eldest of the women to speak. There was an aura of mystery around her and John could tell that there was a special aspect about her that the other two women did not possess. She was a psychic, an astrologer, and the High Priestess of her coven—she mesmerized John.

She began, "John, tonight is the lunar phase we call the **full moon**. It is furthest from the sun and illuminates the half of the earth that is otherwise bathed in darkness. Astrologically, the sun and the moon are in opposition, 180 degrees apart and residing in opposite signs. Since it is late summer, the sun is traveling through Virgo, and thus the moon is in Pisces. This watery full moon is sure to pull on everyone's emotions."

The others nodded at her proclamation.

"Look, there, just above the last of the light of day. Do you see those brightly shining stars?" she asked.

John nodded.

"They are, in fact, the planets Venus and Mars. Today they are in full conjunction, balancing their vibrations in the apropos sign of Libra, ruler of relationship. Here, Venus is in charge, but rather than fighting with her partner, she is putting him to good use, motivating us within our relationships, inspiring us to take right action for the purpose of creating harmony. And her work is timely…"

Without diverting her eyes, the High Priestess pointed directly above. "There, high in the sky, you will find Jupiter, the largest planet in our solar system. He is home in his sign of Sagittarius, where he is most auspicious, most jolly, and most expansive."

John followed her gaze upward, studying the sky.

She continued, "He enlarges everything he touches and today sits 90 degrees from both the sun and the moon. This configuration is called a T-Square and highlights tension and challenge. Being the one in the middle, it is Jupiter's counsel we must seek to resolve the conflict between will and emotion, between the mind and the heart."

John lowered his head and looked into her eyes, but remained silent as she continued to speak.

"Today, we are urged to smile at hardship, to laugh in the face of adversity," she said. "Discord, after all, is only an illusion and exists simply to serve us by expanding our awareness and prodding us along our journeys. John, you **do** understand that your presence here is not by accident, don't you?"

John nodded, but was unsure why. Her words, her impish smile, her stare sent a shiver through him.

The occultist continued, "Two weeks ago, on the night of the new moon, I had a vision. I was meditating during the setting sun and my guides appeared before me. They told me that by the full of the moon, I would be presented a Libra child, one with Sagittarius rising and moon in Pisces. Today, you see, is your lunar return—the full moon is visiting the same spot it occupied when you were born. Venus and Mars are transiting your natal sun, and Jupiter sits on your Ascendant. This is an initiation, commencing an extended journey of spiritual awakening for you. They told me to design a ritual specifically to prepare you for that journey—a journey that can lead to your life's purpose."

"My life's purpose." John mouthed the words without uttering a sound.

"John, I did not share this with the others, but I have been expecting you. The moment I looked into your hazel eyes, I knew you were the Libra boy I was waiting for. I had my sister create a special potion and with your permission I would like to present it to you now. Do you trust us? Do you trust the Universe to guide you on this journey?"

Again John nodded without consciously choosing to do so. He shivered—partly from nerves—partly from excitement. Even so, he felt safe. He trusted these generous, albeit unusual, people. And most importantly, he **was** ready to embark on this **quest**. John placed his hands out to accept what was offered.

"This potion is powerful and disorienting, but John, do not fear; you are safe and supported. Are you ready?"

John nodded a third time and bowed his head in thanks. He knew intuitively to drink the full amount, and although the taste was bitter, he immediately felt a pleasant warmth travel down his throat.

Just then, John noticed the light of the moon peeking above the horizon. As the moon rose higher, so did the effects of the potion. He began to **feel** the moonlight touch his skin, its size larger than he had ever seen before. It seemed to be alive and with a facial expression as if it was communicating with him.

John was transfixed. He couldn't stop staring at the moon. He heard sounds, but couldn't make out what they were. Things seemed to fly passed him. Voices spoke to him as if announcing themselves from the middle of an invisible crowd. His sight blurred, but his hearing grew acute. Every little sound caught his attention: leaves rustling in the breeze, water running in a spring, air moving into and out of his lungs, his heart beating formidably.

From somewhere in the ether there was music and it drew him in. He could distinguish each instrument: a wooden flute, a violin, and at least three discrete drums. Then the drumbeat grew and commanded the majority of his attention; his body, of its own accord, followed the beat. His arms lifted as if gravity had disappeared, and they danced like snakes under the influence of a charmer. His eyes closed and his head fell back. Suddenly, he had the sensation of lying down; *or am I now standing?*

He felt hands on his back, supporting him, his body floating, as if dozens carried him on their fingertips. He felt more relaxed than he could ever remember feeling before, and more at home than anywhere.

He opened his eyes and was looking up at the stars. He saw Jupiter; it seemed close enough to touch, his hands reached up in an attempt to do so. The bright planet remained evasive, just out of reach. He did not catch it; instead, it passed right through, as if his hands were invisible; its presence, however, penetrated his entire body.

The stars began to move. His thoughts seemed separated from his body, as if he was watching himself from above. *I'm floating... on that brook? No, I feel dry, and warm...heat...from where? Oh that crackling of fire, but where did the fire come from?*

The music shifted and now there was chanting: male voices toning low, a female voice trilling high. He was reminded of a bird, fluttering overhead. *There it is...over there.* In his vision, it was the middle of the day and the bird danced as if wooing a mate. The voice rose, and the bird rose. The voice fell, and the bird fell with it. The voice glided, and the bird glided in perfect synchronization.

And then...the singing faded, replaced by a deep, resonating oration. The voice was telling a story, was telling **him** the story of his life...*my life?...a previous life?*

You have been here before...many, many times before. These people, around you, have studied with you before. They recognize you as their teacher. Yet this time, they are here to teach you. They came in advance to help prepare the way, to ready you for this journey, a journey you have been planning for eons.

He saw himself in robes. He saw himself standing at an altar. He saw himself speaking from a pulpit. He saw himself writing on scrolls. He saw his reflection in a pond, in a puddle, in a bowl of water. Staring back, he saw a bearded old man, a woman with long gray hair, a young girl with skin as dark as the night, each with **his** eyes and **his** smile. They knew him; they were a part of him; and now they surrounded him. They smiled as if they missed him, as if he was **their** child who had come home after a long time away.

And then a different face appeared...one with the eyes of the High Priestess. He heard her voice, but her mouth did not move. She reached out and held his hand, leading him up, or out, or in some direction he could not identify. He was guided forward, but could no longer see the High Priestess in front of him.

Instead, he saw a large ball of fire spinning like a top. It was pulled and stretched until a large chunk broke free. The chunk rotated around the ball, spread out and then burst into a collection of small spheres. The orbs cooled and then one glowed with blue light. It had a large brown spot that gradually turned green, first near the edges and then in the middle. The sphere grew and the spot took shape. It looked like an island floating on the water. It **was** an island, but then pulled apart, forming continents that drifted away from each other as the sphere grew larger.

The water became clear and John saw creatures swimming within it. First there were jellyfish, then eels, and then fish with fins. Trees grew on the land and frogs hopped out of the waters toward them. Snakes and lizards followed. The lizards grew larger and larger, and then elephants replaced them, but ones with long brown hair and large tusks. Strange dogs appeared, and then cats, hogs, and horses. There were apes and then odd-looking hairy men. The men roamed the land in groups, much the way the animals did, except they built fires and huts.

In a flash, John fell into the scene, watching it through the eyes of one of the men. The people around him looked normal now, but were wearing animal skins as clothing. Distant fires and thousands and thousands of stars faintly lighted the nighttime.

The stars began to form images. First there was a ram with spiraled horns and raring to charge, then a bull, massive and motionless. Next came a pair of young men, each with an arm draped over the other. The sky rotated and a crab came into view, crawling out of the ocean, then a lion fixing to roar. A woman stood elegantly in her glowing white gown, and then scales, teetering left and teetering right. A scorpion scurried, its tail curled mightily behind it, and a centaur—half horse, half man—cocking his bow and aiming his arrow. Next came a goat with the tail of a mermaid, followed by a man supporting the weight of a large urn. Lastly, a pair of fish swam in formation—then—again—the ram's head appeared, completing the cycle.

John could hear the High Priestess telling him about the Zodiac, explaining each sign and symbol. In a flash, he knew all about Astrology, and yet couldn't focus on any one aspect. He saw images, characters, personalities, and events. Once again, he saw the sun, and watched the fully formed planets spin around it, each moving through phases like the moon, and resonating like the strings of a harp.

He felt as if he were being given instructions and nodded when asked for permission. A group formed around him, he sensed but did not see them. He could not see the men and women from the Magician's house. Not even the High Priestess was among them. He felt a hand from each group member on his shoulders as they spoke to him in turn. They vowed their support and called him by names that he did not know, or could not remember.

The faces faded, and the voices followed. There was no longer sound or music. The heat of the fire dissipated and the chill of the night roused him to wakefulness.

John's mind returned to his body and he found himself sitting in a chair. His new friends stood around him. The youngest of the women held his hand and rubbed it gently. He felt the wood beneath him and the grass under his feet. He felt nauseous. *What was in that potion?*—he wondered

"Water…" he murmured.

He felt a cool goblet pressed into his hand. Three hands were on the goblet, which was raised to his lips. His hand was one of them but was not yet fully under his control.

The taste of the water was refreshing, but his stomach was still unsettled. His mind was waking, but his body was falling asleep. His arms felt heavier with each passing moment. The men lifted him and helped him along. He didn't recall entering the house, but realized he was then lying in bed. Each one kissed his forehead as his heavy eyelids drooped. Images of the day passed before him. At first he knew he was dreaming, but then he forgot. It was night, and then it was day. He was in a horse-drawn wagon and then the wagon became a boat and the forest became the sea…

Δ ▲ Δ

John woke with a dull ache in his head and his body was sore, as if he had labored the entire day before. He was familiar with the aftereffects of intoxication. But at the same time, he knew that what he had experienced was something quite different.

The herbalist sat in a chair near his bed and pointed to the water on the nightstand. She handed him a capsule and told him that it would help relieve his headache and rejuvenate his body. She urged him to drink all of the water and then poured him some more. The youngest of the women walked into the room; she was carrying a dish with two slices of toast. One was coated with purple jam, the other with yellow. Both looked appetizing.

John swung his legs over the side of the bed and ate the toast, not the slightest bit self conscious at having an audience. He was actually pleased by the attention and wanted to ask questions about what happened the night before.

However, before he could speak, the High Priestess appeared in the doorway and gave him a penetrating stare. Her eyes told him to keep silent, and he understood from her gaze that he should not speak of his experience, but rather allow its mystery to work within him. She wanted him to understand that his journey was his alone and no one, not even she, could know even half it. John marveled at her ability to convey thoughts to him telepathically, and just as he formed that thought, she smiled impishly and nodded with acknowledgement.

The women rose, inviting him to follow. They escorted him into the kitchen where the men sat drinking coffee. The aroma was enticing and without needing to verbalize his desire, a steaming cup was placed before him. John glanced down at the mug and noticed that cream had been added. A quick sip confirmed that it had been sweetened to his liking. By now he was becoming used to the magic bestowed upon him and bowed his head in appreciation.

He thanked the Universe for a truly amazing experience.

III – THE EMPRESS

After breakfast, it finally dawned on John that the Magician and the High Priestess were husband and wife and the youngest of the women was their daughter. The sister of the High Priestess was married to the businessman. For a moment John envied this magical family, but he knew that it was not his path to live among them, at least not indefinitely. Even so, when the Magician invited John to remain with them for the next few months, John gladly accepted.

The Magician was not being altruistic. "In three months on the full moon, my daughter, Sara, will be married," he explained. "There is much preparation to be done. We could really use your help."

"I would be honored to be of service to you," John replied. "May I ask who the groom is?"

"The groom is none other than the Emperor himself and the wedding will be the feast of the decade. As you can imagine, this will not be an ordinary wedding!"

"Thank you sir, for your trust in me," John said. He was excited at the prospect of learning more from the magical family. Sara and he were about the same age and he hoped they would become friends.

The days passed. John felt the love and acceptance of a harmonious family. It wasn't too long before he and Sara were comfortable enough around each other to share a joke. He playfully began calling Sara: "The Empress." Although initially meant in jest, the name **did** suit her, he concluded, and not only because she was betrothed to the Emperor.

The more time John spent with the Empress, the more he learned about her special gifts. She had an aura of beauty he had never encountered before. And although her physical beauty was undeniable, it was her grace and creativity that set her apart. John was grateful for those afternoons when he was able to join her in the garden. She was a skilled horticulturalist and was growing all of the flowers that would adorn her wedding. Each bloom was nearing perfection, a feat, John came to understand, since autumn specimens were the most difficult to cultivate.

"Flowers," Sara had said, "are more than decorative; they can be used for healing." Sara then described to John the principals of homeopathy. One day she even walked him through the complete process of creating a remedy from an extract. Whenever she introduced John to a new species, she taught him how its essence functioned to help humans regain balance. Stones and crystals, he also learned from her, had the power to help people in various ways, for example to become more centered and to meditate more deeply.

The Empress was not only gifted with plants and flowers, but animals responded to her poise as well. Whether domestic or wild, all animals seemed to enjoy her company. The house pets followed her around more than any of the other members of the household, and they were content to sleep at her side while she worked. When she tended to her gardens, the butterflies, birds, and squirrels all seemed to come out to greet her.

Even the clouds part from the sun for her—John found himself thinking one afternoon.

It soon occurred to John that Sara gave nearly all of her creations away. "You make such beautiful things," John said, "Why do you not keep them?"

"Creating beauty makes me happy. But what is truly rewarding is sharing it with others," she explained.

"You are going to be an amazing wife and mother," John said.

"Thank you, John. What a wonderful compliment. The Emperor and I want as many children as the Universe will gift to us. I know the Emperor desires sons, but he will love our daughters just the same. He recognizes the power in both men and women. I am sure there are skills he will want to teach the children himself, but I also know that he respects me and will allow me to raise them, especially our daughters, as I see fit."

"As you have been raised," John observed.

"Exactly! Each woman must choose for herself the crafts most suited to her. Among the women in my family, there is no shortage of knowledge for them to learn from."

Inspired by the Empress, John began some creative pursuits of his own. He would rise early in the morning and perform his assigned chores while the days were cool. Later in the afternoon, when the heat rose, he would find a spot of shade and write poetry or sketch pictures in his journal. He wanted to create a wedding gift for his new friend and each day he would sketch or write with the hopes of creating something appropriate.

At the same time, John was discovering more about himself and his innate nature. He realized that when he was in the presence of someone special; their energy rubbed off on him. For example, the more time he spent with the Empress, the more creative and inspired he became. John shared another connection with Sara: both were crossing the threshold of significant change in their lives. In his journal he drew a picture of a beautiful shrub in full bloom being transplanted from a small garden to a large ornate landscape in front of a castle. Underneath it he wrote the title: The Empress.

IV – THE EMPEROR

As the wedding neared, the Empress spent more of her time preparing for the occasion. One day she approached John with a question, "My preparations at home are almost complete. Would you be willing to work with me at the palace? It is time for me to collaborate with the Royal Family."

"Will I be meeting the Emperor?" he asked.

"Of course," Sara smiled.

John was nervous. The Emperor, John had learned, was known throughout the land for his commanding persona. He may have received his position through birthright, but there wasn't a man for miles who would challenge him for it. John hoped in his duties that he would make the Empress proud of him.

The first day John saw the Emperor, he was immediately struck by the man's presence. He was masculine and spoke with a deep, powerful voice. At six feet, the Emperor wasn't as tall as John expected. Many of the military men marching throughout the palace were taller. Yet, when these men stood next to the Emperor, it was as if they lost any height advantage. They seemed to shrink to mere obedient boys in comparison to the authority of his leadership.

Although John was nearly the Emperor's height, he was not built like a soldier. He was aware of this difference and the confidence he had gained in the presence of the Empress began to wane. The grandiose environment of the castle, the stature of the military men, and the commanding authority of the Emperor intimidated him, and made him feel like a child. Sara noticed the change in her friend.

The Empress, on the other hand, remained self-assured in the presence of her fiancé, and although surrounded by his advisors, she did not hesitate and walked right up to him. He immediately gave her his full attention. The Empress stood on her tiptoes to whisper in his ear, and the Emperor turned his gaze toward John in response.

The Emperor dismissed the men he had been meeting with previously and continued by himself down the hallway.

Sara approached John, who stood alone, agape, and confounded. "He wants to have a chat with you—with us—in his quarters. Are you ready?"

John shivered as if a cold breeze blew in through the windows. He remained speechless and gave a tentative nod. The Empress smiled and gave him a reassuring hug.

Sara wanted to say she found endless enjoyment in the ways of men and their sometimes fragile egos, but instead simply said, "I know you see men cower at my fiancé's presence, but let me tell you about the real man underneath. He is as gentle and loving a man as you will ever meet."

"I am sure that is true...where you are concerned," John said, "but I am merely a stranger."

The Empress wished she could tell John everything she knew. If she could, she would tell him that even the Emperor knew fear and discomfort, and that at times he depended on her and her strength to help him remain courageous and focused. John would never believe that occasionally, **she** was the one who barked the commands. Instead, she simply held John close and whispered, "The Emperor is going to love you as I do." She took a step back, looped her arm through his, and led him down the hallway.

When they entered the Emperor's assembly chamber, John was awestruck by the immense size of the room. Everything around him appeared oversized. The Emperor sat in the largest chair John had ever seen. Etched into the armrests was a daunting set of lion heads, which stared out from beneath the Emperor's brawny hands. The throne looked as if it had been carved from a single, massive piece of granite. It had been fitted for comfort with leather that was dyed a rich shade of burgundy. John had a hard time diverting his eyes from the imposing figure before him.

As large as the room was, it was austere. Only four chairs faced the Emperor's throne. Each was constructed of oak with ornately forged iron backrests, representing the signets of the kingdom. The seats were cushioned and covered with deep brown leather, muted colors that contrasted with the vibrancy of the throne. John noticed that behind and around the chairs, was ample room for others to stand. He tried to imagine the meetings that must have taken place in this room. He pictured some of the lands' most powerful men sitting in the chairs, each surrounded by his best knights.

Two types of artwork adorned the walls: weapons retired from days of old and artifacts from distant lands, mostly tapestries. Huge silver sconces illuminated the room. The Emperor watched the young man as he scanned the room. He smiled at the boy's obvious wonder and fondly recalled Sara's description of him: *He is adorable. His innocence is the most genuine I have ever seen. I guarantee you will smile in his presence.*

John's eyes finally found their way to the Emperor's and then immediately changed their expression. The Emperor marveled at how much information was conveyed by the boy's face. John opened his mouth to speak…then hesitated. He remembered it was respectful to speak only after being spoken to first.

"John, welcome. Your reputation precedes you. Apparently you have not only gained the affection of my fiancée," he gave Sara a tender smile, "you have won over her entire family."

John felt the color rising in his cheeks.

"It is my understanding that you are just passing through our great city. Where are you headed? Do you have a destination in mind?"

John was surprised. He did not expect to receive any of the Emperor's attention, but now, here he was, the topic of the discussion.

"Well, sir," John stuttered, "I…uh…don't have a destination."

"Are you intrigued by a particular direction: north, south, east, or west?" the Emperor asked, "What is your time frame?" The man had participated in many campaigns and knew the importance of a good plan.

"Well," John continued," I don't have a direction in mind and I'm not on a schedule either. I mostly just go when and where it feels right to go."

The Emperor raised an eyebrow.

John began to have doubts. *Here I am in front of a powerful and important man. Surely he must find me immature…or worse… irresponsible. Perhaps he is right: Am I avoiding life by wandering about? Is this an inappropriate life for a man?*

"John, I admire your bravery."

John looked up at the Emperor, astonished.

"I would not be fit for this chair, were I not well traveled," the Emperor explained. "When I was your age, I did not have the option to wander of my own accord; the military life was thrust upon me. In retrospect, I see that it was a life that suited me…but I also acknowledge I was not afforded any other choice." He signed. "At this stage in my life, I feel the weight of responsibility. My choices impact a great number of people."

"I do not envy your burden, sir."

The Emperor gave a faint smile. "I do not think many do. Some may covet my supposed power, my wealth, or my fame...but my responsibility? I do not think many desire that." He sighed again. "But I did not ask you here to tell you of my plight; I wish to know more of yours."

"My plight sir?"

"This lovely woman who you have recently befriended is not so easily impressed by the likes of men. Her admirations are more numerous with animals, plants, and children, yet she has not been able to stop talking about this carefree young man who has wandered into her life. I have no reason to be threatened by this new friendship, do I?"

Once again John blushed, he cheeks burned as the color rose in intensity.

The Emperor held his amusement inside, not wanting the boy to see that he was joking. He had not doubt as to Sara's loyalty, but wanted the boy to learn something about the world into which he was entering. Leadership required a discerning nature and through the years, he learned ways of testing others through questioning. He could hardly wait for the boy's impending response.

"Uh...sir...if I may...I...uh...assure you..." John swallowed hard. "I...I have nothing but complete respect and admiration for you and the Empress...uh...your fiancée." John looked over to Sara with pleading eyes. Her countenance soothed him and he regained some composure. "I am here at your service and I completely appreciate the honor of being in your presence...all of you!"

The Emperor observed John carefully as the young man spoke. John felt a flutter in his stomach and the heat returned to his cheeks.

The Emperor smiled a warm toothy smile. "John, you needn't worry. I have no suspicions of you. If I did, that would reflect poorly on the relationship I have with this beautiful woman to whom I am completely devoted. I am teasing you."

Sara's eyes widened with surprise.

"It's true, I am not known as one who teases others, but I have to admit it is fun," and with that the Emperor let out a laugh, which soon had them all laughing.

John relaxed as the joyous sound echoed off the walls.

The Emperor became serious again. "John, I called you here because I have a proposition for you. As you know, our wedding is less than a month from now. There are an increasing number of deeds to be performed, and I would prefer not to pull any more of my men off of their regular duties. I want you to be responsible for these tasks."

"I am honored, sir" John said. He was sincere, but also nervous about his abilities.

The Emperor continued, "You will be provided with food and lodging here in the palace during your service. Sara will be residing in the castle as well for the remainder of time before the wedding, but after today, custom has it that we will not be permitted to see each other until the ceremony. Among the other duties to which you will be assigned, I would like you to serve as our private messenger. Sara trusts you whole-heartedly and I, being an excellent judge of character, trust you as well."

"Thank you sir."

"John, I do not expect you to provided service without compensation. I know many powerful men and women throughout the world. Sara tells me that you seek education through exploration. In exchange for your work here, I can arrange for travel to the city of a trusted ally. You will be welcomed within that city and provided for in exchange for work. I am sure you will find both the experience and the work enlightening. What are your thoughts on this arrangement?"

John was stunned. Not only was he being offered an amazing opportunity; he was also being allowed to proffer an opinion. He could hardly contain the excitement bubbling up through his body. *Is this really happening?*

Yes, believe it my son. This is real.

Did I just hear that?

Yes, you did.

John looked at the Emperor in wonderment. *Am I hearing the*

Emperor telepathically? But as he continued to look at the ruler, all he could see was the man patiently awaiting a response, with no indication he knew John's thoughts. John then looked at Sara, but she held the same expression as the Emperor. Whatever he was hearing, it was not coming from someone in the room. *Who's there?*

Do not concern yourself with that now. You will have time enough to learn more. Are you going to respond to this man who has made such a generous offer to you? Do you accept his proposal?

John responded to the internal conversation and blurted out, "Yes!" He had intended a more eloquent response, but the excitement, not only at the offer, but at the guiding voice, caused the enthusiastic outburst.

Both the Emperor and Sara seemed surprised by the declaration.

John composed himself and addressed the Emperor more deliberately. "Sir, I accept your offer with honor and gratitude. I do not feel worthy of this gift, but I promise, I will make you proud. I am dedicated to you both for the remainder of my time here."

John looked at Sara; he wondered if she had an awareness of the conversation he had had in his head. He guessed that she noticed something because she looked at him questioningly. Her countenance changed and her eyes assured him that they would have time later to discuss whatever he was thinking. She turned to her betrothed and said, "My lord and future husband, I would like to thank you for your generous offer. Make your wishes known and we will happily carry them out."

As Sara addressed the Emperor, John detected something in her words. He realized she was addressing the Emperor in the formal manner; one that would be expected of her whenever someone outside the immediate family was present. She was already employing the public role she would exhibit for years to come. Many would look up to her and seek her out for guidance in matters not befitting the Emperor himself.

Sara then stood and bowed to her fiancé. She looked over to John and nodded, indicating that it was time for them to leave. John bowed as Sara had, thanked the Emperor again, and left the room, allowing Sara a few private moments with him.

When Sara walked out of the room, John fell in behind her and they walked through the castle. John remained silent. He knew she was already viewed as **the** lady of the land. He watched others drop their eyes reverently as soon as they gained sight of her. The respect bestowed upon her was well deserved, not merely for her role, but for the beauty, light, and wisdom that she possessed and shared with everyone. John was grateful he could witness this.

When the two reached the outer courtyard, Sara stopped, turned, and addressed John for the first time since leaving the Emperor's quarters. "You did very well, John. I did not know he was going to make you that offer. He was more impressed with you than I had expected. You are part of the family now."

John stared at her, speechless.

She hugged him, and then stepped back, held him at arms-length, and went right into the business at hand. "John, I will not see you for the rest of the day. This is my last opportunity to spend time with the Emperor before our wedding."

John nodded, but she knew by his look he was uncertain of what was to happen next.

"You will be escorted to your quarters," she explained. "Later on today, one of the Emperor's men will fetch you to discuss your duties."

"When will I see you again?"

"I'm not certain. Maybe in a few days." She saw the look of concern on his face. "Please don't worry; you will be taken care of quite well. This is how it must be. I will send one of the servants to my parents' house to retrieve your belongings." She raised her right hand just above her ear and a servant John hadn't noticed came to her beckoning.

"Will you please escort Master John to his quarters? He will be staying in the honored guest suite."

The slender young woman with olive skin, dark eyes, and glossy black hair nodded with understanding to the Empress.

Sara spoke to John one last time, "I will have the coachman fetch your belongings and deliver them to your quarters."

Before John could respond, Sara was gone.

Δ   ▲   Δ

J ohn followed the servant to his quarters, occasionally glancing over his shoulder to where Sara once stood. He was nervous for what seemed to be the tenth time that day. *What are my duties going to be?*—he wondered and was disappointed when no voice responded. However, once he entered his quarters, he forgot all about his concern as he took in the beauty of the luxurious suite.

The servant showed him around and explained all of the amenities available to him. When they reached the bathroom, and after she showed him where he could find towels, soap, and cologne, John looked down and pointed to what appeared to be a second toilet. He did not know what it was used for.

The servant blushed and smiled demurely. "Sir, that is what is called a bidet."

She then reached down and turned the water on. She looked up at John but he still did not understand. So she leaned over to him and in a light voice said, "The bidet is used after that," pointing to the toilet, "for personal hygiene."

Suddenly, John understood what she was saying and began to blush; then they both laughed. He felt foolish for not knowing what a bidet was, but she was kind and nonjudgmental. He felt a kinship with her and over the next few weeks, whenever he had questions or needs, she was the one he would call on. This woman he realized over time was not a servant, but his friend.

The woman left and John explored the room for a moment, and then realized he was tired. He had just begun to relax when he heard a knock at the door. John rose, went to the door, and opened it. A handsome young man in military garb stood on the other side of the door. The soldier's uniform was perfectly pressed. He stood erect with shoulders back, but less formally then if he had been in front of a superior.

John surmised that the soldier was actually more a boy than a man. He appeared younger than John, which led John to believe that this was why the soldier was assigned to the wedding preparations. *Surely men higher in rank have more important duties to attend to*—John concluded.

And thus began John's new routine. Each morning, the young soldier would fetch him and each day they would work side-by-side. Some days it was just the two of them, but most days there were others.

John saw the Emperor nearly every day as the ruler made his rounds. Sometimes he inspected the work being done; sometimes he assigned new duties. On occasion it seemed he was there for the sole purpose of spending time with his men, bonding with them. These men admired their leader and it showed. He commandeered respect without demanding it. John was impressed by the traits with which the Emperor had that garnered such loyalty.

The men never spoke ill of the Emperor when he was not around; and they deferred to his every whim when he was present. Some of the men were larger, taller, and possibly even stronger than their leader, but they never challenged his authority. John began to see the Emperor differently than he had before when he first met the man in the grand room. He was now able to see the ruler through their eyes, as the guiding, fatherly figure, which was his true character.

John also saw how the Emperor cared for his men. At times, he would pull one aside and talk privately to him. John would reflect on these encounters when he had some time to himself and often realized that the particular soldier selected had seemed a bit off, although not overtly. Still, the Emperor noticed the inconsistency and intervened. The Emperor would put his arm around the soldier as they walked off to discuss in private whatever was troubling the man. In every case, the soldier returned more relaxed, as if a huge burden had been lifted from his shoulders.

As John bore witness to these moments, he found himself envying the future children whom this man would rear. He thought about the Emperor and the Empress and concluded that they were a quintessential father and mother paired together. He saw a father who would teach his boys to be men while adoring his daughters completely, and a mother who would nurture the needs and individuality of any child in her care.

Each afternoon, upon finishing their work, John had a small

amount of time to relax before the evening meal. After a while, the young soldier would knock on his door to escort him to the mess hall. At first, John did not socialize with the others. He was too exhausted; so he just sat in silence while he ate. He was not used to doing so much physical labor and quickly realized why so many of the men were strong and fit. Each night, after dinner, he would soak in the tub to relax his sore muscles.

Over time, John's body began to adjust to the workload and one evening he was determined to get the whole table talking. "I have an idea," he announced to those around him, "why not share a memory of something that has happened to you since joining the military?"

No one spoke up; most continued eating.

"All right then, I'll go first." John then related to them the conversation with the servant regarding the bidet. Half of the soldiers laughed immediately, while the other half looked on with blank faces. John then realized that some of them didn't know what a bidet was either, so he explained his embarrassing revelation and that got the rest of them laughing too.

One-by-one, each told a story. Most were funny, typically mishaps from their first weeks in the military. However, some were more intimate than John had expected. He soon realized he was gaining their confidence. Men were generally slower to let outsiders in than women were; yet, he realized that when they did, they were equally as intimate and vulnerable.

John felt good about his early success. As he and the young soldier walked back to his quarters he said, "What do you think of the idea of me initiating more conversation at the table over the next few week?"

"I think the men would like that very much," the solider responded.

As they shared their thoughts and experiences during dinner; John noticed how much he enjoyed not only their camaraderie, but also feeling a part of a larger group. It had been a long time since he felt that type of connection.

As much as John was getting accustomed to living in the moment, there were times, especially when he was alone in his quarters, when his mind was focused on the past. During these times he would reflect on his childhood. He recalled spring evenings when he played soccer with his classmates. There was a connection among him and his teammates as thy competed against an opposing team. Although they were playing and having fun, they worked towards a common goal—together. They had to rely and cooperate with each other. Granted, there was a bit of competition between teammates, which was healthy, but the team members knew instinctively not to allow it to interfere with the success of the team.

At first John could not understand why this memory came to him. He began to realize that every experience has a purpose. *Playing sports taught me how to bond and cooperate with others. And now I am applying that skill with the soldiers*—he considered. As he recorded this revelation in his journal, a feeling of well-being settled inside of him

Δ   ▲   Δ

J ohn's first week at the castle was coming to an end. He missed Sara, but was enjoying his newfound responsibilities. He was so busy, he forgot about one of his assigned roles—that is until he heard a knock on his door. When he opened the door, instead of the young soldier, there stood one of the Emperor's servants. John remembered him from his initial meeting with the Emperor.

"My master wishes to see you this morning. Please follow me and I will escort you."

John did as he was told and soon found himself, for the second time, outside of the Emperor's throne room. He heard what sounded like the end of a conversation, but he could not make out any words. Suddenly, the door opened and a man rushed by, making brief eye contact with John before heading down the corridor, towards a direction John had never been.

"Ah, John, come in," the Emperor's voice boomed.

John entered and as soon as he stepped over the threshold, the door was shut behind him. Although this was the first time meeting with the Emperor alone, he did not feel nervous because he had seen the Emperor everyday over the past week as he worked side by side with the soldiers. The Emperor invited him to sit, and he obeyed.

"Good morning, John. You seem to have adjusted to military life well. My men appear to have accepted you as one of their own."

"Yes, sir, I do believe I am adjusting to the work. And as for your men, I have enjoyed working with them, sir, more than I had imagined. It is nice to feel like I belong."

"Good. However, now there is other work for you to do."

"Other work, sir?"

"Yes, I have received word from Sara that she is in need of your services. She has a job specifically for you."

"A wedding detail, I presume."

"Most assuredly, although I do not know what she will ask of you. She has informed me that it will require a couple of days. You will be escorted to the main courtyard where she will meet with you. After you have completed her bidding, you can return to work with my men. Is that acceptable to you?"

"Yes, sir."

"Good."

John stood to leave, but the Emperor addressed him again, "And John, one more thing…"

"Yes, sir."

"Bring this to Sara." The Emperor handed John an envelope. A red velvet ribbon was tied around the parchment and a beautiful red rose had been slipped under the ribbon.

John accepted the envelope. He held back a smile, not wanting to acknowledge the Emperor's intimacy. He bowed to the Emperor, and left the room.

The servant had been waiting outside of the door and he led John along the familiar path back to the main courtyard. Waiting there was the smiling face of his dear friend—Sara. John was elated to see her. She hugged him and then pulled back realizing that he held something in his hand. "Is this for me…from my dearly beloved?"

"Yes, indeed. You have been missed—by both of us!" John

replied.

"If I were not so busy every waking minute, I am not sure I could stand to be apart from him for much longer. And as for you, I am happy to see you too! Unfortunately, I must send you off again, but just for a couple of days."

"I am curious. The Emperor said you have work for me, but he did not say what it was."

"I figured that by now you could use a break from all of the physical labor I am sure the Emperor has had you doing."

"The break is welcomed, but I have to admit, I have grown used to the work. I enjoy the Emperor's men and they have accepted me as one of their own. Even the Emperor has noticed!"

Sara smiled at John's obvious pride. He reminded her of a boy displaying satisfaction at having impressed his hard-to-please father. "I am happy that you feel at home here, John. And I hope that your experiences have encouraged you to return after your explorations. You have become the brother I have never had, and it will sadden me to let you leave."

John raised an eyebrow at the mention of leaving.

Sara saw his look and quickly continued, "But enough of that! There is much to do. It is only a week until I am wed!"

"I am here to serve you."

"John, before I ask, I must make a confession."

"A confession?"

"Yes. A couple of weeks ago, when you were staying at my house, I happened upon a poem that you had left out in the open. I did not know what it was until I started reading it, but then I was so taken by it I could not put it down. I have thought of it often these past days and have worked up the nerve to ask a huge favor of you."

"I will do whatever you ask."

"You are kind, but this is deeply personal. Would you be willing to write and recite a dedication for my wedding? Tradition calls for the bride's brother to perform such a duty, and being that I am without a brother, I would be honored for you to do this."

John felt tears forming in his eyes and he quickly reached out and hugged Sara. "I am so happy to do this for you, I only hope that I will make you as proud and happy as I am right now."

"Thank you John. I knew I could count on you. Now allow me to give you some details. A wedding dedication in my fiancé's religion is not an informal undertaking. I was advised by the Emperor's religious counselor to have you work with the Hierophant directly to bring this request to fruition. I know how much you enjoy learning, so I thought this would be another opportunity for you to gain some religious and spiritual knowledge."

"OK…, but what is a Hierophant?"

"The Hierophant is the High Priest of the village. He is the most respected of religious men. As you know, my family is not religious per se, but we are familiar with the religious practices of this land. The Emperor's wedding, being a major public event, must follow religious tradition, so the Hierophant will be presiding over the ceremony. He has agreed to mentor you for your task. I am sure you will find each other most interesting. I can hardly wait to hear back…from each of you!"

John detected uncharacteristic impishness within his friend, more like her mother than her. However, in knowing himself as he did, he too had to laugh at the thought of such a pairing.

"And now our time together must once again close as I have so much more to do today," Sara continued. Just as she had done weeks earlier, she raised her hand and a servant appeared seemingly out of nowhere. In the servant's company, her tone became more formal. "Please escort Master John to the main temple; the Hierophant is expecting him. Then promptly return to me. Thank you."

"And John, these are for you," she said, handing him some papers. Then she hugged him goodbye. She finished up by saying, "I will not expect to see you again until tomorrow evening as you will have plenty to discuss with the Hierophant. I have arranged for you to spend the night there. I will send an escort to you in advance of tomorrow's dinner. Expect her between mid-afternoon and sundown. See you tomorrow and good luck."

John bowed to her, showing the same reverence he had shown the Emperor and then he followed his escort out of the courtyard.

V – THE HIEROPHANT

T hey arrived at the temple in the center of the town; it was located on the main square where John had first met the Magician. John admired the architecture and at the same time marveled at how much his life had changed since he last entered the plaza. Months ago, he hadn't as much as a clue as to where he would be or what he would do even hours in advance. Now he was residing in the palace and befriended by the royal family. All his needs were taken care of and while his responsibilities had increased, they all fell well within work he was happy to do.

The servant bowed to him and set off back to the palace, leaving John staring at the ornate door that loomed before him. Somehow, he knew that behind that door would be another learning adventure. He took one last breath, reached for the oversized brass handle, and pulled the door towards him.

Once inside, John needed a few minutes for his eyes to adjust, and then he saw the many stained glass windows illuminating from the darkness. "So much color. So much beauty," he whispered. The cathedral was dark and cool inside, during the mid-day heat. As he moved around in the dim light, the shape of the building itself pulled out of the darkness. The columns and arches emerged with greater prominence, allowing John to make out the details of the many paintings on the walls.

Along the main aisle, an intricate tile pattern on the floor beckoned him forward and John found his legs responding. The pews on either side were carved in wood of a luscious caramel color, modestly ornate in comparison to the rest of the church. As John moved forward, he noticed patrons sitting in various pews, praying silently. Some sat and others knelt. A few read from prayer books and many prayed with beads wrapped around their hands. Towards the front, and to one side, a woman dressed in black lit a candle among the many others flickering within red glass cylinders.

In another section of the temple off of the main nave, a few men performed a prayer ritual. They were dressed in similar black suits and followed a consistent pattern of motion as they quietly mouthed their prayers. Their hands carved out shapes in the air and then came together as each bowed slightly, only to repeat the entire motion again and again.

John continued to observe everything around him. He had never been in a temple like this before and he was mesmerized. The only comparison he could make was to a small country church he had visited the year before. It had been converted from a barn and was minimally decorated. It was John's first introduction to formal worship. He had grown up in rural lands, populated mostly with farms, with great distances between them. Therefore, formal worship was not a part of the community.

John unfurled a simple map Sara had given him of the temple's interior. Ahead and to the right John found the archway he had been instructed to find. A small note, written at the bottom of the page, told him he would be greeted at the entrance to the chapel by one of the priests and then taken to the Hierophant.

John felt a twinge of anticipation. He headed toward the chapel entrance and was met by a young priest. The priest noticed the papers in John's hands and whispered, "Are you Master John, here to see the Hierophant?"

"Yes I am."

"I am pleased to make your acquaintance. I am Father Mark. Please, if you will, follow me."

John followed the priest through the chapel to a side door and then down a long hallway. Rooms of various sizes lined the hall on either side. A few of the doors were open and as they walked by, John peeked in. John observed meeting rooms on the left with chairs around oval tables, while the rooms on the right were arranged like classrooms.

At the far end of the hallway, John saw a door similar to the one they had just come through. Rather than heading through that door however, Father Mark turned and led John to the last room on the left-hand side of the hall. He pulled out a chair for John and encouraged him to sit and make himself comfortable.

As John waited, he glanced around the room and began leafing through the additional papers he had been given. On one of them he found a checklist and the following items caught his attention: vows, dedication, and parable selection. He wondered: *How many of these tasks are my responsibility, and what does each entail?*

He hoped he would know soon enough and turned his attention to the room. To his right, there was a bookshelf filled with nearly identically shaped books. The titles of the books were hard to make out since much of the gold leaf had rubbed off the spines. On the other side of the room, stood a blank chalkboard. John could not tell if it hadn't been used in a long time, or had just been thoroughly cleaned. The wall opposite the door contained a small window, which was the only source of light.

John felt drawn to the books, but felt it would be inappropriate to look at them so he stood and moved over to the widow. He looked out at a large courtyard that spanned the distance between this wing and another. The wing across the way appeared to contain a school. John saw children in matching uniforms, seated attentively in each of the many rooms. John watched the children and tried to imagine what it would be like to attend such a prestigious school.

Suddenly, and with no sound, John felt a shift in the energy of the room. He turned away from the window and saw a man, who he guessed to be the Hierophant, seated at the table. John looked at him and couldn't figure out how he had managed to enter the room and seat himself without making a sound. He was clearly a holy man. He sat patiently with his hands clasped in front of him; his purple robe, lavishly decorated with religious symbols along the center, was more ornate than the younger priest's; and he wore a headdress unlike anything John had ever seen. The golden material had a sheen that reflected the light from the window.

The Hierophant nodded to John and silently extended a hand toward the chair opposite him. John returned to the seat he had originally occupied and decided to pay this man the same respect he had the Emperor by not speaking until he was spoken to.

The bishop was well on in his years and reminded John of the grandfather he once had. The man's eyes let all know that they had witnessed much and that he was here to offer guidance to all who sought it. Other than that, John found the man's facial expression hard to read. It wasn't as if he had anything to hide, he just was more inwardly focused. The high priest nodded a second time as indication he was about to speak.

"Welcome young traveler. I see God has indeed blessed you in the ways I have heard. Our young bride has asked that I mentor you concerning the tasks of her choosing. I must admit, I was a little hesitant to entrust such responsibility to one who is not of our religion, or any religion for that matter, but alas, her confidence in you has persuaded me. Besides, her family is not religious in the stricter sense, having developed their spirituality in more... personal ways. As for the Emperor's family, they can do no more harm to their reputation than they have already by approving of this rather risky marriage. You may or may not know this, but many who partake of formal religion gain no comfort from those who do not."

"Sir, if I may," John began, "my upbringing was very humble and has not taught me religious ways. My travels have been my teachers, and this very village has been the most profound of them. I am happy to receive whatever teachings you provide, but I cannot promise as to what degree your rituals or teachings will ring true for me."

"Young man, I underestimated you. Fear not, I am not offended by your words. I have lived a long life. I do not seek conversion of you, just as I do not expect the Emperor's new wife to begin attending my services regularly. My undertaking has always been to bring God via this religion to those who seek Him. I do not profess this as the only way to God. Those of you who find independent paths to Him are free to pursue them."

"I do honor your path, sir, and your knowledge. I just was not sure what was expected of me and wanted you to understand."

With that, the old man smiled for the first time.

In that first hour, the Hierophant and the boy spoke of religious sacrament and what **was** expected of him. The majority of the conversation focused on the sanctity of marriage and all of the religious significance placed upon it. However, within the discussion, the boy asked many questions about the religion itself and the priest happily answered them. In this day and age, it wasn't often that the Hierophant got to address one so full of questions. His own passion for his religion was rekindled through the discussion and one hour quickly flowed into the next.

John was fascinated, not only with this specific religion, but by the entire concept of religion. He had never thought of the path to

God as being so structured. He intermittently questioned his own beliefs.

Dear Lord, how has this young man been deprived of your teachings all of this time? Does he not require fostering, discipline, and ritual?—the Hierophant wondered.

"John as part of the dedication to the bride and groom, you need to select a passage from Scripture," the Hierophant said.

"I'm afraid I am not familiar with your scriptures."

"Allow me to gift you with a copy of our Holy text."

"Thank you," John said as he took the leather bound book in his hand. He noticed two scarlet ribbons down the spine of the book.

"Between these bookmarks," the Hierophant explained, "you will find those sections most frequently quoted for wedding ceremonies. Read through them and I am sure you will find a passage that appeals to you."

"I am much obliged to you for your generosity," John said.

"You will also need to convey a personal sentiment about the bride and groom. I am sure the Lord's words will inspire you."

"Thank you."

"You have much to consider before the day is done. Let me show you to your quarters."

The Hierophant directed John to his quarters. The room was one of a number allocated for visiting clergy. As in the room where they first met, this room also contained a shelf full of religious texts. The Hierophant encouraged John to look through them. "Many others have been moved by specific passages from our Scriptures and have expounded upon them. You may find further inspiration among these."

"I look forward to reading them."

"Choose three passages that are of greatest interest to you. Midday tomorrow, we shall review your selections and I will guide you toward the most appropriate choice. Many passages contain multiple meanings and some may be more suited for a wedding ceremony than others."

"I look forward to your assistance."

"Take advantage of the remaining hours before our evening meal to study. Father Mark, who you met earlier, will come to escort you to the dining room. May the Lord be with you."

As soon as John entered his room, he began working on the task at hand. He skimmed through the Holy book, noting potential passages of interest. Some were far too difficult to understand or written about situations he could not relate to. Others were so encapsulated in symbolism that they left him lacking confidence in their intended meaning. He was relieved when Father Mark came to his door to escort him to dinner.

The time before the evening meal had not been fruitful; John hadn't found a single parable that he felt suitable for the wedding. He was still getting a feel for the language of the ancient text. He decided to bring the Holy book with him to the dining hall, and was surprised to find that many of the priests read from theirs as well during the meal.

As John looked around, he thought of his first meal in the military mess hall. That day, he felt just as out of place among those men as he did right now. The thought of trying to pull stories out of these men, as he had with the others, was amusing to him. Somehow, he didn't think his charms would work as well on the priests as it had the soldiers.

After the prayer of thanksgiving, hardly a word was uttered by anyone during the meal. John was relieved, knowing he would not have to reveal his ignorance of their ways.

The meal was simple, but tasty; it concluded with another prayer of thanks. John stood with the others and looked around for his escort. Instead, he was approached by the Hierophant who said, "Shortly after dawn you will be summoned for the morning meal. If you have any needs in the meantime, Father Mark will be happy to assist you."

The young priest nodded his consent.

"Early tomorrow afternoon, I shall fetch you myself and we shall break bread together while discussing your selections. May the blessings of the Almighty be bestowed upon you, my son." And with that, the Hierophant left.

When John got back to his room, he was hit by the quietude of the rectory. During dinner, despite the lack of conversation, one could still hear the sounds of utensils scraping against bowls and plates. Yet in his room, not a sound penetrated the four walls. *I don't think I have ever experienced such a lack of sound before in my life*—he thought.

John reached for the scriptures and before opening the book, held it in his hands. He allowed himself to feel the texture of the leather casing. He opened the book and ran his fingers down the page. The paper was thin and soft, the words raised just enough up from it to be felt with the fingertips. John closed his eyes, flipped through the book, and stopped at random locations. In the subtlest of ways, the different sections **felt** differently. His fingers didn't sense a difference so much as his gut did.

He played with this sensation and searched for a section that felt pleasant. *This is a celebration. Show me a passage that is festive and joyful.* He closed the book again and this time ran his thumb along the edge of the pages from the front of the book toward the back. When he felt inclined, he opened the book and scanned the text.

This time, he found a short story about a simple family. It didn't move him, so he tried again. The second time, he opened to a different section, yet found a retelling of that same story from a different perspective. *That's odd.*

He opened the book at random a few more times and started to enjoy the experience. He stopped looking for an **appropriate** story and just paid attention to where he was led. *Ah, I think I know what this story means*—then he selected another. Instead of looking for how a story applied to Sara and the Emperor, he looked for how it applied to **him**, and that seemed to improve his results. With each story that he read, he found aspects he could relate to. Soon, he stumbled upon a story about an orphan. *This ought to be interesting:*

> There once was a boy, Jacob, who had wandered away from the orphanage where he lived and got lost. He couldn't find his way back through the woods and became frightened. His fear turned to panic, and he ran and ran until he encountered a clearing and a small village. He didn't know where he was, but was comforted by being out of the woods.
>
> After a while, Jacob calmed down and propped himself against the trunk of a tree and watched the people

49

of the village. As he surveyed their daily activities, he created a game for himself. He imagined that his new parents were among the villagers and all he had to do was find them. He began identifying what he liked about each couple he saw.

"There is a man who is strong and can teach me to protect myself against bullies," he said to himself. "And that woman with the sweet smile, she would never yell at me for tearing my trousers."

Soon, the little boy's fears dissipated completely and he stood and strolled into the village. A lovely woman noticed the young boy walking down the street by himself. "Where are your parents?" she asked.

"I have come here to find them," the boy replied.

"Find them?"

"I have been at the orphanage, but I believe the people who are to be my parents live here in this village."

A guard approached the boy and the woman. "Oh there you are Jacob, the orphanage has sent me to look for you."

"It's okay," said the woman to the boy. "I will tell the others in the village about you."

After that day, the little boy played the same game whenever potential adopters visited the orphanage. He looked for what he liked in each pair and pretended that they were awaiting his choice.

Then one-day, the same man and woman he had first seen in the neighboring village arrived at the orphanage. He grew excited. *These are my favorite. I choose them. I am going to adopt them as my new parents.*

The children were lined up for examination and when the prospective couple reached the young boy, they asked him his name.

"My name is Jacob. Pleased to meet you."

They each looked to the other for a moment and then said, "How would you like to live on a farm? It is hard work, but there are lots of animals to play with. We have a daughter and two sons, all older than you. They will be happy to have a new younger brother."

Ultimately, the couple adopted the boy. From the hard work living on the farm, he grew up strong like his father. And many a time while working, he tore his trousers. Each time his mother either mended them or gave him another pair handed down from his brothers; and she never yelled.

No other story John had ever heard touched him as much as the one he had just read. A tear rolled down his cheek. He identified with the boy in the story—and shared the boy's dream from a time earlier in his life. While he read, he pictured Sara as the mother and the Emperor as the father.

Before noon the next day, John found three passages that he was drawn to, and to his surprise the Hierophant approved of all three.

"Parables such as these, speak to each person individually. A story need not resemble the life of those who hear it. If it touches their hearts, it serves its purpose. I see that you are drawn to the first more than the others. Why don't you go with that one?"

John realized the Hierophant was right. His first choice, without question, was the story about the orphan boy. It inspired him and as a result, he knew what he would write in the dedication. He was excited to share it with the Emperor and Empress.

Δ　▲　Δ

T he wedding day arrived quickly and the ceremony proceeded flawlessly. The combined precision of the military and the church ensured that every aspect was executed in a timely and graceful manner. John struggled to stay focused; his dedication kept echoing inside of his head. By now, it was well rehearsed, but he was still nervous. His part came near the end of the ceremony, and he was sure he wouldn't completely relax until it was over. Moments before he was to rise and approach the pulpit, the Magician reassuringly placed a hand on his shoulder.

"They are going to love it!" he whispered.

The walk to the front of the church was not nearly long enough for John. Ready or not, all eyes were on him. He began speaking. His voice quivered, giving hints of nervousness, but did not fail him. He focused on the lines before him and the feelings with which they were written. As he eased into it, he stole glances at the honored couple. Words and emotion flowed from him and many a watching eye blurred with tears.

"Three months ago, my aimless wandering brought me to this village. It could easily have been a lifetime ago. On that day, not far from the main doors of this temple, I met the father of the bride. Little did I know how much my life would change from that moment onward.

"Since then, I have been taught and I have been fed. I have been commissioned for service and I have been sheltered. Far greater than all of these, I have been loved and accepted. Like the boy in that story, I was once a young orphan, having lost his parents at too early an age. And like that boy, I have been taken in.

"To many of us, the Emperor and his bride appear the perfect couple, noble leaders of this beautiful village and inspiration to us all. Their love for each other is obvious, but so too is their love for all of you, for all of us.

"If I died tomorrow and could come back again, there would be no greater gift than to return as one of their children, raised under their guidance and reared among the rest of you. I am so grateful for what this village has shown me and eternally indebted to the most amazing role models a man can have.

"Emperor, Sara...Empress, I wish for you both all the love and joy you give the rest of us, and a long life of happiness and prosperity."

Everyone began to clap and cheer. All shared his sentiment, admiration, and gratitude for the honored couple. John once again glanced over to the newly weds; Sara mouthed a thank you with tears in her eyes and the Emperor nodded with appreciation.

The organist moved into a final melody as John walked back to his seat. The ceremony was nearly over; all that was left was the grand exit: a procession that would lead the royal couple from the church, through town, and to the reception.

VI – THE LOVERS

J ohn skipped the parade and took a quiet, circuitous route to the reception. He desired a little time to himself between the ceremony and celebration. Upon arriving at the reception hall, he was surprised to find a huge ballroom filled with people. The happy couple had not arrived, yet the celebration carried on in full force. He looked around for familiar faces, but found neither any of Sara's family, nor recognized any of the Emperor's men.

However, as he looked around the room, he saw beautiful faces everywhere. Most of the men and women were either his age or a full generation older. Most seemed to know a lot of other people and everyone was having a good time. The music was festive and many of the younger participants, mostly the women, were dancing.

Before John had a chance to decide what to do next, he became aware of a handsome man, maybe a half-decade older, standing next to him. As soon as he made eye contact, the man spoke to him.

"Are you enjoying the reception? The Emperor certainly knows how to put on a party." He smiled at John. "My name is Rafi."

"Good to meet you Rafi. I'm John. This party **is** great! I have never been to one quite like it."

"I figured as much. You looked a little wonderstruck." Then, almost to himself, he said, "In fact, it's really cute."

Rafi peppered John with questions: "Where are you from?" Rafi asked with sincere interest. "How long have you been traveling? How long will you be staying? Where are you off to next?"

John didn't offer much in response, but did answer all of Rafi's questions. Since he wasn't quite ready for his imminent travels, he quickly changed the subject.

After a good ten minutes of basic conversation, Rafi ventured into the more personal, but only slightly. "So, John, have you noticed any girls that you are particularly attracted to? Or...perhaps...a boy?"

John hardly noticed the question's intimacy and simply answered, "To be honest, I have just been taking it all in. They are all so attractive!"

Without warning, and to Rafi's disdain, an attractive woman approached the two of them. She had a similar look to Rafi, but appeared to be closer to John in age. In fact, as she got closer, John noticed that her skin and eyes matched Rafi's precisely. She also seemed to have the same level of confidence as Rafi and didn't hesitate to speak to them.

"Rafi, you must introduce me to this handsome man who you've met." She turned to John. "Hello. My name is Gabi."

"Gabi, allow me to introduce John. John is visiting our lovely town for a little while. John, this is my **little** sister Gabi."

John didn't notice the subtle emphasis Rafi placed on 'little', but the comment wasn't lost on Gabi. She shot Rafi a quick glance, letting him know that she would not be so easily dissuaded. "Oh, that sounds very interesting John. Visiting from some far away place?" She slipped her arm through John's and said, "You must tell me about this while we dance. Would you like to accompany me to the dance floor?"

Rafi glared at his sister. *In a social setting like this, women always have the upper hand*—he bristled. He could not totally blame her, after all, it was more acceptable for a woman and a man to touch or dance out in open society. Rafi still hadn't figured out John's preferences and therefore tempered himself for a bit longer.

Still, he was not ready to just let his sister barge in and carry John off so easily and offered, "Or John, if you would rather not dance with all of the **girls**, I would be happy to offer you a glass of wine. Surely by now you've sampled some of the locals' finest?"

"No not really," John said, confused by the siblings' obvious rivalry.

"I would be happy to select one that you will most certainly enjoy," Rafi said as he placed an arm over John's shoulder and made as if to lead him away from the dance floor—and his sister.

Up until that moment, John had not made any assumptions as to what was happening, but now it was clear that this handsome man and his beautiful sister were vying for his attention. John was taken aback. He knew that in the past he had charmed people with his antics, but this night, he was simply there, taking in his surroundings when these two appeared out of nowhere. He was not used to being sought after in quite this way.

His journey thus far had been exciting and filled with wonderful offers of hospitality. However, prior to this, John merely had to choose whether or not to accept what was offered. This time, he had to choose between **two** competing offers, an unusual occurrence for him. On his left, a beautiful woman locked her arm in his. Her eyes glistened and were inviting. He could feel her skin against his. She was soft, yet athletic, like her brother. And then, on his right, stood a man unlike any he had attracted before. Rafi was clearly tall, dark, and handsome. His frame was square and John could tell that beneath his shirt was the lean, muscular body of a true athlete.

John was naïve in the ways of romance. He had always noticed the beauty in people, all types of people, but had to admit that most of the people he found himself around were either much older, young children, or those he felt a more familial connection with rather than romantic. Here he was at a social event, surrounded by peers, and it was an entirely new experience for him.

He felt the weight of having to make a choice. He could tell the intent behind the offers placed by both Gabi and Rafi. Their competitiveness was obvious and probably existed throughout their lives, but he also felt that they were each genuine in their interest. He sensed that while they anticipated his decision, they were really leaving it up to him. As he stood there thinking this through, neither actually pulled on him, despite not letting him go.

John, if he was being honest with himself, couldn't help but to revel in the moment. He didn't want to choose. He wanted to remain right here where he was, sought by both, but still innocent. Once he made a decision, the innocence was over. He could always decline both offers, but that would be a travesty.

On another level, John recognized that this decision was also symbolic. He was not simply choosing between a dance and a glass of wine—between a beautiful woman and a handsome man, he was choosing between a conventional path and an alternative one.

At the same time, he felt a guiding force egging him on:

The world of man might look on a decision like this with bias, but the world of spirit does not. This is not a choice between a higher road and a lesser one; it is simply a choice. There are many paths that lead to the same place. Right now, in this very moment, you are offered two.

And so, John made his decision in the only way he knew how. He closed his eyes for just a moment and concentrated on what he was feeling. His arm and shoulder glowed with increased awareness. He felt how his energy mixed with each of theirs. In fact, he could feel the completion of the circle of energy connecting through this brother and sister who were so closely linked with each other. Before getting swept away with sensation, he concentrated on what he truly desired and realized that there really wasn't a choice after all. His preference was clear.

The slight tension that had built in his body relaxed and Gabi and Rafi, having both felt it, turned towards him. John removed his arm from around Rafi's waist and ever so slightly turned toward Gabi. Rafi, interpreting this as defeat and yielding to John's wishes, pulled his arm off of John's shoulder. Then John reached over to hold Gabi's hand in both of his. He looked Gabi directly in the eye, thanked her for her invitation, and then declined. "I'm really not much of a dancer and I am curious about the local wine." He lifted her hand and kissed the top of it. "Thank you, but I will be accepting Rafi's offer."

Gabi was speechless. Both siblings were stunned.

Gabi had to admit that initially she had been driven by sibling rivalry; but John's unique looks, had also enticed her. Now she was completely charmed by his innocence and candor. She felt fondness for this gentle stranger and was content with his decision.

Rafi, meanwhile, was beside himself. He had never seen such a display of grace, charm, and chivalry. He was now smitten and grew excited with anticipation.

As Gabi's eyes moved from John's to Rafi's, Rafi moved in to give his sister a hug. He was in awe at what had just happened and whispered a "wow" into her ear as he embraced her.

Gabi echoed his "wow" and then whispered, "Enjoy yourself."

Gabi smiled in her beautiful way and left the men to each other. Halfway to the dance floor, she felt the weight of their stares. She looked over her shoulder, winked at them, and blew them both a kiss, awarding her blessing. With that, Rafi placed his arm back on John's shoulder and led him to a quieter area, making good on his offer to introduce John to the area's finest wines, finest views, and finest company.

As John walked off with Rafi at his side, he felt as if someone watching was nodding with approval. In appearance, he had simply accepted one offer of two, yet in reality, what he was accepting within himself was much more.

VII – The Chariot

I n the middle of a melody, the musicians paused and then moved into a traditional and familiar tune. A few beats later, the large wooden doors at the end of the hall swung open. Two beautiful stallions entered the room, pulling behind them the Emperor's Chariot. As the crowd parted, the ornate coach moved further into the room; the royal groom and his magnificent bride waved to their guests as flowers rained upon them. Cheers and applause thundered, welcoming and congratulating the adored couple.

John watched the display and was quickly lost in the thoughts it sparked. He first contemplated the symbolism of the horses: one black and the other white. The Hierophant would have said that they represented two distinct paths to God, the Emperor's family being religious and Sara's of the occult.

Another might point out the joining of man and woman in marriage, separate and unique, yet connected as the horses were via their reins. The chariot itself was also a symbol wrought with meaning. It literally carried the newlyweds over the threshold into the room, yet was symbolically carrying them from their past into their future, from a life apart to a life together.

John thought about his own life. This day marked a transition for him as well. His future loomed before him and soon he would be literally traveling into it. With the wedding over, so too was his work with the Emperor. The last few days before the wedding, John had made his decision and decided he would travel east. Now all that remained was a single night. The following morning he would be on his way.

Then it hit him—the newlywed's union meant his separation— from them and the village, which had become like home. Tears slowly escaped his eyes and drifted down his cheek.

As John sunk deeper into the realization of what lay just ahead, Rafi squeezed his hand, bringing his attention back to the room. *And what do I do about Rafi?*

The evening **had** been pleasant, and it **was** easy for John to imagine spending more time with this man. *But now? On the verge of leaving?*

The room started to spin and John's chest constricted. It was all happening too fast. He felt out of control. It was bad enough that he was leaving in the morning, but now he had to say goodbye to another person. The pressure grew too much, and he needed to escape.

John turned to Rafi, "I must go. I still have things to prepare before my journey." He gave Rafi a firm, but short hug and quickly made for the door. When he reached the threshold, he looked back, catching the confused expression on Rafi's face; then retreated into the safety of the darkness where he was able to breathe once again.

VIII – STRENGTH

T he next morning, John woke early with a lump of emotion stuck in his throat. He was sad and afraid. For the first time in months, he felt that life was unfair. "Yes, I made the decision to head east and I really want to go," he tried to reason, "but that look on Rafi's face. I know I disappointed him, but what more can I do?"

To make matters worse, the one person who he would turn to at a time like this was no longer available to him. He knew he had to face this alone. *I might as well get used to it. I'm going to be on my own for a long time.* So he decided to get moving.

Walking helped; walking always helped. The movement of his body allowed the emotional energy to flow and thus dissipate. As John wandered, he found himself heading toward a part of town he had never visited before. The newness of the surroundings brought relief, giving him something to focus on other than his anxiety. The street led to the entrance of a park and then transformed into the main path through it. Then, further up, the path forked and a group of signs indicated attractions that visitors could find along each branch.

The sign that caught John's attention pointed the way to the zoo. He had never been to a zoo. In fact, the only beasts John had ever seen close up were farm animals. And so, with a hint of anticipation, he set off in that direction.

It was still early so the zoo was as absent of people as the park had been. All was quiet, except for the animals. John heard intriguing sounds all around. He remembered what it was like on the farm in the early morning hours; he guessed that many of the animals were impatiently waiting for food.

More signs littered the paths, indicating the various animals that could be found. Initially, John couldn't decide where to visit first, but that was before he saw the one that said: "Wild Cats." John had always been fond of domesticated cats and was excited at the prospect of seeing the wild ones.

Once John neared what was affectionately referred to as "Cat Alley," his heart raced and his breathing stopped. In the cages just ahead, he saw them. The first exhibit was the Lion's Den. These kings and queens of the jungle lounged regally about. In front of each, John saw deep red stains where slabs of meat must have been laid out only minutes before. In fact, the smallest of the lions was still licking her chops, likely having just finished her portion. The lions, all squinting with pleasure and contentment, didn't notice John as he passed.

In the second cage, John saw a tiger high up on an embankment, lying on his side and catching the only sun he could find. John could just make out his orange coat, black stripes, and white belly amid the camouflage.

Although excited with what he was seeing, John hoped to witness a little more activity, and was happy to find some in the third cage. There, a bobcat, much smaller by comparison, paced restlessly. She seemed frustrated and etched a pattern within her territory as if looking for something to do.

In the middle of her circling, the bobcat stopped unexpectedly and stared directly at John. Rather than threatening or defensive, the cat merely held eye contact as if looking into him. In that moment, John felt kinship with her. It was as if the imprisoned beast was pleading with John to take full advantage of his freedom, to continue his travels and not consider for a moment the alternative.

For the length of the bobcat's stare, John wondered if he had been led to this very experience as an omen, encouraging him despite the difficulty he was having. As if in response, the bobcat closed her eyes briefly, let out a muffled growl, and then reinstated her ritual pacing.

John, momentarily lost in thought, was then roused by the sound of keys clinking in the next cage. As he walked over to it, he saw the zookeeper, a middle-age woman inside of the cage. John's eyes moved down the woman's arm to her hand, unprotected and stroking the large head of a black panther. The panther's jaw was slightly opened, revealing a mouthful of aggressive-looking teeth. The woman, however, showed no signs of fear and handled the beast as if it were her pet.

How can this woman be so peaceful in the presence of such a dangerous animal?

Sensing his attention, the woman looked up at John and subtly motioned him over. "Good morning young man. What brings you to the zoo at such an early hour? I am not used to onlookers during the morning feeding."

"Good morning, ma'am. I was feeling trepidation and thought a walk would help calm my fears. It's kind of ironic that I would find myself seeking solace among such ferocious animals."

"Young man, irony is an illusion. Your subconscious has led you here for a reason. Seen another way, these animals are ones that feel **little** fear. Maybe you were drawn to them in an attempt to find your own inner strength."

"I've never thought about it that way. And a moment ago, I almost thought that the bobcat was trying to communicate with me too."

"I'm sure she was. These cats are wise animals. On some level, they have chosen to be here in the zoo. They know that through being observed, they can teach humans in a way that they could not in the wild. Our bobcat friend is just a little torn because, while one part of her accepts being here, another part wishes to be free."

"But freedom comes at a price." John lowered his head slightly.

"You are not from here, are you? I can tell from your accent that you are not local. But, from your words, I sense that you too are torn…between staying and leaving perhaps? Oh—you've made a decision, but wonder if it is a mistake?"

John looked at the woman in disbelief. *How could a woman I am just meeting have such insight into my situation?*

"Young man, I understand your confusion, and forgive me. Working with these cats has taught me the gift of telepathy. You are so open; your thoughts are easy to read. But fear not, only those you send out can be detected. Some day, you may come to learn of your own telepathic abilities. Everyone has the potential; it just requires awareness and practice. This panther here can also read you, but rather than your thoughts, he reads your feelings. He senses that you are nervous, for example, and that you fear him, but he also knows that you are a loving being, and therefore, you do not threaten him. He has asked me to invite you to come pet him if you wish. Would you like that?"

John looked at the panther and was overwhelmed by the cat's beauty. He wanted to touch the cat and trusted what the woman was saying, but still felt a great deal of fear. As he debated with himself, he heard a voice in his head, one that was distinctly not his.

Do not seek to eliminate your fear, merely to overcome it. The courageous are not fearless, rather, they are those who find the strength to walk through their fears. Do not repress or deny your fear; it may be a beast, but it can be tamed. Train her to serve you lest she become your master. Accept the cat's invitation, and observe what happens.

John furrowed his brow in further disbelief, but then relented. As he approached the entrance to the cage, the zookeeper opened it from the inside just wide enough for him to enter; she then quickly locked it behind him. John, now inside, pushed back against the bars and clutched at them. The woman, having moved towards the panther once more, split the distance between them. The cat glanced sideways in John's direction, but then lowered himself down to the ground and rested his head. He still kept John in his peripheral vision, but did not look at him directly.

The woman moved in next to the cat and knelt beside him,

encouraging John to approach when he was ready. John's eyes moved across the animal. The fur glistened in the early morning light and appeared soft. Now that John was closer, he could see that the cat was spotted, black on black. His desire to touch the cat grew. He wanted to feel the softness of the animal's fur and the firmness of its muscles. His feet began to carry him forward as he took deep breaths to process the fear. The more deeply he breathed, the calmer he became.

Yes, my boy, breathe.

John moved in behind the woman so he could pet the cat without being near its head and powerful jaws. The fur was as soft and inviting as it looked. Once John made contact with the animal, adrenalin rushed through his body, replacing fear with exhilaration. Here he was petting an animal that few would ever be near, let alone touch.

As John's bravery increased, he moved his hand closer to the panther's head. The cat responded to the gentle touch, moving his head up towards John's hand. John then moved his other hand over to the cat's shoulder. Here he felt the firm, rippled muscles of the cat. One hand moved up to the top of the head, the other down to its paw. John acknowledged these as the two most powerful features of this beast, yet he could not resist. He could feel the cat's vigor beneath his fingers and imagined it traveling up his arms and into his body.

John was now looking at the cat's profile as the panther opened his mouth slightly, again revealing his huge teeth. John felt a trembling under his fingers, which was accompanied by a soft guttural sound. He realized that the panther was purring and was tickled by the thought of it. *Wild cats are still cats!*

The woman placed her hand on John's back to catch his attention. "It is time for me to get back to work."

John nodded and followed her out of the cage. She shut the gate behind them. "Thank you for your wisdom and this incredible experience," he said.

"Good luck on your travels. If you return to the village, please come see me again." She then looked back to the panther and said to John, "He thanks you for your courage."

John faced the cat and bowed, thanking the cat in return.

Although John could easily have spent all day in the zoo, he didn't have the time. He retraced his steps back to the castle. He could not hold off his future any longer.

Δ   ▲   Δ

J ohn met up with the Emperor and Sara in the castle's central courtyard. There, awaiting the royal couple, was the magnificent chariot from the night before. This time John got to examine the vehicle up close. While the servants placed the last of the royal couple's belongings in a second vehicle that would be accompanying them, John paced around the chariot. He ran his fingers lightly over the wooden body and eyed the symbols that decorated it. Working his way towards the front, John petted first the black horse and then the white. He marveled at the strength and beauty of these powerful yet peaceful animals.

The Emperor entered the courtyard and watched John for a moment, then placed a hand on the boy's shoulder to get his attention. For the first time since John met him, there was no talk of wedding plans or work to be done. "Are you ready for your travels? Have you decided to go with your original plan?"

"Yes…I'm still going…ready or not."

"To make your journey easier, I am providing you with food, clothing, two escorts, and a horse-drawn carriage."

"You are too generous, sir."

The Emperor ignored the comment and said, "I have arranged for another court to receive you. Gifts have been placed in the carriage for them."

"I won't disappoint you."

Then, and for the first time, the Emperor hugged him and in that moment John felt loved, appreciated, and protected. He felt like a son who was being sent off for further rearing and knew he would be missed.

The Emperor released John, and Sara, who had appeared moments earlier, moved in for her turn. She embraced John and kissed him on the cheek, then held him a bit longer, not knowing when she would see him next. And then she climbed in next to her husband and waved as they rode out of the courtyard to the west.

John watched them until they were out of sight. He pictured the vast ocean they would visit; one that he had yet to see. He could almost feel the ocean breezes cooling his face while the sun simultaneously warmed it. He thought of the exquisite beauty he had heard much about, where the setting sun met the sea and looked forward to witnessing this for himself someday.

John turned and then noticed that his transportation was waiting for him. His escorts loaded his belongings in with the rest of the cargo, letting him know that once he was ready, they could go. The next phase of his journey was beginning, and this time there was much distance to cover.

PART II – AIR – EAST

IX – THE HERMIT

T he motion of the eastbound carriage cradled John like a soft cocoon oscillating in the breeze. He wasn't ready to mingle with his escorts, who he did not know, so he kept to himself inside the cab. He pretended the coach was being moved along by an invisible hand rather than drawn by regal horses and steered by the Emperor's men.

John was no stranger to being alone. The isolation thrust upon him was, however, a stark contrast to the months prior. The cozy compartment gradually closed in around him. Before long it encased him like the hard shell of a crab.

Unlike his time in the village, each day dragged on lethargically. He had withdrawn into seclusion by choice, but the more reclusive he became, the wider the chasm between him and the others grew. The thin wall that separated him from his escorts became an abyss he could not bring himself to cross.

His journal served as his sole companion. He could say anything to those pages, which allowed him to express his thoughts and feelings without judgment. Two weeks into his journey he wrote the following:

> I grew accustomed to the constant companionship
> when I was in the Emperor's village. I miss the
> daily flow of events, which naturally unraveled as
> we prepared for the wedding. Now each day runs
> into the next with hardly a change in the scenery.

The catharsis of expressing himself through his journal chipped away at his shell. One day, he felt ready to emerge from his solitude. The first attempt to socialize, however, was thwarted.

For a month, John had not tracked their progress from within his protective chamber. The afternoon he climbed down from the cab, he was met with gloomy skies and cold temperatures. The higher plateaus introduced him to the most severe weather he had ever seen. He had never experienced a hard freeze before and could not tolerate the scathing wind. He was forced to retreat back into the carriage. He bundled up to fight against the cold, but could not rid himself of it. A constant shiver caught hold of him and then gave way to a high fever. His extended time sequestered from the others thus continued.

John was exhausted and felt imprisoned by his condition. He slept for most of the day. Being alone no longer provided safety. His mood followed the course of his body, plunging him into sadness and depression. The only thing that seemed to give him comfort was reminiscing about his time in the Emperor's city.

As he wrote in his journal, he remembered something Sara's aunt had given him: the herbal tincture of Goldenseal. She had advised him: *It is not uncommon for spiritual quests, as the one you are about to embark on, to be physically straining. In stretching your awareness, you'll be stressing your body, too. If at any time you feel your strength waning, you can stave off sickness with this Goldenseal. Take it each morning and evening until you feel rejuvenated."*

It is probably too late for it to do any good—he thought—*but I will try it anyway.*

Δ   ▲   Δ

T he next day, while John was drifting in and out of sleep, he opened his eyes and saw an old man sitting across from him.
Am I dreaming?—he wondered.

The man was very thin, and despite the cold, wore little clothing. *I must still be dreaming*—John concluded, but as the scene was quite vivid, he wasn't convinced.

The figure in front of him looked old and young at the same time. He sat in an awkward position, but showed no sign of discomfort. His wide eyes looked deeply into John's, and without moving his lips, he spoke to him:

Dear boy, your fortunes will fall and rise three times before you see me again. At that time, you will be ready. One must first experience the outside of the Wheel before he can begin to strive for the center.

The old man snapped his fingers and disappeared.

John's body jolted from the dream. He dismissed the vision and thought, *Did we just hit a ditch?* He sat up, stuck his head through the window, and called out to his escorts, "Hey! What happened? What did we hit?"

At first, the two simply looked at each other and laughed. Then one yelled back, "We've not hit anything but smooth roads all day. That fever of yours has you hallucinating, my friend."

"My fever!" John instinctively put a hand on his forehead, then mumbled, "but wait, I don't have a fever any longer." He scanned his body, but couldn't find a single thing wrong. The cough was absent, the body aches relieved, and he could breathe through his nose for the first time in days. "Well I'll be! That Goldenseal really **does** work."

X – WHEEL OF FORTUNE

With his health back to normal, John made a second attempt to climb out of his solitude. When he felt the carriage slow down and come to a halt, he clambered up the front and joined the others. At first, the men were wary of John's presence, but in no time he had them talking. Both had made this journey at least twice before, and began telling him what to expect.

"As you most likely noticed, we spent the first month traversing the rather monotonous desert plains of the Middle East. Now that we're into our second month, the terrain offers more variation in scenery, and, as you have learned, it is cooler."

"I have to admit, I wasn't expecting it to be **this** cold."

"The good news is, we are now roughly halfway across the Middle East. In about two weeks, we'll reach a village, which many consider the western edge of the East. Our plan is to spend three or four days there to break from travel. After that, it will take just over a month to reach our destination."

From that day on, John spent an increasing amount of time with his escorts. He learned all about their families, their interests, and the distant places they had traveled to. As he got to know the men better, he became more outgoing.

John's returned resilience was accompanied by his love of music and he introduced his travel companions to songs from his youth. The three sang and laughed the days away. The music, the stories, and the companionship made the days pass quickly. The consistency of the undeveloped terrain and the easy camaraderie of his travel companions lulled John into a comfortable complacency. He was therefore surprised when a remote village seemed to pop out of nowhere.

His companions smiled at the shock on his face. One of them explained, "This spot is the crossover point. Over time it has developed as a trading post between the West and the Far East. At any one time, there are at least as many travelers passing through as full time residents."

John took in the bustling scene in front of him. He observed that many of the travelers looked different than those he had encountered thus far. And they spoke languages he had never heard before. *I am clearly a foreigner here*—he thought. He realized he was excited for the first time since leaving the Emperor and Empress. He wrote in his journal:

> Four nights in a bed, twelve hot meals, and plenty
> of people to meet and query! This sojourn is going
> to be the best of both worlds: all of my needs
> attended to, yet as free as if on my own.

The day of their arrival to the post left them with only enough daylight to find lodging and then eat before settling in. The meal provided was the best they'd had since leaving the Emperor's palace. However, it was the luxury of a bed that each longed for even more. Between the much-missed comfort and the anticipation of the following day's activity, they were happy to retire early. As John drifted off to sleep, he made a mental note to not oversleep, as he had plenty of plans for his first day and wanted to get an early start.

At first light, John was up and out wandering the village. His natural charm and sincerity allowed him to meet the people in this village as easily as he had when he jumped off the back of the farmer's wagon. Since this was a resting point for travelers, most of the other visitors were, like him, taking a break from their travels. As a result, they could afford leisure conversation with a stranger. And even the locals seemed open to conversing with a curious and outgoing boy who had traveled from the West.

John soon realized that the Eastern lifestyle carved out more time for contemplation than in the West. He also noticed that talk of spirituality and religion was commonplace. The locals were more open to discussing their own beliefs and less threatened by the beliefs of others. This reminded John of his conversation with the Hierophant.

Although the Hierophant had stated that he was open to alternative paths to God, he did mention that most of the others in his order were not. John recalled what he had said: *Western religions typically do not make room for alternate spiritualities, and although many are similar, they still compete for the souls of man.*

Here, in the East, John didn't experience anything of the sort. When revealing his lack of religious affiliation, he was met with a complete absence of judgment. One man responded, "The Buddha acknowledges all paths to enlightenment."

The outpost gave John a good sample of what he might encounter at his destination. He knew from three days of casual conversations with both travelers and locals that he had made the right decision to travel east.

John revealed to his journal:

> I want more than brief discussions about belief. I want to explore Eastern mysticism. But to do so I have been told it is best to study with a spiritual teacher: a guru.

However, every time John asked if there was someone he should seek specifically, he always received the same answer:

"When the student is ready, the teacher will appear."

John was confused. *These people seem so open and friendly, but I wonder if they are teasing me with this clichéd response?* After further consideration, he discerned that the Easterners were sincere. *It must simply be their way to talk in riddles*—he concluded. Nevertheless, he was frustrated by the lack of straightforward responses.

Four days in the village was a balm to his body and spirit. He felt healthy and rejuvenated—still—his soul craved wisdom. As kind as everyone he encountered had been, he could not get past the redundant response that he was going to have to wait until **his teacher appeared**.

While John and his escorts prepared to leave, John received some encouraging news. He learned that the Himalayan region was the spiritual capital of the East and there would be much to learn there.

As the carriage moved down the road out of the village into the next leg of their voyage, the escort driving turned to John and said, "There are three segments remaining to our journey. Each will last about two weeks. First, we will cross the rest of this wide valley that separates the Middle East from the Far East. Next, we will skirt along the southwestern edge of the Himalayan Mountains. Finally, we will ascend a mountain pass that will lead us to our destination."

The first few days of their resumed travels were relatively uneventful. This allowed John time to write in his journal and reflect on his time at the trading post and his conversations with the other travelers. With every entry, the phrase that frustrated him kept reappearing on the page:

When the student is ready, the teacher will appear.

John wondered if his recent illness had somehow impacted his memory. *I feel as if I am forgetting something, but what?*—he wondered one evening. Then, just before drifting off to sleep he remembered the image that had come to him in his feverish dream and a shiver ran through his body: *Your fortunes will fall and rise three times before you see me again.*

He felt self conscious about speaking to his escorts about his dream and instead sought comfort with his journal. He replayed the dream in his mind and tried to give words to it on the pages in front of him. It was through this exercise that he recalled a reference to a wheel. He then wrote:

> Oh no! Is something going to happen with the carriage? Is my dream an omen of misfortune?

John began to feel a wave of despair. He reached into his pocket, pulled out the Black Obsidian stone, and rolled it around in his fingertips until his trepidation softened. He flipped the page and sketched a wheel in his journal; he then found himself penciling animals around it. He stared at the drawing and considered what it all meant, but try as he might; he could not shake the thought of potential problems. Whenever he closed his eyes, he pictured the carriage disabled and the three of them stranded on the side of the road. John knew such musings could be harmful and he recalled the Magician's admonition: *If you keep worrying about misfortune, you will eventually walk into it.*

John decided to stop repressing his fear and shared his concern with his escorts. But when he told his companions about the dream, instead of relieving his fear, he activated theirs.

"We have not seen anyone on this road for days," one said.

"We are low on food and cannot afford to be stranded right now," the other one said.

The three rode on in silence as each fought egregious images that raced through their minds. John continued to finger the Obsidian in his pocket, but the imaginations of his companions would not be silenced.

The driver attempted to be more cautious by shifting the carriage further from the downhill side of the road because his imagination had them running off of the road and crashing to certain doom. However, instead of avoiding turmoil, his reaction to his fear actually created a problem: a boulder, which jutted out from the escarpment, clipped the center of the rear wheel, snapping the pin that held it in place. The wheel hung on for a while, but then popped off the axel. This would not have been catastrophic, in and of itself, except for the fact that the wheel, once off, rolled down the hill behind them and disappeared from sight.

The Emperor's men were capable guides and loyal subjects, but they were not indoctrinated in the workings of the Universe. Therefore, they could not understand or accept responsibility for their own part in creating the mishap. Instead, they looked accusingly at John. They blamed him for what had happened because he was the one who had foretold the accident in the first place.

Although they were angry with John, the two escorts could not rebuke him. They had been given strict orders by the Emperor to take care of the lad. So, instead, they vented their anger at each other. Venomous words were exchange regarding the driving skills of the one at the helm, and this escalated into shoving. A moment later, they were rolling in the dirt with fists flying. Because they found a physical outlet for their anger, it dissipated quickly. One helped the other up out of the dirt and then they started attending to the supplies that had been thrown from the carriage.

John had not witnessed the altercation because he had wandered off in the direction the wheel had gone. There was a slight curve in the road and he thought there was a possibility it might be laying just beyond it. As he walked, he thought of the dream again: *Your fortunes will fall and rise three times...*

"This was most certainly the first calamity," John mumbled. "Will there actually be a rise in fortune for each fall?" This possibility brought him hope, and then confidence that something good could actually come of it.

With no luck after rounding the bend, John headed back to his companions. When he saw them with dirt on their clothes, he looked each one up and down, puzzled. The two simply laughed, but said nothing. John then noticed their bruises and figured out what had happened.

As John stood there facing them, his eyes moved beyond the men and the carriage. Up ahead and just within sight, the road forked. *How did I not see that before?*—he wondered. *The right side is surely the main road as it appears obviously well traveled, but the left side is narrower, it must lead to something close*—he figured.

John tossed his stone up in the air and then from one hand to the other as he took in the scene before him. The weather was relatively mild and the sun was still high in the sky. He estimated that he had at least four hours of sunlight left to explore. He decided to take a chance and investigate. With anticipation, he trotted toward the narrow road.

As he passed the men, one of them said something, but John merely nodded. Intent on his mission, he had not heard the declaration.

Thirty minutes later, John found himself staring at a homestead. He guessed the hut on the left served as the residence since the structure on the right looked like an Eastern version of a barn. He saw chickens, goats, and other animals roaming the yard and then a short man wearing a straw hat. The man carried a workman's tool in one hand and beckoned to John with the other. The man's energy was welcoming and John obeyed.

As John approached, the man spoke out to him, but in a language John did not understand. He recognized the language as one he had heard in the village. The man, detecting John's lack of understanding, tried a second language and then a third, finally finding one that John comprehended.

John was born of mixed race parents and was exposed to multiple languages. His mother died when he was ten. Hearing his mother's language now, after all of these years, stirred images from his youth. But the memories had to wait; he needed to focus on the man in front of him. John had to concentrate not only to understand the man, but more importantly, to express what he wanted to convey. So, in the simple words of a ten-year-old boy, John explained how, "their wagon broke."

The little man's command of the foreign language was nearly as limited as John's, but he nodded with understanding.

The man and John walked side-by-side back to the handicapped carriage. When they reached it, John was surprised to find it upright. He wandered over to his companions to ask them about it.

"I told you we had a spare. Didn't you hear me?"

John shook his head, embarrassed.

"We still have a problem, though," the man continued, "The pin that holds the wheel on was destroyed. If we try and go anywhere, we'll surely lose this one just like we did the last one."

Just then, the little man wandered into view, startling the others.

"John, where…did you find this man?"

"There's a turnoff up ahead, so I followed it and found Mr. Lam's place thirty minutes up the road. He has come to offer his help."

Mr. Lam bowed to the men and they nodded in return. He walked over and methodically inspected the carriage. He compared the damaged wheel to the others and figured out the problem. Then, moving around towards the back, he suddenly and without warning, struck the carriage with his hammer. Another swing, a crack, then some prying, and he broke loose a seemingly worthless piece of wood. He walked over to the damaged wheel and hammered the makeshift peg into the hole where the pin had been.

He told John that the peg would hold long enough for them to travel back to his house where he could fix the wheel more properly.

John roughly translated Mr. Lam's analysis to the others.

Knowing he could not fix the wheel before nightfall, Mr. Lam invited the three for dinner and a night's rest. As he said this, he gestured the act of eating and sleeping for the others to understand. Both men smiled and nodded appreciatively.

The four men climbed into the carriage and headed to Mr. Lam's home…more cautiously than necessary. The escorts silently prayed that the wheel would stay on. Mr. Lam, on the other hand, sat quietly with his eyes closed and his hands resting in his lap. John simply reflected on the day's events.

One escort said to the other, "How fortunate we are. We will get the wheel fixed properly, plus enjoy a hot meal and a good night's rest!"

John overheard the comment and thought, *This is surely a turn in fortune, but is it this the first or the second? Does the miraculous healing count?*

By the time they reached Mr. Lam's residence, it was nearing dusk. As they entered the hut, the aroma of Asian spices filled their nostrils. Mr. Lam introduced the men to his family. The evening passed with little conversation but a lot of eye contact. Mr. Lam told John that his children had never seen men of their race before.

He, himself, had been to the Middle East when he was young, but that was many years before when he had been in the military.

John translated for his companions, which helped to establish a kinship between everyone in the hut.

Since the house was very small, it was explained that the guests would have to sleep in the barn. The men did not mind; they were grateful for a comfortable place to rest. The occasional animal sounds were soothing to John and he quickly fell asleep.

The next morning, John woke before the others and wandered around the property. Many of the animals were awake and eyed the stranger as he meandered. John saw the carriage in the yard and realized that Mr. Lam was already up and working on the wheel. As John walked over to it, he could see the man was hammering in the new pin, which he had crafted to match the others. Rather than disturb Mr. Lam, John quietly watched, admiring his focus and patience. It was clear that Mr. Lam was enjoying himself as he hummed while he worked.

John shifted his weight slightly, which made a bit of noise, and Mr. Lam noticed. He turned, smiled brightly, and greeted John. "Good morning, my friend. Did you sleep well?"

"Completely! Thank you so much for your hospitality and kindness. Have you fixed the wheel already?"

"Oh yes, the wheel will be as good as new. It is like a puzzle," he said with excitement. "To work with my hands and to solve mechanical problems is a comfort to me; it is a **moving meditation**."

Many of the man's words were beyond John's basic vocabulary, but he was still able to understand the essence of what the man was saying.

John and his two companions were back on the road a short while later. They felt confident with the repairs and their luck overall. In fact, the rest of the trip transpired without a glitch.

Intermittently, John would remember his dream with a twinge of worry that something else would go wrong, but would then remind himself that, at least so far, each problem was followed by a solution.

PAGE OF SWORDS

A few days later, as the sun neared the high peaks to the west, the men entered the outer reaches of the city. Instantly, they were surrounded by people heading in all directions. At this time of the day, many of the merchants were preparing for the late afternoon winds that swept off of the mountaintops as the sun's rays retreated behind them.

Once the sun set completely, the winds would die back down, but during that hour of transition, it was best to secure any items that might fly away. John's escorts, having been to this city previously, were familiar with the daily phenomenon. They would have preferred to arrive an hour or two earlier, but were, nevertheless, happy to be traveling in daylight.

Although the city was populous, it did not cover a great area. It took them less than the remaining daylight to reach the palace, which was visible as soon as they entered the city limits. John looked around in awe as they drew closer. The architecture in this Eastern mountain city intrigued him, but nothing compared with the royal residence.

The palace was not surrounded by a wall, as was the Emperor's castle. Clearly, it was not designed for war. However, it still conveyed power, just of a different sort. The design was fascinating to John because it seemed to defy nature. The materials looked light enough to float on air, yet even during the windiest part of the day, the structure held firm. It channeled the gusts so well, in fact, that once in the central courtyard, the air was still.

The Emperor's men brought the carriage to a full stop and climbed down from their perch. John looked around but saw no one. There were no guards at the gate, and even inside the courtyard, not a soul passed through. John looked up at the windows that faced the courtyard and noticed the beautiful fabrics that decorated them. As his eyes followed the perimeter of the courtyard, his peripheral vision caught sight of a young woman approaching them.

The first thing John noticed about the young woman was her dress. The fabric had the same sheen as the material of the draperies, but with a different color and pattern. The dress was both simple and elegant. Its simplicity was that it was fashioned from a single piece of cloth, but the cut and tailoring was elegant. It fit her athletic figure perfectly.

John guessed her to be about sixteen years of age. Her hair was straight, nearly black, and hung down naturally around her shoulders. Her eyes, a deep dark brown, conveyed a maturity that far exceeded her age.

Before John said a word, the young woman bowed deeply as a greeting and introduced herself, "Welcome. I am Vinita, the only daughter of the Queen and King. Your arrival has been anticipated. It is nice to see that you have endured the journey safely. Please follow me and I will take you to the Queen." She then looped her arm in John's and escorted all three into the palace.

Once inside, Vinita led them down a grand hallway that intersected another perpendicularly. As they neared the end, Vinita paused as if taking notice of something disconcerting. John could almost sense it too, but being unfamiliar with the environment, he had nothing to base his feeling on. She signaled the men to hold still and keep silent, then crept further down the hall with the poise of a cat approaching its prey.

KNIGHT OF SWORDS

Suddenly, a young man leaped out from around the corner. Instantly, the two were engulfed in a flurry of mock battle. John watched with amazement, each strike blocked by a hand or foot. The boy had an advantage over Vinita in height and strength, yet still could not sneak a blow past her guard. She was clearly on the defense, yet was in no way losing ground.

Just when it appeared that the Queen's daughter was faltering, she surprised them all with a most skilled maneuver. Jumping into the air, she planted a foot at the center of the boy's chest and sprung backwards off of him towards the men, landing first on her hands and then round to her feet. The boy was knocked off balance and thrown to the floor, yet gracefully rolled back up to his feet, resuming a posture of readiness. It was only then that he noticed the guests silently observing the scuffle. He blushed with embarrassment, and then quickly composed himself.

Vinita broke the silence to explain. "This is my brother, Rajesh, first born and only son of the Queen and King."

Rajesh bowed his head slightly.

Vinita continued in a casual manner, "He is my **impetuous** brother who never tires of keeping me on the defense all day. I **so** look forward to his eighteenth birthday when he will be sent to university, freeing me of his daily attacks." Vinita smiled at her brother, a sweet smile that clearly conveyed she had gained the upper hand over her sibling.

QUEEN OF SWORDS

U nexpectedly, Vinita's smiling face turned serious and she dropped her eyes submissively. John turned to discern the cause and saw the Queen approaching from the far end of the hall. A quick glance at Rajesh confirmed John's suspicion that he too had assumed a humble and submissive stance.

As John watched the Queen's approach, he marveled at how her walk possessed an air of authority. She gave Vinita and Rajesh a disapproving glare—a mother silently scolding her children. She quickly regained her composure and slowly shifted her attention to John and the Emperor's men. The tension in the room remained, although she was smiling. Then her stance visibly softened. John found that as her body relaxed, so did his. The three men quickly bowed to the Queen.

She nodded in response and then spoke, "Welcome to my country, my city, and my home. Vinita, you are excused. Rajesh, come with us. Men, if you would, please follow me." The Queen turned, and continued back the way she had come.

Instinctively, John trailed a few paces behind, afraid of being too close. He continued to observe her posture: stiff, upright, and with shoulders back. He had never seen a woman walk with such a commanding presence. The closest example that he could think of was the High Priestess. She too emanated an aura of power, which she derived from her knowingness and her access to the inner workings of the Universe, and which gave her confidence. The woman in front of him was more like the Emperor, a leader, and radiating that similar demeanor of authority, albeit in a female way.

John then thought of females in the animal kingdom, specifically the lioness and how ferociously she protected her cubs. His mind flashed with images of myriad female beasts taking stands to defend their young. Among the visuals, he heard four words:

Behold the Alpha Female.

The inner voice caused John to pause momentarily. *Alpha Female?* He knew he had never heard the term before, but for some reason, he knew what it meant. The Emperor exemplified the Alpha Male, and now this Queen was illustrating to him what the female counterpart was like.

The Queen led the men into a large receiving room and sat in one of two oversized wooden chairs. As with the Emperor's receiving room, intricate symbols had been carved into the furniture. Each chair was unique, yet both were adorned with a curved sword placed just above the head. The Queen made herself comfortable and eyed her guests.

The Emperor's men took their seats and focused their attention on the Queen. John's inquisitive nature took over; instead of sitting, he turned his head to explore the entire room. It took him a few minutes in the silent chamber to realize that the Queen had been waiting for him. Slightly embarrassed, he sat.

"I trust that your travels were smooth and without challenge, yes?" the Queen said to the three. She raised an eyebrow, and added, "Maybe a bit of delay in your arrival, but not enough to prevent it?"

The men looked at each other, but no one said a word.

"And John, I trust all went well at the wedding from your vantage?"

John merely nodded.

"Good. Now, on to more pressing subjects." As the Queen spoke, John couldn't help but steal a glance at the empty chair. The Queen noticed.

"Fear not, you will be acquainted with the King later. He is attending to things as men do." The Queen sensed John's confusion and continued, "John, this is not Kathmandu. Although kings run much of the rest of the world, this small part of it is still run by women. The Capital City does not sanction our matriarchal ways, but thankfully, they do not exert themselves upon us either. Thus, my daughter will succeed my throne, and her daughter after that.

"It is my belief that we have enjoyed an extended period of peace as a result, that, in conjunction with our devotion to Quan Yin and the Buddha. Although we participate in simulated combat via our martial arts, we believe that the true battle is only with the self. Once one comes to accept this, then all external obstacles can be prevailed by turning inward, rather than fighting others.

"But enough of this. There will be sufficient time for you to learn more of our ways later. Rajesh, provide entertainment for Master John as I have some business matters to discuss with the Emperor's men. Stay within the confines of the palace. I will send for you when I am ready."

As John walked out of the room, he felt for his companions, knowing they were at a disadvantage with the Queen. He then turned his attention to her son, who, at seventeen, had obtained the stature and strength of a man, while retaining the face and personality of a boy.

The energetic Rajesh guided John through the palace with a quick pace. John realized Rajesh was excited to have a male peer present. It was clear that he lacked the companionship of boys his age and was eager to share his passions with one. As they walked, his mind darted from subject to subject just about as fast as his body carried him from place to place. They finally reached their first destination.

"This is the sparring room where my sister and I train with our Sensei twice a week," Rajesh explained. "He is from Japan, but knows many disciplines. Would you like to learn some of the basics? I can teach you?"

"Rajesh, I have to admit, you and your sister put on an impressive display. How could I say no? It looked like so much fun!"

Rajesh was thrilled to have a pupil. "First, we need to learn some tumbling. This is to keep us off the floor as much as possible." Rajesh demonstrated and John watched. He then explained important details and demonstrated again. Finally, it was John's turn to try. He was a fast learner. Although not as athletic as the boy or his sister, he mastered the move without much difficulty.

Rajesh was pleased and continued with more challenging moves. John was again able to imitate Rajesh, although not as gracefully. Rather than being impressed with himself, John couldn't help but wonder—*How could it be that I am learning this so quickly?* With doubt in his mind, he attempted the next tumble, which proved to be a grave mistake. Because of his mind's distraction, John's focus was compromised and he did not hold his body as instructed. He landed with his leg askew, which caused him to twist his ankle. He screamed as he crashed to the floor.

What have I done? What a fool I am to have attempted these moves so soon! His self-deprecating thoughts were briefly interrupted by the memory of his dream: *Your fortunes will fall and rise three times before you see me again.* As he winced in pain, all he could conclude was that this injury was another bout of bad luck. He prayed his ankle wasn't broken.

Rajesh felt concerned for what had happened and tried to console John. He knew his mother would not be pleased with the turn of events and decided to run and get his father.

KING OF SWORDS

A few moments later, Rajesh returned with his father trailing behind. The King knelt next to John and began examining his leg. His actions were methodical and without emotion. He held John's leg firmly while thoroughly testing the range of motion of his ankle, moving John's foot until John screamed.

The King silently considered the extent of the damage. He came out of his deep thoughts and articulated instructions to his son. Rajesh ran off quickly to fetch the requested items and returned in a flash. The King began to brace John's leg. As he worked on the injured limb, he explained his process to John and his son. Although John wished the man handled him more gently, he found confidence in the King's apparent knowledge of physiology. Once the King determined that John could be moved, he and Rajesh lifted him off the mat. The two supported all of John's weight as they carried him off through the palace. The pain in John's leg continued to throb and as soon as he was laid out on a bed, he passed out.

ACE OF SWORDS

For the next 36 hours, John drifted in and out of consciousness. The first time he roused, he saw that his leg had been wrapped and elevated in a sling. John fought to remain lucid, but the effect of whatever herbs he had been given was too strong.

The next time John woke, he felt as if he had just been talking with someone he knew well. The few aspects of the dream that stayed with him quickly slipped away as the pain pushed back into his awareness. The discomfort was constant, but had transformed into a dull chronic ache and was no longer all-consuming. In fact, it left just enough room for John to sense his hunger. He looked to his left and saw a tray with food and water. A few bites and gulps was all he could muster before falling back to sleep.

The third time John awoke, he felt an odd sensation running through his body. It wasn't pain he felt, but rather warmth. The heat originated at his foot and traveled up towards his knee. Beyond the knee, he felt a buzzing vibration that moved all the way up to his head. Waves of energy then began to travel throughout. His head oscillated gently and his eyelids fluttered, but would not open. In his mind's eye he saw swirling colors and silhouettes above him. Then he felt as if someone was leaning down towards his face peering into him intently.

With a bit of effort, John forced his eyes open enough to see what was happening in the room. The silhouettes were gone, replaced by a single man standing near his feet. The man's hands hovered above John's injured leg and moved as if caressing something invisible in the air. John was sure that he could feel within his leg the movement of the man's hands. When the man's hands approached his knee, his entire leg began to quiver. When they moved back down to his ankle, his foot rocked back and forth. It felt as if invisible strings connected the man's hands to John's body, allowing the man to move him like a puppet.

John's eyes grew heavy and again his consciousness waned. Just as he was falling back asleep, he thought about the man and was certain he had seen him before, *but where?*

Δ   ▲   Δ

T he next moment in John's awareness had him lying on the grass with the sun shining down on him. He looked around and saw puffy white clouds floating by. A voice echoed, instructing him to stand up.

"I don't want to stand, it is going to hurt," he heard himself say.

Do not worry my friend, just stand and see for yourself.

John complied, and not only was he surprised that he felt no pain...he actually felt nothing at all. *How odd*—he thought.

He looked around—nothing...no trees...no hills—just white. He looked down. There was no grass beneath his feet. *Am I standing on a cloud? How could this be?* Suddenly he had the sensation that he was falling. He threw his leg out to catch himself and his whole body jerked.

John, now completely awake, looked around the room. No one was with him, however fresh food had been placed next to his bed. A little bit of light filtered into the room, but John could not tell whether it was dawn or dusk. *How long have I been in this room? And what was that dream about?*—he wondered.

He clearly remembered tripping, which is what woke him. He looked down at his leg, but the brace was gone. *A brace **had** been there, hadn't it?* He moved his foot slightly, but there was no pain. He tested it a little more, still no pain. *OK, let's try standing*—he thought. Then he remembered the voice from his dream: *Do not worry my friend, just stand and see for yourself.*

OK I will—he decided.

He swung his feet down to the floor then pushed up off of the bed. He first stood on his good leg, and then shifted his weight slowly to the other. *Still no pain; how strange. Do I dare try jumping up and down?*

"Go ahead and see for yourself?" came the reply, not from his mind but from within the room.

John spun around so fast he nearly lost his balance; he placed a hand on the bed to keep from falling. The voice John heard, he realized, was from the man of his feverish dream in the carriage. He opened his mouth to speak, but only half-garbled words came out.

"Go ahead, my friend, jump up and down. Test it out. You will find that your ankle has completely healed."

John blinked twice to make sure he wasn't seeing an apparition. "But...you...you are the man from my dream."

"I thought you might remember me from when I visited you. I am sure you do not remember visiting me though. Do you?"

"I...I visited you?"

"Yes, you actually came to me first. When the student is ready, the teacher appears, but it is the student that calls out to the teacher. Your intention to learn is very strong. Are you aware of this?"

"Are you saying that my desire to learn has called you as a teacher?"

"It is not just your desire, my young friend. Your desire is where it begins, yes, but it is your **intention** that holds all of the power."

"My intention?"

"You demonstrated your intent by traveling all of this way. Idle desires in and of themselves do not bear fruit. At this time, I ask that if you **truly** wish to learn more about Eastern mysticism, that you come stay with me for a while."

"Stay with you? Where?"

"In my cabin just outside of the city. Your progress in this area requires undivided attention, at least for a while."

"But I just arrived. Wouldn't it be rude for me to leave so soon? I hardly got acquainted with the Queen's family before I was injured."

"I have already spoken to the Queen and I have her consent to commence with your learning."

"You have?"

"Yes, but only if you concur. It is tradition here for one to apprentice with a guru once he or she has come of age. You are old enough to decide for yourself. Is this acceptable to you?"

"Yes. Absolutely!"

"Good. My intuition told me that you would be amicable to this, so I took the liberty to have your men collect the minimum of your belongings. You will not be in need of much."

John followed the Guru's eyes, looked down, and saw his satchel on the floor. He smiled to himself at the thought of being back down to his trusted old pack.

"We should go. We have a long walk ahead of us."

Δ   ▲   Δ

F or the next few hours, the Guru led John across the city in the opposite direction from where he had entered just days earlier. They headed northeast, further in towards the mountains. The Guru walked slowly, methodically, and in total silence. Occasionally, he would nod as a greeting to a passerby, but he neither raised a hand nor spoke a word.

The trek reminded John of the day he had met the Magician, his first spiritual teacher. The way the two walked, deliberately and in silence, their presence and serenity, all felt similar. Even the Hierophant shared these qualities.

By late afternoon, the two had traveled out of the city limits. They rarely encountered others now as they ventured further up the mountain pass. They walked among the giants but did not climb them. As the forest grew thicker, John felt that they were nearing their destination. Sure enough, deep in the forest, they came upon a small grass hut nestled between some trees. In fact, the trees appeared to have been planted in formation as supports for the hut, rather than the hut being added among them.

"Have you lived here a long time, Guru?"

The Guru nodded in response to John's question, but did not speak. John began to wonder if he overstepped some boundary, but felt no judgment from his Guru, and so quickly dismissed the thought.

"My friend, as an outsider to this culture, I do not expect you to know of our customs, so I will break silence this evening to explain what you may expect for the next ten days."

John shook his head for a moment. *Why is it that all of my spiritual teachers read my mind so easily? Am I an open book to the spiritually endowed?*

The Guru smiled for the first time since they'd met, and then began to laugh. He laughed so heartily that John couldn't help but laugh himself. For five full minutes, the two men laughed and held their stomachs, tears streaming down their faces.

"Thank you for sharing your joy with me. Joy and laughter are the most healing of expressions that a human can experience. Never lose the ability to laugh with your whole being." The Guru returned to his demur demeanor and signaled John to follow him into the hut.

The hut consisted of a single room that served as kitchen, dining room, living room, and bedroom. The kitchen area contained a simple wood-burning stove. A teakettle and iron pot sat upon it. The bedroom/living area contained nothing more than two futons. In the final corner, John saw a tree-stump that had been fashioned into a small table with seat cushions surrounding it. Although the quarters were simple, they contained all that was needed...with one exception.

The lack of indoor plumbing is a small price to pay for spiritual growth—John reasoned.

The Guru sat at the stump and motioned for John to join him. Then he began to speak, "My friend, in the time that has passed between when we first, shall we say, met, and now, you experienced life on the outside of the Wheel of Fortune. As the Wheel turns, fortunes rise and fortunes fall. Many men live near the rim of the Wheel; it makes for an exciting ride. However, at any time, you can move towards the center of the Wheel. Once at the center, the motion of the Wheel will have no effect on you. The Wheel of Life cannot be stopped; peace is found only at the hub, namely being centered within one's self.

"For this time we are together, I will teach you how to reach the center of your Wheel. In the beginning, you might only be able to stay there for a short while, but over time, you can learn to remain there as much as you like."

All John could do was nod. He wondered how long it would take to master the skill.

The Guru did not respond to John's thoughts, instead he explained the daily routine. "Each day, we will rise 30 minutes before dawn. We will drink tea, but not eat. In this way, we will be fully lucid by dawn. From the beginning of dawn until shortly after sunrise, we will sit for the morning meditation. After meditation, we will prepare and then eat our first meal. From sunrise until early afternoon is the only part of the day when we eat. No more food will be consumed after our mid-afternoon snack.

"The late afternoon is dedicated to outdoor activity, the gathering of wood and food, or perhaps a leisure walk. In the early evening, we do chores in and around the hut. Each night, we will perform yoga exercises for an hour, and then meditate for an hour before retiring."

John nodded, trying to memorize the routine.

"For the first ten days, this will all be done in silence."

"I won't be able to ask you any questions?" John asked, nervously.

"There will be no talking at all."

"I don't know if I can be totally silent," John admitted.

"I will teach you two meditation techniques that will assist you in tempering your urges. The first requires a mantra; it is simultaneously the most simple and the most difficult."

"A mantra?" John asked.

"Yes, a mantra is a phrase specifically tailored to an individual. Its purpose is to help you focus. You will repeat the mantra in your mind over and over without following any other thoughts. Each time extraneous thoughts enter you mind, and they will, permit them to pass on through. If at any time one of them catches hold and you fall into a chain of thought, you are to gently return your focus to your mantra."

John knew this would be difficult. Thoughts constantly rolled through his mind. "What is my mantra?" he asked.

"I will discern the most appropriate words for you. They are yours alone, hold them close."

John knew he would need to think about it to find the right one. "What is the second technique?"

"I will place an object in front of you. You are to focus all of your attention on that object. You may think about any aspect of the object, but nothing more. All superfluous thoughts are to be released, and then return attention solely to the object in front of you."

John guessed this second technique would be easier than the mantra, but it would probably depend upon the object.

"Take the rest of the evening to do as you please. Our routine will begin in the morning. I suggest you relax and get an early night's sleep."

John had had a long day, but after crawling into his futon, he discovered he was not ready to sleep. His mind flashed images of the mountain city. Intermittently, he thought about the meditation techniques. He repeated the mantra the Guru had given him, to make sure he had memorized it adequately. The more he thought about his situation, the more excited he felt. Here he was, exactly where he had hoped to be, learning Eastern mysticism from a master.

As tired as his body was, John's mind could not rest. He had been with the Guru for less than a day, and all the new information he had gained was floating around his head. His mind was trying to process all he had learned and as a result generated symbolic images. The scene of their trek into the mountains took shape as the background. Each of the new ideas he was learning became clouds floating across the sky. Sporadically, a crow would fly by, cawing out his mantra. More and more clouds filled the sky, blocking out the sun as it neared the western horizon.

A hand appeared, stretching out from one of the clouds. It clutched a giant sword in its grasp. The hand held the sword still for a moment, then whipped it across the sky, generating a mighty wind. John felt the wind on his face and squinted his eyes against it. It reminded him of that first afternoon, when the winds rushed down from the mountaintops.

The winds subsided, just as quickly as they appeared, leaving the sky clear. The sword, still clutched by the giant hand, was again held stationary; the sword's blade reflected the setting sun, casting rays of light in all directions.

Once again, John squinted. This time his eyes responded to the light. The color of the sun shifted from a brilliant yellow, to a shimmering orange, to a glowing red. In the reflection, John could see the sun's shape morph as it began to dip beneath the horizon. Just as the last of the sun was about to disappear, a bright green flash shot out from the sword, temporarily blinding John, and then causing the entire image to fade into a deep dark grey. A moment later, his whole body shook.

John opened his eyes just as the Guru removed his hand from his shoulder. Long shadows, created by a single candle burning near the wood stove, shimmered against the walls. John rubbed his eyes and tried to rouse himself further. He caught the sound of water nearing a boil, which confirmed that morning had arrived.

The Guru retrieved the kettle from the stove, poured the hot liquid into the two cups, and laid them out on the tree-stump table. The smell of the tea began to fill the room. John climbed off of his futon and made his way to the table; a shiver rumbled through his body in defense of the morning chill. Before sipping his tea, John warmed his hands around the mug.

The Guru sipped his tea as he watched John from above the rim of his mug. His eyes looked watery in the candlelight, yet conveyed a seriousness that made John look away self-consciously. As John drank the tea, his taste buds adjusted, shifting the flavor from bitter to savory. The caffeine soon took effect and he felt his energy rise.

The Guru finished his tea, rose from the table, and moved over to his futon. He placed his body in what John would come to recognize as the lotus position. He looked over to John and then towards the window, indicating that dawn had broken and that it was time for their first meditation. John obediently scrambled over to his own futon and approximated the Guru's position as best he could.

The Guru then nodded slightly towards John and softly closed his eyes immediately entering a meditative trance.

TWO OF SWORDS

J ohn closed his eyes and the battle ensued. A part of his mind obediently recited his mantra while another complained. His mind drifted down to the discomfort in his legs and he forced it back. It focused on his stomach, growling with hunger, and again John moved his mind back to the mantra.

John tried to intensify his concentration, but random thoughts continued to steal his focus away from his discipline. As before, one part of his mind chanted while the other berated him for his inability to properly meditate. John continued to wrestle with his mind, but with little success.

After almost twenty minutes of this internal struggle, something began to shift. John's breathing fell into rhythm with his inner voice. Half of the mantra fell within the in-breath and the other half with the out-breath. His body relaxed and began to rock, alleviating the discomfort in his legs. The rocking motion gave John the sensation of floating, and this created an image in his mind. As he was instructed, he observed the image as objectively as he could.

The scene in front of John took the shape of a desert landscape reminiscent of what he had seen as he crossed the Middle East. The land was barren and littered with large boulders. As he floated forward, he began to compare the feeling of his motion to that of the carriage. He caught himself analyzing and gently returned his focus to his mantra and watched.

In the distance, a band of color appeared and morphed into a body of water stretching to the horizon. As he approached it, a silhouette appeared and took shape. The figure that emerged resembled the Queen's daughter. She was seated in the lotus position, precariously balanced on top of a boulder. She was blindfolded and balanced two large swords in front of her on arms folded across her chest. The right hand held its sword towards the left and the left hand towards the right. Behind her, the sky looked stormy. Waves crashed against the large rocks that jutted out of the water, a threat to anyone who dared to enter the sea.

As John drew closer, his forward movement slowed and then stopped. He continued to float gently up and down, but moved no nearer to the girl or the ocean. Although the girl held her balance, John felt the tension and struggle, as if at any moment she would have to drop the swords or jump off the boulder. The sky darkened, as if warning him to heed the dangers that lay beyond the edge of the sea.

Dusk settled in behind the girl. A sliver of a moon glistened above the horizon. John remembered that in Islam, this first visible phase of the moon marked the beginning of the lunar month. The conscious, logical portion of John's mind grew stronger and brought him out of the trance. *Is this an omen? Are there dangers forthcoming?* As he studied the image before him, he came to the realization that he was at a threshold; once he crossed it, there was no going back.

Although the sea looked ominous, John knew he must proceed in spite of what lay ahead. In that moment, John had an urgent desire to share the vision before him with his Guru. He wanted his teacher to give him insight into its meaning and his interpretation. Instead, he resigned himself to the notion that he would forget all about it by the time he would be allowed to speak again.

Δ   ▲   Δ

For the next two days, John's morning meditations alternated between little and no success, and no new visions came to him. His mind seemed to be gaining strength against him rather than relenting to his will. Then one night, within a dream, John found himself walking along a curved path. A tall hedge had grown along either side, and John could not see beyond its height. As he walked, it appeared that he was heading directly towards the hedge itself. *Is this a dead end?* He then realized that he had reached a fork; the path split left and right.

John did not hesitate; he chose the path to the right and ran down it. He wasn't sure if he was running with urgency or just for the fun of it, but soon he came to another dead end. No, it was another fork. *Hmm, this feels familiar.*

This time, John took the path to the left and again ran down it. Again he came to yet another fork. *Is this the same fork?* He stood there for a moment and looked down in each direction, then at the hedge that marked the fork itself. *I feel like I keep returning to this same place.*

He looked down each path again, and now saw a different scene. The ocean lay in the distance; storm clouds loomed above it. It was the same in both directions, yet oddly, it was cloudless and calm where he was in between.

Something was familiar about the ominous ocean scene. It was then that he remembered his vision from days before. It was the same scene as then, just from a different vantage. Suddenly, a voice resonated "Which way will you go?"

John turned and saw Vinita standing next to him. She was dressed as she was in his first vision, but her eyes were uncovered and she no longer held the swords. As he noticed this, his perspective shifted. He realized that he was not looking at her with his own eyes because he was the one now blindfolded; he was the one holding the swords.

Again she asked her question: "Which way will you go?"

"Which way **should** I go?"

"This is not a question of should, merely a question of will."

From the perspective of his dream, John looked left...then right...and finally looked directly at the back of his blindfolded self...the hedge before him. Then...his sight went dark.

"You must choose. You must lay down a sword and remove your blind. The sword you lay down will be the path abandoned," the girl's voice said softly in his ear, "The one that remains represents the direction chosen."

But John could not choose. He had already peered down both paths and could not see a difference between them. He had already traveled left and right, only to end up in this same place. *What am I missing? Is there something more?* Then...John heard what he thought was his Guru's voice.

Wake up, my boy. It is time to meditate.

This time the voice was real and roused him from his sleep. "Wake up, my boy. It is time to meditate."

That's it, John realized. That's the answer! Seek within. There is a third choice!

John sat up and accepted the tea handed to him. As he looked up at his Guru, he realized that he could not have heard his teacher speak…both were still remaining mute.

John felt the dream pulling away and mentally reached for it before it was gone. He forced himself to remember what the girl had said to him…and that voice. He sat to meditate and fell quickly into a serene and tranquil state; one he had been unable to achieve for the past two days. The trance remained without vision or conversation, yet flowed effortlessly.

THREE OF SWORDS

T hat night, during his evening meditation, a new vision appeared. John was out in the forest. It was dark and cold. He was afraid and his heart raced. He heard hooves trampling the ground behind him. He ran—ran out of fear, trying to find the safety of the hut, but he could not find it. He could feel the beast drawing nearer. A sword appeared in his hand and two others on his belt. Then a voice spoke out to him: "You cannot outrun it; you must slay the beast. Three swords to the heart is the only way to defeat it."

The galloping behind John grew louder. He stopped and braced for the attack. He turned swiftly and raised his sword defensively. The beast, which had lunged into the air, fell directly onto John's upheld sword, piercing itself in the chest.

Three swords to the heart is the only way...

John let go of the first sword and reached across his body to retrieve the second. Before the fear returned, he impaled the beast a second time, close to where the first sword had penetrated.

John then examined the wounded beast. The body was horrific, but the face was that of a man. John saw pain in its eyes and sadness, which filled him with compassion. Compassion led to empathy as he began to feel the beast's pain.

The face transformed and became that of his own. Then the body morphed into his body, but dressed as he had in his youth. John began to cry and wondered why he had been made to pierce his own image.

He knelt down next to the wounded figure and reached for its face. The eyes opened and looked directly at John, pleading for mercy. John's hand drew within inches, but then the boy's sad expression shifted and gave way to a smirk and then laughter. The face changed into the mean face of a spiteful man. John recognized the man, but before he could place him, he transformed back into the vile beast. The laugh echoed dauntingly. The teeth of the beast were long, sharp, and yellow, and his breath was hot and rancid. The beast's hand flew up, catching John's throat. His ugly green nails drew blood as they pushed into John's skin.

"Empathy is your weakness," the beast growled in a raspy voice.

John had to act and now; it was the beast's life or his own. His left hand pulled at the beast's claw that clutched at his throat while his right hand reached for the last of his swords. As soon as his hand grabbed the handle, it fell free from its scabbard. He lifted the sword as high as he could and then drove it down into the beast between the other two swords.

The beast's hand went limp and fell from John's throat. John quickly replaced it with his own. He let go of the sword and peered into the beast's vacant eyes. The face transformed back into the mean and familiar man, but only for a moment before once again becoming his own. This time, the body remained that of the beast.

Is this beast disguised as me or is it reflecting some part of my own being?—John wondered.

Without knowing the answer, John began to mourn for the creature. He knew he had no choice but to slay this beast, yet he still felt remorse. The pain in his heart grew and this time, the tears were real. The sensation of them flowing down his cheeks roused him from his trance. He soon began to sob uncontrollably and fell into the anticipating arms of his Guru.

The Guru held him tenderly, stroking his hair gently as the sobs continued. John couldn't find the origin of all of the pain, but some part of him knew that it had to pass through him this way, lest it never leave. For the first time in his life, he was truly letting it go.

Was this part of what the young woman was forewarning me about? Was this the first trial of many?

The Guru gently laid John down on the futon and John brought his knees up close to his chest. He then moved in behind John and held him until the boy cried himself to sleep.

FOUR OF SWORDS

T he next morning, John woke of his own accord. The sun was already shining in through the window. He had been allowed to sleep late for the first time since staying at the hut. He looked around the room, but his Guru was not there. A cup of tea rested on the floor near him and was still warm.

John sat up and started drinking the tea, recalling the dream he had just woken from. A lasting image stayed with him of a knight lying still. The odd thing was that the dream was both first person and third person at the same time. In the one view, **he** was the one lying on a bed, resting after an odious battle. In another he was standing beside the body, looking down at it. In this second view, instead of a bed, the body was laid out on a tomb, encased in knight's armor, its face hidden by the metallic mask.

John's mind returned to his meditation from the night before. The intense emotion was distant now; all that remained was solace.

John climbed out of the futon with cup in hand and wandered out into the morning light. The weather was the most pleasant he had seen thus far in this Eastern country. As he made his way around the hut, he found his Guru sitting quietly in a patch of sunlight. The old man held his hand out and was feeding four small rabbits. Upon seeing that John was awake, the Guru got up and led John back into the hut with an arm around his shoulder. John knew that he had been allowed extra rest because of the emotional release the evening before, but he also knew that it was now time to get back to their routine.

Δ ▲ Δ

J ohn had had a breakthrough, and over the next few days he realized he was reaching his first level of mastery. Now the yoga, the meditations, the entire routine flowed with little effort. But four days later, John began to feel restless. *Is this it? Is this as far as I am going to go?*—he wondered.

Before retiring, John decided to say a quick prayer. He asked for a shift, a change, something to stimulate his interest and further his learning. Little did he know what the Universe had in response.

FIVE OF SWORDS

T he next evening, John woke in the middle of the night. His heart was racing and he was wet with sweat. Another horrible dream filled him with fear. This time, no images remained...only emotion.

As John lie there in the dark, he began to shiver, partly from the cool air against his wet skin and partly because of the fear that haunted him. He listened for his Guru, but heard nothing. *Is he still there? Is he alive?*

Suddenly, John was overcome with paranoia. *If anything happens to this man, how will I find my way back to the city? I do not think I could do it on my own. Does anyone even know I am here?* The Guru said he had spoken with the Queen, but John had no proof that they knew where he was.

John wondered where all his fear was coming from. *I feel threatened, but why?* He looked back into his memory and while he couldn't remember anything specific, he did find the emotion somehow familiar. *Is this what is meant by déjà vu?*

For the next hour, John tossed and turned, unable to sleep. The fear and the panic kept gnawing at him. He had been alone plenty of times within his travels, yet not deep in the forest of a strange country. He tried listening for the Guru again, but again, heard nothing except animal noises outside of the hut. And these brought him no solace.

Somehow, John managed to fall back asleep. In this latest dream, he found himself standing near a young boy. The boy was waiting outside of a government building, and was scared. A trial was taking place and activity could be heard. John knelt next to the boy and offered him comfort.

"Are you OK, little guy?"

"I'm scared. There is a mean man in there. What if he gets free? He will come after me because I told on him. He said if I ever told anyone what he did to me, he would find me and then I would **really** be sorry."

"Don't worry, little guy. He is tied up. They caught him and they are not going to let him go. You are safe now."

"But what if he escapes? What if he finds me?"

"Let's hope that that never happens. Do you remember what he did to you?"

"Yes." The boy grimaced.

"I will tell you a secret: in remembering what transpired, you can better heal from it. If you hide it away and pretend like it never happened, it will be much harder to overcome. It will follow you around and make you sad and afraid. Then you will be my age and not know what all of the pain is about. You don't want that to happen, do you?"

Δ   ▲   Δ

For the first time in days, the Guru needed to wake John when it was time to get up. Even awake, the dream stayed with him. In fact, the dream stayed with him all morning and prevented him from meditating with any success. *Who was that boy and what happened to him? And why was I telling him it was better to remember?*

When John wasn't thinking about the morning dream, he was thinking about the feeling he had in the middle of the night. *What am I worried about? Was that another premonition of looming disaster?* The hairs on the back of his neck stood on end.

John's inability to concentrate lasted throughout the next day and was evident. He was frustrated with himself and was afraid of disappointing his Guru. Although there was only one day of silence left, it felt like an eternity and was excruciating.

The Guru determined it was hardly worth it for John to sit for another fruitless meditation. He decided it was best to break silence a little early. In the middle of the afternoon, he uttered the first words in nearly two weeks.

SIX OF SWORDS

M y friend, what is troubling you so much that you can hardly wait a few more hours to speak?"

The Guru was braced for a verbal deluge, but did not expect an hour would pass before John conveyed all that troubled him. John told him about the latest dream of the little boy, and the nighttime of fear that preceded it. As John related one story, another popped into his head. Before they knew it, John had reviewed the entire ten-day period, including all of the visions, dreams, and emotions he experienced.

John finally finished his tome and asked, "Guru, I don't think I'll be able to concentrate on my meditations without your help; is there anything you can say to me to help me understand all of this?"

The Guru had observed John's shifts and emotions during the past two weeks but was still amazed how much John had processed and released. He appreciated John's unique interpretations. He understood well the process of one getting acquainted with the inner self. Many of his students had a similar unfolding, but each was distinct. There was nothing he could say to the boy that would reveal what was trying to make itself known to him. John would have to travel that road further.

Instead, the Guru told John that their routine would be interrupted for the next several days. "At dawn we will commence a brief sojourn. Movement restores harmony," the Guru said.

The words stayed with John, holding some unknown significance.

In lieu of their usual ritual, the men spent the rest of the afternoon preparing for their trip. They gathered food for the journey and packed makeshift housing for their nights away from the hut.

Before their evening sit, the Guru told John it was time for another lesson on meditation. The Guru reviewed the first two methods taught and explained to John that they were two variations of a single type of meditation. "This is what is known as **active meditation** because one actively controls the direction of his mind. In each method, one focuses the mind on something specific (a mantra or an external object) and is to persistently let go of all other extraneous thought.

"The second type of meditation is **passive meditation**. Here the mind is not focused in a particular direction, but is instead allowed to observe whatever shows up. As with active mediation, there are two methods."

John first learned that upon resuming the meditative position, he was to relax and observe any thoughts that were present. As before, one would often experience two minds. The **first mind** held thoughts and the **second mind** observed them. The challenge was to remain within the observing second mind and not lose oneself in the thinking first mind.

This new form of meditation sounded easy to John, at least until he sat to practice it. Instead of passively observing the first mind, John found that he could not help but fall into the thoughts that showed up there. Once catching hold of a random thought, John could lose five or ten minutes following the chain without even realizing that he was no longer observing.

When he did become aware of what he was doing, and thus activating his second mind, he struggled to find something for the second mind to focus on. His second mind wanted to be like the first mind, analyzing what it observed. Often, the first mind would think a random thought and the second mind would notice and then think thoughts in response. The two minds would thus enter into a sort of dialog.

The challenge of the second mind was to remove all judgment. When the thoughts in the second mind judged how well, or not, John did, he fell out of observing and into thinking.

And it got even more interesting when John's mind split into three. The first mind provided a random thought. The second mind observed the thought, but then created thoughts relating to the observation. Meanwhile, a third mind, a true observer, watched the other two. Therefore, John's first attempt that evening, and second attempt the next morning before sunrise, were both relatively unsuccessful.

Δ   ▲   Δ

T he men silently set off on foot, commencing their journey. In a couple of hours they reached the edge of a lake. John hadn't noticed they were approaching a body of water until they were upon it because a thin layer of mist hid it from sight. Oddly, the mist seemed to dissipate right as they reached the water's edge.

The lake didn't resemble any that John had seen before, as trees grew right out of the middle of it. In fact, the forest seemed equally as thick over the water as it was over the land. *Is this actually a lake or a recent flooding of some sort?*—John wondered.

His question was soon answered as his attention was directed towards a small boat that had been tied to a tree not two yards from where they stood. The presence of the boat indicated that the water must have been there for a little while anyway.

The Guru invited John to climb into the boat first and then handed him their packed belongings. John was directed to place the bundles in the center of the boat and to sit at the bench near the bow. The Guru then untied the boat, grabbed a pole that had been resting against the tree, and climbed into the stern. Using the pole, he pushed the boat away from the shore and further into the water.

John watched his teacher guide the boat with the long pole. He figured the lake must always be shallow to allow for movement in this way. He had been on boats before, but ones that were rowed rather than guided in this fashion. He soon found facing backward uncomfortable and turned his attention to where they were going rather than how they were getting there.

A short while after leaving the shore, the abundance of trees gave way to a clearing. John looked back to check on his Guru and saw him resting comfortably now, rather than propelling the boat as he had been. Apparently, the natural current was now strong enough to guide them along unaided. John looked forward again and could see they had actually been on a creek that was emptying into a river.

The river was a different color, a dark mixture of blue and green whereas the creek was brown. Where they met, a clear line delineated the two waters. The line curved out gracefully in the direction of the river's current. As their boat entered the river, it too followed that graceful arc turning with the direction of the dominant flow.

For the next couple of hours, the sun intermittently peeked through the clouds as they gently floated downstream. Both sides of the river were clearly visible. The left bank, the side they had entered from, was forested and lush, the river forming the edge of the forest. The right bank sloped gently up and away from the river. Hills could be seen in the distance and the fields that lay in between were covered with grass. Occasionally, they saw animals grazing, cows, horses, and goats. John expected to see farmhouses and looked for them, but then sat back and watched the scenery pass.

A bit later, the Guru spoke for the first time that afternoon, "How is your state of being?" he asked.

John was caught off guard. It was so rare that his teacher asked him a question like that. He took a moment to think about it, but found himself saying the first thing that came to mind. "I feel at peace."

"Harmonious, yes?"

"Yes."

"Inner wisdom is without bounds. You may not be aware of this, but you were practicing the second form of passive meditation. Occasionally, your mind *thought* about what you were observing, but for the most part, you simply observed.

"Now you know what passive meditation feels like. This state is a natural state, experienced when in new places and when observing that which has not been seen before."

John felt pleased with himself that he had mastered passive meditation, but the Guru had more to impart to his student.

"The challenge is to observe familiar surroundings in this same manner, including the habitual thoughts that pass through one's minds daily," the Guru explained. "In your morning and evening meditations, continue to practice by observing your thoughts passively. However, throughout the day, practice observing your **environment** passively. Stay in the present moment as much as possible. Let go of judgment, expectation, or analysis. Merely observe what is in front of you. Look at as much detail as you like or simply feel the whole of it, but firstly observe."

For John, this part of his learning was fun because he was happiest when he was flowing through life and experiencing new places, new people, and new cultures. The weeks prior had been so inwardly focused that he, ironically, felt less like himself. Now that he could look outward once more, he felt relaxed and at peace. In spite of his struggles, he **was** learning and gaining proficiency.

The feelings of comfort and peace stayed with him through these days. He found himself remembering how he had felt months ago when he was traveling without purpose or destination. He tried to remain focused on the present, but couldn't help looking back now and again.

Even his formal meditations flowed better now. He found that once he related observing thoughts to observing his environment, he was better able to remain passively within his second mind. His first mind would continue to produce random thoughts, yet his second mind grew stronger in its ability to watch without judgment.

SEVEN OF SWORDS

A few days into their sojourn, John and his Guru parked the boat for more than just the night. After a brief walk from the river, the two happened upon a cabin similar to the one they had left. In fact, inside, John had to look twice everywhere to find any differences. This was clearly another home frequented by the Guru and the two quickly fell into the familiar routine.

This time, however, the men spent more of the daytime out and about than before. A small village was nearby, so rather than feeding off of the land, they acquired what they needed in town. The Guru had students in the village who offered food and necessities in exchange for lessons in yoga, spirituality, and guided meditation.

One afternoon, while the Guru attended to a group of his pupils, John wandered through the village. A particular road that snaked along the river caught his interest. For the most part, John was doing as he was taught and passively observed the new surroundings. It was then that he noticed a boat traveling on the river, guided by two men. The boat seemed to be heading toward him and the shore. For a moment, John thought that they only started approaching after seeing him, as if **because of him**, but he quickly dismissed the thought as unlikely. *Surely they're just heading into the village.*

Still, something didn't feel right. The men did not look like other villagers, or even those from the main city. They wore clothes that reminded him of the West.

Before John had a chance to sort out what he was feeling, one of the men waved and then called out to him. John didn't understand what he said, but it seemed as if he was asking for assistance, so John moved a bit closer to the water. As the boat pulled up to John, the man in the front extended his arm as if asking to be pulled ashore and John instinctively did the same. It was then that everything sped up.

The first man grabbed John's arm and pulled him into the boat. John protested and struggled, but was roughly pushed to the floor. The second man moved in behind him and held him down. All the fear John felt in that dream the other night was nothing compared to what passed through his body now. Being unable to understand their demands only made it worse.

The first man grabbed him by the lapels and pulled John towards him, yelling into his face. He peered deep into John's eyes with his own, which were filled with hate and rage. Dissatisfied with John's undecipherable response, the man threw him down, snatched his satchel, and then began digging through it. John instinctively reached up to retrieve his bag, but the second man held him down again.

The first man rummaged through John's belongings, intermittently pulling an item out for closer inspection. Sometimes he would throw it back in the bag, but he mostly tossed the unwanted items over his shoulder into the river. With each possession lost, John felt further violated, his cherished memories shattered and destroyed.

The man finally found what he was looking for, but not enough to be satisfied. He held the coins up to John's face and demanded more. John silently looked into the man's eyes, but said nothing, knowing it was of no use. There was nothing he could say and nothing he could offer the man. Everything he owned was right there and was being taken from him already.

The second man pointed at John and said something to the first and they both laughed. It was then that John realized that he had urinated in his pants. Now, he not only felt violated, he felt humiliated.

Why is this happening to me?—raced through his mind and he fought to hold his tongue. When he could no longer swallow his words he blurted out, "What do you want from me? Why are you doing this to me?"

The men looked at each other and laughed even louder. The first threw John's satchel at him and mumbled something to his cohort.

The second man, following orders, let go of John and then kicked him as if telling him to get out of the boat.

John needed no further prompting. He grabbed what was left of his belongings and jumped out of the boat into the mud along the river's edge. He was silently relieved to be covered in mud as it hid what would otherwise be an obvious wet spot on his pants.

The men did not give John a second glance, and they traveled further down the river as if nothing had happened.

EIGHT OF SWORDS

John, traumatized by the whole event, ran back to the hut without stopping in the village to meet up with his Guru as planned. He wanted to keep running until he was out of the village, out of the city, out of the whole country. He wanted more than anything to be back in the Middle East and out of, as he thought of it, *this whole stupid part of the world*.

But the hut was his only refuge and he felt he would be safer there than anywhere else. Although it was still light outside, he tore off his muddy clothes, climbed into his bed, and clutched his satchel and curled up around it.

When the Guru returned some time later, John was awake but pretended to be asleep. He was angry with the man for bringing him to this mean and ugly village; for not being there when he needed him; and for not protecting him from the villains.

The emotion in the room was thick, and the Guru knew instantly upon entering that something was wrong. He sensed foreboding during the walk back to the hut, wondering why John had neglected their rendezvous. The village was too small for John to have gotten lost, and intuitively, he knew that John was back at the hut. But only upon entering the cabin did he realize, at least energetically, the extent of what must have occurred.

Twice, the Guru began to say something, but refrained. He searched his own intuition as to the most appropriate way to offer assistance. Empathically, he could feel what John felt, a mixture of pain, embarrassment, and anger. He could feel that some of it was directed at him, but he also saw beyond the immediate. He concluded that something serious had occurred to upset the boy, but now was not the time to discuss it. First the boy needed to feel, and then release, the emotion. After that, when he was ready, he would speak of his own accord.

The Guru decided to brew a tea that would at least help the boy sleep. His intuition guided him in the selection of herbs. He listened to his own body as he tuned into the boy lying in the corner. Once the tea was ready, he placed it next to John's futon and touched him lightly on the shoulder.

John, still angry, at first refused to acknowledge the offering. But then the aroma enticed him and he relented. As he rolled over and sat up, he stole a glance at his Guru, sitting in meditative silence with his eyes closed. This afforded John enough freedom to drink the tea while remaining unobserved. Just in case, he faced the window away from his teacher.

John, simply wanting the day to be over, looked forward to sleep. As he stared out the window, he watched the sky turn from dusk to complete darkness. He didn't care how early it was; he just wanted to be free of the whole day. *If I am going to be trapped in this awful place, at least let me slip into unconsciousness.*

Soon enough, his mind crossed the boundary between wakefulness and sleep.

NINE OF SWORDS

I n John's dream he sees himself as a little boy. He wakes and is lying in bed. He is wet, and his bedclothes are soaked. As soon as he realizes what he's done, he is overwrought with fear. His boyish mind fills with dread over the punishment he'll surely receive for wetting himself **again**.

When he was younger and wet himself, his mother would comfort him. She'd change his clothes, remake the bed, and assure him that one day he'd outgrow the horrible habit. And he had, at least for a while, but that was before she died.

Now that the bedwetting has returned, his uncle's intermittent beatings have grown more frequent. John instinctively did not like his uncle, but once placed in his care, the wariness became fear... justified fear, because at times, he is beaten so severely, he fears for his life. He misses his parents, but hates them for dying and leaving him with this evil man.

And the punishments are even worse when his uncle is drunk. One time, he was literally thrown out of his bedroom window and locked out of the house, left to sleep in the cold air in his wet clothes. Another time, when he dropped and broke a dish, his uncle grew so angry that he smashed a second plate against the boy's knuckles. The bruises were still evident and tender to the touch.

As he looks down at his hands, he recalls the promise he made to himself that night. He swore that he would run away rather than endure one more beating. *Am I brave enough to do it, to leave right now in the middle of the night?*

He may have also asked himself, but did not: *Am I brave enough **not** to run, knowing that I will be beaten again?*

The sky, still dark to the east, tells John that he has time. He listens for a moment and hears the sound of his uncle snoring in the other room, and that consoles him briefly. *When my uncle drinks, he never rises before the sun*—he concludes.

First things first, get out of these clothes. He moves over to his bureau and picks out fresh clothes, day clothes, rather than nightclothes.

Am I going to do it? With each piece of clothing he puts on, he wonders further. *Am I really going to do this?*

Fully dressed, he now gathers belongings he had previously set aside just for this occasion.

In the dream, he's watching the younger version of himself and the sight of the clothes he is wearing strikes him. The adult John recognizes them, realizing that the clothes the boy wears are the clothes **he** wore for years after that night. He stares at the boy's face and recognizes it, not because it was his own from years past, but because it is the face of the boy he dreamt of the week before.

That boy I was talking to, at the trial, who was afraid of the evil man...oh my God...that boy was me! I was the one who was beaten repeatedly. I was the one who lost both parents and was condemned to torture at the hands of a raging and alcoholic uncle.

John's semi-lucid state figures out that the traumatic day he has just endured is reminiscent of those from years ago as the boy in his dream. The robbery sparked the memory; a memory that he repressed and long forgotten; one that now brings with it so many other memories that he wishes had been permanently erased from his mind.

But nothing can be erased from memory.

The dream continues and the boy is discovered. His uncle is roused from sleep, needing to use the toilet. Just as he begins to undo his pants, he hears sounds from the boy's room. He stands in the doorway for minutes before the boy notices him. This is enough time for him to remove his belt and for his anger to build.

John can do nothing to warn the boy in his dream. Even if he could call out, the dream speeds up, too fast for clear details to be relived.

His drunken uncle stands in the doorway, belt in hand. The boy sees him and is frozen with terror. The fear that fills John as he watches the boy causes the dream to shift and he again views the scene through the eyes of the boy he once was.

His uncle lunges at him, swinging the belt. John feels the sting, but not with the same intensity as he felt it years earlier. The boy kicks and hits the man between his legs. His uncle, clutching at himself, falls to the ground and drops the belt. The boy, closer to the door than his curled up uncle, grabs his bag and darts out of the room and out of the house. He runs—runs without stopping for what feels like hours.

Exhaustion takes over and he collapses in a pile of leaves on the side of the road. His chest heaves painfully, his lungs burning from a lack of oxygen. The pain grows and some part of him realizes that he is not remembering pain, but actually feeling it. It hurts to breathe and he feels as if he is suffocating.

He feels a hand on his chest and panics: *Oh my God, he has found me! My uncle is going to kill me now!* But when he opens his eyes, he sees his Guru's concerned and caring face. He hears screaming, only later realizing it is coming from his own mouth: "I can't breathe! I can't breathe! It hurts to breathe!"

TEN OF SWORDS

A s John woke more fully, he realized that the pain he was feeling was real. An acute spasm in his back was the source. With each intake of air, the stabbing ache amplified. John's body, needing more oxygen, expanded his lungs only to encounter greater pain. He struggled to hold still, and gasped for air.

The Guru, unable to break the spasm, placed two fingers in just the right spot and applied pressure. The pain from his touch went virtually unnoticed until John slumped forward...unconscious. The Guru knew it wouldn't last long and quickly headed out for assistance.

The next time John woke, he realized that there was another person in the room. It was a short woman with shiny black hair. She was wearing a straw hat, not on her head but resting against her shoulders. Her clothes were as shiny as her hair with intricate designs and beautiful colors. She placed various items on a tray next to him, but he could not make out what they were.

The woman and the Guru removed John's shirt and then rolled him onto his stomach. The woman spoke to the Guru in melodic tones and then the Guru told John to relax. As the woman explained what she was doing, the Guru translated:

"Chi, life force, circulates in the body like blood. It travels out from the chakras and along meridian lines. The experiences in life, be they mental, emotional, or physical, can cause blocks, imbalance, and lead to stagnation. Sometimes, the stagnation of chi manifests as disease, other times pain. Through the use of small needles, we stimulate the chi to flow freely once again, relieving pain and promoting the natural healing processes of the body."

One by one, the woman inserted her needles, twisting each for a moment before inserting the next. A needle was placed near John's neck, then another on each shoulder. Two sets were inserted along either side of his back and then the last of them near his elbow and wrist.

All in all, ten needles were inserted into John's body and spun. The position of lying on his stomach was difficult for John, the pain felt as if he was being stabbed in the back right behind his heart. In a flash, he pictured his lifeless body lying in a pool of blood, pierced by swords rather than needles.

A short while later, the woman removed the needles and massaged John's back. The sharp stabbing pain had already lessened to a dull ache. She rolled him onto his back and inserted additional needles. She then rubbed her hands together and placed them on his chest. She explained through the Guru, the second part of the procedure. John learned she was not only an acupuncturist, but also a Reiki master. With her focused intention, she conveyed healing energy to John's body through her hands. She'd found that the combination of acupuncture and Reiki worked best for those she treated.

John soon felt heat emanating from her hands and this soothed his pain further. His breathing grew calm and he found himself relaxing into a meditative state. He wondered if it was just his imagination, but felt waves of energy flowing from one needle to the next. It was like the gentle vibration felt when humming. His body twitched, first his left leg, then his left arm. His right leg rocked and then he heard ringing in his right ear. Her hands gently rested in one spot, heated up, and were then moved to another.

John continued to drift in that place between wakefulness and sleep, finding himself within a dream or vision. He was lying on a cushioned table, but the room was different. Instead of the woman and his Guru standing above him, others surrounded him. He couldn't make out their features; instead they were merely shadows outlined in a bright glow. He sensed that they were there to help him and he felt calm.

One of them looked into his eyes as if looking deep inside of him. Above him and off to one side, he heard a voice reading from a book. The voice spoke with a serious steady tone…no emotion, just the reciting of words to convey information. The story was neither embellished nor emphasized and the shadowed beings listened intently, emanating compassion to what was being read.

Suddenly, another face appeared before John, but this one had familiar features. Telepathically, the being asked John if he was ready to let it go. John knew that this was in reference to the information that had been read from the book, information he knew, yet at the same time was not fully remembering. But he did understand what was asked and nodded.

"Yes, I am ready to let this go," he found himself responding.

"In letting this go, you can no longer hold on to the illusion. You cannot pretend that it did not happen. You will no longer be able to repress the memory. Are you prepared for that? Are you prepared to remember it all?"

"If that is the way it must be, then yes, I am ready."

"Then it is so. Let it be written in the Records."

The one who had read from golden-edged pages began writing upon them while the shadowed beings formed a circle around him. Each placed two fingers of each hand underneath John and without actually lifting him, caused his body to rise up above the table. He heard a prayer being recited and then felt as if he was thrown up into the air. When he landed, his body jolted awake.

John looked around the room, but the woman, her needles, and warm hands were gone. Across the room, John saw his Guru meditating, swirls of golden light circulated around him. John also saw a river of silver flow out of his Guru's chest and across the room to his. He blinked, but then it was gone.

In his memory, there were glimpses of the vision he had woken from, along with an echo of that distant voice reciting from the book. He couldn't hear the words, but remembered how they felt. He thought about the two questions he was asked and then remembered the pain in his back.

And then he remembered the beatings. The dream, he realized, was actually a memory of what had really happened. He now remembered it all and clearly. As he recalled those years with his uncle and those years on his own, he felt no pain. He now understood the tone of the reader; it was neutrality. And as he thought of his uncle, he felt the same.

Δ ▲ Δ

T he next day, John felt well enough to be up and about. He actually felt almost completely better, but didn't trust it fully. Although he and his Guru more or less followed their normal routine, John knew intuitively that something was different. He felt it and waited for his Guru to say something about it. But nothing was said until the next day. After the mid-day meal, John's Guru asked him if he was interested in a walk; a short while later, they set off.

During the walk, John's Guru began talking to him in a way he had not before: "My boy, you have completed the first phase in becoming a true spiritual warrior. You now know what it is like to battle your mind, tame your mind, and seek beyond your mind. The mind is like a child, meant to be taught and guided, not controlled or manipulated. It has purpose and will work with you once you learn how to work with it.

"You have met your subconscious and now know some of what had been hidden there and for some time. And you have learned how your conscious and subconscious together partake in your manifestations, be they illness, experience, or emotion. There are no enemies **out there**, only reflections of misguided thoughts **in here**."

"But what about the thieves?" John asked. "What did I do wrong to make **that** happen?"

"My boy, the **Perfection of the Universe** is difficult to see. To the uninitiated, it can materialize as an arduous task or a poignant challenge. You see only what was taken, not what was given in its place."

"Even so, did it have to be like **that**?"

"It was not the way it **had to** have been, nor the way it was **supposed to** have been, yet it was perfect the way it was nevertheless."

"I guess the first problem is fearing men like that to begin with…and the second problem…is feeling violated by their actions."

"I would say the first problem is believing there is a problem, and the second problem is experiencing that belief over and over again. Your fear is not the problem; it is there to show you your innermost thoughts. The entire Universe conspires to help you get from where you are to where you want to be. It is not wrong to be where you are, but it is an illusion to think you are someplace else."

John raised a questioning eyebrow.

"You are not always expected to see the **Perfection of the Universe**, but you will see it more as your awareness grows. For now, you have gained knowledge and it will soon be time to put that knowledge into practice, out there in the world. It is time to be more in your body and less in your mind. The body is where we find pain, but also where we find pleasure. It is another of our greatest treasures in this reality. With the mind, we can visualize anything, but only through the physical body can we truly **experience**.

"And on that note, may I suggest that we break fast and treat ourselves to tea and some biscuits?"

PART III – EARTH – NORTH

KNIGHT OF PENTACLES

John looked up and was surprised to see the expanse of the city emerging from beyond the last filtering of trees. He had been so engrossed in conversation with his Guru that he hadn't noticed it approaching. Just up ahead, and to the left, a Japanese style teahouse sat invitingly. The establishment marked the boundary between the forest and the city.

As they neared the teahouse, John found himself fully enjoying the energy of the city. He was thankful for all that he had learned from his Guru, however he was happy to be among people again. *It's curious*—he thought—*I feel less lonely, despite being surrounded by strangers.*

John could see that a garden stretched around to the back of the teahouse and expected to be led there, but to his surprise, his Guru chose a table nearer the street. *This is unusual*—John thought as he eyed his Guru suspiciously. He then turned his attention to the hostess, who was pouring them tea, and hoped he had kept the thought to himself. They sat quietly, drank tea, and watched the ebb and flow of strangers.

John glanced at his master, more causally this time, and thought about what had been said during their walk. The Guru's focus, however, was inward, almost as if he were meditating. His eyes were open, and he took an occasional sip of tea, yet his energy was contained. John turned his sights back to the bustling street, which lured his interest.

He watched the many brown-skinned faces come and go. Suddenly, a flicker of color caught John's attention. It wasn't the color of fabric, for there was plenty of that in the crowd. It was the color of hair that attracted his notice. There, in a sea of dark brown hair, a single head with wheat-colored hair stood out in the distance. The man stood head and shoulders above the crowd, which allowed John to also ascertain the man's fair skin. His bright blue eyes scanned above the crowd and then locked onto John. His face shifted with recognition. John and the stranger were not acquainted with one another, but the sight of another foreigner induced feelings of camaraderie.

As the wheat-haired man approached the teahouse, John's Guru stood. John began to rise but his Guru held out his hand as if to say, "Please, stay seated."

John complied and the Guru moved away from the table. The newly vacated seat did not remain empty long.

The blue-eyed man continued his approach without hesitation. He came up to the table and pointed to the chair. John did not recognize the words he spoke and instinctually responded in French, *"Je ne comprends pas ce que vous avez dit."*

The man sat down and with a noticeable accent responded, *"Parlez-vous anglais?"*

John nodded.

"Wunderbar! My French is not very good." The man smiled and stretched out his hand. "My name is Johannes."

John shook the man's hand. "Good to meet you Johannes. I'm John. What brings you to the Nepal?"

"My father sent me here on business; I'll be glad when my work is done and I can return to Europe. I am from Germany. Where are you from, John?"

"Well, that's hard to say. I have been wandering for so long, I don't know that I can call one place or another home."

"So you like to travel?" Johannes asked.

"I **have** been to many wonderful places and have seen many wonderful things," John said with a hint of uncertainty. He told Johannes about his arduous journey across the desert; then more confidently spoke of the Emperor's kingdom.

Johannes began telling John about the various cities he had visited on behalf of his father when a woman from the teahouse approached their table. She set a cup in front of Johannes and filled it with tea. She then placed a small plate with two cookies in the center of the table next to the candleholder.

John expected the woman to refill the Guru's cup, but when he glanced down at the table, the cup was nowhere in sight. He did not remember the Guru taking it with him, but he had to admit his attention had been on the stranger and not his teacher. John looked around but could not find his Guru; he was disappointed because he wanted to introduce Johannes to him.

"I love these fortune cookies. They are everywhere in the East. In anticipation of Western visitors, they have included English translations. Here, pick one." Johannes lifted the plate for John to choose.

John selected a cookie and Johannes took the remaining one. John watched as Johannes broke the cookie in two, revealing a small piece of paper. Johannes was obviously familiar with the Eastern custom.

"Now make sure you eat some of the cookie first lest your fortune not come true. Then you can read of your future."

John did as he was told. The cookie, light and simple and not very sweet, was a nice companion to the tea they had been drinking. John unrolled his fortune and stared at it. Johannes continued talking, but John didn't hear a word the man said.

Johannes noticed John wasn't listening and stopped in mid-sentence.

John continued to be distracted.

"Well, out with it then," Johannes said. "If your fortune is so significant that you don't even hear a word I am saying, then let's have it. Read it to me." Without waiting for John to reply, the German reached over and took the piece of paper from John's hand. He quickly read the short sentence and placed it on the table in front of them.

John looked down at the fortune, looked up at Johannes' questioning face, and then looked around—confused.

Johannes picked up his own fortune and read it out loud: "When two legs become four, twice the distance is covered in half the time." He looked up at John, "I am not sure what that means. I think yours is better, even if they mistranslated it. You've heard that one before, right? It's supposed to say, 'When the **student** is ready, the **teacher** appears.'"

But John knew it wasn't a mistake. **His** teacher was gone, and wasn't coming back; he knew that now. That's why they came here. That's why they needed to be near the street. That's why he left right when Johannes arrived.

ACE OF PENTACLES

J ohn dropped his head to his chest, and when he did, he saw the bag his teacher had been carrying lying next to the table. *This is strange*—John thought—*why is his bag next to my chair?* John reached for the bag and then realized it was his own satchel. *How could I not recognize my own bag?*

John picked up the bag to inspect it more closely. Something else caught his attention—a pendant was sticking out of one of the side pockets. It was a simple coin, which had been attached to a piece of leather.

The image on the front was a circle separated into two halves by a curved line. One half was smooth, the other rough. The two semi-circular shapes implied movement and seemed to flow one into the other. At the same time, they fit perfectly together like pieces in a puzzle. Each half resembled an open hand—the fingers at one end and the palm at the other. In this way, the two halves together looked like one hand resting on top of the other, as in a handshake.

On the back of the coin, John noticed two symbols he had been taught by his Guru. The one on the left meant teacher; and the one on the right—student. As John moved the coin around in his hand, he noticed something interesting. The symbol for teacher and student were the same symbol, only reversed! *Could this be how the fortune was mistranslated?*—he wondered.

He placed the coin on the table and Johannes picked it up. When he put it back down, John noticed something else. Johannes had placed the coin next to the metal candleholder. From where John sat, he could see the coin and its reflection simultaneously. In the distorted reflection, the symbol for student and teacher were flipped and attached, which John soon recognized as the symbol "to teach." The design of the candleholder actually allowed for an additional reflection, which showed the symbols, combined in another way, forming: "to learn."

It all makes sense now—John realized. *When the student is ready, the teacher appears...and...When the teacher is ready, the student appears.* John was excited by the revelation as the concept took root in his mind. *The teacher teaches and the student learns...*

but all students eventually become teachers...and all teachers learn from their students. Students need teachers...and teachers need students...and the cycle continues just like the black and white shape on the front of the coin. Each half flows into the other, and becomes the other.

Just then, Johannes' voice brought John out of his thoughts. "Where are you staying, John?"

"I haven't even thought about it," John replied.

"I just had an idea. My business here is just about done and now that I have a load of goods to bring back to Germany, I could use another set of hands. Are you interested in heading back to Europe with me? I was going to hire a man from here to come back with me anyway. I would be happy to hire you if you are available."

John smiled. "You do not know how available I am. As luck would have it, I just finished my studies here today and I am ready to move on to the next endeavor. I hadn't even considered my next move. You cannot imagine just how fortuitous it is to be meeting you right now."

And with that, the two men shook hands and began their joint venture.

TWO OF PENTACLES

T wo days later, with the goods secured, the men were on their way to Europe. During the first part of their journey, John learned all about his new friend, who was a few years older.

"My father insisted that I complete my studies in business. I resisted at first, but I have to admit, I really do enjoy all aspects of business affairs. I have a good mind for it."

"What do you mean?" John asked, impressed that Johannes seemed to know what work suited him.

"When it came time for me to write my thesis, I designed a project that not only advanced my education, but served my father's company as well. After exploring a number of options, I settled on one that could expand my father business in a new direction."

"That sounds rather ingenious." John asked. *I wish I had special talents*—he thought in response.

"It did not happen quickly," Johannes explained. "It took me months to research and develop the idea, and I had to write up all of my suppositions and support my conclusions in detail. Once it was written, I had to submit it to my professor for review. Then I had to defend my ideas in front of a committee—like an attorney in a courtroom. Only after I had made my case to them, could I take the business plan to my father."

"He was impressed, I'm sure."

"Oh yes, very impressed. So much so, that after graduation, he appointed me to lead a new venture for his company. That is what brought me here to the East." Johannes spoke confidently, but not arrogantly.

For days, Johannes spoke of the specific details of his plan and how he had implemented them thus far. He was clearly passionate about his career; each minute detail was considered and decided upon. John could see that Johannes was gifted in his ability to bring fresh ideas to pre-existing situations.

John was also impressed at how Johannes seemed to juggle his responsibilities with the rest of his life. He told John that he did not ascribe to, "All work and no play," despite having worked the entire time he was studying for his degree. John was in awe at how Johannes squeezed work, study, and pleasure into the confines of a twenty-four hour day.

John could not help but compare himself to his traveling companion. He reflected on his own life and was torn. On the one hand, he was happy to be on the road again, traveling to new places, learning new things, and meeting new people. Life was once again flowing of its own accord. Yet, on the other hand, he felt that he wasn't using any of the knowledge his Guru had taught him. Since taking the job with Johannes, he had virtually no time to himself and was not meditating or practicing yoga. Johannes was such an engaging speaker that John wasn't even observing his surroundings as they passed from town to town and village to village.

Johannes was extroverted and had a strong personality. Rather than compete, John simply followed along passively. He allowed himself to be dependent upon Johannes' expertise. Johannes was familiar with the countries they were traveling through, so he established the route and the daily routine. He decided when and where they stopped, when they ate, and when they rested for the night.

John thoroughly enjoyed the new companionship, and he found it too easy not having to think much. But at the same time, he felt as if he was losing his sense of self in the process. With all that John had learned from his time with the Magician, the Emperor, and the Guru, he was still shy, and oftentimes introverted. Again with Johannes, he was listening, but not talking…learning, but not teaching.

One night as he tried to fall asleep, he thought back to the teahouse and the fortune cookie. *Aren't I supposed to be teaching Johannes and not just learning from him? Wasn't that the message in the fortune cookie? Aren't I supposed to be putting my newfound knowledge into practice as my Guru had foretold?*

John liked Johannes, his passion for work, and his ability to balance his work and leisure time effortlessly. He appreciated having a job, yet also felt a twinge of resentment towards the overly structured work plan as laid out by Johannes. John couldn't seem to balance his **own** desires with those of another, especially when the other was outgoing and well established.

John thought back to his relationship with others he had met thus far in his journey and discovered a pattern. He found that his personality seemed to shift in reaction to whomever he was with at the time. Rather than being clearly who he was, his **genuine** self, he merely became the opposite of his companion.

THREE OF PENTACLES

S uddenly, without realizing it, John had shifted into the mode of his second mind. This time, instead of observing his thoughts, he was observing his **actions**. *I am **less** in my mind and **more** in my body. I **am** applying what the Guru taught me…I just hadn't noticed—until now.*

With this newfound revelation, John set his intention and was soon able to figure things out for himself, without having to take direction from Johannes. He found that he **could** carve out time for meditation and contemplation, which he did before going to sleep and again after waking.

A few days later, they stopped to rest in a glen outside of a village. "Let's go for a walk," John said, spontaneously. The words were as unexpected to him as they were to Johannes, but were received openly. As a result of the utterance, exercise became a part of their evolving routine.

A few days after that, John once again found himself contemplating his purpose before drifting off to sleep. *I **do** know how to manage the various aspects of my life...I **do** know how to incorporate what I have learned from my travels in the East. As long as I keep practicing and pursuing my path, my ability will grow. Maybe some day I'll find **my** purpose in life.* He drifted off to sleep feeling confident.

John also began to notice what he had to offer to others. On another day, instead of going for a walk, John suggested they do yoga. This time, he had planned the suggestion. As it turned out, Johannes was familiar with yoga, but had never tried it, and was curious. He was excited to learn the benefits of yoga and was an eager student.

During the next phase of their journey, they alternated forms of exercise and each time they did yoga, John would teach Johannes a new pose. John had first thought that his advantage would be short lived, since Johannes was quite athletic, but in fact, Johannes never quite gained proficiency over the precise positions. John thus remained the expert and would often assist Johannes with a pose before moving into his own.

Further along the journey, John made the connection between Johannes' mental focus and his own practice of meditation. He came to understand that Johannes' work was his meditation. The clarity he obtained in creating solutions and plans was achieved through that focus. John saw how Johannes instinctively lived within the second realm of creation. His thoughts and ideas were formed, molded, and perfected in his mind first, and only put into motion after. By the time Johannes set out to execute a plan, he did so with complete confidence, his overall success assured by forethought.

And in noticing this, John was once again reminded of how much he learned over the past year. Through observing Johannes' talent and skill, he was becoming aware of his own abilities. And thus, throughout the trek from the Far East to the eastern edge of Europe, John came to understand in detail how his new friend had reached a level of success so early in life.

This revelation further fueled John's interest and he wanted to know more. "What was the single greatest influence in your life?" John asked Johannes one day.

"I can't say there is one event, but I think my father has had the greatest influence on me."

"I'm curious. Tell me more about him: how he founded his business and how he built it from the ground up."

Johannes simply responded by saying, "Ask him yourself; you're going to meet him soon."

KING OF PENTACLES

J ohannes and John entered the city of Kiev towards the middle of summer. This was where Johannes and his father had agreed to meet.

Upon first glance, Klaus Müller simply came across as a more mature version of Johannes, both in appearance and behavior. However, upon closer inspection, differences became evident. For one, Herr Müller was shorter than his son, and broader both in face and frame. This gave him a more masculine look beyond that gained with age.

The younger Müller had inherited his father's astuteness, however the older was also decisive. Johannes weighed and analyzed options extensively before drawing conclusions, whereas his father considered alternatives for only a moment before deciding. His years of experience showed and his confidence was unmistakable, yet he exuded practicality with every word he spoke. It was obvious; Klaus Müller was a man who knew how to get things done.

Unlike Johannes, his father was not formally educated in business. It was never his intention when he was young to establish a large corporation; he simply found success in his every undertaking. Klaus was naturally gifted with an intuition for ingenuity. In his early years, within each line of work he engaged, he learned to take advantage of opportunities as they presented themselves. He was a doer more than a thinker. He gained skill through action and improved his proficiency with every iteration. When new ideas crossed his mind, he quickly tested them out rather than perfecting them in his mind. In this way, instead of presenting a plan, he presented results, and always at a profit. It was for this reason that he quickly found himself rising in levels of responsibility.

And as it turned out, more fruitful opportunities always presented themselves, pulling him away from one business and into another. By his late-thirties, he realized it was time for him to venture out on his own. At that point, he had impressed so many, that it required little effort to bring together a team willing to carry out his undertaking. Many he had previously worked for, now worked for him and were happy to do so.

His consistent leadership motivated all who worked close to him, ensuring the success of everyone. How could they fail when each was inspired to pursue their individual best? And through the gift of synergy, the whole was clearly greater than the sum of its parts.

Despite his resolve, Klaus Müller was a caring man. As John watched the interaction between father and son, he couldn't help but think back to his time with the Emperor. As with the other, one witnessed hardly more than a hand placed on a shoulder, yet something about the subtle display of affection was perceptively heartfelt. Herr Müller was patient, listened attentively to his son, and then responded in an authoritative, yet supportive tone.

Maybe that's why Johannes is so comfortable with himself— John concluded. *He has a strong role model, someone who is both encouraging and experienced.*

What warmed John to the man most was how quickly Klaus Müller accepted him as a member of the clan. When Herr Müller first met John he welcomed him with a two-handed handshake; John could feel his sincerity in that gesture.

Like father, like son—John thought. The family resemblance between Johannes and his father was more than skin deep. Johannes had inherited some of his father's talent and all of his passion, but then developed his own unique gifts from there.

FOUR OF PENTACLES

A fter the two parties joined, John soon learned that Johannes' younger sister was traveling with their father. Johannes' sister was much younger than Johannes and John observed that the two did not relate to each other much. The affection typically found between a brother and sister was not present, or at least not apparent. *They seem like two individuals who just happen to share the same parents*—John observed.

John could not articulate it, but there was something else that was odd about the situation, which seemed to set Johannes and his sister apart. She was treated differently and her guardian always accompanied her, even though she was under her father's care—as if she was being protected from something.

John was never introduced to her, and she did not acknowledged his presence.

John's curiosity grew and he was anxious to interrogate Johannes. However, the formality of the situation prevented him from broaching the subject in front of the others. *I will just have to wait patiently for the right time to pull Johannes aside.*

In the company of Johannes' father and sister, the trip took on a whole new feel. They now traveled in luxury. No expense was spared to make their journey through Eastern Europe as comfortable as possible, staying in the finest accommodations and eating the most flavorful meals.

At their first meal, John almost laughed when Johannes' sister was seated at the head of the table. *Why is the most successful businessman in all of Germany deferring to his young daughter?*— he wondered. Yet Johannes' father seemed completely comfortable with the arrangement. Even Johannes showed no resentment to playing subservient to his sister.

That first evening struck John as odd in many ways. Johannes' father occasionally spoke with his daughter and with his son, but never addressed them together and they hardly uttered a word to each other. The formality didn't seem to fit with Johannes' personality. John just could not imagine Johannes being brought up this way.

After dinner, the travelers were each shown to their rooms.

Johannes' father had a room on the top floor of the hotel, as did his sister and her guardian. The three entered the lift first and due to its size, occupied all of it. Johannes looked over at John and suggested that they take the stairs since they were only four flights up.

Neither of the young men were winded from the climb, and walked down the hall without as much as heavy breath. Johannes unlocked the door and then held it open for John to pass.

The room was beautiful. As John walked in, he glanced into the bathroom; *the marble alone must have cost a fortune*—he thought. Further into the room were two beds, both large and well dressed. Beyond that, he saw a pair of French doors leading out to a small balcony. Sheer drapes filtering the light did not prevent the occupant from enjoying the view of the majestic city.

John stood in the middle of the room and waited for Johannes to select his bed first. He noticed that their bags had already been brought into the room and were lying on the floor between the matching desks. Much to John's surprise, Johannes selected the bed further from the window, affording John the bed with the nicer view. John later would realize that his bed would be bathed in light all evening while the other retained a modicum of darkness. After sitting on his bed, John looked over at Johannes and broke the silence.

"OK, I have been dying to ask this all day. What is the situation with your sister? She is treated like a queen!"

"That's because she'll be one some day."

"Uh...really?"

"I was hesitant to tell you this, but my stepmother is the Queen of Heidelberg. Isabella is actually my half-sister. The Queen and my father got married when I was eleven years old, a few years after my mother died. I've been away at school for much of my half-sister's life, so I don't really know her that well. Since she is the royal heir, her guardian and servant always accompany her. And she has always been home-schooled, so even though she has been traveling with my father, she is still tutored."

"What is it like being in the royal family? It doesn't seem to fit you."

"Well, I keep it at arm's length. The Queen chose my father more because of his success than from love. She wanted a partner who would win favor with the city, and my father was well known and well liked. He is a practical man and marrying the Queen was a business opportunity like any other. They like each other well enough, and respect each other completely, so who am I to judge? But I don't think of the Queen and my half-sister in the same regard as my father. And I certainly do not envy that lifestyle. I would not want to be the heir for any amount of fame or money. I am happy focusing on our business and leaving the politics to the women."

"I guess that's why I was not introduced to your sister—uh—Isabella. I guess there really is no reason for her to be acquainted with me."

"Oh, that's not it at all. You will be introduced to her, but not before meeting the Queen. The custom is always that one must first be presented to the Queen and meet her approval before being introduced to Isabella.

"You know, I don't know my sister very well, but there isn't a thing about her I dislike. For a girl so attended to, she is not spoiled, but rather very down to earth. She has never acted above me; she just plays along as she was taught. In royalty, from what I can tell, there is a lot of emphasis on appearances. Luckily she is neither burdened nor flattered by it."

Δ   ▲   Δ

D uring their time in Kiev, the men met often and primarily discussed the itinerary for the next part of the trip. John's excitement grew with the mention of each city planned on the route.

That last night in Kiev, John asked Johannes, "With all of this talk about Heidelberg, when do you think we'll arrive there? I can hardly wait."

"Well, we have all of Eastern Europe to cross, so we should be arriving in Germany by early autumn. I suspect that we will be passing through the Black Forest at high season, right as the leaves begin to change."

"What do you mean change? What happens to them?"

"Oh I forgot, in your travels you have only seen desert and evergreen forests. You have never been exposed to diverse vegetation.

"In Northern Europe, the forests are deciduous; they lose their leaves in the winter. In the autumn, before the leaves fall, they change color from green to varying shades of yellow, orange, and red. In the Black Forest, the display of color is amazing! Many travel from different regions to witness the foliage. In celebration of the beauty of autumn and the bounty of summer, we have our highest holiday at that time. It is called Oktoberfest. I hope you like beer because Germany has the best in all of Europe, if I do say so myself, and we'll be drinking plenty of it!"

Δ   ▲   Δ

A s they left Kiev, the traveling party turned to the southwest and eventually crossed into Hungary. In this part of the world, countries and cultures were relatively close together. John was amazed that there was less ground to cover from city to city, and was pleased when they found themselves nearing Budapest much sooner than he had expected.

The sun was setting in front of them right as they entered Pest, the eastern half of the city, and oh what a sight it was. This city was easily the most beautiful that John had ever visited. Kiev may have been considered the eastern edge of Europe, but in Budapest, one surely felt as if they had fully arrived. John looked forward to experiencing as much of it as he could.

They were to remain in Budapest for a full week, the longest stop in their journey so Klaus could attend to one of his businesses there. Given that Johannes wasn't involved in that part of the business, he and John were free to spend a leisurely week in the city. Since Johannes had been to Budapest many times before, he knew all the fun things to do and the sites to visit.

Johannes was becoming more and more like a big brother to John. They were similar in many ways: both had a thirst for learning, even if in different fields. The two seemed to have the same level of energy for whatever endeavor was in front of them. They tired of conversation at the same time, and needed the same amount of physical activity and exercise. As they walked around the city, or danced in the wee hours, one always suggested a break when the other was contemplating the same thing.

John had never been in such a diverse city. He noticed that there were just as many handsome men with dark features as with light, and each type seemed to attract attention from others equally, both from men and women. He and Johannes made new friends easily wherever they went, be it enjoying the sights throughout the city or in the bustling nightclubs. And since the Hungarians were used to visitors who could not understand a word of their unique language, many spoke other languages, which one or the other was able to understand or translate.

Although Budapest was both enticing and exciting, John's primary interest was in Klaus and Johannes' business. *Yes, the Hungarian people are as beautiful as their city*—he considered. *And yes, there are plenty of sights to see, history to explore, food to eat, and wine to drink, but*...he was reticent to finish the thought.

Truth was, when he was without his companion, John found himself retreating within himself. The few days he was on his own, he attended tours or explored the natural beauty of the city, but he befriended no one.

Although these inner thoughts seeped into the forefront of his consciousness, John didn't explore them further. *What am I afraid of?*—he asked himself, but didn't really want to know.

But he knew his trepidation came from his relationship with Johannes, which was the first of its kind for him. *Why does this kinship I have with Johannes feel so different than what I felt with Sara?* But no answer came to him. With Sara, there was no attachment, no envy, no jealousy, but with Johannes, there was a twinge of all of these.

The last night in Budapest, Johannes was eager to venture out one last time, but John could not muster the thought of it. He just wanted to stay in and rest up for the next leg of the journey.

However, he was annoyed that Johannes went out without him. *Why do I care what Johannes does?* Again he found no answer, yet still could not shake the irritation. Instead of resting, as was his reason for staying in, he merely tossed and turned…and brooded.

The next day, as they gathered their belongings, John remained silent and aloof. Johannes noticed something was up and eyed his friend suspiciously for a moment, but neither broached the subject.

The time in Budapest had quenched Johannes' thirst for a little rest and reprieve, but now he was ready to get back to business.

FIVE OF PENTACLES

A number of days later, as they entered the outskirts of Prague, a heavy rain forced the caravan to stop for the night outside of the center of town. John was frustrated and disappointed. He had heard a great deal about Prague and was eager to see as much of it as he could. He knew he wouldn't have much time to spend there, between the work and the travel schedules. The rain was not helping matters.

John's mood matched the dark clouds and cold rain. He felt a connection with the city he was yet to discover. Even on the outskirts, the somber beauty of Prague was evident and distinct from Kiev and Budapest.

The next day brought more rain. The buildings, John observed, had been constructed with stone that blackened with age. This gave the city a heavy, almost sinister feel. Even the architecture was more haunting than the other cities he had visited. The overall effect was that Prague felt colder.

*Well, it **is** colder*—John thought as he watched the rainwater gush down the city streets en route to the river. The rain lasted the rest of the day and well into the next morning. Johannes kept himself busy with work, but John didn't have enough to do to keep himself occupied. Then, towards midday, one of Herr Müller's assistants knocked on the door and entered the room. Johannes looked up from his desk and the two spoke briefly.

After the assistant left, Johannes announced, "We have a lunch meeting to attend, but after that we are headed to Old Town Square —rain or no rain."

John followed Johannes into the dining room. During lunch Johannes and his father sat next to each other, discussing the latest order of business. On either side of them sat their respective assistants. John had no official functions and was furthest away from the conversation.

John could not help but feel that his life lacked purpose. *Just what is purpose?*—he wondered. He wished that his Guru was with him to offer him guidance, but he knew that his teacher would encourage him to look inside of himself. John tried to understand his feelings of alienation. *Maybe I'm just bored*—he reasoned. *Perhaps if I had something useful to accomplish I wouldn't feel so inept.* As John tried to decipher what to do, the lunch meeting dragged on...and he moped.

John feared the rain would never end and they would be stuck in the periphery of the city indefinitely. Despite its glacial pace, the time of departure did arrive and the party ventured on toward the center of town. Although the initial storm had passed, the downpour gave way to a light mist, and the penetrating chill shifted into a refreshing cool. *Maybe there's hope for the day*— John thought.

As they traveled, John felt the city tightening around them with the increased density of the buildings and roadways. Prague was smaller than Budapest, and to John, it felt much older. As they neared Old Town Square, a tower rose up above the other buildings.

"What is that? John asked, pointing to the tower.

"It is called the Powder Gate. It is the eastern gate of the old city.

To John, the tower looked more like a building than a gate, although it did have an archway fashioned through the middle. It sat at an odd angle to the road and the surrounding buildings, as if the city started to grow in one direction and then changed its mind.

Like much of Prague, the tower was stained from age, and flickers of gold showed brightly against the dark background. Just as they were about to pass through the tower, John realized that the gold he saw formed parts of the many figures strewn throughout the façade: a scepter in one hand, a sword in another, the angelic wings attached to many, and in at least one case: scales.

After passing through the arch and into the old city, John turned to look at the other side. Directly behind the massive structure, the waxing gibbous moon could be seen rising above the part of the city they had just traversed. Seeing the moon this way took John back to that full moon night at the Magician's home. For a moment, his perception shifted and he felt as if the energy of that evening was reflected in the face of the moon. It seemed as if that ceremony had just happened the night before, as if in a dream. Then, just as quickly, his perception shifted back and with it came a newfound yearning to explore the city.

To Johannes, Prague was nothing new, and being that he had plenty to do, he allocated the remainder of the afternoon to focus on work. Since the weather had lifted by the time they had settled in to their newest lodging, John set out to explore on his own.

Despite how similarly Prague and Budapest were laid out, they felt different. Both spanned a river, hilly on one side, and flat on the other, with beautiful bridges linking the two, yet in Prague the hills were slighter and the roads narrower.

The hotel was located a few blocks from the river just off of the Old Town Square. In fact, given the bend of the river, one could easily reach it heading north or west. John decided to first head west and figured he could follow the river to the north and circle back around.

However, once in view, the world-renowned Charles Bridge was too much to resist, and so John amended his plan. He crossed the main thoroughfare that edged the river, paused to take in the scene, and then ambled across the classic bridge to the other side. After a short jaunt through the myriad arts and crafts stands littered along the western bank, John doubled back, strolled across the bridge once more, and then allotted additional time to admire the views up and down the Vltava.

A number of clock towers were within sight and after glancing at one, John realized it was later than he thought, so he picked up his pace and followed the bend in the river north and then east. A few blocks further, he turned south and headed back toward Old Town Square.

John soon found himself in what was likely the oldest part of town. Churches and temples were abundant in Prague, yet the one up ahead on the corner looked far simpler than any other he had seen. As John walked passed the temple, he saw men and women bundled up and lying on benches, under hedges, and along a wall. They looked cold and distraught, their skin weathered far beyond their years, and their hair matted and tangled. The scene caused a pit to form in John's stomach. He didn't like seeing people live this way, in abject poverty, most especially on a cold, wet day like this one.

Instinctively, John reached into his pocket to count the coins he had there, but intuitively, he knew he didn't have enough to give to everyone. So he crossed the road away from the unfortunate locals, turned left, and intended to shoot over to another block. However, in doing this, he put himself right in the path of a young, lame, homeless boy begging for money. It was impossible to avoid him. The boy had already noticed John and was no more than ten paces ahead. John knew it would be too obvious if he crossed the street to evade him.

John didn't like the discomfort he felt in the boy's presence. *Why am I feeling this way? Surely it is not the boy's fault that he is impoverished.* John felt both guilt and obligation.

SIX OF PENTACLES

J ohn liked to help people when he could. *Wasn't I just longing to be of use this morning?*

The boy stood in front of him, hand extended out, trying to speak to him in one language and then another.

I can't just walk past and ignore him, can I? What choice do I have?

The child seemed to be in genuine need, but to John, giving the boy money didn't feel right either. *If I had food, I would have been happy to share it with the boy, but money? Besides, I don't have much of that to begin with.*

So many different thoughts ran through his mind: *What if this boy is only pretending to be lame as he leans on his makeshift crutch? What if he has full faculties, and has his sights on pilfering my belongings?*

With no more than two steps to go, John tried to shake the

fearful suspicions and reached for altruism. He fingered the coins in his pocket and tried to discern their worth by feel. He wasn't used to the local currency or its relative value, so it was of no use. *I am going to give too much...or too little, I have no way of knowing which. And I can't pull it all out in front of the boy to try and figure it out.* Ultimately, he picked a coin at random, dropped it into the boy's outstretched hand, and kept walking.

For some reason, the gesture did not console John. He was walking away from the boy now, and as far as he could tell he was not being followed, yet the increased distance added no comfort. *Something is not right*—he thought. He was afraid to look back, but couldn't hold off any longer. He had to shake the threatened feeling that gripped him and hoped the scene behind him would console him.

It did not.

What John witnessed was worse than he could have suspected. Two other boys, fully abled, were now harassing the boy with the crutch. The poor boy clearly wanted to keep the coin he had received, but the others were determined to heist it from him. The disadvantaged boy caught John's gaze and looked at him with pleading eyes, but then one of the ruffians turned and leered at John intimidatingly.

John felt he had no choice but to continue his withdrawal. *The two tormenters could easily overtake me if they wanted. The last thing I need is another altercation in a foreign country*—he reasoned. This city was no match to that modest Eastern village and John recognized that his first choice had to be in favor of his own safety.

John quickly rounded the corner and didn't look back. He soon reached the square, but was immune to its beauty. In fact, he abandoned any plans to explore the plaza and instead raced back to the hotel. He needed to put some more distance between himself and that horrible scene. *Surely Johannes will be done with his work and able to offer some comfort and distraction*—he hoped.

When John reached the hotel, he spotted Johannes enjoying a glass of wine in the bar. John pulled up a stool and silently plopped down onto it.

Johannes looked at John. *He seems even stranger than the other day*—he thought, but was not about to ask why. Instead, he returned his attention to his drink.

John did not offer an explanation. He was embarrassed by the incident and didn't want to give it any more power by talking about it. And yet, for the remainder of the day, the apprehension stuck with him.

XI – JUSTICE

That night, in a dream, John found himself walking through what he imagined to be the Black Forest, but the images were from the Nepali forest, which created a denser, darker version.

As John trudged through the abundant growth of trees, he felt heavy and weary. *Now I know why they call it the Black Forest*—he thought as he strained to see stars in the sky. To the west there was light in the distance. He squinted, trying to determine its source. He could decipher the edge of the forest was just ahead, and seemingly in no time, he reached it.

In his dream, the topography of the cities of Budapest and Prague merged and upon leaving the forest, John found himself at the eastern end of a replica of the bridge he had crossed the previous day. Before entering the eastern gate of the bridge, John looked out over the river. He couldn't see the water because a thick layer of mist blanketed it in both directions. The river appeared to be similar to the Danube and the Vltava, yet John somehow knew this one by a different name, the Dämmern.

John entered the bridge and began walking towards the western gate, which could easily be seen towering over the far end of the bridge. The bridge's surface was lit by the evenly spaced gas lamps, which traversed the span. Between each lamp, an ominous sculpted figure stood dark and motionless, peering down at John as if passing judgment on his past or recent wrongdoings. John walked slowly, noticing the familiar feel of the cobblestones beneath his feet. With each step, the sky grew lighter as in the early stages of dawn.

Beyond the western gate, instead of seeing the familiar scene of Mala Strana in western Prague, John saw a steep, lush terrain that more closely resembled Buda, the western side of Budapest.

John had only visited Buda once during their time there. After crossing the Széchenyi Chain Bridge, and a strenuous climb up the many staircases that ascended the hillside, John was rewarded with a spectacular view of the Danube and Pest, nestled along its eastern edge.

Similar to that day, John crossed the remainder of the bridge and climbed the mountainside, except this time, he was not only surrounded by lush greenery, he was also treated to elegant white statues, fragrant flowering shrubs, and a meandering waterfall. But John did not see buildings until he reached the top of the mountain. This mountaintop city, which he somehow knew by the name Lumière, did not resemble any he'd seen in Europe, the East, or in between. All of the buildings were constructed of a brilliant white marble, pristine and unweathered.

The main plaza was wide and at least twice as long. At the opposite end, a classically architected building sat higher than the others. Huge stairs lead up to the main floor and massive columns supported the stately roof at least four stories above it.

Although there didn't seem to be any sunlight, the city glowed brightly as if lit from within. John walked across the plaza, looking left and right at the buildings that flanked it and intermittently at the tile work beneath his feet.

A moment later, and without climbing the stairs, he reached the ground floor of the enormous courthouse. A statue, many times larger than any he'd seen thus far, towered over him: an elegant woman, blindfolded, held scales in her left hand. In her right hand she clutched a sword seemingly too large for her. The statue itself was carved from a single piece of marble the same color as the building, her sword and scales forged of gold. Her silk blindfold shifted lightly in the breeze. The scales, true to form, oscillated gracefully.

Despite the clearly feminine figure and pose, John felt intimidated by her presence. Something in the way she gripped the sword let him know that she knew how to use it and was strong enough to wield it if need be.

Master John, welcome.

The voice was deep, yet nevertheless female. It seemed to come from all parts of the building at the same time. John looked around and then up at the statue. The blindfold had disappeared and the woman's eyes peered down at him compassionately.

Thank you for visiting my home. It is not often that one comes here willingly. Many who seek justice, silently wish for it to only visit their peers. They are quick to assign Karma to others, but fear the day it knocks at their door.

"Madam Justice. Tell me, do I continue to carry a heavy burden of Karma? Have I not released the worst of it?"

My dear son, you misunderstand the workings of justice. You are thinking as men do, and thus judge yourself as men judge. You need only remember that you are the creator of your own reality and that manifestation is pure and exact.

Consider for a moment your recent time in the cities along the Danube and the Vltava. Do you not recognize the lessons of your own making? Do you not see your own reflection in the faces of your peers? Have you not yet deciphered the origin of these experiences?

"Please, Madam Justice. Tell me what I am neglecting to see," John begged.

In Budapest, you closed yourself off from the others to protect yourself. Then in Prague, you found yourself on the outside looking in, wanting and longing to feel connected. Does this surprise you? Forget not that the walls that protect are the very same that imprison.

Many a time, you have said to yourself, 'Everything I want is right there, but I cannot have it.' We invite you to recognize both sides of that statement. Yes, everything you want is right in front of you! As part of creating what you desire, you have first created it out there, but then in recognizing that it is not yet in here, you throw up your hands in defeat.

John lowered his head knowing that what she said was true.

Were you incapable of creating it for yourself, Master John, you would not have the ability to see it. In gazing upon an image of your desires, you are given the opportunity to make it a part of your reality. The journey is not meant to end there and thus you needn't resign. Your reaction to that which is observed is merely that which remains to be resolved. Within those ill feelings is evidence of your underlying thoughts, your outmoded and self-defeating beliefs, and the roadblocks you have yet to remove from your path.

John lifted his head feeling hopeful.

We now invite you to recite the first part of that statement alone. 'Everything I want is right there. Everything I want is right **here**!' Even if it is not all that you desire, it is being shown to you for a reason. When it appears, the time is ripe to proceed further.

John mouthed the statement.
Madam Justice continued:

For a moment, let us revisit your time with the boy you encountered near the temple. You saw only his poverty and his need. In that regard, he reflected your own perceived lack. You felt sorry for him because you had been feeling sorry for yourself. Had you not been feeling despondent already, you would not have **stumbled** upon him. And yet, in giving to him from a place of guilt and obligation, you seemingly caused him (and thus you) more pain and misery. This caused you to sink deeper into regret and hopelessness.

John dropped his head again, this time embarrassed.

Doubt us not; charity is an illusion. There is only creation and expression. You cannot give to another what is not rightfully theirs. You cannot receive from another what is not rightfully yours. What you give another that is not rightfully theirs will disappear from them.

What you call 'giving' is nothing more than creating and expressing. What you feel when you give is what you are creating for yourself. If you feel joy in giving, then you are creating more joy. If you feel guilt for not giving enough or not giving something specific, then you are creating for yourself more experiences of guilt and later resentment, which is woven of the same fabric as guilt. You create what you create and the entire Universe exists merely as the delivery system of that creation. When you express who **you** are, you become a part of that delivery system, giving to others the experiences they have created for themselves.

Giving and receiving is an illusion. There is only expressing and experiencing. The difference between expressing love and experiencing love is the apparent direction. Love expressed feels like it is flowing out of you. Love experienced feels like it is flowing into you from the outside. Yet this again is an illusion. There is only one, **THE ONE**, and that is the source of all love. You cannot give or receive love, only express and experience it...or not.

John rubbed his head, attempting to absorb all of what was being imparted.

'Not' is also an illusion. If you are **not** experiencing something, you are **not** intending it and not attending to it. **Intention** and **Attention** are one in the same. If there is any question as to what your intention is, observe where your attention is.

The words 'give' and 'receive' are more appropriately replaced with 'create' and 'experience'. What you are not willing to give to yourself, you will not receive from others. What you are not willing to create for yourself, you will not experience. If you do not love yourself, you will not be loved by others. If you do not respect yourself, you will not be respected by others. If you do not honor yourself, you will not be honored by others. If you do not trust yourself, you will not trust others. If you do not stand up for yourself, others will not stand up for you. As you love yourself, you will experience love from all sources. As you respect yourself, you will experience respect from all sources.

John felt the burden lift from his shoulders.

Go, now, and further your journey of experience. Remember, do not hide yourself from the truth—**you** are creating your own reality. Justice is blind in that she does not discriminate. But Justice is also omniscient for she sees every thought, intention, and emotion. Remove your blind and journey with your eyes open! Behold your power and worth—for you are created in the image and likeness of The Omnipotent One, and thus creating as He does where there is no limit of power or lack of perfection.

SEVEN OF PENTACLES

J ohn woke with renewed hope. The events of the previous days were no more than a distant memory. He had one full day to explore Prague and then it was back on the road.

At breakfast, John learned that Johannes had completed his work and was interested in accompanying John on his adventure. The two started in Old Town Square and then headed across the bridge to visit the castle in Mala Strana, which was located on a moderate sized hill. The castle gardens treated its visitors to a panoramic view of the rest of the city. From their perch, John could see both towers of the bridge, the Powder Gate, as well as some of the taller churches along the Square. He was amazed how the dark city transformed into an ocean of red-tiled roofs when viewed from above. The complete bend of the river was also visible, and John lost himself for a few minutes watching long boats glide up and down at a leisurely pace. The day went by too quickly for John.

Δ ▲ Δ

E arly the next morning, they were back on the road. It took no more than a few days to cross into Germany. It was evident in each town they passed that Oktoberfest preparations were well underway. The entire country was gearing up for the much-awaited celebration. The group crossed through Bavaria quickly. This meant that Johannes and John could take the scenic route through the Black Forest. Herr Müller and the rest of the group were eager to return home, so they stuck to the main road.

As the two entered the forest's canopy of trees, John's first impression was that the Black Forest did not resemble the one from his dream. He then asked himself—*What Forest? Which dream?*

John became enthralled by his surroundings. He began counting all of the colors on display. The damp earthy smells, the still warm enough to be comfortable air, and the abundance of color all made for a most luscious serenity. Even the stride of the horses became more relaxing than it had been throughout the previous stages of their trip.

Johannes said, "You know, I love the Black Forest, but most especially this time of year. Whenever I wander through, I relax in a way I never do otherwise. These trees live a long time. They're in no hurry since they have nowhere to go. So much of my life is about accomplishing something. It's nice to come here and let all of that go for a while. Do you know, when I listen carefully, I swear I can hear the forest growing! Or maybe it's just breathing."

John was enchanted by Johannes' comments and looked around with a heightened interest. Instead of just noticing the color, he looked at the trees, the birds, and the ground animals that scurried about reacting to the horses' trot.

John remembered something his Guru had taught him back in Nepal. It was called the Planting of Seeds meditation, n*ever more powerful than when surrounded by tree*s. As he recalled the meditation technique, he told Johannes about it, "First, imagine yourself as a tree. You can be an evergreen, a fruit tree, or one of these, what did you call them?"

"Deciduous."

"Right, deciduous. OK, so imagine that you are a tree. Feel the parts of your body from your roots deep underground to your branches high in the sky. Think about the function and purpose of each part: your roots for collecting water and nutrients from the soil; your trunk, which supports your weight and carries food and water up and down; your connective network of branches; and ultimately each and every leaf or needle that gathers sunlight for energy.

"Feel yourself mighty and beautiful. You are a tree, but you are also a man, and that man has wants and desires. Look at them. Why do you desire this item or that experience? What will it feel like when it arrives?

"Feel the desire, and then mold it into a seed. Place it inside of a cone, a piece of fruit, or a pod. With each seed you create, the overall desire grows. Life will be grand indeed when all of these wishes are fulfilled. As the tree that you are, hold the cone, fruit, or pod in your branches. Channel energy from your roots below the ground, up through your trunk to the containers and the seeds held within them.

"You can image one cone or fruit with a bunch of seeds, or separate containers for each. Go with whatever visual shows up in your imagination.

"And when you are ready, let them go. Just like these trees, which are now letting go of their leaves, let go of the containers, let go of the seeds. Watch them fall to the ground or float off in the breeze. Soon they will reach the earth and be buried in the soil. Thank the earth for nurturing your desires during their gestation, through the late autumn and winter and up to the spring thaw.

"And then, in your third eye, peer into the future and see them sprout! Know that it is only a matter of time before the seeds of your desires become wishes fulfilled."

John inhaled deeply and let his breath out with a prolonged sigh. He was so focused on the meditation, he forgot to place actual desires into his seeds, but deep down, he knew he didn't need to. The Universe knew what he wanted...probably better than he did.

EIGHT OF PENTACLES

A fter the visualization, the two rode on in silence until they came upon a perfect spot to set up camp. The trees formed a circle, almost as if they were planted that way, and there was plenty of room in the middle to set up the tent.

They tied up the horses to adjacent trees and then pulled out their gear. This would be the first time that the two had camped since Asia.

"Now I know I always set this stuff up, but do you want to learn?" Johannes asked.

"Yeah. Show me, oh master of the woods." John giggled. Something about the forest made him a little giddy, or maybe it was that meditation. *Of course, the energy building toward Oktoberfest could be partly responsible too*—he surmised.

After the tent-pitching lesson, the boys wandered the area in search of dried leaves and twigs for a fire. With the change of season, being further north, and deep in the forest, it was going to be a chilly night, perfect weather for a fire. Johannes put his hand on John's shoulder to get his attention.

"Here."

"What is it?"

"Eat it. Don't chew it; it tastes awful. Swallow it."

"It's not going to kill me, is it?" John asked with a smile.

"Trust me. I'm the master of the forest and I have more to teach you. OK, now take a swig of this, but not too much. That's the good stuff."

John took a sip and felt a burn all the way down to his stomach. It was pleasant. Johannes then did the same.

"So, now what?"

"Well, while we're waiting, let me teach you a thing or two about the medicines of the forest." Johannes laughed and John followed. He knew that Johannes was imitating John's Guru based on earlier conversations.

"See that one? …Noooo. That one is not for eating. It is not even good to touch, but this one over here? That's what I just gave you. That's the magic kind, which you'll see for yourself soon enough." Johannes looked around, but didn't find any more specimens. "Let's head back now. I need to teach you how to light a fire before we start hallucinating."

John couldn't tell for certain whether Johannes' last comment was a joke or not, but he didn't ask. He trusted Johannes, like a brother, so whatever he was up to, it would be OK. It turned out that Johannes was joking about teaching John to start a fire. He had a sparker and with two strikes caught the leaves on fire. In no time, the kindling was burning and then the larger sticks.

The two sat next to the fire, not quite across from each other, but not right next to each other either. This way they could see each other without turning away from the fire. Johannes leaned back against his remaining gear and looked up to the sky. It was now dark enough for them to see the stars and the moon.

John looked deeply into the fire. He watched the flames dance. He saw mostly yellow, lots of orange, and just a bit of blue. And at the very tips, he caught glimpses of green now and again. The branches below glowed red.

And then it hit. John's head expanded and his body tingled. The sound of the fire grew so loud it became a roar.

So this is the magic.

At first, the effect was similar to the potion he had taken a year earlier, but then it shifted. He looked over at Johannes, now sitting up and staring at him. Johannes was wide eyed and had a smirk on his face, certainly feeling the effects of the mushrooms as well. John's eyes locked onto a swirl of smoke that wafted at Johannes' side, reflecting the glow of the firelight. Two black orbs formed within it. John squinted questioningly and then tilted his head as the orbs morphed into a pair of eyes. Soon an entire face emerged.

As more details appeared, John at first thought he was looking at a woman, adorned with golden cuffs on her wrists, rings on her fingers, and pendants around her neck. But then, as the body took shape, he realized that the musculature was decidedly male and dressed in a warrior's garb, unlike anything he had ever seen. Actually, the man was mostly undressed and parts of his body were painted with intricate designs.

John's eyes dilated with intrigue. Instead of fading, the image grew more pronounced and everything else blurred. What sat before him and next to Johannes was a being from a different time and place. John nodded to the warrior, and the warrior nodded back, his eyes, prominently outlined in black, stared at John with an intensity that made him shiver. And then, the warrior looked to John's right and then to his left, apparently acknowledging two others. John could not see them, but could hear them, and slowly began to make out what they were saying.

"...and so I feel that it is almost time. Do you both agree?" the one on John's left said in a female voice.

A male voice on his right responded, "Yes. I too feel as you do. In my assessment, his mind and body have been adequately prepared."

"Good. We've already selected his next teacher, one whose heart is wide open and eager to take on an apprentice. This will facilitate his next phase of learning."

"As you wish, so it shall be…"

The conversation faded, or rather, was drowned out by a deluge of stimulation. The forest came alive. John could see energy flowing up and down the tree trunks, the leaves forming dim points of lights high above. John looked at his friend and saw butterflies of light fluttering around him. He could no longer see the warrior, just a pillar of light in his place. John looked around at the circle of trees and noticed columns of light among them. Additional columns stood next to each of the horses. The energy followed the contour of the circle and spiraled up towards the leaves. Another wave spiraled down, crisscrossing the first. The swirling made John dizzy and a little nauseous, so he laid down flat on his back and closed his eyes.

Johannes shifted and rested his foot against John's. In an instant, John felt a spark that morphed into a tingle and traveled up his leg. He then noticed vibrations rising up out of the ground along the length of his body. As John focused on the sensation he thought: *Ahh, pure experience*—and then didn't think at all.

NINE OF PENTACLES

T he two indulged another full day and night in the forest, but then used the following morning to travel the short distance to Heidelberg. They emerged from the forest late in the afternoon, high above the old city and across the river from it. The view of the city from that vantage was spectacular. The city was wedged between the modest River Neckar and another forested hillside. A beautiful arched bridge stretched across the river, which they would soon traverse, gaining access to the city limits.

Although many beautiful buildings formed the skyline, the most impressive one was the Queen's castle, which had been inhabited by her family for generations. As they drew near, Johannes pointed out the part of the castle where they would reside during the Oktoberfest celebrations. Johannes, being a modern man, maintained his own apartment separate from the castle, but typically spent the holiday with his father and the Queen.

Flags flew high above the castle, indicating the countdown to Oktoberfest. Each day, a different flag was flown. Any German-born could tell from them how many days remained until the celebration commenced.

"Two days 'til Oktoberfest," Johannes exclaimed with excitement.

The week of celebration always brought out the young boy in

Johannes, and John smiled at the sight of him. Johannes was happy to be home after such a long time away, but it was the holiday that had him most excited.

When they reached the castle gate, a guard addressed Johannes. *"Herr Müller, willkommenes Haus.* We have been awaiting your arrival." The guard spoke to Johannes for a few moments before Johannes thanked him and then passed through the gate.

John nodded to the guard and followed.

John listened in, but did not understand the German. He was initially surprised when Johannes was addressed as Herr Müller, but then reminded himself that Johannes and his father would share that description when addressed formally.

"So what was that all about? Is everything OK?" Despite hearing German for months, John could not quite get the right intonation of the sound.

"Oh, that? It's nothing. He was just welcoming me home. My father had left word for us to head to the dining room upon our arrival."

They walked through the main courtyard and then entered the castle through oversized iron doors. Another pair of guards stood watch; John supposed it was more out of formality than necessity.

In walking through the halls of the castle, John noticed touches of beauty everywhere. He examined the vibrant colors and rich textures, the elegance and proportion. The richness of this Central European castle far surpassed anywhere else John had been on his travels.

They entered the Great Room and dining hall. The table alone was magnificent. Silver candelabras spanned the length of the table, which sat at least three dozen people. The two walked past the formal dining table toward a side room that appeared to extend beyond the outer wall. This room, more intimate in size, contained windows on all sides, and was situated for a modest-sized party. A round table sat in the center of the round room and accommodated twelve patrons with plenty of room between them.

Upon entering the room through the archway, John noticed Herr Müller (senior) sitting with four others; two he recognized as Isabella and her guardian. Isabella sat to the left of her father, and on her left was most assuredly the Queen of Heidelberg. She was elegantly dressed and adorned with glittering gems and white gold. A second young girl sat to the Queen's left, and on the opposite side of her was Isabella's guardian.

Before sitting, Johannes brought John around and presented him to the Queen. As it turned out, this was not nearly as formal an introduction as John had expected. Johannes then sat next to his father and John sat next to him.

John soon learned that the second young girl was the Queen's niece. The Queen's younger sister had died in childbirth and since her husband had passed earlier that year in a freak accident, the baby girl was raised within the royal family.

As John watched the equal attention and favor paid to both of the young girls, it warmed his heart towards the Queen. She not only served as her niece's caregiver, but also treated her with the same love and affection as she did her own daughter. He was happy to see a girl with the unusual misfortune to have been orphaned at such an early age placed in the company of such care and affection.

Throughout the meal, John couldn't help but notice the elegance of the entire setting. The china alone must have traveled more than twice as far to get there as he and Johannes had. The silverware was heavy and shined with a recent polish. And the crystal sang intermittently when inadvertently touched by another object on the table.

The formally dressed servants moved efficiently around the room and with grace. Plates were whisked away the moment their usefulness had passed, and used forks, spoons, and knives were rapidly replaced with fresh ones. When a new course arrived, all of the dishes were laid down in unison.

Despite the abundant luxury, the whole scene was simply a normal meal for the members of the royal family. It surprised John how comfortable he began feeling around the extravagant display.

And the luxury did not end with the dinnerware. The food itself, unlike anything he had ever tasted before, was pure heaven. The sauces, the cheeses, the meat so tender it fell off of the bone. John found himself eating more than he thought he could, and savored every bite.

When the meal was completed, having served its purpose, John was free to meet Isabella formally. In response to his earlier request, Johannes had arranged for the four of them to spend some time meandering the castle gardens and become more acquainted. This was the last day of rest before the celebration began.

PAGE OF PENTACLES

W ithin minutes of their gathering, John was relieved to see the young girls being just that, young girls. They told John of their favorite flowers and rushed him over to view them. They showed him the Koi Fish pond and told him the names they assigned to the largest ones. The girls had an appreciation for nature and found beauty in the simplest of things. Playing along the water's edge, as they had done many times before, they still found things to marvel at.

A moment later, Isabella and Beth each grabbed one of John's hands and dragged him to their favorite part of the garden. Almost hidden in the corner was a life-size sculpture of a dragon. The dragon, as the girls related, was a friendly dragon and protector of the city. Its majestic wings permitted the large beast to fly high over the city and was said to warn of intruders in the ancient times. The girls loved the dragon and climbed upon its back as if ready to take flight. They both told John of a shared dream they had had where the dragon carried them to distant lands. They both hoped someday to visit those lands, once they figured out where they were.

The description of the dream reminded John of those he had had during his time in the East, ones he hadn't even shared with Johannes. Soon he found himself telling the girls all about them in the best dramatic voices he could muster. The girls watched him with their blue eyes wide. John then told them of the day he first met Johannes and how divinely orchestrated it felt. He was surprised at himself for sharing such intimacy with two young girls, but was equally surprised at their interest. These girls were clearly not ordinary girls.

"You know, John, Beth and I were sisters once, real sisters with the same mother and father!"

"What do you mean?"

"In a past life, when we lived up North on the Baltic Sea. We both remember! Our rooms were right next to each other and had views of the sea."

"How much of that life do you remember?"

This time, Beth replied. "I remember more than Isabella does. She mostly only remembers when we were young, but I can remember when we were older. We married brothers, both fishermen. They were gone a lot, so we mostly only had each other."

Isabella, awaiting her turn then said, "I think I died first because I remember Beth taking care of me when I was sick, but that's that last I remember. This time, I'm going to take care of her if she ever needs it." Isabella reached over and hugged her older cousin as they sat atop the dragon.

Eyeing John and then Johannes, Isabella said, "I think you two were brothers the same way we were sisters. You look so much alike and your names are even similar. I bet you were twins!"

Suddenly, and without warning, John felt sick to his stomach and it showed on his face.

"Hey John, are you OK? You look a little green." Johannes moved over next to his friend.

"I am not sure what it is, but I suddenly don't feel well. I better head in, I might have to throw up."

"I hope it wasn't anything you ate. Did you eat anything that I didn't?"

"Not that I know of. Why don't you take me in, Johannes? Isabella, Beth, I am so glad to have had a chance to meet you, and your dragon and Koi Fish friends. We'll have to do this again."

John and Johannes quickly headed out of the garden and back into the castle. John's room was just down the hall from Johannes'. On the way, Johannes instructed his servant to bring them some tea. However, even before the tea arrived, John felt back to normal.

"I don't know what that was all about. That sort of thing happened to me in Nepal a few times. It usually happened after I had a profound dream or vision, one that was emotionally painful. But this time, I don't know what triggered it. It just sort of came out of no where."

"Do you think it has to do with what Isabella said?"

"I don't know. I am not going to worry about it though, these things have a way of making themselves known, sooner or later."

Johannes stayed with John a bit longer, to ensure that he didn't need anything else, and then left for his own room, wanting to prepare for the next day's events.

TEN OF PENTACLES

As John rested, alone for the first time in what seemed like months, he thought of his parents. John's father was French and taught him his language, as well as English. John knew that he had distant relatives in France and was excited to know that Heidelberg, in Western Germany, was close.

John's mother was the beautiful Middle Eastern woman he could hardly picture any longer. He wondered if she could see him now and if she was proud of him. She too was in love with the idea of Europe and confessed that that was part of the reason she had fallen in love with his father. She had always dreamt of going to Central Europe with him and her son. "I made it, mother! I'm in Europe now and only a short distance from *le pays du père!*"

In reminiscing about his parents, John couldn't help but think about his uncle. It was strange for him to think about that man and not feel hate or anger. And those memories that popped up sporadically since leaving Asia, they all felt so far away.

The many friends John had accumulated during the past year became his new family. *Has it already been a year?*

He thought about Sara and felt calm. He couldn't imagine her in better hands. He smiled remembering how he used to call her the Empress. He found himself unconsciously rubbing his stomach and then questioned whether Sara was perhaps pregnant at this very moment. Technically, she could even be a mom already. She did tell him that the Emperor was anxious for her to bear him a son.

I have learned so much that I would like to share with them. I have seen so many interesting cities and traveled through wondrous countries. And now I am in Europe!

As John grew sleepy, one final thought flashed through his mind. All of the luxury he had witnessed here in this castle was nothing compared to the wealth of family and friends. John felt blessed by the many who loved him. The only way it could be better would be to have them all in one place.

Δ ▲ Δ

T he sound of bells tolling and trumpets blowing woke John up the next morning. He was surprised that the celebration was starting so early. He soon learned that the early start only occurred on the first day of the festivities.

The first morning was all about the children. The bells and trumpets announced the start of the celebration and within a few hours, all gathered for a parade. Many marched in traditional costumes. Musicians, acrobats, and balloons abounded, all surrounded by and geared toward the children.

Oktoberfest started as a carnival, but quickly evolved into an adult celebration. Each day, the festivities started later and went further into the evening until, on the last night, it continued all night long. The earlier part of the week was more about food and was dedicated to the summer bounty, but as the week went on, it became more about a final indulgence before winter.

The one thing that remained the most consistent throughout the week was the music. Oktoberfest started and ended with festive music. Musicians from different countries came to Germany just for this particular week, enjoying an endless audience.

John had been forewarned to pace himself. He didn't want to wear himself out too early and so each day, he would partake until some part of him told him to rest. He wanted to see and experience it all, even if just through observation. It was important to him to make it through to the end. The last night, he was told, would be the most fun, the most magical, and the most active.

Although beer was the advertised focus for the week, the last night was also known for another treat, one that was strictly for the adults. Not everyone partook, but enough did, which gave the air a cloud of aroma; a scent that while legal in some countries to the north, was only tolerated in Germany during the last night of

Oktoberfest. Many related this night to *Le Mardi Gras* in France and *Carnavale* in Italy, a night when the common mores were suspended, if only unofficially.

Johannes warned John that it was going to be a long night, but little did he know that it was a night that would change the course of their lives significantly.

QUEEN OF PENTACLES

D ays later, John continued to vacillate between moments reeling with emotion and times when he was emotionally shut down. He could not understand what had happened or why, and in his lack of understanding, he felt hurt, abandoned, and lost. All he knew for sure was that Johannes was gone. *One day, I am having the time of my life and the next, I'm, alone and distraught. Why did he have to leave like that? Couldn't he have just talked to me?*

John asked the questions over and over, but received no answers. The only person who could explain it to him was gone. John came to realize that he had to face that fact, accept the situation, and find the wherewithal to carry on.

For days, he did not leave the confines of his quarters. After that, he sought out Herr Müller. He wanted to distract himself from his misfortunes with busywork. Klaus had accepted him as part of the family and was grounding and supportive. In his presence, John felt better, but each evening, the sadness returned. Klaus offered quiet, fatherly comfort, but John needed to talk to someone and didn't feel comfortable opening up to Johannes' father.

He thought about Sara and how she was the one peer who could shift his perspective better than any other person he encountered. What he needed now was the kind of nurturing he only got from women. He needed to talk about how he was feeling, and the only woman he knew in all of Germany was the Queen herself.

Without knowing how she would react, John set out to seek the Queen's counsel. She had opened her home to him and had treated him well since he'd been residing there. He sensed in her a stability and maturity that he needed right now. *Besides, what other choice do I have?* And so John requested to meet with the

Queen.

The aftermath of Oktoberfest meant that activity throughout the city was low. As a result, the Queen had time for him that same afternoon. Upon meeting, John could see in her eyes an understanding that needed no words to be communicated. This woman was astute and held a strong awareness as to the goings on within her home, castle, and city.

John sat in her presence and yet the two remained silent. He wasn't quite sure what to say or how to begin. As he mulled it over, she patiently observed the emotion welled up inside of him. Then, for the first time in days, the tears returned.

The Queen took this opportunity to speak. "John, as you know, I am a practical woman. I do not make decisions rashly or in the midst of intense emotion. In you however, I see a young man whose emotions flow freely. I've kept an eye on you since Johannes' departure and have had my suspicions confirmed that you have been indeed affected by it considerably.

"I know it is none of my business what happened between the two of you, but I do see how distraught you are over it. I suspect that you are beating yourself up more than is warranted. It seems to me that Johannes has fled from his responsibility to you as a friend. There is nothing so wrong that cannot be faced and worked through. He is likely avoiding some aspect of himself, I'm sure, because he has done that before.

"While it may be pertinent for you to intermittently review these recent events to learn whatever there is for you to learn, you must first balance this current state of emotion so you can more clearly see what really transpired and why. I am sure you are blaming yourself over Johannes' departure, but do you really know the truth of it? Have you really discerned your part in this? Or are you merely looking at this through old eyes, and guilt ridden beyond due cause?"

John nodded his head and realized that he had been blaming himself completely for what had happened. He couldn't help but think that this was just another occurrence within a painful pattern in his life. Besides, he had come to accept the Law of Attraction as taught to him by the Magician, and so reasoned that this was fully of his own creation.

The Queen went on. "I see a lot of similarities between the two of you, but I also see you as one who is more willing to face what comes. Have you given yourself credit for that? You must look at this correctly, John. Johannes was the one who ran away, not you."

John listened, thinking all the while that he made the right decision seeking the Queen's advice. Her guidance was working; she was getting through to him, offering him a new perspective, a reprieve from the incessant replaying of self-deprecating thoughts. He found his emotions subsiding. *Maybe she is right. Maybe this isn't entirely my fault.*

The Queen continued to soothe John without ever inquiring on the details of what occurred between Johannes and him. Once she sensed that John's emotions had calmed sufficiently, she allowed the conversation to draw to a close. She told John to give it some time, and then to return to her in a few days.

And so John continued to spend his days working for Klaus and his evenings contemplating a course of action for himself. He knew that remaining in Germany long-term was not an option. It was just too difficult to be in Heidelberg surrounded by Johannes' family without Johannes.

Things certainly didn't turn out as I expected—he thought.

The trip across Eastern Europe filled him with anticipation for what lay ahead. Each day flowed into the next and he had felt that it could have continued that way forever. It was not that he expected Heidelberg to become a permanent home, but he never anticipated that things would have turned out as they had.

So now what?

He tried to not view his time in Europe as a complete failure; he had seen and experienced so much after all. And, he was still learning through his work with Herr Müller. But he also knew he had to formulate a plan.

It doesn't look like a solution is going to fall into my lap this time. I am going to have to make a decision and take some form of action, but what?

Days went by and then for no logical reason John decided to return to the Queen. This time, he was not emotional. The conversation centered more around his plan for the future rather than how he was feeling.

"I have given it a lot of thought, but alas, I still do not know what I should do," he said to her.

"Well, John, what is it that you most want to do?"

"I'd really like to find Johannes and talk to him about what happened." *What?* John could hardly believe what came from his own lips.

"You sound surprised by your own answer."

"I guess I am. I had been asking myself that same question for days, yet only now do I realize the answer." For a moment, John thought about what he was deciding. *Yes, I have to give this a shot to see what understanding I might gain from confronting Johannes directly.*

The Queen offered regret that he would not be staying in Heidelberg, but John sensed her words were offered superficially. Her physical gestures implied a support of his decision that she was not conveying verbally. Deep down, he knew that she approved.

Where she expressed legitimate regret was in not being able to provide him an escort. She had no one to spare and thus could only provide him with a horse and enough supplies to get him to the great sea of the South. When Johannes departed, he had left little information as to where he was headed, but she suggested that John travel to Crete, the largest of the Greek islands. "Johannes prefers to work the winter months there, where the weather is much milder than here in Germany. That is the most likely place to find him."

Despite the odds working against him, John felt he had to give it a try. *I just have to.*

PART IV – WATER – WEST

XII – THE HANGED MAN

J ohn kept himself busy preparing for his voyage to *the great sea in the middle of the earth*. He found himself thinking of the Mediterranean in those terms as if to instill a greater purpose to his mission. In reality, he was averting his attention away from the great sea of emotion in the middle of his heart.

After studying a map of the region, and considering a number of alternatives, John decided that the Rhine River Valley, which ran south along the eastern side of the Franco-German border, was the easiest path out of Germany. He estimated that after about a week of travel, he could turn to the west and head into France, skirting around Switzerland and more importantly, the Western Alps. He knew, because it was nearing winter, it would be best to avoid mountains. This time he would be traveling alone and could not risk getting sick.

France. John ran his fingertips over the country's image on the paper as he thought about his father's birth land. Despite it being a lifelong desire to visit the country, he could not muster any excitement about it now. The fact that he was fluent in French gave him little, if any, comfort.

John's determination and focus in light of the Queen's counsel had allowed him to hold his emotions at bay. However, once he was on the road, with the city retreating behind him, the painful deluge of abandonment returned.

I can't believe I'm leaving so soon—he lamented.

Johannes and John had arrived in Heidelberg only a month ago, but so much had changed—both internally and externally. For example, it no longer looked or felt like autumn. The Black Forest was now devoid of color and the sun set earlier in the afternoon than John was accustomed to. The calm, mild, and sunny weather gave way to a dull, gray, and chilly scene. It was not lost on John how symbolic all of this was.

The Rhine River soon became John's newest friend and companion. Often, when he stopped along its banks for a brief rest, he would shed his tears into its waters. Although John frequently saw people traveling north and south on the river, no one ever noticed the lonesome traveler on the western shore.

Yet the Rhine wasn't the only one observing John that first week. Along the eastern bank of the river, the Black Forest, which continued south, also kept track of the lad's progress. The trees, the river, the gentle rocking motion of his horse, and the German countryside all did their part to nurture the sadness-ridden boy. With each passing day, he cried less and soon began to settle into his time alone.

John had not been by himself since before that fortuitous meeting with the Magician. He missed that part of himself: the adventurous boy who hadn't a plan, a destination, or even a hope. *When you have no expectations, there is nothing that can disappoint you*—he considered. Although he did not have a rigid schedule now, he did have a destination and a hoped for outcome.

He weighed the possibilities: *There is a small chance of success...but a much greater chance of failure. I might not ever find Johannes...or worse...I might find him only to be rejected outright.*

Rather than wallow in those thoughts, John committed himself to the road in front of him. He had weeks to travel before reaching the sea that stretched all the way to the Emperor's land. To pass the time, he started drawing on all of the skills and knowledge he had gained over the past five seasons.

The afternoon that John turned west, leaving the Black Forest and the Rhine River behind, he made the conscious decision to leave his suffering behind as well. His Guru had said to him once: "Pain is often unavoidable, but misery is optional." So he ceremoniously washed his face in the Rhine one last time before following the setting sun toward the homeland of his father.

As John crossed into France, he thought about what he was leaving behind. He was sacrificing all that Germany had provided for him via this quest. He was trading security, apprenticeship, and family to pursue what he felt he needed to do. And yet, in looking forward, he had no regrets. *I would make the same decision again*

—he affirmed. He now felt better about his decision than before.

With renewed purpose, he assigned himself another task; he set out to find a quintessential French village where he could experience his father's culture and practice a language he had not used regularly since youth. Before rushing into the nearest village, John also decided to reinstate the practiced discipline of meditating twice each day. For months he had submerged himself into the physical experiences of life, and he had seemingly lost his way. He now needed to rise above the chaos in his mind and transcend the pain in his heart.

With Germany retreating behind him and Switzerland still well to the south, John penetrated further into France. An unusual warm front rolled in from the west and the seasonal procession seemed quickly to reverse direction. John was not familiar with the typical weather patterns of Central Europe. Rather than make any assumptions as to how long the warm weather would last, he suspended his travels to enjoy it. *A walk in the warm sun would be ideal right now!*

His body was stiff from riding horseback and he figured the movement would do him some good. He could easily continue on his way by walking along side his horse rather than riding atop it. He allowed himself to let go of the need to make specific progress, and strolled leisurely for maximum enjoyment.

By early afternoon, the sun was high in the sky and the day reached its warmest. John was ready to break from walking and decided to do yoga, which he hadn't done in months. The warmth of the day would certainly help him stretch out his muscles. Afterward, he could relax and maybe even nap in the late-day sun.

Mimicking the routine taught by his Guru, John started with sun salutations. The muscle memory within his body moved through the poses easily. His mind, not needing to expend much effort, relaxed into the rhythm. He had forgotten how good it felt to work his body this way. In fact, he felt so good by the time he completed the salutations, he moved right into the more challenging positions, something he didn't expect to attempt on his first endeavor.

The warrior poses were more a challenge of strength than balance, yet he succeeded in holding each one for an adequate amount of time before moving on to the next. After those, he moved into poses like Tree, Eagle, and Dancer. These required a greater amount of balance. He found that the more he balanced his body, the more he balanced his emotions. He soon reached a calm stillness he hadn't experienced since arriving in Central Europe.

Something within John propelled him forward, and as a final challenge, he moved into the position his Guru called Sirsha-asana: a headstand. With his forearms flat on the ground next to each ear, he stretched his legs straight up to the sky and held this position for a minute or two. His Guru could hold that position indefinitely, but John never mastered it. And he certainly wasn't going to now. In as controlled a manner as he could, he rolled down into a seated position and onto his back. He then lifted his legs straight up over his head again, but this time into a shoulder-stand, what his Guru called Sarvanga-asana.

John liked the shoulder-stand better because he could hold it much longer. He recalled that he used to be able to meditate a full 20 minutes in this position. Today, he found that if he opened up one leg, he could relax into it better, so he bent his right leg and crossed his right foot behind his left knee.

He had never assumed that position before, and it felt... different. His awareness shifted. He felt tranquility all around him. He imagined that his consciousness was expanding, touching the surrounding hills and farmland. His horse, reacting to the shift in energy, knelt down and rested. An unfamiliar sensation tingled throughout his body, first along his skin, and then all the way to his spine. He could feel waves of energy moving up and down the length of his body.

The specific sensation that he was not alone then enveloped him. In his mind's eye, he saw twelve druids in a circle around him. Six priests and six priestesses dressed in white robes stood shoulder to shoulder, each man between two women, each woman between two men. Their arms were down by their sides and they were holding hands.

The scene then took on motion. The druids unclasped their hands and crossed their arms in front of their chests, the right hand extended left, the left hand extended right. They then held hands once again and slowly lifted their crossed arms up above their heads. One by one, each turned around to face out from the circle, never letting go of the hands of their neighbors.

In unison, all of the women turned to face in. A moment later, when they turned to face out again, the men turned to face in. Finally, they all faced in, unclasped their hands, and uncrossed their arms. They kept their hands above their heads and pointed their palms toward the center of the circle where John continued to hold his modified Sarvanga-asana position.

Within John's inner sight, the Druids' palms gradually began to glow. Rays of light radiated from them and traveled towards the center of the circle…in slow motion. Inch by inch, the light extended further toward him until each connected with John's left foot extended above his head.

The beams of light disconnected from the Druids' hands and moved further into John's body. He could feel the radiance travel down his leg all the way to the top of his head where it circled back up his spine and into his bent right leg. His body vibrated around it.

Suddenly, a flash of lightning cracked out from his right foot into the direction it pointed. John's vision followed the bolt of lightning as it flew over the earth. Somehow, he knew the direction the light was traveling, mostly north but also west.

John's sight moved faster than the bolt of light and overtook it. Further ahead, he could see what appeared to be another circle. As he drew closer the image became more focused. John realized that it was not a circle of people, but a circle of stones. A stone altar sat in the center. John correctly guessed it to be his destination.

The circle of stones was deserted. The dim lighting suggested it was just past dusk or the very early dawn. His perspective switched from the moving beam of light to the stationary altar. He now looked out from the center at the approaching light.

As soon as the bolt arrived, the whole circle lit up with life. People, again dressed in white robes, surrounded the altar in all directions. Many carried torches. They chanted and moved in concentric circles, each flowing in the opposite direction from the one before and after. All eyes focused on the altar in the center where John now lay.

John's body held the same position on the altar as in reality. His left leg was straight and his right leg bent, but instead of extending up in a shoulder-stand, he was flat on his back. His head was still bent and peered down the length of his body. Then his vision blurred.

XIII – DEATH

J ohn felt no fear, yet he sensed that a treacherous occurrence was imminent. The energy of the scene surrounded him, but was distant. *What am I doing here?*—he asked from atop the altar.

In response, the vision once again shifted. He now saw from the perspective of one in the crowd. Instead of a white robe, his was black. His face was mostly concealed within an oversized hood; all of the others turned away from him and shielded their eyes. A path soon cleared to the altar.

John glanced down at his hands. He reeled from the image. In place of flesh, he saw the bony hands of a skeleton clasping a long dagger. It was coated in dried blood. John moved his fingers; the skeleton's fingers responded as if they were his own. He brought his free hand up to his face, but felt only the hard, cold bones of a skull.

John raised his eyes, or rather his eye-less face, and scanned the crowd. An unfortunate wretch, who gave into his curiosity, caught sight of the glowing red orbs that occupied the hooded figure's eye sockets. He quickly fell to the ground and screamed with his hands clasped over his now burning eyes.

John turned his gaze towards the altar. Relieved, he did not see his own body lying there. In its place, the body of a young boy assumed a similar position, except his head was back against the stone and his eyes were blindfolded. The boy's body heaved with terror, but John, within the skeletal frame he possessed, felt no fear whatsoever. He felt no compassion for the boy either, and none for the now dead man with the burned out eyes.

The malefactor John emulated knew what needed to be done and was prepared to perform the deed without hesitation. He stepped over the dead body at his feet and drew closer to the altar. He then whispered to himself or possibly for John's benefit, "The boy and his fear must be executed...without fail."

John occupied the skeleton's body and had access to its

consciousness. He knew that the execution was, without question, what needed to be done. All of the onlookers were waiting for the sacrifice, begging and pleading for it to be carried out. To them, death was as natural as the winter. It was a rite of passage. It would set them free.

But this did not stop John from pleading. *This boy, he is so young, and so afraid. Why does his life have to be sacrificed? The fear is not his fault. Does he have to die because of it? Is there not fear in the eyes of all who watch?*

"All save the one in the black hooded robe," came a reply.

Argue as John did in his mind, he still felt the right arm rise up; the bony fingers clutched the knife firmly. He was inside of the being but merely observing its actions; **his** will held no power over what was to transpire. The hand rose slowly and deliberately, but came down with force and velocity. The blade sliced through the flesh until scraping the hard stone surface below it. The young body convulsed repeatedly, then went limp and lifeless.

It was done. A life had been ended and along with it the fear, pain, and suffering it had harbored. The hooded face peered down to examine the body. John didn't want to look, but as this was a vision, he had no eyes to shut to it. He couldn't avoid seeing what was laid out before him. Yet what he saw gave him relief. Yes, a life was ended, but not the boy's. It was not a human body there on the altar, rather the carcass of an animal: a goat.

The skeletal master evaluated the execution. By his assessment, it was deemed a success. He raised the dagger, now dripping with blood, and in a deep reverberating tone, proclaimed to the crowd, "The transformation is now complete."

The white robed figures no longer moved within their concentric circles. They now stood in place and cheered.

John no longer felt fear among them, only joy.

XIV – TEMPERANCE

An establish routine of yoga and meditation began to help John cope with the intermittent, albeit growing less frequent, waves of pain, fear, and panic. Some days, John thought or even believed that he had surpassed the worst of it. But then another episode would wash over him. When he did fall back into the pool of his emotion, he nearly drowned within it.

John wondered whether the cycle would ever end. Since leaving Heidelberg, he was certain of only one thing: his understanding of the purpose of human emotion was completely lacking.

"Why does it have to hurt so much?" he asked his horse, or anyone who might be listening.

Another disappointment was that traveling through northeastern France was not nearly what he had hoped. The people he encountered were nice enough, but his command of the language had them treating him as any other. Even the novelty of speaking French wore off as it very quickly became like speaking his native tongue. The French countryside was lovely, even given the time of year, but the simplicity of life there made each village seem very much like the previous. None of the towns inspired him to stay for any length of time and thus he continued on his way.

Two weeks after leaving the banks of the Rhine, John happened upon another river. He jumped down from his perch and walked his horse over to the river's edge for a drink of water. He sat down on the ground and pulled out his map. He scanned the paper, trying to discern his location and mumbled to himself, "I vaguely remember there being rivers in eastern France. Which one is this?"

"*Pardon, monsieur.* May I help you?" A Frenchman, who noticed John with the map, walked over to offer his assistance.

Slightly startled, John jumped to his feet. "Yes please. Can you tell me which river this is?" he asked.

"But of course! It is La Saône." The Frenchman announced the river's name as if addressing a crowd.

"Can you show me on the map?" John asked, handing the map to the Frenchman.

"Certainly. Let's see…there is Le Rhône and…**here**. This is where we stand presently." The man held his finger on it for John to see. "Where are you traveling to?"

"Well, Crete eventually, but that's a long story. I do need to get to the Mediterranean, though."

The Frenchman eyed John for a moment, curious about the "long story," but then returned his gaze to the map. "If you travel south," the man pointed to the left along the river, "in a week or two, you will encounter the beautiful city of Lyon. It is situated at the junction of La Saône and Le Rhône…here."

John examined the map where the man's finger now pointed.

The Frenchman continued, "Lyon is one of France's largest cities. Le Rhône continues south from there. It is a popular shipping route, delivering French exports, especially wine, to all of the Mediterranean."

"That's how I shall go, then," John said confidently. *"Merci beaucoup, monsieur."*

"Pas de problème! Bon voyage! Et bonne chance!"

As the Frenchman walked away, John thought about the man's parting words. *Luck, I can use more of **that**!*

Δ   ▲   Δ

L yon was precisely as the Frenchman described: a thriving and beautiful city nestled between two majestic rivers. The vibrancy of the city immediately drew John in. Without any consideration, John opted to remain in Lyon for an extended rest from his travels. The intrigue simply needed to be explored.

I deserve at least this much—he reasoned.

Before long, John found a small inn that rented rooms by the week. *Perfect*—he thought with growing optimism.

The first few days, John meandered the city streets without purpose. The stimulation of city life revitalized his energy and rejuvenated his spirit. It was large enough to attract diverse and cultured peoples, but retained a small town feel within its many quaint and homey neighborhoods. The center of Lyon occupied a thin strip of land between the two rivers and was flanked by two hills. Fourvière formed the western bank of La Saône while Croix-Rousse pushed the rivers apart just north of downtown.

One day, John decided to climb the hill of Fourvière and discovered a prominent basilica at its crest. After a brief tour of the cathedral, he sat on the steps and looked out over the city. He marveled at the way the manmade structures interacted harmoniously with their natural surroundings. Here, man had not simply dominated nature, but rather maintained an equilibrium within it; one that most other cities failed to achieve.

The theme of balance kept jumping out at him: the balance of river and hill—water and earth the Magician would say, and there being two of each; the balance of man and nature; and the balance of activity and serenity.

He then considered the rivers themselves. La Saône came from the north and Le Rhône from the east. He related them to Heidelberg and Nepal and his experiences there. Down from his perch the waters mixed and merged. Further south, one could not distinguish the waters of one river from waters of the other.

"That's what I need to do!" John exclaimed audibly. *I need to integrate what I learned from **both** places. It's not just about finding the center of the Wheel inside of me. It's about tempering my inner feelings with my outer experiences. I can't simply run off and be by myself every time I feel overwhelmed.*

And then a truly profound thought occurred to him. *Is that what Johannes did? Is that why he ran off?*

John savored the insight just as he savored the expansive view that lay before him. He wished he could maintain his balance throughout times of challenge. *Maybe if I hadn't over-indulged that last night of Oktoberfest...if I had kept my bearings, I wouldn't have ended up with the mess I created.* But if he were being truthful in that moment, he would have to admit that it didn't quite feel like a **mess**. His quest was in and of itself an experience, and one that he could now appreciate.

Maybe that's it. Maybe life is balanced for me, just in an oscillatory sort of way, and over longer stretches of time. Is conflict required to inspire the pursuit of something greater? Isn't it challenge that leads to adventure and ultimately fulfillment?

John had been able to calm his emotions through solitude and the rhythm of his travels, but it was only in this current state of contemplation that he attained this latest shard of wisdom. He felt truly blessed. And he began to feel excited at the prospects that lay before him...in both time and space.

The goal need not merely be the reaching of my destination, but ought to include everything along the way.

KING OF CUPS

J ohn decided to re-emerge into the human community of which
he was a part. *Everyone I have grown to love were strangers
at the start*—he reasoned. So for the remainder of his week in
Lyon, John mingled with the people around him. He struck up
conversations without hesitation whenever the opportunity was
presented. He shared of himself and his journey, and found others
sharing of themselves in return.

As if responding to his efforts, his luck began to change. He felt
more like his old self again: charming, friendly, and attracting
attention and affection wherever he went. He was thankful for what
each day brought. He enjoyed the company of the new
acquaintances who surrounded him and as a result, learned more
about life in Lyon than he had expected.

Two days before his rent expired, John found himself making a
spontaneous decision. He decided to sell his horse and travel the
rest of the way to the sea by boat.

Earlier that day, John had been walking through Vieux Lyon, the
oldest part of the city at the base of the Fourvière Hill. He had
spotted an open-air market and paced up and down among the
vendors waiting for something to draw him in. Most of what he
saw were countrymen selling goods from farms that lay just
outside of the city. However, one man stood out among them.

The first thing John noticed about this man was his volume, in
both senses of the word. He was a large man who spoke with much
exuberance. His voice was louder than any other and was
frequently yelping out with glee and amusement. His full cheeks
were rosy, a combination of the cool air and the cheerfulness that
billowed from within him. When he spoke, his arms expressively
shaped the images he portrayed.

Those around him attempted to keep a bit of distance from him,
probably for their own safety, yet found themselves pulled in by a
large hand on their shoulder or a long arm around their neck.

John assumed the man was speaking French, but his accent was
far too melodic to be native. His intonations were emphatic and
many-a-word was trailed by an extra 'ee' or 'ay' sound. Something
about this man was completely lovable, much in the way a

grandfather is to a child.

Even from a number of paces away, John could see a sparkle in the man's bright blue eyes. John moved in a little closer and found himself drawn even further in as if by a rip current. Suddenly, with a bearish hug and a kiss to both cheeks, the few in front of John were dismissed. Now nothing stood between John and the jolly man save the warmth that surrounded him.

"Buon giorno, mon ami! Come va?" The man introduced himself as Signore Feliciano Nuoto, but told John to call him Felizio. Upon hearing his name, John understood why the French he spoke sounded so strange; it was mostly Italian, with just enough French to be understood locally. Felizio then moved right into his sales pitch and began introducing John to the Italian food selections he was selling.

Most of his items were various types of pasta. John was nearly overwhelmed by the abundant varieties. Each one had a beautiful name he was not familiar with, but when translated for him made perfect sense, based on what it looked like; "Little ears," "little hair," "butterflies," and "fountain pens."

Felizio explained, "The women of Italy long ago learned that the way to a man's heart was through his stomach. Every time they wanted more of their husband's attention, they invented a new type of pasta. Ever since, Italian women have been over feeding their men and boys with love and food." As Felizio said this, he patted his own belly and laughed at how loved he apparently was.

The topic of love moved Felizio into an emotion that readily showed on his face. "I miss my wife and family. I am so looking forward to returning to *Napoli*, especially since it's getting cold here in France. Tomorrow is my last day to sell goods in Lyon. After that, I will be sailing down the Rhône to the *Mediterraneo*. I will spend a few days in Marseilles, as long as my goods last, and then set off to *Italia* to be home for the winter."

Since no other potential customers approached him, Felizio began telling John all about his family. He spoke of his wife and two children, his sister and three brothers, and all of his nieces and nephews. The entire family lived in and around Sorrento, overlooking the Mediterranean, and just outside of the large Southern Italian port of Naples.

When John mentioned that he was traveling to Crete, Felizio's face lit up. He threw he arms around him and said, "Come with me to *Napoli*, my young friend. It is on the way to Crete and is about half the journey from here. In Marseilles, after selling the last of my goods, I was going to spend some days buying supplies for home, but if you are with me, perhaps you can buy the goods while I sell, or vice versa. Then you can see my beautiful country and meet my beautiful family. That would bring Felizio so much joy. Will you come with me and provide this weary old man some company?"

How could I say no—John thought—*to an offer given with such an open heart, let alone such a strong hug?* And so, in that moment, John decided to sell his horse and sail with Felizio to Marseilles, the Mediterranean, and Italy.

Δ　▲　Δ

J ohn's final days in Lyon flew by quickly as he had a purpose, and tasks to complete, before they set sail down the Rhône. He did carve out a little bit of time to enjoy the city, which mostly entailed long, French dinners, then a brief stroll before retiring. Before he knew it, he was bidding the city *adieu* while watching it sink into the northern horizon as they drifted downstream.

John warmed up to Felizio quickly and felt comfortable aboard the schooner. The boat was not that large, so it was good that he felt as comfortable as he did with the convivial man.

He soon noticed that Felizio's disposition was different now that they were out of the market. His one-on-one personality was calmer and more introverted. He spoke more softly, yet when a particular comment tickled him or brought out his passions, he quickly returned to his exuberant self, even if just for a moment. At times, hours of quiet would pass, each respecting the other's inner space, but once conversation ensued, Felizio was quick to share with John the aspects of his life he held so dear.

One moonlit evening, Felizio started singing in what he later described as the traditional Italian way. He serenaded the moon, the water, and whoever was within the sound of his voice. Felizio was a romanticist. When some scene or event touched him in a special way, a common occurrence, he shared his emotion with whomever he was with. He explained to John, "Romantic experiences are not just to be shared between lovers. I spend too much time away from home to not enjoy the sharing of life with companions and strangers."

But the romance of the evening made John feel sad. He started to think of Johannes, which reignited a bit of pain. This time, the pain was not so much about Johannes or what happened, but stemmed from a belief that whatever was blocking him from a successful relationship would block him forever. *Am I doomed to a life of solitude?*

Felizio noticed that his young friend's emotion had shifted and he stopped singing. He debated whether to console him or remain quiet. After thinking for a moment, he turned to John and with a large hand on the boy's shoulder, asked him, "Do you want to talk about what is bothering you?"

Not quite ready to divulge what he was thinking, John merely replied, "I'm a little sad; that's all."

ACE OF CUPS

F elizio, a man so attuned to the full spectrum of emotion, knew instantly what the source of John's sadness was, albeit not specifically. His own relationships had taught him the larger portion of the romantic wisdom he now possessed. And years as a father and an uncle gave him ample opportunity to share it with the youth in his life. He was sure he knew just what John needed to hear.

"My young friend, there are many out there who will tell you that the first phase of a relationship is the most critical in determining whether that relationship will last or not. I do not disagree that this part is significant indeed. Yet there is one phase that is more so; the phase that **precedes** the meeting of a potential partner is even **more** crucial. It is the way that a person opens up to love **before** a suitor enters the picture that has the greatest effect on that individual's chance for success."

Before going on, Felizio gestured for John to wait while he descended into the galley in search of props for his discourse. As John sat in anticipation, he could hear Felizio clanging pots and pans, rustling bags and boxes, and shifting whatever lay in his path, all the while whistling gleefully. A loud pop clued John to at least one thing Felizio was up to. A moment later, this was confirmed when Felizio emerged with a freshly opened bottle of wine and three glasses.

Felizio placed two of the glasses in front of John and left the third at his side. The first of John's glasses was empty, but the other contained a little bit of liquid. John opened his mouth to ask Felizio about the second glass, but the man's large hands quickly told him to sit back and be patient.

"My friend, what you see before you are two glasses. They represent *due regazzi* not unlike you." Felizio brushed John's chest with the back of his fingers. "Everyone seeks and desires love. This *vino*," he held up the bottle, "is the love they desire. Oh the joy to be filled with such *amore*, the luscious color, aroma, and flavor. What glass, uh man, would not desire such pleasure?"

As Felizio spoke, he waved the bottle of wine under his nose and then over to John for him to enjoy. He poured some wine into his own glass, swirled it around, and upon completing his thought, tasted the wine like a true connoisseur. After thoroughly savoring his first sip and agreeing with his own words, Felizio accepted the wine as favorable. He kissed the tips of his fingers emphatically, and then continued.

"Now each of these young men seeks love and will soon find it, but notice how one is empty while the other is not." Felizio touched one glass and then the other. "Which do you think is better prepared for love?"

Pointing to the glass with a little bit of liquid, John replied, "This one?"

"Per che?"

"Why? Well, because he has a little bit of love inside already?" The intonation of John's voice gave away his lack of confidence.

Felizio lifted the glass John had chosen and said, "Smell the contents of this glass. Does that smell like love to you?"

John leaned forward, placing his nose just above the glass, then quickly pulled away, making a face. The rancid smell of the vinegar stung the inside of his nose.

"What you have here is a man who is carrying something inside that is unpleasant, no? It is the spoiled remains of a previous relationship. Even if he clears most of it out," Felizio poured half of it overboard, "he will still taint the new love that enters."

Felizio poured a little wine in each glass and encouraged John to taste. John first tasted the pure wine and enjoyed the rich flavors he found there. He then sipped from the other glass and indeed found that the small amount of vinegar was still enough to override the flavor of the wine. It was too tart to drink and caused him to smirk once again.

"*Amico mio*, to open up to love, it is imperative to clear out anything that is old. It is only the empty chalice that can receive and retain the full *bellezza* and *piacere* of love. Either vessel can hold wine, but only the one is worth drinking from. Wouldn't you say?"

John nodded pensively.

"My friend, there are thousands of varieties of wine out there and many eager to pour you some. Make it your goal to be the empty vessel. By all means, fill your glass with a little of this wine and a little of that. Taste the Chianti and the Pinot Grigio alike. Give yourself time to determine exactly what wine best suits you, but in between, be sure to empty out your glass every time. Keep yourself clear, and that will allow you to sample the true essence of whatever wine is given. Then, when another drinks from your cup, they will taste your **true** love and have the best opportunity to choose or not what **you** have to offer."

John stared at the two glasses absorbing the full impact of the metaphor presented to him. He was fascinated by the simple yet elegant truth of it. It was clear to him now that he was not empty, nor had he been when he arrived in Germany. His pain was not just about what happened there, but the accumulation of all that came before. His glass was ever filling with the sour remains of past disappointments.

He turned to Felizio and asked, "How does one clear out their glass?"

"This, my friend, is the right question to ask, and is the work of a true warrior of love. Only the love of God and self can clear out all that taints your glass. Forgiveness siphons out the vinegar and God forgives everything. Seek to forgive all who have poured something unpleasant into your cup, and forgive yourself for carrying it around. Enjoy the romance of life and appreciate whatever love is given and in whatever way, be it romantic or platonic."

Felizio then grabbed John's nose and John recoiled, giggling.

"And always trust your nose. You didn't have to drink the vinegar to know how it would taste. We always smell the wine first and only when our nose agrees, do we sip. Romantically, your nose is here." Felizio pointed to John's stomach just below his naval. "I am not talking about the butterflies you might feel when you are nervous; I am talking about warnings you get, deep in your gut. Your nose smells the wine before it enters your glass, and by developing your sense of smell, you can help keep your glass clear, saving you the time and effort to clean it."

Felizio poured himself more wine and filled John's good glass.

"Now, enough of this seriousness. The moon has moved a full hour and we have not taken notice. It is time for us to celebrate this beautiful moment." Raising his glass, Felizio proposed a toast. *"Salute per l'amore, il piacere e la felicità!"*

"Hey, what's that last word?" John asked.

"*Felicità?* It means happiness."

As the two men sipped their wine and sang to the moon, John thought how much Felizio's name sounded like the Italian word for happiness. *That can't be a coincidence*—he concluded.

TWO OF CUPS

T he next morning, John woke with a dull ache in his head. He was still in his clothes from the night before, but a blanket had been laid over him some time after he passed out. *Who knew when that was!*—he wondered. He then held his head, laughed, and softly said, "No *amore* leaves one with heartache, but too much *amore* gives one a headache!"

As John came more awake and to his senses, his nose detected wonderful aromas: the strong smell of freshly brewed coffee mixed with that of home cooking. His head complained about the previous nights drinking, but his stomach growled loudly for the delicious food he smelled.

He stood up and quickly fell back down. He was still developing his sea legs and in his second attempt, stood more cautiously. He recalled the first thing he learned from Felizio upon entering the boat: *One hand for you and one hand for the boat, at all times.* Felizio did not always follow his own command, but the last thing he wanted to do was to have to fish John out of the river. John thought that fair enough, so the least he could do was comply.

John wandered down to the galley and found Felizio with an apron on and cooking. John wondered: *Are all Italian men as in touch with their feminine side as Felizio. Maybe in Italy, things like cooking and wearing aprons are not even considered the way of women as they are in other places.* John then wondered what Felizio was wearing on his head: a puffy and flimsy mass of white fabric.

John clumsily made his way into his seat at the table.

Felizio heard the commotion and stopped whistling. He greeted John with, "*Buon Giorno*, my friend. Did you sleep well?"

"I slept like a rock!" John said imitating an expression he picked up in one of the European cities he'd recently traveled through.

"I'm glad to hear it. Are you prepared to taste some of the fine cuisine of Chef Felizio?" Felizio took a bow, but was careful to not drop his hat.

"Yes sir! What's on the menu for this morning?" John responded, playing along.

"To drink, we have *caffè latte*. Actually, as we will be drinking French coffee on our trip, I should say *café au lait*. And for the main course, I have prepared a *frittata*, as good as my mama makes."

John watched the ease with which Felizio worked.

Felizio placed a carafe of coffee on the table, which he had set earlier. He then placed another carafe next to the first. This one, he explained, contained steamed milk. He eyed his frittata one last time. Finding that it had arrived at perfection, he slid it out of the pan and onto a plate. He placed the plate at the center of the table and then waved his hand over the entire spread for John's benefit.

John smiled brightly. He examined the frittata; it was beautiful. It was obviously made with eggs, but had pieces of red, green, and white within it. Upon closer inspection, John could make out peppers, cheese, and onion, plus a few other vegetables he couldn't quite identify. He was so entranced by the display in front of him that although Felizio had begun talking, John did not hear what he was saying.

He turned his attention back to Felizio and caught the discourse mid-sentence.

"... and so, I thought I would further cheer you up today by telling you of the day I first met my dear Lorita. *Ti piace?"*

"Yes, yes, I would **love** to hear about that." John responded.

"My friend, you remember me telling you about *la Isola di Capri*, the beautiful island near my home town of Sorrento, *sì?"*

"Yes, I remember."

"Well, it is just off the coast. In the summertime, my brothers and I would often head over to the island, how do you say, 'looking for trouble,' namely with women who didn't know us. Well, one day, we had wandered the island for much of the afternoon and into the evening. By this time, most of the visitors milled about the western side of the island waiting for the sunset. The scene was *molta bella!"* Felizio kissed his fingers; he then paused to sip some coffee.

He continued, "My three brothers and I stood around watching people gather. Then my younger brother whistled at a *donna bella* in the distance. My two older brothers quickly saw what Nardo saw and began mumbling lewd comments to each other. But for me, time slowed down."

Felizio placed a hand on his chest over his heart and went on, "I saw her just as she turned to look our way. She saw all four of us, but it was my eyes that she locked onto. This woman was clearly the most beautiful woman I had ever seen." Felizio looked up nostalgically, then stared deeply into John's eyes, raised one eyebrow, and said, "And let me tell you, in Italy, there are beautiful women everywhere!"

John, captivated by the story, stopped chewing...and then

gulped, waiting for Felizio to continue.

"She was older than me, probably closer in age to Marcelo, the oldest among us, but she only had eyes for me." Felizio smiled proudly, then laughed in that jolly fashion that always brought John back to that first day at the open-air market in Lyon.

"You should have seen the looks on my brothers' faces, even my younger brother, who often teased me because I had not the machismo of my *fratelli*. Throughout my entire youth, I anticipated the day when I would have my turn among my brothers, and this day was it." Felizio lightly slammed his fist on the table.

John laughed.

"I knew Nardo within his immaturity was about to yell something, so I caught his throat with my hand and stifled all sound." Felizio mimed choking his brother as he said this. "Nardo was a wise guy, but he knew that I had more strength in my hand than he did in his whole body. So he quickly shut up and silently rubbed his neck after I let go."

"What about the other two?" John interjected.

"Marcelo and Luca looked on, but did not challenge me. Lorita, meanwhile, held eye contact with me for a bit longer, then turned back towards the setting sun. She leaned against a stone wall, crossed one foot behind the other, and rocked it gently. Her body language suggested to me that she was relaxed and approachable. She turned her head about halfway to listen for my approach, but didn't turn the rest of the way to look at me. She was too classy to invite me to come talk with her in an obvious way, but I knew what she was conveying. An average man who did not comprehend her subtle clues was just too simple for her."

"So what did you do?"

"Without saying a word, I left my brothers and walked over to her. I leaned against the wall next to her, but not too close."

"Did you talk?" John's eyes widened.

"Indeed. We discussed the beauty of the scene before us, but nothing more. The only personal information we shared with each other was our names. We stood there for the remainder of daylight, watching the sun disappear. The sky turned from yellow to pink to lavender and finally the deep indigo of nighttime."

"She didn't just leave then, did she?" John asked.

"No. We left together. I walked her back to the main port on the east side of the island. She caught the last ferry back to Napoli and I took the one to Sorrento. The last thing she said to me before boarding her boat was that in summer, she often visited Capri on Saturdays."

"I bet you went to Capri every weekend for the rest of summer!" John grinned, picturing the younger version of the man in front of him.

"Indeed! I did not miss a single Saturday on the island all summer. Some days, the weather was not good enough for her to make the trip, but most weekends, she was there. I would spot her walking in the gardens or down by the cove. If I didn't find her sooner, I could always catch her at sunset in the same spot where we met."

While Felizio talked, John cut a slice of *fritatta* and placed it on Felizio's plate. He then fetched himself a second portion.

Felizio thanked John and went on, "Most of the time, we merely talked. Occasionally, while expressing a thought, she would place her hand on my forearm and stroke it gently just once before pulling away." He rubbed John's arm to demonstrate. "When she did that, time stopped for me altogether. There was so much love, affection, and trust conveyed in that simple touch."

"Why so coy and so subtle? You both liked it each other, right?" The suspense of the story was almost too much for John.

Felizio ignored John's prodding. He took another sip of coffee and continued at his own pace. "Little by little, I learned of her situation. She was, in fact, ten years older than me…and she was married."

John slumped slightly in response to what Felizio said.

Felizio paused for added effect, and then went on. "It became clear why nothing more than conversation transpired between us that summer. It was not that she was unavailable to me emotionally; it was that her marriage had not yet been resolved. She had already decided to leave her husband, and rightfully so, but until all was completed, she would not open up to me fully."

John took a deep breath, and sighed.

Felizio nonchalantly sipped his coffee and continued. "Lorita and I did not need words or even kisses to convey our feelings.

Mine showed clearly on my face and with her, they could be found deep in her eyes. Her emotions were always there for me to see, but I had to learn to decipher them. I soon discovered that she was this way because her emotions were not for all to see. Only those who took the time to learn her unique language of expression would be privy to the fountain that flowed within her."

"But wasn't it frustrating?" John empathically felt frustration just waiting to hear what happened next.

"You might think that a boy of my age, very near to what you are now, would have grown frustrated by such limitations, but not me. Being in her presence was so rewarding; the sight of her, the smell of her, the sound of her voice fulfilled me. I knew that it was only a matter of time before we could be together. Knowing that you are wanted and chosen by the object of your affection is one of the most calming conditions one can experience."

As Felizio basked in the memory of that distant summer, he began eating the *fritatta* on his plate for the first time. John suspended his questions and permitted the man a moment to eat.

THREE OF CUPS

F elizio and John finished breakfast and began clearing the table. John poured himself another serving of coffee and sat back down.

While Felizio washed dishes, he reinstated his story telling. "As it turned out, my sister Tessa knew Lorita's sister Alessandra. They both attended an all girls' university in *Napoli*. Lorita also has a younger sister my age: Cassandra. Alessandra and Cassandra so wanted Lorita to be happy that they were overjoyed when Lorita and I got engaged the next summer. In fact, it was Cassandra's idea to throw us a surprise engagement party. The three maidens planned the whole event.

"One Saturday late in June, I took the ferry over to *Napoli* to meet with Lorita as I normally did. Ferries made a continuous loop between Sorrento, *Napoli*, and Capri in both directions. This enabled me to escort Lorita from *Napoli* to Capri and back. A few times, Tessa accompanied me because she started spending her Saturday's with Alessandra. So, when she joined me that morning,

I didn't think anything of it.

"Anyway, that particular day, both Alessandra and Cassandra waited for the ferry with Lorita. They told Lorita that they were going to spend the day on Capri as well. So the four women and I headed over to the island together. As soon as we landed, the three younger women ran off, waving to us as they did."

"You didn't suspect **anything**?" John asked with surprise in his voice.

"Had I been paying attention, I might have. For example, I would have noted that my three brothers were likely to be on the island that day as well. I knew they were hanging out together, looking for trouble as they usually did. That morning, I overheard Luca mention that they needed to catch the 10:00 a.m. ferry, so I assumed that they were going to Capri. However, the realization that all of our siblings were on the island at the same time never occurred to me."

"And Lorita didn't suspect either." John said, half saying, half asking.

Felizio shook his head and went on, "After the girls left, Lorita and I meandered the island along our more or less typical route. A few weeks prior, Cassandra had accompanied us, asking all sorts of questions about our days on Capri; she must have been gathering information to make sure we would happen upon the *festa* unchaperoned. Sure enough, after a stroll through the *piazza*, Lorita saw a tent and we both heard music playing. It sounded like an anniversary party or maybe a wedding. Lorita wanted to check out the happy couple and suggested that we take a closer look. As we approached, we could tell that something was about to happen because the music stopped and everyone gathered close together on the far end of the dance floor facing away from us. We had to move in closer to get a look at anyone."

Felizio, now done with the dishes, sat at the table across from John. He extended the pause, again for effect, but also to sip more of his coffee.

John prodded impatiently, "And?"

"All at once, everyone turned around and yelled, *'Congratulazioni!'* and the band started to play again. Tears came to our eyes, seeing everyone in our families gathered together, just for us. We were truly surprised and touched by the celebration."

Despite already knowing the result of the endeavor, John's heart filled with what was likely a mere taste of the joy Felizio and Lorita must have felt that day.

He could visualize the scene Felizio had described. The three conspirators, seeing their plan was a success, celebrated amongst themselves. With a drink in hand, they danced as if around an invisible May pole. One, two, three times they swirled, their left hands clasped together in the center. To complete the ritual, they raised their right hands and brought their flutes of *Prosecco* together. Felizio's sister, Tessa, toasted the union of the two families and thus made official her joining of the sisterhood.

Felizio concluded by saying, "And then our sisters danced over to Lorita and me, encircled us, and bathed us with kisses and hugs." His eyes started to water. The bliss of that moment, of that full day was still with him and flowed readily from him.

John saw how much this man loved his wife and family. He truly believed that Felizio deserved all of the love he received from them as well.

The emotional waters within Felizio calmed again and he returned to telling John all about the engagement party. He spoke of the food, the music, and the distant relatives whom he didn't see often. He spoke of his brothers and how they pulled him aside at one point. Only when the four men were separated from the others did his brothers offer their sentiments.

Luca, the quietest of the four, was the one chosen by the others to speak on behalf of the three. "Dear brother, we're sad that you're leaving the clan of bachelorhood. No more days roaming this island looking for beautiful woman to whistle at." As Luca said this, he glanced at Nardo, the only one who ever did, in fact, whistle at women.

They all laughed, except for Nardo, who turned beet red with embarrassment.

Luca became serious again and said to Felizio, "We are very happy for you, Feliciano. You deserve every bit of happiness you have found with Lorita. May the two of you retain this happiness for years to come! And may you both be an example to the rest of us."

The three brothers raised and clinked their glasses, then looked Felizio in the eye conveying their consent.

Felizio remembered that moment as fondly as any other that day. "Although that was the only time my brothers had opened up to me to that degree, I have never forgotten it. That experience showed me that my brothers did indeed love me. And from then on, I could more easily see their love in all of the subtle ways it was expressed."

FOUR OF CUPS

I n the southwestern sky, the sun began to dip behind the hills. John, with Felizio at his side, watched until the entire disk was hidden from view.

The older man put a hand on the younger man's shoulder and said, "I hope you enjoyed our last sunset on the Rhône. This time tomorrow evening we'll be watching it from the city of Marseilles." He watched a moment longer, but then took advantage of the remaining light to ready the boat for the evening.

The two men enjoyed the last of the day's sunlight in silence, each lost in his own thoughts. John reviewed various images from Felizio's stories while Felizio thought about his family and calculated the number of days that separated him from them.

John's mind kept returning to the party on the island of Capri. He heard the music, smelled the food, and pictured all of Felizio's family in his mind. He imagined what it would feel like to have that kind of family. In his fantasy, he substituted familiar faces. He saw Sara as his sister and the Emperor as his oldest brother. Felizio himself was his father, but the Queen of Heidelberg played the role of his mother. He then saw Johannes. At first, it felt as if Johannes was his brother, his twin, just like Isabella had said that day, but then Johannes became his mate, his partner. He pictured holding Johannes on the dance floor with all of their family surrounding them, in joy, in bliss, in love.

As his heart opened to the image of Johannes in his arms, he was taken back to that final night of Oktoberfest. The scene in his mind shifted from day to night. He was no longer fantasizing, but remembering. The music transformed and became the harder, faster music of the Germanic club style.

Johannes was still in his arms on the dance floor, but this time he saw it as it had really happened. They were dancing, the two of them among a bunch of others.

Earlier, Johannes had handed John a cup with that look in his eye. "Drink up," he said, and winked.

John could still remember the sweet taste of the brew followed by a hint of bitterness.

Within the joy of the moment, the group formed a circle, each with an arm around two others. When John began to feel that familiar onset of intoxication, he thought to himself—*here we go again!*

Yet this time it was different. This formula was not meant to cause hallucinations. Instead, it blocked inhibitions. It was more for the body than for the mind. John's body began to tingle and he felt vibrant and awake.

The circle dissipated. Each broke free to dance with complete abandonment as the drug took effect. Some shut their eyes and waved their hands in the air, while others smiled and laughed as they stared at each other.

The music shifted…slowed into a more melodic tune and this brought the circle back together. It was a welcomed break from the exercise and an excuse to touch each other. John noticed with intense curiosity how different the skin of others felt. He then put a hand on his own arm and found that his skin felt just as vibrant and alive.

The circle slowly pulled a part, but John kept an arm around Johannes and held on to his shoulder. The effect of the drug was strong with John and grew stronger.

John's grip on Johannes relaxed. He started leaning on his friend, for support more than anything else. In response, Johannes moved his arm around John to keep himself from getting knocked over. That's when he noticed that John was faltering.

Johannes turned to face John and put his other arm around him. Holding him up, he said, "Are you OK?"

"I'm fine. In fact, I never felt better!" John was being sincere.

Johannes soon realized that John was not supporting his own weight. "John! John, stand up! Come on, you're going to fall over!"

John tried to no avail. "I…I can't."

"Here. Keep your arm around me and hold on. I am going to get you off of the dance floor. Stay with me John; I don't want to have to carry you."

Johannes supported most of John's weight and guided him to a dark corner on the grass away from the crowd. He helped John lie down and sat beside him. He wasn't overly concerned, but didn't want to leave John's side nonetheless.

John was lost in the high. His eyes were opened, but unfocused. His arms swayed with the music and his head rocked back and forth. The rest of his body was limp. He moved a hand over to Johannes and placed it on his leg. "Thank you Johannes. Thank you for bringing me here and being my friend. I'm having the time of my life." John sat up and tugged at Johannes with what little strength he had. "Can I have a hug?"

Johannes' inhibitions were lowered enough by the drug to allow himself to be pulled over towards John. He held him lightly and then relaxed into a full embrace. Johannes was hesitant, but he did feel love for John. In fact, the love he felt was different than anything he had felt before.

As Johannes started to move away, John held tighter. "Wait. Stay with me. Hold me."

Johannes, now free of John's grasp, turned to him and said, "John, no! I can't."

Δ   ▲   Δ

W ith the weight of Felizio's hand on his shoulder, John's mind returned to the here and now. He realized it was completely dark.

"Are you hungry my friend?" Felizio asked as he patted his stomach. "How about I teach you a little bit about Italian cuisine?"

John nodded and followed the older man down to the galley.

Felizio had already chopped all of the vegetables and was about to begin cooking. That's when it occurred to him to fetch John. "I'm going to prepare a traditional Italian supper *come nona*, like grandma used to make. In this pot, I am assembling the *Ragù*: a tomato sauce with fresh vegetables and a bit of meat. In the second pot, I will boil the pasta. Tonight we'll be having *farfalle*, one of my favorites! Don't they look like butterflies?" He smiled brightly, almost like a little boy.

John pulled up a stool to watch Felizio cook. He so enjoyed the man's company: his openness, his zest for life, his affectionate and generous spirit. In that moment, Felizio's intention was to teach John to cook, but John knew he was teaching him so much more.

Δ   ▲   Δ

T he next morning, they arrived at Marseilles via the sea. John was surprised to find that the Rhône did not actually pass through Marseilles, but rather emptied into the Mediterranean at Saintes-Maries-de-la-Mer, just west of the grand port city.

The energy of the city was active and frenetic. John felt chaos all around him, but had no way of knowing that it was unusual for the old port.

After they docked and secured the boat, the two men wandered up to the nearest square. John soon noticed that there was water everywhere. Apparently, the city had been flooded by a passing storm. Luckily for John and Felizio, the storm passed to the east of them days earlier, but the city of Marseilles had not been spared. The storm surge created waves much larger than normal and carried them ashore. Many of the buildings along the coast had been flooded, causing much stress for the locals.

John and Felizio missed the worst of it; however, their timing couldn't have been better. That day was the first day the markets had reopened and as it turned out, Felizio's goods were in high demand. A number of people who lived near the port lost all of their food supplies and were in need of everything that Felizio had to offer. What would have normally taken days to sell was gone in just hours.

Rather than split up as they had originally planned, John and Felizio worked side-by-side to handle the onslaught of customers. Felizio dealt with the money while John packed the goods. John had to go back to the boat a number of times until there was nothing left to sell. By mid-afternoon, they were packing up and closing down their table.

Since the whole market had been swamped with activity from the increased demand, John and Felizio asked around and found others who could use extra hands. Felizio helped one merchant by unpacking vegetables to keep up with the rate they were being sold. John, on a number of occasions, helped shoppers carry goods from the crowded market to their cart or wagon.

The day was full, more than either had expected, and was completely satisfying. Each was satiated with the abundant feeling of having accomplished so much in such a short period of time. Not only did all of Felizio's goods sell, but they sold at a premium, so the men decided to indulge in the city that night. Not all of the port's restaurants were open, but the ones that were operational were bustling.

Over dinner, the men discussed the remainder of their journey. Within the conversation, John offered a suggestion, "Why don't we stick to our original plan and stay in Marseilles for the full four days. Surely, plenty of people need help recovering from the storm. We'll offer our assistance to anyone who will accept it."

Felizio nodded in agreement. "What a splendid idea! I have friends in the city and wanted to check on them anyway. We'll start with them and then ask around."

Δ　▲　Δ

The next day, Felizio and John visited all of Felizio's friends and found them faring rather well. Most of them lived above the port and were therefore not affected by the flooding. A few had things that needed attending, but with John and Felizio's help, all was repaired in no time.

With Felizio's friends taken care of, the men decided to help out whomever they could. They walked through different neighborhoods and eventually stumbled upon one near the older part of town. This area was low lying and was more severely affected by the storm. Many of the residents were poor to begin with, but due to the flooding, they were now homeless. The waters hadn't yet receded, so there wasn't much John and Felizio could do for them.

As they headed to higher ground, they came upon a woman yelling out continuously.

"*Géraud! Où es-tu mon petit ange?* Where are you my little angel? Mommy is looking for you, sweet boy."

"*Salut Madame.* Can we help to you?"

"*Oui, oui! S'il vous plaît!* My little Géraud is missing and I cannot find him. The winds were blowing so hard, and then the rain and the waters came. It was the middle of the night and there was no light."

"It's OK Madame. We'll help you. Can you describe your son?"

"No, no; not my son. My little dog. He ran off when the storm came and we had to evacuate. I cannot find him and I have been looking for days. He has never been away from home this long. Our street is still flooded, so he cannot go back there. I don't know what to do or where else to look."

Felizio took the woman's hands in his and held them. His touch consoled her and her body softened. She had been trying to be strong, but now that she hesitated, all of the emotion came flooding out. As soon as she started to cry, she lost what little control she had had and fell into Felizio's arms sobbing. She kept saying, "I'm so afraid he is gone. I can't go on without him. What will I do without my little angel?"

Felizio allowed her time to release the emotion. All of the fear and all of the stress and trauma of the previous days poured out of her. John marveled at how comfortable Felizio was with the display of emotion. John himself, felt compassion for the woman, but his empathy got swept up in the current of her emotion. Her pain and her search churned up his own like a river flowing into a pond.

John caught himself and felt guilty for thinking of his own problems *at a time like this. I am being selfish.* He became angry with himself for not thinking only of this poor woman and how he could help her. He then reasoned that Felizio was comforting her, so there was nothing for him to do just yet. *Oh, this helping people business is hard sometimes. How do you separate your own pain from the pain of others?*

Felizio continued to hold the woman, all the while keeping his eyes on John. He knew that John was struggling and fighting within himself. He was well aware of the burden John carried and on top of that, he could see the boy reacting to the present situation.

The woman's tears diminished and her sobs grew calm and infrequent. She lifted her head off of Felizio's shoulder and wiped her eyes. John could see the relief that had already washed over her even without a solution to her grief. Now that she was ready to speak again, Felizio asked her name and she responded. "Sophie Beauvaire. *Enchanté.*" As she said this, she smiled as if meeting them in an ordinary setting. John guessed that this was a conditioned expression of greeting.

"Madam Beauvaire, we are only visiting Marseilles, but are happy to help you find your dog while we are here. OK?"

"*Merci beaucoup, Messieurs.* But please, call me Sophie."

"It is our pleasure, Sophie. I am Feliciano Nuoto, Felizio to my friends. And this is my traveling companion and friend John, or if you prefer *Jean.* He is heading to Crete via my hometown of Sorrento near *Napoli.* He is a fine young man and resourceful. I am sure we'll find little Géraud. Don't you worry."

The three of them walked through the neighborhood while Sophie described Géraud to the men. Her description of the dog was so detailed that John was able to picture him clearly. She also described his personality, and as she did, the image in John's mind came alive. He saw the dog's tail wag, and watched him sniff around like he was searching for food. John then saw a hand with a piece of meat. He could almost feel the joy within the dog as he quickly snatched it up.

The thought of food made John realized that he too was hungry. He looked up at the sun and saw that it was high in the sky above the port and to the south.

"Felizio, Sophie, are you hungry? I just had a thought. Since Géraud has been on his own for a few days, he must need to eat. Maybe he wandered over toward the port where there are a number of restaurants and food stands. The smells alone would attract anyone who is hungry. I thought we could head over there, have lunch, and then ask around to see if anyone has seen Géraud in the last day or two."

"That is a wonderful idea, John. Let's do that. Sophie, have you had a descent meal since the storm?"

"I have been worried sick looking for my little angel. I can't even remember the last time I ate."

"Well come with us. We will take you to one of the finest Italian restaurants here in Marseilles. They are one of my better customers, so you will be able to taste some of my pasta. Whenever I come to Marseilles, I deliver them my very best. Now, let me tell you about the pasta."

John smiled and then laughed to himself. Once Felizio started in on his sales pitch, it was going to take a while. John looked over at the other two and saw how Sophie was taking it all in. She walked between the two men and kept her eyes focused on Felizio. Felizio, in return, kept looking at her as well, but occasionally made eye contact with John. Sophie at one point was looking straight ahead and at that moment Felizio winked to John. He was simultaneously distracting and entertaining Sophie, and let John in on his secret.

They arrived at the restaurant and sat at a table outside along the street. Felizio ordered *antipasti* and a bottle of wine for the table. When the appetizer arrived, he directed Sophie's attention to it.

"See these olives? Taste." He place one in Sophie's hand and popped a second into his mouth. "Mmm, *molte deliziose!* I brought these all the way from Italy. My brothers grow them. You will not taste better anywhere!"

John's mind began to wander and returned to the image of Géraud that he saw earlier. Without thinking, he picked up a piece of meat and then let his hand fall below the table. His mind continued to drift as he sipped his wine and relaxed. In the distance, he could hear Felizio telling Sophie about his family, but didn't follow the familiar story. Just then, a dog grabbed the meat out of his hand.

Before he could say a word, Sophie screamed with joy. "Géraud! Where have you been?"

Géraud had gulped down the meat and then quickly caught his owner's scent and started licking her legs. Sophie picked Géraud up and held him in her lap. She let him lick all over her face. She was so happy to be reunited with her little angel. Felizio and John silently watched the joyous reunion.

Throughout the remainder of the meal, Sophie and Felizio shared stories and John just observed, listened, and ate. Afterwards, they wished Sophie and Géraud well and found others to help in their remaining time in Marseilles. Soon, they set sail for Italy.

Δ   ▲   Δ

T he first night at sea and all the next day, John rested; he was tired. He felt emotionally drained. The weight of their entire visit to Marseilles permeated deep inside of him. He had witnessed much loss, and much pain. Yes, Sophie and Géraud had been reunited, but not everyone's story ended that well. He couldn't help but think of the poor who lived in Sophie's neighborhood and how their lives would continue to be a struggle.

As the sadness seeped in, he thought once again of Johannes' last night in Heidelberg: It was early morning by the time they had returned to the castle. They were both exhausted and still well within the effects of intoxication. When they reached John's room, they fell on the bed and passed out.

John woke up a couple of hours later when the sunlight poured into their room. He pulled off his shoes and did the same for Johannes. He nudged Johannes and told him to get properly into bed. Johannes, still half asleep, pulled off some of his layers and then crawled into bed. John closed the drapes to block out the light and then did the same.

Johannes was lying on his back and had taken his shirt and

trousers off. When John crawled in next to him, he turned towards Johannes and placed a hand on his friend's chest. He could feel Johannes' heart beating and the gentle rise and fall of his breathing. With his fingers, he traced the contours of Johannes' torso. John wasn't sure if he was awake until Johannes brought his hand up and placed it on top of John's.

The intimacy of the moment sparked John's desire. A yearning egged him on and this time, Johannes relented. John caressed Johannes' taut stomach, and Johannes' body responded. Giving in to his own pleasure, Johannes guided John's hand further down his body, encouraging John's exploration. John shook with the fear of overstepping the invitation. Then it was too late; he couldn't stop himself even if he wanted. If Johannes had boundaries, he would have to set them because John was not going to.

At one point, John placed his face against Johannes' chest. Energy flowed freely between them, their flesh melding. Between the drug-induced intoxication and that of love, the boundary between them vanished and John felt Johannes' heart as if from the inside.

His own heart began to pound as a rush of passion raced through him. He felt more love and desire for this man than he had ever felt before...for anyone or anything. He wanted to give Johannes as much pleasure as he felt just lying there next to him.

Johannes began breathing more heavily. John pushed further and further and Johannes yielded more and more. John read his friend's body well and guided it toward ecstasy. He knew when to advance and when to retreat. He wanted the moment to last forever. He had never felt so connected, so fulfilled. Every part of Johannes' body excited him and nothing was seemingly off limits. He felt a freedom of expression that he had never felt before and lost himself inside of it.

Johannes placed his hands on John's shoulders and squeezed them firmly. The muscles up and down his body started to flex, which excited John even more. John looked up at his friend and found Johannes staring down at him. In the dim light, his eyes were like black orbs filled with intensity. Something told John to continue before losing the moment. Johannes shut his eyes and threw his head back.

Their bodies moved like waves and the rhythm quickened. Johannes' breathing grew louder, and then went completely silent. His head swung left and right and then straight back. From shoulders to toes, his body tensed and trembled repeatedly, then completely relaxed.

The excitement sent John past his own threshold, falling on top of Johannes, his body convulsed violently. He wrapped his arms around Johannes and held him with all his strength while the intermittent tremors continued.

The physical pleasure faded, but the emotional pleasure only continued to rise for John. By giving into the needs of his body, he was now able to focus fully on his heart. He continued to explore Johannes' body with his hands, but this time with a soft, caressing touch. Johannes' body was now fully relaxed and John's soon followed. Sleep pulled at both men and soon prevailed.

FIVE OF CUPS

T ears rained down John's cheeks and Felizio noticed. The memory of that morning, which should have been filled with bliss, was awash with pain and sorrow. It was the last time John saw Johannes.

It's not fair. How can life give one a sip of the greatest pleasure in one moment, and then take it away the very next? Everything that John had ever wanted was right there and was then swept away by a tsunami.

Felizio placed a large hand on the boy's shoulder and asked if he was ready to talk about it. Felizio knew to not pry too much, but felt the boy was ready.

And John was ready. He told Felizio all about Johannes, right up to that very afternoon when he woke alone. Johannes had not only snuck out of John's room, but he had in a stealth move, departed Heidelberg altogether. Not even his father knew much more than that. Apparently, Johannes left word that he was heading to the Mediterranean to take care of business, but nothing more.

The Queen suggested that Johannes might be found in Crete, but nothing was certain. John didn't know for sure if he would ever find Johannes and did not know what would happen if he did. "If I don't find him in Crete, I doubt I will return to Heidelberg. I don't even know what the whole point is. There isn't anything I can say to Johannes that I haven't already said."

John paused, and sighed. "Right before we fell asleep that night, I told Johannes that I loved him. All he said in response was 'I know.'"

John kept playing that night over and over in his head. If only he did this or didn't do that. He kept thinking: *This is my fault. I should have known that Johannes is not like* **me**. *I shouldn't have allowed myself to fall in love with him. All I did was ruin our friendship.*

"He could have been the brother I never had. Even Isabella said she pictured us as twins in another lifetime."

Felizio listened to the boy and let him ramble on. Some people needed to cry; others needed to talk. In either case, they all needed to get it off of their chest and Felizio was a good listener with a broad shoulder to lean on.

Once John said all that he needed to say, Felizio descended into the galley to fix lunch. About ten minutes later, he returned with a tray of bite size *panini*.

As they ate, Felizio said, "Do you remember my friend, François? We helped him clean up his basement the other day? Do you remember how sad he got when he discovered that some of his wine was ruined?"

John remembered that François had told them it was his favorite stock and he had been saving the last of it for a special occasion. During the storm, the case was knocked off of the shelf and three bottles broke open, spilling the cherished wine all over the floor. The whole time he cleaned up the broken glass, he lamented the loss and mumbled how one couldn't find that specific vintage any longer.

John nodded at Felizio's question, but continued to cry.

"Well, François kept focusing on the three bottles that were broken. It was only afterwards, when you pointed out to him that two remained that he began to cheer up. All was not lost for François. His youngest son was soon to be married and he still had two bottles for the occasion. You got him to see what was saved from the storm rather than what was lost.

"Now it is time for you to do the same for yourself. In every situation, there is always what was gained from it. You said that your time with Johannes was the most special you ever experienced. If you could share something like that with him, then you certainly could share that with another. That experience showed you what sweet love you have to give. That is what you can focus on."

John stopped crying and wiped his eyes.

"And there is still hope. You might still find Johannes in Crete. Maybe the situation was too much for him to deal with then, but maybe after spending time thinking about it, he will be able to see it for what it was. I am not trying to get your hopes up, but I do want you to see this situation fairly. Yes, three bottles of wine may have broken open and spilled, but there are two left."

John felt a little bit better and could now see that all was not lost. *I do miss Johannes and what we shared that night...and our friendship. But Felizio is right; I do find wonderful people wherever I go.*

"And besides," Felizio continued as if reading John's mind, "If Johannes hadn't run off and you hadn't set off after him, you never would have met Felizio and you wouldn't be on your way to *bella Italia* right now! Eh?"

Felizio's grin was contagious and John smiled, despite the lingering sadness. He did enjoy Felizio and did look forward to seeing Italy and meeting the Nuoto family.

SIX OF CUPS

The next afternoon featured perfect weather for sailing: the waters were calm and the sails were full. John sat at the front of the boat facing back while Felizio steered. It had been a while since he had written in his journal, so he took advantage of the smooth sailing to get some writing done. Something about the day had him in good spirits. He found himself looking back on the many adventures he'd experienced. Each fond memory seemed to spark another further back in time. The hours passed by as he wrote and reflected on his experiences.

John was deep in a memory from long ago when Felizio's

beckoning interrupted him. When he glanced up to look at his friend, he saw land flanking both sides of the boat. He quickly spun around and saw water ahead as far as he could see. He turned back to Felizio questioningly, pointing both left and right. Rather than screaming across the boat, Felizio waved John over and waited for his young friend to make his way to him.

"This is my favorite part of the journey. The island to the north," Felizio pointed to his left, "is Corsica. It is a part of France. And this one, to the south," he pointed in the other direction, "is *Sardegna*. It is one of the two large islands that are a part of my motherland."

"Where is the other one?"

"*Sicilia* is southeast of here. If we turned to the right instead of staying straight, it would take us only a bit longer to reach than my home. *Italia* has been trying to kick *Sicilia* to the curb forever, but it never leaves." Felizio chucked at his own joke, and then laughed heartily.

John stared at him blankly. "I don't get it," he professed.

Felizio handed John the map he had tucked away near the helm. He pointed a finger at the island of Sicily and then the peninsula of Italy. The joke became blatantly obvious and John smiled with understanding.

In a more serious tone, Felizio added, "These islands here sit halfway between Marseilles and *Napoli*. They are a welcomed change of scenery, no? I always get nostalgic when I sail through the Strait of Bonifacio."

"How come?" John asked.

"Sardinia is where my family vacationed regularly when I was a child. I first learned to sail during those trips back and forth to the island. Occasionally, we would visit the north island for a day, which enabled me to practice the French I learned in school. The French name for their island is *Corse*."

As Felizio thought of those summers, he uttered a thought out loud, but mostly to himself. "Just about every year in August, the Nuoto brothers would cause a little more trouble in Sardinia than they did the year before."

John watched as subtle emotions flashed across his friend's face.

Felizio then explained further, "Most Italians take the entire month of August off from work. We spend as much time as we can on the beautiful Italian beaches. Greece is the only Mediterranean country with more coastline than Italy, but Italy's beaches are far prettier."

Of course you would think that—thought John referring to the obvious bias Felizio had as an Italian. The grin on his face gave away his thoughts.

Felizio quickly retorted, "So you think I only say this because I am Italian, eh? Wait until you've been to both countries. Then you can tell me which you think is more beautiful!"

John tried to keep a serious face, but couldn't. His grin grew wider than before and he broke into all out laughter. Felizio quickly followed, laughing at himself gleefully.

After the two men calmed, each holding his own stomach from the laughter, John noticed that they had already passed the narrowest part of the straight. It didn't take long for the islands to retreat from either side of the boat, but it did take longer for the nostalgia to recede. For the remainder of the day, Felizio told tale after tale of his many adventures on the islands in those years past.

KNIGHT OF CUPS

The days of sailing between the Strait of Bonifacio and the mainland glided by as smoothly as their boat on the sea. The Italian coast came into sight just as they turned south toward *La Baia di Napoli*. John could see a pair of small islands up ahead just off of what appeared to be a peninsula jutting out to the west. When he asked Felizio if either of them were the island of Capri, he was a little disappointed to find out that they weren't.

"*Pazienza*, my friend. We will see Capri soon enough. But first, we're going to take a slight detour. Before we head to Sorrento, I want to check on Paolo."

Felizio explained that Paolo was attending *La Università degli Studi di Napoli Federico II* in Naples. It was the beginning of his second year and Felizio couldn't shake the feeling that his son needed him.

A few hours later, John and Felizio docked among the much

larger boats in the port of Naples. John was overwhelmed by the size of the port and the city behind it. Naples was easily the largest and most industrial city he had ever been to. The port was alive with activity that made Marseilles seem like a ghost town in comparison. John had to remind himself that Marseilles was not up to normal operations when they were there due to the storm, but he doubted it could ever compare to the commotion he was witnessing as they made their way toward the city.

John looked around and couldn't help but notice that many of the men looked like Felizio. Any time he saw men conversing, he saw the familiar hand motions he had grown accustomed to these weeks since Lyon. The voices he overheard were equally as emphatic. *These Italians are a passionate bunch! A shy man must really stand out in these parts.*

And the Italian language was beautiful. When Felizio spoke to him, he heard an Italian word here and there, but to listen to the melody of full-fledged Italian as it was shared among the locals was music to the ears. Sometimes, he just listened to the sounds, not trying to understand any of it. Then a familiar word would catch his attention and he would suddenly begin to understand a modicum of what was spoken.

As he suspected from the words that Felizio used, Italian and French were far more similar than he would have guessed. In fact, he found it rather easy to read the Italian signs posted around the city. On paper, the two languages were more similar than when spoken. He would later find out that once you understood the common conversions, you could easily learn one language when knowing the other.

John imagined what it would be like to stay in Italy and study the language and the culture. *Maybe if this trip to Crete doesn't work out, I'll return and settle down for a while.* But then John thought of Sara and he missed her as well. *That's it! After Crete I will return to the Middle East. I can always come back to Italy later.*

John found the aura of the university intoxicating. Once they entered the campus, the air was filled with learning, which only excited John further. John was a student of life, but he often fantasized of being an actual student attending a university like this one. The architecture alone was awe-inspiring. *And even in late autumn, the weather is quite nice in Naples.* He guessed that there would be snow on the ground by now in Heidelberg. He then wondered if the milder weather would be too much of a distraction from studies, but then quickly dismissed the thought once he saw the main building of the university. He at once pictured attending classes and studying in this building regardless of the weather.

Felizio apparently knew his way around campus, only occasionally asking if a particular building was this or that. It would have taken John days to find someone in a school this size. From what John overheard, Felizio was looking for buildings dedicated to particular studies. John guessed that he must have known what courses Paolo was taking and figured he would find him that way.

Sure enough, it was only an hour later when John heard a young male voice yelling from across the courtyard.

"Papà! Papà!"

The young man came running over with books under his arm. He placed his books on the ground and then gave his father a strong hug. One of the things that John loved about the Italian culture was how freely men expressed affection to each other. In the Middle East, a grown son would never be seen greeting his father this way, at least not in public.

The father and son spoke a few sentences in Italian before Felizio switched to French introducing John to Paolo. Without skipping a beat, Paolo switched to French as well and addressed John.

Paolo's French was better than his father's and John did not hear even a hint of an accent. *Paolo's French may be better than my own*—John thought.

Paolo told his father that he wanted to say goodbye to his friends, but that his classes were done for the day. He could allow a few hours' break before getting back to his studies in the evening. When Paolo returned, he and his father simultaneous asked if the other was hungry and the three men laughed.

Of course, in Italy you have to catch up over a meal!—John concluded.

Paolo rattled off a few suggestions and Felizio picked among them. It was clear that Felizio wanted to treat his boy to a meal beyond what he would normally eat at the university, so they headed a few blocks further from the edge of campus and found what appeared to be a fairly nice *trattoria*.

SEVEN OF CUPS

O n the way to the restaurant, Paolo shared with the two men some of what he was learning at the university. It was obvious what Paolo's interests were. The course he was most excited about was art history. The class covered art, literature, architecture, and music, tying them together through significant periods of European history. The course was designed to introduce students to a variety of areas they could subsequently pursue in more depth.

By the time they sat at the restaurant, the topic switched from one of Paolo's interests to another: girls. During the *antipasti* alone, Paolo described a number of girls who showed interested in him and a list of their positive traits. At the moment, he was only *un amico* with each, but they were pressuring him for a more intimate involvement.

As Paolo described the difficulty of picking between his admirers, his mood grew somber. He suddenly realized a common theme within this pressure to choose. He segued back to the topic of his studies and explained that the deadline to choose a major was fast approaching. He had a mere two weeks to decide among his many interests. All throughout the meal, Paolo told why he liked one subject and then why he liked another. Just as he started to convince himself on which one would be best, he found reason to choose another.

"It is no different than with the girls. How can I choose one beautiful girl over another when I like them all!" he exclaimed holding his head in his hands. "They make us choose our major now, but only give us two chances to change before spring. After that, they make us jump through hoops if we want to change it again."

John quickly sensed that it was for this reason Felizio was guided to visit his son. It was clear that Paolo sought direction from his father and John knew first hand how sound Felizio's advise was.

Surprisingly, Felizio just listened and did not offer suggestion. As John observed more, he realized that Felizio was having a hard time relating to Paolo's situation because with him, he never had to choose. He only loved one woman his whole life, and as for work, there was room enough for all that he liked.

John observed that Paolo still benefited from his father's presence. He clearly felt better just being able to share his dilemma with his father. And he hadn't asked Felizio for any specific advice, at least not so far.

Felizio ordered *cannoli, biscotti,* and *tre tazze di caffè espresso,* but before the desert and coffee were served, Paolo became uncharacteristically quiet. Thoughts of his struggle churned in his head and he began to feel it more strongly. Felizio reached across the table and placed his hand on top of his son's for comfort. All he could say was, "Give it some more time, my son. You still have a couple of weeks to decide."

Slowly and increasingly, John felt the urge to speak. Up until that point, he merely sat back and listened. He saw significance in the father/son reunion and didn't want to interfere, yet the need to speak continued to grow and he didn't even know what to say.

Just then, Paolo, with an exasperated tone, blurted out, "I will never figure out what I want. I am so bad at all of this. I never know what to do."

We disagree.

John said the words, but he didn't know where they came from or who 'we' were.

Both Paolo and Felizio looked at him questioningly.

John continue cautiously, "I know this is going to sound really strange, but I feel as if someone is trying to say something to you through **me**, Paolo. Do you want to hear the message?"

Paolo looked at his father and his father looked at him as if to say, "I don't know either, but let's see what he has to say." Paolo looked back at John and said, "Yes, go on."

John closed his eyes and moved his focus inward. He had

witnessed his Guru channel, and so knew what was happening, but he never thought that he might have this same ability; he didn't really know what to do. In his mind, he kept hearing the same words over and over, *'Dear boy'* — *'Dear boy.'* John somehow figured out that they were waiting for him to say what he was hearing, and thus echoed what he heard.

Dear boy. Fear not. You do not remember us, but we know you well. In fact, we know you better than you know yourself. We have been with you for a long time, more than these 19 years that you have called yourself Paolo. We know who you **really** are and we are here to assist you.

Do you know why you are drawn to so many of these arts that you study? You are drawn to them because you have studied them before. You have painted, composed, and written. In your studies, those pieces that most affect you, bringing you to tears, are often those that you yourself have created in previous times, as men with different names.

Dear boy, do not fear the choices that are laid out before you. They are like fairy gold; they glisten and excite you, but are not true options for you now. The time is not ripe. You will know the right choice when the time comes. Only one study is calling to you this time around. It is not a logical choice, but one that will be felt with the heart. In fact, you have already made the choice, you have just forgotten.

In university life, there is so much emphasis on the mind. Even when studying the arts, you are taught to analyze style and motif. The men who wrote your texts have claimed to know what was in the mind of the artist.

On the contrary, my boy, it is not with the mind that men create art. Often, men know not what they are creating until their eyes gaze upon the completed work. Ha! You do not read **that** in your history books now do you? It is the ego of the artist that keeps him silent on this. Do you think one would be honored if they admitted that they knew not what they were creating until it was done? It is the fear that inspiration will visit them no more that causes them to keep its auspicious ways to themselves.

You have been an artist before and you will be one again. It is your heart's desire to create beauty and this **will not** be stifled within you. But you must let go of the whims of lesser desires. As you have noticed, it is similar with the women who court you. You cannot choose because you have not yet been given the right choice. Until your heart decides, you will remain ambivalent.

The heart lives neither in the past nor the future. The heart lives only in the present. That is its gift. The heart only chooses in the present; it does not plan ahead like the mind. As you walk along a narrow path, there is no alternative but to proceed forward or pause. Ah, but once you reach a crossing, only then must you choose.

You know an intersection approaches, but you have not yet arrived. Enjoy the sights, the smells, and the sounds on your journey. Fantasize about the possibilities. Know that your heart is far wiser than your mind and allow it to make the choice for you, and at the exact right time. This is the way of the **truly** inspired.

John opened his teary eyes to see Felizio and his son staring at him intently with wide eyes and opened mouths. He knew he had channeled, but the looks these men gave made him nervous.

"What is it? Why do you two look like you just saw a ghost?" he asked.

"Do you know the significance of what you just did?" Felizio responded.

"Well, I know I channeled a message for Paolo, but am I missing something?"

"My dear friend, the fact that you spoke such wisdom is special enough and we are both grateful for it. But did you not notice that you said all of that in perfect Italian? ...But you do not know Italian!" Felizio said.

"Really? Oh my God! I understood everything I was saying, but it was as if I was listening and not speaking. I had no idea that it was Italian being spoken from my lips!"

As Felizio and John continued to speak of what just happened, Paolo remained silent. Occasionally, he would take a bite of dessert or a sip of his cappuccino, but he remained mute. Awkwardness settled over the table as each man processed the event in his own way.

After dinner, Paolo said goodbye to his father and then turned to John and said, "It was really nice meeting you, John. And I am going to think about that message for a while, I assure you." He then ran off to study with his friends.

John was certain that he noticed a sense of ease within Paolo that was not there earlier. He hoped that the message helped Paolo.

At this point, he owed so much to Felizio for all the kindness and wisdom shared. *Maybe in this small way, I am returning the favor via Paolo.*

Felizio watched his son disappear into a crowd of students. He felt content with the visit. Whatever had urged him to come to Naples had been satisfied, he was sure of it. He now looked forward to sleeping in his own bed next to his beautiful wife for the first time in months.

The two men made their way back to the port and were to sail shortly after. The trip across the bay would only take a couple of hours as Sorrento was within sight across the way.

As soon as they sailed out of the port, Felizio directed John's attention to an island ahead and to the right. "See that rocky island over there? **That's** Capri, the island were I met my dear Lorita. Maybe before you head off to Crete, we'll take you there. The views from the top are *bellissimo!"*

PAGE OF CUPS

F elizio and John soon arrived at the small port near the center of Sorrento. As they secured the boat, they heard a young girl's voice yelling from a distance.

"Papino! Papino!" It was Carina, Felizio's daughter. *"Papino,* I have been looking out for you everyday from my window. When I saw your boat sailing into port, I just knew it was you! I've missed you so much, *Papino.* I knew you would make it home before my birthday!"

"My sweet Carina, I would not miss my little girl's birthday for anything. I have brought you gifts from France, but you will have to wait until the big day arrives. In the meantime, meet my new friend Gianni. He speaks hardly any Italian at all, though. Have you learned enough *francese* to say hello to him?"

"Bonsoir, Monsieur. Je m'appelle Carina. Comment allez-vous?"

John smiled at the formal French such as taught in school. *"Salut Carina. Enchanté! Tu es très joli et très sympathique.* You are very pretty and very nice."

Carina looked at John, not knowing what else to say, or how to say much more; instead, she turned to her father and started talking rapidly in Italian.

With the boat secured and a bag over a shoulder, the men followed Carina up toward *la casa di Nuoto*. Sorrento was built on a steep hillside and as they started up one of the many staircases away from the port, Carina held her father's hand. When John came up along side them, Carina reached over and held his hand as well. He happily accepted being welcomed into the family by its youngest member.

At first quietly, and then out loud, Carina counted the number of steps as they ascended. When they completed the first few staircases and walked along a level street, Carina explained to her father that there were 60 steps to go. Felizio looked over to John and translated what Carina had said. She then turned to John and said in French, "There are 120 steps from the port to our house."

"You counted each and every one of them?"

"Yes! Many times."

When they reached the next staircase, Carina would count the steps, in Italian, and John would echo what he heard. For the most part, the Italian numbers were similar enough to the French for him to understand what she was saying.

Thus began John's first of many Italian lessons from the youngest Nuoto. Throughout his days with the family, she would point to various objects and say the Italian word out loud, giving John a chance to mimic her. It was a game between the two of them, but one where John got to learn and Carina got to teach. This made her feel proud and John was happy to be learning Italian in the process.

When a particular word was especially difficult for him, she repeated it to him as many times as it took for him to get the pronunciation right. She would then test his progress by quizzing him every now and again, pointing to an object she had taught him earlier saying, *"Che cosa è questa?"* or simply *"Che cos'è?"*

After John started learning many of the items around the house, he took his turn as teacher, testing and expanding her French. *"Qu'est-ce que c'est?"* he would say pointing at a household item. Since she had already possessed some basic French, he took the liberty to teach her not only words, but also some of the more complex sentence structures. At times, he was taken aback by how quickly she progressed.

John soon realized that part of Carina's immediate interest in him was due to the absence of her brother. This was only the beginning of his second year away and she missed him terribly, especially when he didn't make it home for three or four weeks at a time. It had been about that amount of time since she last saw Paolo, and she craved fraternal attention.

QUEEN OF CUPS

B ut on that first day, when John, Felizio, and Carina approached the Nuoto home, John looked up and saw the woman he had heard so much about. Lorita was standing in the doorway with a broad smile on her face. She wore an apron similar to, but more feminine than, Felizio's and the aroma of fine Italian cooking drifted out from behind her.

At first glance, John was struck by Lorita's apparent age. Felizio had so clearly described Lorita as she had appeared when they first met years ago and thus John's mental image was of a younger woman. Once he adjusted, he found Lorita as beautiful as Felizio had declared. Yes, she was a woman in her fifties, but her elegance was ageless. Her eyes still held the sparkle of the younger woman she once was and the lines on her face only added a sense of wisdom to her beauty. As she held his eye for a few moments, John guessed that she was less shy and reserved than she had been.

Lorita's briefly held observation of John was quickly replaced with an all out expression of joy at seeing her husband for the first time in months. She embraced him, and then kissed him, holding his face in her hands.

Felizio pulled her to him and held her close while caressing her hair. Had John not grown so accustomed to this family's display of affection, he might have been embarrassed at witnessing such an intimate expression of love.

Lorita's awareness of John resumed, reminding her that a stranger, at least to her, was present. She stiffened slightly, greeted the visitor, and invited him into their home.

Felizio introduced John to Lorita with a quick explanation of his

French and Italian. Lorita's French, to John's surprise, was also better than her husband's. Her accent was minimal, and she almost never inserted an Italian word when speaking. She switched between the one language and the other with such ease that even John, a man of four languages, envied her grace.

Carina disappeared into the house with John and Felizio's bags as Felizio and Lorita led John into the dining room where the table had already been set. As one would have guessed from the delicious smells in the house, dinner was nearly ready.

"Lorita, are you making what I **think** you're making?" Felizio asked his wife.

"Yes, Feliciano. I had a feeling you would arrive today and thus prepared your favorite: *Il pollo alla cacciatore,*" Lorita, for John's benefit, added, "a stew made with chicken, onions, peppers, and mushrooms in a red wine tomato gravy and served over rice."

John's eyes widened and his mouth watered with anticipation.

Lorita excused herself to finish preparing dinner and Felizio invited John to follow him down to the wine cellar.

"Come look at my *collezione* and we'll pick out a bottle of *vino*."

When the men returned, the ladies were preparing the table; Carina placed an additional setting for John while Lorita set platefuls of *caccitore* at each setting. Carina then filled the drinking glasses with sparkling water while Felizio opened and served the wine. Everyone flowed around each other in a way that suggested this was the family custom.

John could not help but think that this was possibly the best meal he had ever eaten in his life. The meals at the castle in Heidelberg were impressive, but they could not compare to homemade Italian. The weeks with Felizio had hinted at the Italians' command of cuisine, but Lorita's food removed all doubt.

The dinner conversation was mostly between husband and wife, catching up on months of history. Lorita spoke of the extended family, rattling off many a name that John was familiar with from Felizio's stories. And the majority of what Felizio spoke of was those events that John himself had witnessed.

To be expected, the conversation about Paolo lasted the longest. Felizio spoke mostly in Italian, as his command of French was not good enough to describe the subtle emotions he witnessed within his son. At one point, he eyed John, contemplating whether to discuss **that** part of the meeting between the men, but decided it was a bit premature. He didn't want to put John on the spot, recalling how long it took for John to open up during their first weeks together.

Intermittently, Lorita would switch to French to ask John a question to keep him from feeling left out. Soon, the information on Paolo ebbed, allowing the conversation between John and Lorita to flow into the light interaction of two people getting acquainted with each other. Occasionally, Felizio would offer up some facts about John he was told along the way, but only those that were not in any way personal.

After dinner, Carina ran off to complete her schoolwork before going to sleep. When they were sure that Carina was out of range, her parents softly spoke of the pending birthday celebration that was to occur in a less than a week. As John listened in, he was happy to know that Paolo would be returning home for his sister's ninth birthday. He looked forward to seeing Paolo again. He was curious to hear how the big decision would work out, but he also had to admit to himself that he longed for some fraternal interaction.

EIGHT OF CUPS

A couple of days later, shortly after Carina left for school, Felizio went off to deal with business matters. Before leaving, Felizio suggested to John that he and Lorita spend some time getting to know each other better. John liked the idea and figured that he could also meander through the neighborhood a bit to not wear out his welcome.

Lorita sent her husband off with a kiss to both cheeks, and then returned to the kitchen. When she emerged, she held two metal carafes and invited John to join her in the dining room. Just as when Felizio served coffee, one carafe held espresso and the other steamed milk. This time, however, Lorita described the Italian custom.

"Has Feliciano explained to you why we serve coffee this

way?" she asked John.

"Not specifically, no."

"In Italy, we have a number of coffee drinks. They are always made with espresso. With some, we add water, and with others we add steamed milk. The unique ratio of espresso, steamed milk, and foam form the myriad varieties."

"Interesting," John replied while he considered which drink he wanted to try.

Lorita concocted a *macchiato* for herself and demonstrated the technique. "So John, Feliciano tells me that you are traveling to Crete in search of a friend. That sounds ambitious," she said.

"Perhaps. At the time, it was the only thing I could think to do, but now, I am not sure what I hope to gain. A part of me feels like giving up, but I have invested this much time and distance that it would be a waste to quit now. Right?"

"John, there are times in life when the best thing a person can do for themselves is to walk away from some situation or other...even after years. Allow me to share a story with you. Feliciano is not my first husband."

Although John already knew this, he was quite surprised that Lorita was bringing it up. He was curious, and gave her his full attention.

"My first husband's name is Mario. I met him when I was very young. We were in school together and I was in love with him from the moment I saw him. I was instantly drawn to him and the feeling was mutual. But Mario was very different than Feliciano. He hardly showed his feelings at all. At the time, that made him safe for me. I would have been too scared at that age to be with someone as expressive as Feliciano. With Mario, it was easy to not express my own feelings. I could hide all of my vulnerability as he hid his own."

Lorita unwrapped a loaf of bread and began cutting it into small slices.

"At that time, it was not common for girls to approach guys, and since he didn't show any affection toward me, nothing happened for years. He wouldn't take a chance with me and I wouldn't take a chance with him. We were both too afraid."

Lorita handed John the dish of butter and he began spreading some on his bread.

"By the end of our schooling, something in me told me that it was my last chance. I had to go out on a limb or we would never get together. Intuitively, I knew he had feelings for me, but I was afraid for my vulnerability. I decided to ask him if he had a date for the school dance, and as it turned out, he didn't. I told him I didn't either and then he asked if I wanted to go with him.

"That was it, once we danced together and I felt his hands in mine, I knew what I felt and I knew what he felt. We dated for the rest of the school year and then got married the following fall. In those days, it was common for girls to marry shortly out of high school, so we were more or less just following the trend."

Although John listened intently, he decided to try making himself one of the coffee drinks Lorita had mentioned.

Lorita took a sip of her *macchiato* and continued, "All throughout the first years of our marriage, Mario withheld his feelings. As I said earlier, this was good for me because it enabled me a pace I was comfortable with. I loved him, but I didn't let him inside. He never asked, so I never really told him how I truly felt.

"After five years, I started to change. I decided that I wanted to have children, but I wanted to be closer to my husband before starting a family. So I began to open up to him. I started to show my love for him in ways that I hadn't before. Instead of opening up to me in return, he closed off. As I moved closer, he pulled back. He started working more and avoided spending time with me. When he was home, he was tired, and didn't want to go out or even talk. Even the physical intimacy was all but gone from our relationship.

"So, for two more years, I worked on solving the problem. I felt that I had invested too much time with him to just give up. The church always taught, 'Till death do us part,' so I was committed."

John's first attempt at a *cappuccino* ended up as too much foam.

Lorita noticed the look on his face and motioned for him to hand her his cup. She assembled the drink without thinking about it and went on with her story. "In our seventh year of marriage, it became too difficult. By then, it felt like I was living with a stranger. Mario retreated so far into himself I couldn't reach him at all. I so longed for an expressive relationship, for physical and emotional intimacy. I still loved Mario, but it became clear that he could not go where I wanted to go.

"So, after seven years of marriage, I told Mario I was leaving. By this point, my sisters had completed their schooling and were out on their own. I decided to move in with Alessandra near the center of *Napoli*. I figured the time apart might open him up. Maybe if he saw what he was losing, he would come around. But it did not work. Instead, Mario just buried himself in his work, and when he wasn't working, he was drinking with his friends. That last year, if I didn't reach out to him, I didn't hear from him at all. So, towards the end of our eighth year, I asked for a divorce.

"Here I was, approaching thirty and becoming a divorcée. But I didn't cry. I had already shed too many tears and there were none left. I looked back on the eight years stacked up behind me and was ready to leave them all behind. I wasn't giving up; I was letting go."

As if on cue, John dropped a piece of buttered bread and it landed in his coffee. He fished it out and popped it in his mouth, deciding that the combination of coffee and buttered bread was in fact delicious.

Lorita picked up a slice of her own bread and held it up to John. She nodded and dipped it into her own coffee following John's lead. After taking a bite, she said, "I like it that way too!"

She then commenced with the best part of the story. "It was at that time that I started spending Saturdays in Capri. I still remember the day I met Feliciano as if it were yesterday. He was young, but was so handsome. And above all else, he was expressive. He wore his heart on his sleeve and that was exactly what I so desired. I knew instantly that this man was all of the things I kept asking for, that I hoped Mario would become. If I never let go of Mario, I never would have found Feliciano. And when I found my Feliciano, I found my *felicità*."

"Felizio's name means happiness, doesn't it?" John asked to confirm his suspicion.

"Indeed! His parents named him well!" Lorita stated.

She then brought the story back around to John by saying, "So, John, whatever you are looking for, keep looking for it. You may find it in Crete or you might not. Give what you can to this endeavor, and when you are ready, let it go. Your heart will let you know when enough is enough."

For a moment, John thought back on the day he first met the Magician. He remembered the discussion about manifestation and saw how it applied to Lorita and Felizio's marriage. This gave him hope. The relationship between Sara and the Emperor served as his first role model of partnership. In this second case, he saw how Lorita and Felizio created the specific aspects of their relationship ahead of time. Felizio kept his glass empty and knew that Lorita was everything he wanted when he saw her; and Lorita, who did not get what she wanted with Mario, found all that she most desired in Felizio.

John couldn't help but notice that the theme of the day was expression. *Has Johannes ever expressed love to me? Isn't that one of the things I desire? And what about that night, anyway? Yes, it felt wonderful to express my love for him, but was he just allowing it to happen because he was intoxicated?*

John was clear that he didn't want to chase a fantasy, but he wasn't exactly ready to let it all go just yet. He had told himself that he would go to Crete in search of Johannes and let it all go after that. He realized now that before getting there, he should be certain, at least to himself, what he hoped for.

NINE OF CUPS

A fter another hour of conversation, Lorita excused herself to start getting ready for her day. She told John that she needed to start preparing for the weekend.

"Saturday is Carina's ninth birthday. We asked her how she wanted to celebrate. We said, 'Carina, would you like a party with your friends? Or would you rather have a gathering with all of your cousins, aunts, and uncles?' She, of course, wants both, so Saturday is her party, and Sunday will be the family gathering. You are welcome to accompany me as I run errands, but by all means, do not feel obligated. I can give you recommendations if you would like to visit places of interest in the area. There is no shortage of things to do here."

John decided that some time on his own would do him some

good, so he opted to go out exploring. He assured Lorita that he would be all hers once he had an afternoon to himself. He thanked her again for the wonderful company, for sharing her time, her story, and her wisdom, not to mention her home. He hugged her for the first time and then ventured out.

If there was one wish John had for his time in Sorrento, it was to visit Capri. The images in his mind from Felizio's stories weren't enough; he had to see for himself the beauty of the island. So he headed down to the port and caught the next ferry to the island.

En route, John could not decide which view was better, the view of the island as one approached or the view of the coast from the water. Felizio assured John that the Amalfi Coast of Italy was known throughout the world as the most beautiful. From the water, it **was** a sight to behold.

Upon reaching the island, John sought out the locations on the island that Felizio had mentioned in his stories: the stone wall where they first met, the gardens they walked together as they courted, and the place where the surprise engagement party was held. On the one hand, he felt like a kid on a treasure hunt, but on the other hand, he almost felt guilty as if spying on the actual events as they were happening. When he was sure he found a location, he could almost see the younger versions of Felizio and Lorita.

Then it hit him. *It's Carina's birthday tomorrow! I had better look for a gift for her.* It was late in November and the days were short; John figured he should head back down to the port on Capri. He noticed a number of shops there on his way in and was sure he could find an appropriate gift among them. *What would a girl of nine want for her birthday?*

When he arrived at the first shop, he found himself drawn to a number of items made of stone. *Surely there is nothing here Carina would want...* but he couldn't shake the feeling that kept him looking. *Why do I keep circling back to this part of the store?*

He realized a particular chess-set appealed to him most. The pieces were carved out of a lightweight stone that was smooth to the touch. According to the description, the set was the Roman gods against the Greek gods. Of course the characters were mostly the same, but with different names. When examining the chess pieces, one could make out subtle differences between the opponents, besides the obvious color difference. The stone felt the same, but the Roman pieces were a stark white while the Greek pieces were a light blue.

Although John didn't know how to play chess, he had heard of the game and knew that it was a battle of strategy. *To whom does this chess set want to go?*—he asked himself. Suddenly he saw an image of Paolo in his mind. *That makes sense. Who would enjoy chess more than university students?* He didn't know when Paolo's birthday was, but decided to buy the chess set anyway. *Always trust your intuition,* he reminded himself.

Two stores later John found a gift that felt right for Carina; it was the most beautifully illustrated Tarot cards. When John picked up the deck, he was instantly brought back to his own ninth birthday. That was the year before his mother got sick. His was given a set of cards for his birthday and recalled how much fun he had doing readings for his friends and parents.

Just to be on the safe side, he decided he would buy two gifts for Carina. If Felizio or Lorita didn't want her to have the cards for whatever reason, he would keep them for himself.

Without thinking, and before completing his decision, John found himself doing something he used to do with the cards when he was younger; he cut the deck and looked at the bottom card of the top half. As he studied the card, he strained to remember its meaning. A plump man with a smile on his face was featured. His grin was broad and his expression smug. Above and behind the man, nine cups were lined up on a shelf in the shape of an arc. *Ah, yes, the wish card! This is the card of hopes fulfilled. If you had asked about something desired, this card says that it will surely find its way to you.*

A short while later, John sat on the ferry. His bags of gifts sat at his side. He enjoyed the view and thought more about the Nine of Cups card. He wondered if there was additional significance to gain from it. And then it hit him. His father had drawn that card for him on his ninth birthday. *That's when he told me it was the wish card.*

His father had said, "Whenever you look at this card, fill each cup with a wish and know that they will all come true. Nine wishes for your ninth birthday." *How appropriate that I would remember this on the eve of Carina's ninth birthday.*

Nine is the number of completion, and when you see nine three times together, the completion will be profound and divine.

John was not sure where that last part came from, but in either case, it sat with him the rest of the way back to Sorrento.

In the evening, while having dinner, Felizio brought out his gifts for his daughter. He gave them to her a little early so that she could have them for her party.

Carina swiftly tore open her packages, starting with the largest. The first box contained a beautiful dress in the style of Paris. Felizio hadn't traveled all the way to Paris on this last trip, but thanks to a Parisian merchant he encountered in Lyon, he didn't have to.

The next two boxes were much smaller. When Carina opened the larger of the two, she found a beautiful silver necklace. Her mouth dropped open silently. The silver pendant contained a small yellow stone that shown brightly. Carina lifted it out of the box and then held it up to her father.

As Felizio place it around her neck, he said "Topaz is the birthstone for those born in November. During the Middle Ages, only Royalty could afford it."

In the last box, as John had guessed, Carina found a pair of earrings that matched the necklace.

Excitedly, Carina looked at her mother and said, "Does this mean I can get my ears pierced now?" Carina had been pleading with her mother to get her ears pierced for a year now, and Lorita kept saying, "You are not old enough yet, my dear."

Lorita smiled at her daughter and said, "I was going to make you wait until you were ten, but after your father brought these home, I couldn't argue. They are so beautiful, and you have been so good these past months while your father was away. We'll have them pierced next week, but you can wear your necklace and dress tomorrow for your party."

John eyed Felizio, referring back to their earlier conversation, and then revealed a fourth box for Carina to open.

"Carina, I bought you a little gift myself. Open it and I will tell you about it."

Carina opened the box more cautiously than the others. Between her not knowing John well and the way he introduced the gift, she didn't know what to expect. A moment later, she pulled out the cards and started flipping through them. The Tarot deck John had selected was specifically designed for children and was decorated with vibrant colors. She paused at one card that illustrated a woman in a purple dress adorned with jewels. The gem around the woman's neck looked a lot like the Topaz in Carina's necklace. She showed first her father and then the others. She then saw the parrot on the woman's arm and giggled.

John had spent a little time studying the booklet that came with the cards, and because Italian resembled French, he was able to remind himself the meaning of many of the cards.

"That card is all about riches," he told her. "It usually refers to material wealth, such as when receiving beautiful gifts. In fact, every card in the deck has a special meaning, and when you lay them out in a particular pattern, you can do readings for yourself and friends. When you are young, it is mostly for fun, but as you get better, your intuition will perceive guidance from the cards. Sometimes, people use Tarot cards for **divination**, to see future potentials."

Carina continued flipping through the cards and when one struck her in a particular way, she showed the others. The cards intrigued her, more so than John had expected, and this left him feeling satisfied. *Who knows what this will lead to? She might play with them for a while and then set them aside, or maybe they'll become an ongoing game to help her develop her intuition. Only time will tell. But I am happy that she seems to like them well enough right now.*

Δ   ▲   Δ

The next morning, the house was astir with activity. Lorita was in the kitchen cooking *Lasagna* and baking *Anisette* cookies with the birthday girl as her assistant. Since Paolo had taken the first ferry over from Naples, he had arrived early enough to help. Felizio was the only one absent. He had run out to pick up some last minute items needed for the party.

With the setup complete and the party about to begin, Paolo suggested that he and John find something to do for the day. John decided that now was as good a time as any to present Paolo his gift.

"Before we head out, I have something for you."

When John handed Paolo the nicely wrapped box, Paolo looked back questioningly. "It's not **my** birthday today. Mine isn't for another four months!"

"That's OK. I saw this and couldn't walk away from it. Something seemed to tell me that you would like it."

Paolo removed the twine and lifted the top of the box off. The chess set pieces were laid out so that one could see all of the figures. One by one, Paolo lifted out a piece to examine it more closely before placing it back in the box.

"This set is the Roman gods against the Greek gods," John told him.

"The Roman king piece must be Jupiter," Paolo said pulling it out of the box.

"It is. And the other is...Zeus." John strained to remember. "He even has a lighting bolt in his hand," he added pointing to it.

"We studied art from Greek mythology in one of my classes." Paolo said recognizing the design. "I have never played chess and I don't know all of the names of the pieces." One shaped like a building held his attention the longest. "I really like this one," he said handing it to John.

"They call that the rook or castle," John told him.

"It is modeled after a building I studied in my Architecture History class," Paolo said. "It is called the Pantheon and is located in Rome. The Greek version is another one I've studied. The Parthenon is located on the Acropolis in Athens."

"They have the same name?" John was confused.

"Almost! The **Parthenon** is the Greek temple dedicated to the goddess Athena. The **Pantheon** is the temple in Rome."

"I'm not sure I'd be able to remember which is which." John

said, already straining to remember.

"Here's one way to keep them straight. There is only one 'r' in each phrase: 'the Pantheon of Rome,' and 'the Parthenon in Athens.' I saw the Pantheon a few years ago when my class visited Rome. I would like to go to Athens some day."

"I would love to see **both** of them!" John said, hopeful. "There is a booklet in the box beneath the chessboard. It says what each piece is modeled after, in case you cannot figure any of them out. It also explains how to move them across the board. It sounds complex...too complex for me to understand in Italian."

"Thank you very much John. This is great! I have been curious about chess since I started school. I see people playing all the time in the square or in the library. I'm not sure if any of my friends know how to play."

"You're welcome Paolo. Your father and now your mother have been so kind to me, it is the least I can do. Besides, this particular set excited me because this is the closest I've ever been to Rome, and I'll be heading to Greece from here. This set sort of marks this point in my life." John knew he would remember his time in Sorrento for the rest of his life.

"All of this talk about ancient times gives me an idea," Paolo exclaimed excitedly. "Let's go to Pompeii. It is not too far from here so we can be back by evening. Pompeii was a Roman city destroyed when Mt. Vesuvius erupted in August 79 AD. We can see strange and interesting relics from that time period. You're going to love it!"

The boys headed out, and within a couple of hours, arrived at the entrance to Old Pompeii. Merchants, selling reproductions of artifacts found in the ruins, lined the street on both sides of the gate. Paolo suggested that they visit the site first and then peruse the merchant stands after.

Before they reached the gate, one of the merchants called out to them, *"Signore! Parla Lei italiano?"*

Paolo answered, *"Sì. Sono italiano.* My friend here is visiting, but he understands some, more so each day."

"I noticed that you were speaking in French."

Following the conversation, John interjected, "French is my father's tongue. I also speak English."

"But you do not look French."

"I am from the Middle East. My mother..." John was nearing the limits of his Italian, but he guessed the merchant understood what he was trying to say, and left it at that.

"Will you be staying here for a while? Are you, by chance, looking for work?"

John looked at Paolo for help and Paolo translated for him. John had caught the gist, but not enough to answer what was specifically asked. John replied to Paolo and Paolo translated.

"My friend is traveling to Greece, eventually, but is not on a set schedule. Why do you ask?"

"Tell your friend that my brother owns a gift shop. He speaks French, and is looking for some help for the next four weeks during the holiday season. We get a lot of tourists here that speak different languages, and I am sure he would be interested in hiring your friend...if he is willing to work for the full four weeks. Have him think about it and if he is interested, he can find my brother here." The merchant handed Paolo a card. "My name is Vincenzo." He pointed to his name on the card. "My brother is Giuseppe. If I am not there, tell him that I sent you. My brother is always there."

Paolo agreed to explain to John everything he had said. He then told the merchant that they were going into Old Pompeii and would stop by afterwards, if John had any questions.

On the way into the ruins, and before he forgot any of the details, Paolo explained Vincenzo's offer.

John was surprised that he understood as much of the conversation as he had and grew excited at the prospect of staying in Italy for a little while.

Paolo then said, "If you stay for a whole month, I am sure you'll be able to speak quite a bit of Italian. You have learned so much just in this last week."

"Well, Carina has been teaching me Italian and I have been teaching her French. It has been a lot of fun. She is quite the little girl."

Once inside the archeological dig, the conversation switched to the site at hand. Paolo, having been a number of times, played tour guide and explained to John the sights around them.

At the end of the tour, John pointed to the address on the

business card and said, "Do you know where this is?"

"Yes. We'll practically pass by there on the way home."

"Can we stop in? Do we have enough time?" John asked.

"Sure."

As they walked out through the gate, they saw Vincenzo watching them with anticipation. John looked at the man and said, *"Andiamo là adesso. Grazie mille.* We are going there now. Thank you very much."

John and Paolo walked the dozen blocks to the gift shop in virtual silence. It was the first time they were silent since their adventure had begun. John was mulling over questions in his mind, planning ahead what he might want to ask.

When they arrived at the gift shop, John immediately recognized many of the statuettes as those that Vincenzo had been selling near Old Pompeii. As promised, Giuseppe was in the shop behind the counter.

"May I help you find anything in particular?" Giuseppe asked.

Responding in French, John showed Giuseppe Vincenzo's card and echoed much of what Vincenzo had told them. Giuseppe's expression immediately switched from the more formal shopkeeper to one of a long forgotten friend.

"My boy, let me give you a tour of my shop. As you can see, it is empty now, but starting in about a week, there will be a dozen people in here at any one time; too many for this old man to handle by himself. Even when my brother is here to help, I could still use a third."

Giuseppe showed John the various sections of the shop, explaining many of the responsibilities that would be his if he accepted the job offer. Asking Paolo to keep an eye out for customers, he took John into the back and showed him the stacks of boxes that held all of the items he hoped to sell the last month of the year.

A moment later, their tour was interrupted by the sound of Giuseppe's name being called by Paolo from the front of the shop. Apparently a couple of tourists wandered in and were asking for some assistance. While Giuseppe helped his customers, John gestured for Paolo's attention.

"Paolo, look at that. It looks just like a piece from your chess set...Mercury is it?"

"Yes, and there is Michelangelo's David. You see that everywhere in Italy. The real statue is in *Firenze*."

"What is that odd building?" John asked pointing to another.

"That is the Leaning Tower of Pisa. It is located up North, not too far from Florence."

Wandering into the Greek section, John said, "And there's that building from Greece again, the Pa...Parthenon." John had to use Paolo's mnemonic.

"Very good!" Paolo was excited that John remembered correctly. "It was built in the 5th century, B.C.E." Paolo then began to describe all of the architectural features of the Parthenon that made it such a significant building.

Giuseppe interrupted, placing his hand on John's shoulder.

"So, my boy, is there anything else you would like to know about the shop?"

John asked a few questions and then told Giuseppe he would come back on Monday to let him know for sure if he would accept the job. He was most certainly interested, but wasn't quite ready to make the decision.

As the boys headed back to Sorrento, John began to speak, "Paolo, I am constantly amazed at how much knowledge you have of art and architecture. How do you retain it all?"

"It interests me. I love it, in fact."

This reminded John of Paolo's studies. "By the way, have you come any closer to choosing your field of study?"

Paolo's demeanor shifted suddenly.

From this, John guessed what Paolo was going to say. For a moment, he regretted broaching the subject.

Paolo answered John's question by saying, "I'm afraid not. I have been trying to remember all of what was said in that message, but it is hard to trust that it will work itself out. I mostly don't think about it. I have to decide soon...this week. I have an appointment with my advisor on Wednesday."

"I have an idea. Why don't you talk to me about the different options? Sometimes, when you hear yourself speak, it helps."

Paolo's mood lifted a bit. "OK. First, as you have already noticed, I love art history. It is easy for me to remember all of the periods and styles because it all interests me so much. But the problem with being an Art History Major is what do you do with it? I don't want to be a college professor or work at an art gallery, not that there is anything wrong with that. I just feel a strong urge to be **creative**. In your message, when they said that I created various forms of art, it felt so true. I know I can be in my head about art, analyzing it and talking about it, but that is not enough for me. At the same time, to just paint would be too much in the other direction. It would bore me after a while. I need something for my head *and* my heart."

"Have you thought about being an architect? All that knowledge of the history of architecture would help you create beautiful neoclassical structures or what have you. And, since there is a technical aspect to architecture, it would keep your mind busy. Form and function: heart and mind."

Paolo stopped walking and grabbed John's arm saying, "Why didn't I ever think of that? The architecture school is a different college within the university, but there are some architecture students in my art history class. You know, I was thinking of taking architecture history next semester. It follows my art history class, but is specifically tailored for the student architect."

John started to become as excited as Paolo was.

Paolo then said, "A number of years ago, when my sister was younger, my uncle and I built a dollhouse for her. I lost hours in the creativity. I had all of these ideas and kept adding details to make the dollhouse more beautiful. I wanted it to look like some of the buildings in our town, but different at the same time. Carina loved the dollhouse, still does, but I don't think she sees it the same way I do. It's just a dollhouse to her."

"You know, sometimes we learn of our path early in life and forget. Maybe you knew you were to be an architect back then?"

John listened to himself and couldn't help but wonder how much of what he was saying was actually meant for him. Paolo was too deep in thought to notice, but John was certain that he was tapping into something.

TEN OF CUPS

By the time the boys returned to the house, all evidence of Carina's birthday party had been whisked away. Lorita was preparing dinner and Felizio was enjoying an *aperitif*. As soon as Felizio looked at the boys, he saw the excitement that surrounded them and knew something was up.

Paolo, hardly able to contain himself, said to his father, "*Papà*, come to the kitchen. We have some news to tell you and *Mamma*."

Lorita turned to see who had entered the kitchen. She saw three anxious faces awaiting her attention. "What? The *cotolette di pollo alla milanese* is almost ready. Are you all **that** hungry?"

"*Mamma*. I have some good news for you and *Papà*. John and I both do. John was offered a job today, and I figured out what I want to study at school."

"Well, I guess we all had ourselves a productive day," Lorita said to her son. "So tell me about what you decided first, and then we'll let John talk about his job offer."

While Paolo spoke of his decision, Lorita employed the men's assistance. She handed each a bowl of food to place on the table. John, knowing the story already, went into the other room to fetch Carina for dinner.

By the time Paolo finished his discourse, everyone was seated and had already begun eating. Part of what took so long was that Paolo explained to his mother the channeled message John conveyed when they were in Naples.

Lorita graciously let Paolo tell that part of the story, not letting on that she already knew about it. Felizio had mentioned it to her days earlier.

After Paolo finished, and while he consumed a few forks full of pasta, Felizio filled the glasses with wine and proposed a toast, "To my son the architect, and my adopted son, the prophet!"

"John," Lorita added, "I guess it is official. The man of the house has spoken. You are officially a member of the family now. It's your turn. Tell us of your news."

John beamed brightly, more from Lorita's comment than from the job offer. "Well, just before entering the old city of Pompeii, a merchant, noticing we were speaking in French, called us over. He told us about his brother's gift shop. We visited the shop on the way back and the shopkeeper, Giuseppe, offered me work. He's looking for a helper to get through the holiday season. He specifically wanted someone who could speak other languages. I am excited about the job, even more the idea of staying in Italy. But I don't want to impose. I could pay rent since I will be earning some money."

"Now John, none of that nonsense," Lorita retorted. "You heard Feliciano. You are a member of this family now and you are welcome to stay as long as you like. Besides, you have been my husband's assistant for weeks; you have been tutoring Carina in French; and now you have apparently been more help to Paolo than any of his counselors at school. The way I see it, we owe **you!**"

Paolo added, "I hope you are ready John, because tomorrow you are going to meet the whole clan! I think I'll introduce you as Gianni Nuoto, just to see how everyone reacts!"

In response to Paolo's comment, everyone started laughing.

John had to admit that he liked the sound of it. *In two years time, the orphaned boy has gained two families. I have my Italian family and my 'sister' Sara and her family. Who knows how many kids she'll have by the time I see her again. And if Johannes doesn't hate me, and if I ever see him again, I might have a little bit of family with him as well.*

Δ   ▲   Δ

T he next day, John wasn't as prepared for the activity as he had thought. An Italian nuclear family was one thing, but the extended family was quite another. The volume alone was startling. He had thought Felizio was loud that first day he met him, but as it turned out, Felizio wasn't the loudest among his brothers. For example, while they were playing cards, it was no mystery who was winning and who was losing. The whole neighborhood probably knew!

With the women, it was a different story. Escaping was the tricky part. They had gathered together over coffee and had commandeered John, Paolo, and Carina. With each one, an aunt looped an arm through one of theirs and held on with a firm grip. John, being the new one, had an aunt at each arm. After a while, and seeing the pleading looks on their faces, Lorita dragged her sisters and sister-in-law away, freeing them up to mingle with the cousins. Paolo and Carina each gave their mother a pair of kisses in thanksgiving. John gave Lorita a hug, but got a pair of kisses in return.

The cousins were not organized into any one group. The youngest were running around and playing games. A straggler or two would visit a parent inquiring about sweets or spying on the card game. The oldest of the cousins joined the ranks of the higher generation. At times, one would sit in on the card game, giving one of the men a break to go check on the women and kids.

John and Paolo formed an island floating in the middle of the sea of family. It seemed that all of the other cousins were either a decade older or a decade younger. Paolo explained to John that it was nice having him around so that he wasn't the only one of his age.

Despite the fact that coffee and dessert had already been served, Lorita soon came out with a cake in celebration of Carina's birthday. The whole family stopped what they were doing to sing to the nine-year-old. The men never left their card game, but sang and yelled from across the way. Everyone was served a piece of cake whether they asked for it or not, and few pieces went untouched.

While everyone ate cake, Carina opened up gifts from her cousins, aunts, and uncles. With each one, a number of cheers, "oohs" and "ahs" were heard from the onlookers.

To John, the day resembled many of the stories Felizio had shared with him during their journey. Without exception, all the names now came with a face. *With a family like this, you always know where home is.*

The next morning, over breakfast, Paolo proposed a suggestion that he had woken with, "*Mamma, Papà.* As you know, I get four weeks off between semesters. John will be done with work by then, and Carina will be out of school for the holidays. Why don't we take a trip? Since I will be studying architecture, I would love to go to Greece. In the first part of my Architecture History class, we will be studying classical designs, most of which are in Greece and Italy. We can take *Zio* Nardo's boat. I know he will not be using it. Yesterday, he mentioned that he is taking the holidays off this year. And this way, we could take John to Crete."

Lorita looked at her husband. "Feliciano, how do you feel about getting back out on the water so soon?"

"With my family along? I'm all for it!" he replied. "I am sure I can get in a day or two of work and bring in some extra money as well. I think this is a fantastic idea! It will be Carina's first time in another country. What do you say, Carina?"

Carina responded by running over to her parents and giving them each a hug and a pair of kisses.

Felizio looked first at Lorita, and then at John and Paolo, and said, "I guess the women are for it. So men, are we in?"

John offered an emphatic *"Sì, sì, sì!"* in his best Italian imitation and everyone laughed.

Felizio finished the discussion proclaiming, *"Grecia,* prepare yourself, *La Famiglia Nuoto viene!"*

PART V – FIRE – SOUTH

XV – THE DEVIL

W ith the sun on his shoulders and the island of Crete receding behind him, Johannes looked to the south. *These past six weeks have been productive—he thought to himself—but I will be happy to be free of them.*

Most years, Johannes labored at an easy pace when in Crete. He kept his days short and spent many an afternoon on the beach enjoying the soft, late-autumn sunshine. *After all, why be on an island and not enjoy what it has to offer?*

However, this year he had thrown himself into his work with abandon. At first, he was content keeping busy; business was booming and he knew his father would be pleased. *At the very least, it will get me out of trouble for running off in the first place* —he reasoned. Nevertheless, six weeks chained to a desk were enough. *The additional profit I created more than compensates for a much-needed vacation—he justified.*

Rather than stay on the island and loll on the beach, Johannes had decided that he needed a different kind of fun. A bustling city with an active nightlife was in order, some place near enough to Crete, but outside of the region of his work. Cairo, Egypt fit the bill.

As he had packed his bags, he continued to argue with himself. "I am old enough to do what I want without consulting my father," he had said out loud trying to convince himself. *But then again, I do **work** for the man*, came the internal reply. It was sometimes hard to separate the father from the boss!

The short trek across the southern Mediterranean lasted just long enough to put him in a new frame of mind. Once he was in sight of the Land of the Pharaohs, he was ready to have some fun.

Each time Johannes came to Cairo, he noticed an increasing number of Europeans walking around the markets. *Before long, my secret oasis will be overrun with tourists—he thought—but not today!*

The value of the European currency, as compared to that of Egypt, was still good enough to afford him the finest luxuries there. Johannes was not a shy man, and he certainly pampered himself whenever he could, but in Egypt, he felt like a king! The myriad pleasures Egypt had to offer were not only affordable, they were legal. *Talk about guilt-free indulgence!*

Johannes entered his room, dropped his bags, and walked out onto the balcony. "This room has to be the best I've rented in Cairo thus far," he whispered to himself.

The sun hovered above the southwestern horizon and the great pyramids of Giza. The scene was breathtaking. For a moment, Johannes wished he had someone to share it with. Then images of Cairo's nightclubs filled with beautiful strangers flashed in his mind and he was once again content with his independence and freedom. For the next few weeks, nothing would direct his activities save his own inclinations…or so he thought.

Johannes watched the sun slowly disappear behind the pyramids. He felt pulled toward them. "There will be plenty of time to visit them later," he said in response.

Johannes' intention for his first days in Egypt was to actively explore Cairo's nightlife. He couldn't care less whether he saw the sun again for days. In preparation, he unpacked his belongings and laid down for a short rest. After a brief nap, he indulged in a good meal to sustain him for the long night ahead.

Johannes started the evening crawling from one pub to another. Then he wandered through a more active part of town and sought out a new and exciting nightclub. Every year, some came and some went, which kept things exciting for the once-a-year visitor. One particular club caught his attention and piqued his interested. *Osiris Nights, how can you go wrong with a name like that?* Johannes walked in and then the real fun began.

The hours passed like seconds. Before long, Johannes found himself staggering home with the Egyptian sun nearing the horizon. He felt light-headed and a bit off balance. He quickened his pace to retreat from the imminent sunlight, which was just too much to handle.

I know it has been a couple of months, but have I grown that intolerant to alcohol?

The rest of the way back to his hotel, he kept trying to sort it out. *Who was that man who went on and on for a couple of hours? He acted like he knew me. Kept saying, 'I know you better than you know yourself,' like he'd been living inside of my head for years now.* Johannes then questioned whether the experience was real or if he had hallucinated the whole thing. *I didn't smoke **that** much did I?* Something about the entire evening felt very much otherworldly. In looking back, he concluded that the weirdness started when he walked into the *Osiris Nights* club.

He rubbed his head, tore off his clothes, climbed into bed, and committed himself to forgetting all about it.

Δ   ▲   Δ

F or much of the month of *Diciembre*, John was an *operaio*, a workingman. The routine intrigued him.

This is the way most men live—he observed.

He could still recall the words the Magician had said to him long ago. *See those merchants over there? They live in what I will call the first realm of creation. They create with their hands. They work hard: they till the soil, plant seeds, and tend to their crops. They harvest their bounty and haul it to markets like these in order to earn a living. The farmers **believe** they can support themselves in this manner and therefore they do.*

John didn't think that he had lost his ability to manifest in the third realm. *Isn't that how I found this job to begin with?*—he asked.

Yet, with each passing day, less and less of the unexpected seemed to occur. It was as if the routine itself was rooting him more into the first realm of creation, casting all of the magic of the third realm aside.

And how does the common man deal with this work life routine? From what John could tell, many of them actually re-enforced their connection to the earthy side of life, digging the hole deeper. To cope with the drudgery of work, many bought a variety of items, items that had no practical significance. To pay for these things, those same men had to work: it was a vicious cycle. Some men indulged—or overindulged—in earthly pleasures and the pursuit of them. And still others sought escape through various forms of intoxication, just to get away from it all. Yet even this seemed to embed them further into the rut.

Intoxication—John noticed—*merely increases one's tolerance for being in the hole, thus lessening the incentive to climb out of it.*

For the most part, John had no judgment about all of this; he just considered it all with curiosity.

For the time being, he emulated those around him. He had extra income for the first time in his life and with the surplus of money, he found himself wanting to buy things he didn't really need. He reminded himself that the extra money would come in handy while in Greece and this kept him from squandering it on belongings that would just weigh him down on his travels.

Ah, Greece. He was eager to visit the ancient nation. And he was especially thrilled that he would have his new family along with him. *I feel indulgent: first, this extended jaunt in Italy, and now a vacation in Greece.* The two were certainly delaying his arrival in Crete. *Am I subconsciously procrastinating in some way, allowing all of this distraction to keep me from facing my fear? And what if I never find Johannes? Will I be able to simply let it go and move on?*

John's mind mused over the questions while he restocked shelves in the back of the gift shop. He was accustomed to his tasks well enough now to not have to think about them much. This left his mind free to wander.

Meanwhile, a couple of English speaking tourists perused items nearby. John hadn't heard English much since leaving Germany and wondered if his thoughts about Johannes were sparked by it. As he overheard the conversation next to him, he couldn't help but comprehend what was being said.

The two were dressed in expensive clothes and spoke with a tone of pretentiousness. Many of their comments were offensive. John was certain it hadn't occurred to them that someone could understand what they were saying. They not only ridiculed many of the items they looked at, but also made snide remarks about Giuseppe.

See, this is the problem with money; it gives some people the idea that just because they have more of it, they can be rude to those who have less.

John was incensed. He couldn't help but get caught up in the situation and struggled to walk the fine line—addressing the rudeness, but not partaking in it.

He walked over to the couple and asked in English if he could be of assistance. He maintained as pleasant a voice as he could, but the glare in his eyes gave away some of what he was feeling. He hoped that they would detect his displeasure and realize that their rude comments had not gone unheard.

The couple looked at John. A flash of guilt showed on their faces, but was quickly replaced with an air of condescension. "We were wondering if you had items of *higher* quality than what we see here?" the woman said.

"Well, ma'am, items are priced according to their quality. The highest priced items can be found towards the back. They tend to not be as popular among the average tourists. Would you like me to show you where they are, or can you find your way back there on your own?"

John regretted that last comment. *Damn it! Rudeness is contagious and now I am being rude in response to them.* He hated stooping to such a level and quickly made up for it.

"I would be happy to show you the best we have to offer. If you follow me please." He spoke these last two sentences as sincerely as he could muster, despite himself.

The couple began looking through the section John had shown them and he moved away from them, not wanting to overhear any more of their conversation. This time, they spoke more quietly than before. John guessed that some of the items met their **high standards** because they walked up to the front counter with a few in hand.

John wandered up after them and told Giuseppe that he would tend to the couple since he spoke English. He spared him the details of what had transpired earlier.

After the couple left, Giuseppe excitedly addressed John, "It is so good that items from the back are selling. They are the most expensive, but afford me the highest profit. I wish I had more customers like them."

John shook his head subtly and mumbled in English, "If you really knew the likes of them, I am not sure you would say that."

"What was that?" Giuseppe could not understand what John said.

"Oh, I was just agreeing with you. This sale definitely makes for a good day. I am glad that you are happy, Giuseppe."

John went back to unpacking statues, but now, all he could think about was life in the Western world. He had been in Europe long enough to discern the pros and cons of it as compared to the Middle East and the East. Yes, commercialism did help ease the burden of life in many ways, but he feared that too many people lost track of what he felt was more important. *Success is measured in figures on a balance sheet rather than in good deeds done for one's fellow man.*

He remembered his Guru describing the physical world as, "merely an illusion."

It certainly feels real, John considered. *It's rather hard and quite harsh at times.*

"Be **in** this world, not **of** it," his Guru had said.

John never quite got what that phrase meant until now. That couple showed him what being **of** this world represented.

I guess the physical world does get a hold of you. And once it has you in its claws, it is hard to escape.

Giuseppe interrupted John's inner conversation, beckoning him. *"Gianni, vieni qui!"* These days, John and Giuseppe spoke almost exclusively in Italian. Only when John hesitated would Giuseppe switch to French. "Try one of these!" Giuseppe offered John a truffle. "These chocolates are the best! Don't you agree?"

As John's taste buds basked in the pleasure of the chocolate, he thought about the benefit of this rather realistic illusion. "Yes, they are excellent," he replied. "Can't say I've had better."

"Well, here my boy, have another. This is to celebrate our excellent sales receipts today."

Life is funny—John thought. *One can find good and bad in almost anything in this world. Giuseppe saw only the good that came of those people, and why shouldn't he? He was unaware of their insolence having neither heard them nor able to understand what they had said. He is a man with simple pleasures and he is happy when life offers them to him.*

John remembered when he had that perspective. Recent experience, it seemed, had stolen away some of his innocence. It was like with language. Now that he understood Italian, it's musical quality faded into words and meaning. He could no longer hear it as a foreigner when he wandered through town. He now understood what was being said around him, and was affected by it.

John studied the satyr statue in his hand and raised an eyebrow at Pan's obvious and excited state. "I guess it's all in how you look at it, eh?" He said this more to Pan than to Giuseppe, who had already gone to the front of the store to further calculate his profits for the day.

KNIGHT OF WANDS

Horus beamed with pride. The **Veil of Uncertainty** was a tricky thing to work around, but he felt he had navigated it perfectly. *After all, one has to guide a skeptic as best one could.*

He wondered how long it would take Johannes to realize that there was no Osiris Nights club in Cairo. Maybe he wouldn't wander down that same road again or even notice if he did. Maybe he would just think that the club went under just like that, after all, it was Cairo and those sorts of things happened all the time.

Horus just hoped that he had been able to impart some gentle guiding influence. Johannes had gotten himself to Cairo as urged, but there was still work to be done. *And we can't afford him running off again*—Horus thought. Of course, **he** couldn't condemn Johannes' impetuous behavior. Within many of his own lives, he caused himself more grief than was necessary by impulsively rushing into or running away from situations. A little patience would have saved him from years' worth of challenging experience. *But that is what life is about after all, right?*

Horus was happy with the progress he had made and figured it was a good time to tell Isis about it. She would be pleased with him and that always felt good. He pictured Isis clearly and with intent, which allowed him to call her to him...*or maybe she is having me convey myself to her*. He was never sure which it was, or how exactly it all worked, but he trusted the results nonetheless.

Horus had a lot to learn about being a spirit guide. He had only recently stopped incarnating himself and Johannes was his first assignment. Isis emphasized how important this particular lifetime was for Johannes. "You need to stay alert and not be too shy about asking me for help when you needed it," she advised him.

QUEEN OF WANDS

I sis patiently waited for Horus to notice that she was with him. He still imagined that it took time for things to happen here and therefore didn't notice his creations immediately.

She smiled at the irony. Horus' lack of patience caused him to make decisions hastily, yet he didn't allow himself to see just how quickly everything manifested. *If he took more **time** to discern and less to notice, things would happen faster for him than they do now!*

Isis considered tapping Horus on the shoulder, but decided against it. *He'll come around on his own*—she thought. She was in no hurry. The longer it took him to recognize her presence, the more she could observe him. She already knew all that he wished to tell her, but of course, she wouldn't let him know that. At this stage, it was better for him to continue believing that he specifically needed to convey information linearly. This enabled him to decide when to call on her and what to discuss. Later on he would learn more about instantaneous claircognizant communication.

Isis loved Horus and she loved her place in the Universe. Her purpose was to radiate pure love and wisdom to all who called upon her. *How could it get any better than that?*—she wondered. And because she was known by so many other names, she was called on frequently. She just wished the human population would be done with the whole god/goddess designation. They saw themselves as separate and unworthy as a result, which kept them from utilizing the guidance and support they always had access to.

They didn't comprehend that they too were gods and goddesses, no different save for the human sheath.

And then, of course, there was that whole "my god versus your god" battle that had been going on for eons. *Why can't they notice that **god** and **devil** are really nothing more than alternate spellings of **good** and **evil?**—*she mused. *Could it be any more obvious?* She thought about how humans theorized the workings of the Universe. They looked at experience and called some of it good and some of it bad. They then personified their own concepts, and started giving them names and mythologies...or religions. They took tales of simple, albeit extraordinary lives, and turned them into legends... or parables. It had all served their evolution, of course, but she felt there were easier ways.

Humans. If she hadn't been one herself, she might not have had as much compassion for them as she did. "The veil is thick," she uttered to herself as she remembered what it was like on the other side of it.

Horus finally came around to noticing Isis, and addressed her. "Mother, I have called on you to give you the news you have been waiting for. Johannes has arrived in Cairo. As of now, his intention is to remain there for a few weeks."

"This is good to hear," she responded "Is there anything else you would like to share with me?"

"Yes, and for this I am very proud. Johannes has been indulging in hallucinogens, completely within his own devices of course, but this has allowed me to slip some guidance through the veil. The uncertainty of information gained this way is sufficient enough to remain within the laws. I appeared before him and we had a nice chat. He was very receptive to what I said to him."

Isis paused, more for effect than necessity. She wanted to test whether Horus truly trusted his own judgment or if he would succumb to doubt. He held steady, and so she continued. "It is good that you took advantage of the opportunity. We'll have to wait and see whether he absorbs the information or dismisses it. One never knows for sure in advance. Continue to work with him as you see fit and we'll be in touch when it is time for further synchronization."

"As you wish, Mother."

Isis smiled to herself. Horus' interactions with her were still overly influenced by that one specific lifetime. He still thought of her as his mother. It certainly added a little fun for her, for the time being. Soon enough, he would begin to see himself more on par with all else, but that was still forthcoming.

ACE OF WANDS

T he remainder of John's time working in the gift shop passed quickly. He could hardly believe that the end of his stay in Italy was upon him. The festival of *Natale* marked his last full day in Sorrento. They planned to set sail early the next morning.

This year, Lorita's sisters hosted the holiday feast. Ever since Lorita and Felizio's engagement, the two families merged and celebrated most of the holidays together. Normally, when her sisters hosted, Lorita would help out, but this year, she had plenty of preparations of her own to attend to.

Unlike typical family gatherings, this one seemed to come and go too quickly, at least from Felizio's perspective. On the eve of their vacation, the holiday became hardly more than a meal with the family. With full stomachs, the five departed early to get a good night's sleep before their early morning departure.

The voyage was as much a part of the vacation as the destination. It would take two full days to reach Greece and most of a third to reach Athens. In the interest of time, Paolo and Felizio had split the evenings into shifts, thus enabling them to sail straight through. Lorita always stayed up with Felizio and John with Paolo.

For John, the whole trip introduced him to new places. He spent hours watching the coast flow by whenever it was visible, inundating Paolo and Felizio with questions about what he was seeing.

Carina often sat by his side, as this was her first trip as well. She would occasionally interject questions of her own, but mostly she just watched and listened to the others.

After they were out of sight of the southern tip of Italy, and before the western edge of Greece came into view, John and Paolo passed the time playing chess. The other family members frequently spied on the game and couldn't resist offering one or the other a recommended move. Even Carina picked up on the game and could determine who was winning by examining the board.

As soon as they reached the Greek isles, the majority of time was once again spent admiring the scenery. None of the passengers knew the Greek islands well enough to play tour guide as they sailed through them, so all admired what they saw and pointed out especially interesting sights to each other. In addition, Paolo started providing expedition ideas for their time in Athens.

During the last month at school, Paolo had spent what little free time he had, researching the architectural marvels he hoped all of them would visit while in Greece. Athens alone offered days' worth of exploring. When he suggested they dedicate their first day to the Acropolis, everyone agreed. They had all seen models or drawings of the magnificent Parthenon and were excited to see the real thing.

Felizio estimated that they would reach Athens late that night and thus allotted all the next day to explore the city. As expected, they arrived after midnight. Carina and Lorita had already retired, but John and Paolo were awake with anticipation.

Athens was not as populous a city as Naples, but was easily twice as dense. Greece, as a nation, commanded more coastline than any other on the Mediterranean, and as a result, homed more sea vessels—by a long shot. All of the major ports in Greece operated 24 hours-a-day, seven days a week.

The port in Athens, being one of the largest, was astir with activity even at that late hour. Given that the winter solstice had just passed, Paolo estimated that they could get five full hours of sleep before sunrise. The three worked together with incentive. They secured the boat quickly, and then retired for the remainder of the night.

The combination of the anticipation of the next day and the distant clatter of activity within the port made it difficult for John to sleep soundly. All through the early morning hours, he would catch maybe an hour of sleep and then rouse briefly before catching another hour. Because of the frequent waking, he was able to remember many of his dreams.

One dream that kept reoccurring haunted him during his lucid interludes. In each version of the dream, John was wandering around in the dark carrying a torch. The torchlight formed a yellow sphere of shimmering light around him. Within it, he saw nothing but the sandy ground that he walked upon. A feeling of uneasiness accompanied a sense of urgency. He was looking for something, or maybe someone. Perhaps he was trying to get somewhere and was having difficulty finding his way in the dark. Although John's dreams contained an aura of disquiet, he didn't consider it outright fear. It more resembled anticipation, but of the unknown. John interpreted the dream to mean that he was being led forward, but he also felt that he needed to proceed with caution.

At times, he would hear a deep distant voice calling to him. It seemed to be saying, "I am Ra," or "Ra-Atum," but neither phrase had meaning to him. In fact, when John woke the first time, he wasn't even sure he actually heard words. It could have been just a feeling, a reverberation of excitement or anticipation.

When John fell back asleep, he was once again surrounded by torchlight. In the second dream, he could feel how dry and warm the air was, despite it being the dead of night. He could feel the sand between his toes, not the grainy sand of a beach, but the softer sand of the desert.

The third time John woke, realizing that he had fallen back into the same dream, he sat up and searched for more meaning. *Is this dream expressing my anticipation of our exploration of Athens?*—he wondered. *If so, why is the location clearly different? Athens is a city, not a sandy desert.*

The dream reminded him of the Middle East, *but why the darkness?* And although he had been to many places in the Middle East, he couldn't identify the location in his dream. It depicted someplace he had never been; he was sure of it.

John eventually fell asleep a fourth time, but didn't fall back into the reoccurring dream as before. In fact, this last time, he managed to sleep through to morning and only woke because of the increased rocking of the boat.

XVI – THE TOWER

P aolo was the first to awaken. As soon as the dawn was light enough to read by, Paolo pulled out his map. He looked out at the surrounding city and tried to establish where they were exactly among the various docks. As it turned out, they were ideally located within the main port. A single grand boulevard would take them directly from the boat to the base of the Acropolis.

When John rose from bed and groggily joined the others, not only had Paolo already plotted their itinerary for the day, but Lorita and Felizio had finished preparing breakfast. John guessed from the glint in everyone's eyes that he was the only one to have had such a fitful sleep. The fresh coffee soon took his mind off of the restless night, and before long, John was as energetic and excited as the rest of them.

The walk toward the center of Athens was a welcomed change of pace. All were happy to be on land again. Furthermore, the Acropolis was easily seen high above the city. It provided a constant incentive.

Before ascending to the level of the Acropolis, the Nuotos found themselves walking directly past the ruins of the *Olympieion*. With Paolo's pleading, they decided to visit it first.

"This, the Temple of Olympian Zeus, as it is also known, is the remains of the largest temple in Greece. Construction was started 600 years before Christ, but was not completed until around 130 AD." Paolo was reading from a small notebook he had filled with pertinent information for the trip. He smiled brightly as they walked around the temple ruins, proud to play tour guide for the others.

Paolo's love of architecture was clearly piqued by the classic ruins. John found the energy contagious and felt inspiration growing within him.

At one end of the temple, a dozen or so columns stood clustered together. Some were still connected by the few horizontal roof pieces that remained. Toward the other end, two columns stood apart from the others. Gazing to his left, John wandered down for a closer look at the isolated columns. As he stared at one of them, a feeling of déjà vu moved in and around him. Paolo noticed the intensity of John's gaze and walked up to him.

John turned to his friend and shared what was on his mind, "There is something about this column that intrigues me. It reminds me of something I've seen before. When I looked at the others together, I wasn't hit with the same sense of familiarity, as I get with this one alone. What it reminds me of is similar in height and shape, a standalone monument perhaps, but I can't quite see it in my mind. I can't think of anywhere I've been where I would have seen something like that though."

John moved around the column, eyeing it from different angles. When he reached a place equidistant to the two of them, he stopped and motioned to his friend. "Paolo, come here!"

Paolo joined him and observed the column.

John asked, "When you look at these two columns, what is the first thing that comes to mind?"

"From here, the two columns look like a gateway. In fact, it reminds me of many of the churches in Italy where the main entrance is marked by a pair of columns."

"Exactly. That's the same thought that I had, yet I am not as familiar with Italian churches as you are so I was a little surprised that image popped into my head. From right here, the relative position of the columns is significant, but the columns themselves aren't right. What I am sort of seeing in my mind looks different; something about the tops is not right."

"The capitals? These capitals are of the Corinthian style, and are thus more ornate than many of the other styles we'll see here in Athens. Can you describe to me what you are seeing?"

"Well, that's just it. I don't see a cap at all. What I mean is that the columns I see in my mind come to a point at the top."

"Are you sure you are not thinking of Obelisks? Obelisks are not rounded like these columns, but square. And at the very top of each is what looks like a pyramid."

"That's it! That's what I am thinking of!"

"Well, one can occasionally see obelisks in Italy, Rome for example, but they are neither Greek nor Roman in origin. I believe the Egyptians first created them."

"Hmm," John responded, unsure what to make of it. He stepped back to take in the entire temple ruins. He tried to imagine what the temple would have looked like intact. It helped him to focus on the columns that were clustered together and so he moved over toward them.

Slowly, an image formed in his mind, blending in with the site as it stood. Soon, the undamaged temple appeared before him in all its glory. With it, John saw a number of people dressed in the fashion of the time similar to the Greek gods chess pieces.

The imagined scene began to take motion. It shifted and shook. People began screaming, then running off in terror. They threw their arms up over their heads for protection. The temple itself was moving. Small pieces cracked and fell to the ground, followed by larger ones. A section of the roof gave way and the vertical columns began to sway. At the far end of the structure, the columns rocked more and more until one, and then another, fell to the ground and shattered.

The image of the falling columns disturbed John deeply and he shook his head to erase the image from his mind. Paolo saw the strained expression on John's face and looked at him questioningly.

"Paolo, do you know what happened to this temple?"

"No one knows for sure, but it is believed that an earthquake caused most of it to collapse."

"That's really strange," John said, "because I think I just saw that in my mind. I was trying to visualize the temple in tact, but once I did, it started to shake and then collapse. I assumed I was seeing an earthquake."

"Well, Mr. Psychic, have you had visions like this before?"

"Very funny, but yes, I guess I have. I've never had any way of confirming any of them though."

"Well, I am just glad that they were able to preserve what little of it remains. I find it so inspirational! It seems to have aroused your psychic vision too!"

"Yeah, I guess." John wasn't sure this was a good thing.

John and Paolo rejoined the others, who by this point were anxious to eat lunch before ascending to the Acropolis. The Parthenon could easily be seen from where they stood and everyone was excited to get a closer look.

They walked not much more than a block before finding a restaurant that featured a perfect view of the Parthenon. As they sat at the table, each realized how happy they were to be off of their feet for a bit. Due to the smells emanating from the kitchen, their hunger quickly heightened. This was to be their first of many delicious Greek meals and they were not in a hurry to rush though it.

Felizio ordered the appetizers and Lorita requested a large Greek salad for them to share. The *Dolmas* were too bitter for Carina, but she enjoyed the *Spanakopita.* For the main course, each of the boys opted for a *Gyro;* Lorita ordered a *Kabob* plate for her and Carina to share; and Felizio settled on the *Moussaka*, which contained eggplant and minced meat. Despite the abundance of food, they simply **had** to try a Greek desert. The *Baklava* was sticky and decadent, but no one complained.

Greek food was different enough from Italian to be a treat for the Nuotos; for John, it was similar enough to that which he grew up with to be nostalgic.

After the thoroughly enjoyed lunch, the five were ready to be on their feet again. They knew that the view from the Acropolis would be spectacular and used that as motivation to climb up the hill despite their full stomachs.

Upon reaching the top, all but Paolo was surprised to find that there was so much to see. The Parthenon was one of a number of beautiful ancient buildings scattered across the hilltop. The hill upon which the Acropolis was built was not the highest in Athens, but nevertheless featured panoramic views of the surrounding area.

The family chose the Temple of Athena Nike as their meeting place and gave themselves a few hours to explore. Carina stayed with her parents, and the boys wandered on their own.

John and Paolo decided to stick together, visiting each building in succession. Paolo wanted to examine specific attributes of each structure. John alternated between enjoying the architecture and admiring the view of the city from the myriad perches. At the Parthenon, John spent most of his time on the steps facing south, looking out towards the sea.

Without intending to do so, John found himself sinking into another vision. This time, what he saw was an ancient city, much smaller than the current city of Athens. Distant hills, presently coated with buildings, were lush and green in his vision. From the Acropolis, the outer walls of the old city were conspicuous. The air was clear and ancient vessels could be seen approaching and departing the main port.

From the southeast, movement caught John's attention. He turned to get a better look and saw it approaching. He couldn't comprehend what he was seeing. He marveled at how solid ground could move like that; much like the leading ripple in a pond after a rock has been thrown into it. Once the wave reached the Acropolis, the ground shifted violently beneath his feet. The first jolt brought him to his knees. The ground rocked front-to-back and then side-to-side. Again, he heard screams and rumble all around him.

This time, it was Paolo's hand on his shoulder that shook him from his daydream.

"I just had another one…another vision of an earthquake!" he said to Paolo. "Why is this place stirring up these visions within me?"

"I don't know, but come on, let's go see the *Erechtheum*. You can tell me about your vision on the way."

As they wandered over to the north side of the hilltop, John described the details of his latest vision.

"As long as you keep seeing the past," Paolo said, "I wouldn't be too concerned. It would be different if you were having premonitions. That earthquake had to have happened over a thousand years ago."

"Yeah, you're right," John agreed. "I'm not going to worry about it. It's just a little alarming because when I have a vision it feels like I am there! I am not just seeing things, but experiencing movement and sound as well."

In an attempt to stave off the visions, John tried to remain focused on the activity of the people around him. The visions only seemed to occur when his mind wandered. However, his plan did not work completely. Instead of falling into flowing scenes as before, he now saw snapshots of the past. Images flashed in his mind, suggesting enough movement for him to deduce the events portrayed. *This is less disconcerting*—John thought, appreciating the slight improvement.

In every case, John saw Athens in the past…just before and during what he guessed to be a single catastrophic earthquake. The less he resisted the visions and flashes, the more clearly he could see the ancient city. With practice, he became more emotionally detached from the scenes and could more easily examine them. He described to Paolo details he saw in the ancient structures that were not evident from the ruins. He told of buildings that had existed where none remained.

"That building over there," John said, "used to have beautiful white cloth draped around some if its columns. And over here, there used to be a beautiful statue on a stone pedestal."

The remaining days in Athens, John continued to have visions and flashes, but only among the ruins. He felt a growing purpose to them, but could not figure out what it was. On their last day, the family boarded the boat as the setting sun dipped behind the southwestern hills in the distance. There was a twinge of sadness within them, knowing that their first destination would soon be behind them, but it was mixed with anticipation for the next one.

The second stop on their Greek tour was Santorini. The island was small, so they planned to stay only a day or two. It was on the way to Crete from Athens, so they deemed it a good choice. Paolo, of course, had researched the island, which was previously known as Thera, and looked forward to it more than the others.

As they approached Santorini the following morning, everyone noticed how high above the water the city was. The white buildings of Fira, when viewed from the distance, gave the impression of snow-capped mountains. As they drew closer, they could see a road that led down to the port where a cluster of buildings lined the water's edge.

"Wait 'til you see the view from the city," Paolo said to the others. "From what I have read, it is one of the best in the Greek islands."

By the time the family reached Fira and found housing for the night, it was late in the afternoon. From what they were told, the sunsets in Santorini were the best around and not to be missed. Following a recommendation, they made their way to a restaurant that featured unobstructed views of the west along with fine dining. Their timing couldn't have been better. They arrived at the restaurant with no more than 30 minutes left of sunlight.

With each passing minute, the sun drew closer to the horizon. It became increasingly red as it did so. The reflection on the bay gave the appearance of a fiery, molten pool. As John stared into it, another vision came.

Aboard an ancient sailing vessel, the sun was setting near a tall pointed mountain. A trail of smoke could be seen emanating from its peak. Suddenly, the volcano erupted in flame and smoke. The mountain ripped open. Half of it slid into the ocean while huge amounts of ash and smoke mushroomed out of its remains.

The initial blast was silent, due to the distance, but a moment later, it roared. It was deafening, like thousands of simultaneous thunderclaps. No sooner had the sound clamored than the gale force winds followed, stronger than a typhoon. The blast of air tore the sails from the ship and capsized it. All of the sailors now viewed the scene from within the water or upon the overturned hull.

The cloud of soot expanded in all directions, quickly blocking what little sunlight remained. Within the darkness it rained, but it was not water falling from the sky; stones, flakes of ash, and glowing orbs of lava descended upon them.

John, still focused on the west, lay witness to the sea rearing up into a wall of water. The fast approaching wave lifted them higher and higher, nearly pushing them into the dark cloud. Then, just as quickly, they slid down the backside of the wave.

John's perspective then shifted. He was now on the shore of an island looking north. This time, the distant and muffled thunder was heard in advance of the approaching blackness. The cloud and the wave raced southward. The cloud was visible first, but the wave surpassed it, stretching up out of the sea. As the wave approached the land, it kept rising and soon blocked out the northern horizon and the approaching black cloud.

Before the tidal wave crashed ashore, a new scene appeared before John's eyes. He was now in the desert, pyramids surrounding him. He was atop one of the tallest among them, looking northwest, trying to discern the origin of the unusual thunder. An imminent storm neared, evident from the dark, billowing clouds. The storm approached faster than any he had ever witnessed before. Something told the scout this was not an ordinary storm.

John woke as if from a night dream. He opened his eyes and saw his legs stretched out beneath the table. All of the Nuotos stared down at him, holding his hands and wiping his face with a damp cloth. He felt a warm wetness on the side of his head, and then intense pain.

"John! What happened?" Felizio asked.

"Are you alright?" Lorita asked.

"You passed out," Paolo told him, "You fell out of the chair and hit your head on the ground. Are you OK?"

John didn't say a word. He blinked his eyes slowly and waited for the nausea in his stomach to subside. The pain in his head, at first pounding, was now receding into a dull ache. Slowly, he rolled onto his side and pushed himself up. Paolo and Felizio then lifted him off the ground and back into his chair. Each kept a hand on a shoulder to make sure he was stable.

Carina, thankful that nothing worse had happened to him, pushed past the others and gave John a big hug.

"Did you have another vision?" Paolo asked John.

"Yes, I did. Three actually! Did you know that all of these little islands here used to be one huge mountain? It was a volcano and when it erupted, it completely ripped apart. In the first vision, I saw it from a boat just east of here. But then I saw it again from a large island to the south. Crete maybe? Finally, I was seeing the soot and hearing the thunder from Egypt. I am guessing because there were pyramids."

"I'm sorry, John, I wasn't thinking. With all of those earthquake visions you've been having, I guess I should have warned you. I read of the eruption that happened here somewhere between 1650 and 1550 B.C.E. It affected all of the eastern Mediterranean. Some believe that it influenced weather all across the globe! They think it may have been the greatest eruption to have ever occurred in the history of mankind!"

"Yeah, I think a warning would have helped." John smiled to indicate that he was teasing. He wasn't sure that foreknowledge would have prevented the rather intense visions anyway.

"Did you say you saw the eruption from Crete?" Paolo asked.

"Yeah, I guess. I mean, I didn't see the eruption itself, it was too far away, but I did experience the aftereffects. I am not sure why I thought it was Crete, since I haven't been there before. But it **felt** like it was Crete, if that makes sense."

"Well, that's interesting because when I looked up Crete in my history books, it spoke of the Minoan people who lived there. Historians believe that the eruption here led to the downfall of the Minoan culture there. After the eruption, the Greeks flourished by comparison. You see, the majority of the soot blew south and east. The mainland of Greece was less affected. This volcano more than likely changed the entire course of history in the Mediterranean."

John rubbed his head and looked out over the bay. He could see it now; Santorini Bay was actually the caldera of the collapsed volcano. He saw that the remaining islands formed a ring around it.

The food then arrived at the table. John's brief nausea was gone and he was happy to eat. He was also happy that the conversation had been interrupted; he didn't want to think about the eruption any longer, nor any other historic facts for that matter.

John was exhausted after the meal. The stress of the prior occurrence took its toll on him. He was ready to retire for the evening. Luckily, everyone else was satiated by the day and content with settling in for the night as well.

Δ   ▲   Δ

Johannes woke within a rumble of activity around him. Carts, camels, and people passed him by with hardly a notice. The noise pounded through his head…as did pain. He tried to sit up, but the dizziness overtook him. He immediately laid his head back down.

He looked around to assess the situation. He was clearly lying in the street within a busy part of town. He guessed it was mid-morning, because he couldn't imagine he'd slept long amid all of the noise, even in his current state.

He attempted to sit up again, a little more slowly this time, and was able to. His head hurt, but so did his jaw. He opened his mouth and determined that his jaw wasn't broken. He reached up to his face and found it covered with dried blood. He not only remembered the punch, but the reason for it, too. *I guess I deserved that one!*

What he didn't think he deserved was the rest of the punishment that followed. He felt around for all of the places where he was bruised: the back of his head, his lip, the ribs on both sides, and his stomach. *Thank God they didn't break anything.*

He searched his pockets, but didn't expect to find anything. Certainly, his foes couldn't resist stealing his money after beating him silly. If he had only listened to that inner voice that told him to stay away from that woman. He should have guessed that a woman like that would not have been alone; he just didn't expect her mate to have a clan of thugs working for him.

Of course, if I hadn't been so intoxicated...and bold, I might have been able to escape without the beating. After all, I only flirted with her, right? He thought back and tried to determine if his actions were in fact respectful; it was all a bit too fuzzy for him to remember.

He took all of this as a sign that the party was indeed over. *I guess I've taken this binge a bit too far. I don't have a death wish after all.* He looked up to the clouds and said, "OK, I can take a hint. Help me get back to my hotel and let me get some proper sleep. Then I'll find a more constructive way to spend my time here in Cairo."

Horus watched Johannes get up and whispered, "Turn to your left. Your hotel is to the left."

Johannes looked to the right and then to the left as he tried to figure out where he was and how to get back to his hotel. The sunlight reflected off a sign and caught his attention. It shifted again and now he could make out what it said. He recognized it right off, which set his bearings. "I need to go to that restaurant again," he said. "That meal was delicious."

PAGE OF WANDS

S eth and Horus drifted along with Johannes as he stumbled down the street. Horus turned to Seth and said, "I never would have chosen that outcome for Johannes, but I guess he needed a swift kick in the hindquarters to wake up and see what he was doing to himself. I saw it coming, but he didn't heed my warning."

"You certainly got the more difficult one of the two," Seth replied. "John challenges me, but in a different way. He hears a little now and again, but he sees so much better. I realize that when I take him into the Hall of Records, he can see and feel what I am showing him…in more detail than I ever imagined! I've been doing some research to figure out what to show him to, you know, nudge him along. And being that he is so emotional, I've had to find things that would leave an impression; otherwise he'd just shrug off the visions and forget the dreams. The Akashic Records are amazing! Have you spent much time scanning them?"

"Only when I was in my life reviews," Horus responded. "Isis has encouraged me to visit the Records more, but I haven't been drawn to them just yet. Johannes keeps me pretty busy as it is."

"Well, if you are interested, I'll take you on a tour. John is asleep right now. As soon as he enters the Astral Plane, I am going to divert him to a specific place in the Records."

"But why is John asleep?" Horus asked. "Isn't it the middle of the day?"

"It is for Johannes, but not for John." Seth put a virtual hand on Horus' shoulder. "Are you still getting tripped up on the nonlinear time thing? These two will not have to sync up in time until they are sharing experience. Speaking of that, we need to start working on a plan, because if we are going to get the two of them into the same place at the same time, we need to be in cahoots."

"Well, my friend," Horus said putting **his** hand on Seth's shoulder. "Johannes is already in Egypt, so **we** are merely waiting on **you**."

Seth looked away embarrassed. "Yeah, yeah, don't bug me about it. That's the reason for tonight's trip into the Akashic Records. John still thinks Johannes is in Crete. He'll be there in a day or two. I need to make sure that he moves on from there quickly. I am going to entice him a bit more, but he has to make the decision to go to Egypt **on his own**; he has to **want** to go."

"Seth, now hold on. I have been thinking about something and I'm curious," Horus began to rub his chin. "Why do you think we got this specific assignment?"

"Well, I think the first part is obvious; it is about **us**: you and me."

"Yeah, we **have** had lifetimes not getting along very well; so I guess we do have things to work out between us."

"Precisely! **We** have to work together in order to effectively help **them** work together. I was not exactly happy about having to work with you at first, Horus, but at least now we can't maim each other any longer. Ha!" Seth laughed, but Horus didn't exactly appreciate the humor; he was still working on forgiving himself for that particular transgression.

Seth then added, "Have you noticed how similar in personality you and Johannes are?"

"Yes, wise guy, I've noticed," Horus retorted. "I've been a bit rash with my emotions and impetuous in my actions…just the way he is. How easily we see personality flaws within another." He put a finger to Seth's chest and said, "But let's hope John isn't too similar to **his** guide. I wouldn't want to see him murder anybody!" Now it was Horus' turn to laugh and for a good few moments.

Seth just kept quiet.

Horus added, "I still don't get how you went from killing Osiris to becoming Ra's favorite and protector. That never made sense to me."

"Can we please not rehash old lives right now?" Seth interrupted.

"Yes, sir! But there is one thing I have noticed that you and John have in common," an impish grin appeared on Horus' face, "your taste in mates!"

"What can I say?" Seth responded proudly. "I've always been partial to same-gender relations. What's it to you? It is not like **you've** never tried it."

"Yes, I know, but I have never fully submerged myself into it in any of my lifetimes, just dabbled a bit here and there."

"And look at who **you're** guiding!" Seth said, pushing a finger into Horus' chest. "Speaking of dabbling, is Johannes ever going to deal with what happened between them?"

"I don't know." Horus shrugged. "I just don't see Johannes choosing that path. I mean, he likes women enough, too much if you asked me. Why should he pursue a relationship with a man? It is not his primary inclination, at least not as far as I can tell."

"And he **shouldn't** deny his true self, but, you know, given the way these two are connected and how they feel about each other, if he just kept an open mind, he might get something out of it. Physical expressions of love don't have to be something specific. I think he would be quite surprised at how amazing it could be. He enjoyed the experience; did he not? I think the **idea** of it is what wigged him out."

"Seth, look back on your lives. Were you ever **that** open when you were on the Earth Plane?"

Seth thought for a moment. "Maybe not, but I am now! And on this plane, we don't even have to choose a gender. We can be whatever we want and switch as often as we like." Seth shifted into a beautiful young woman and danced around Horus provocatively. "I notice that you seem to always choose the male form. Or do you only do that with me?" Seth teased.

Horus observed Seth as a woman. He had to admit that he/she was quite attractive. He then crossed his arms and said, "For better or worse, Seth, I like being male. I just feel more comfortable with it, at least for now."

"Well, Horus, it suits you. I have always liked you that way anyway." Seth allowed himself to flirt with Horus more demonstrably. "I just think you don't let yourself explore as much as you are free to." Seth started to run a finger down the middle of Horus' torso.

Horus attempted to resist Seth's advances, but was having difficulty. Pulling away slightly, he said, "You're the one who always reminds me that I have all the time in the world. So what's the hurry?"

"You have all the time in the Universe, but there is no reason you have to wait." Seth placed a hand on Horus' chest. "There is no time like the present. Of course, the reality is that there is no time **but** the present."

Seth suddenly remembered his duties. He quickly flipped back into his male image and kissed Horus lightly on the cheek. He grabbed Horus' hand and said, "Speaking of the present, I can feel that John is sleeping soundly and about to enter the Astral Plane. I need to catch him before he falls into a dream of his own making. Come on, let's go."

Seth started to drag Horus away, but then hesitated. He turned to face him squarely and said, "And be nice! I am going to bring John to a specific place in the Records, but he is not to remember that we were there, OK?"

Horus looked Seth in the eye. He raised an eyebrow, glanced down at his sides where Seth held onto him, and said, "Sure thing, boss. **I'll** behave."

TWO OF WANDS

T he dim glow toward the eastern horizon hinted of the approaching day. It didn't, however, provide John enough light to make out his surroundings. Above the hills, the crescent moon rose along side Venus, each growing more inconspicuous as the daylight amplified. So far, the only discernible topography John could make out was the mountain range that shaped the southeastern horizon.

Turning to the north, John saw a second torch ahead, the only other one besides the one he was carrying. With dawn approaching, he could barely see along the path he was walking, which led directly to the second torch.

As John drew closer, the shape of the temple emerged out of the darkness. The fire hung above its entrance. Looking back in the direction from which he had come, the dawn light began to stretch across the river valley below him. *I had better pick up my pace if I am going to reach the temple before sunrise.* Urgency egged him on.

John strained to make out the details of what he saw. A silhouetted pair of obelisks towered above the structure. Statuesque figures flanked the entrance of the temple, their backs leaning against the obelisks. Feline versions of the same protected the lower portion of a grand staircase.

Nearly out of breath, John arrived at the foot of the steps. He looked back to determine if he had enough time to catch his breath before ascending the stairway. The hills to the west were now clearly visible and one could also see the far-away peaks beyond them. As John examined these peaks, he noticed their consistent geometric shape and figured they were a few of the many pyramids in the area. He marveled at how each was centered behind the lowest portions of the southwestern hills, which would have otherwise blocked them from sight. *Could they have been specifically situated that way just to be seen from this temple?*

The brief rest brought new life to John's legs and he sprinted up to the temple entrance. Standing between the obelisks, the two statuesque guards stared down at him. Rather than appear threatening, as they did from a distance, they seemed now to regard him with approval. Their hands were pressed together as if in prayer, and their heads bowed slightly, their line of sight directed to visitors of human proportion.

John greeted each with a bow and then turned back toward the south. Although the sun could not yet be seen from where he stood, it had just begun shining on the pyramids. Each reflected the sunlight so as to clearly display their characteristic geometric shape. John now knew why he needed to reach the temple entrance before sunrise. It was as if each pyramid in succession paid homage to the temple by reflecting the early morning light.

The sun reached the edge of the peak that obscured it and inched further. John imagined the sun as a great being, climbing the backside of the mountain and then peering out over the valley before him. The image in John's mind shifted as the sun rose higher in the sky. He now saw the luminescent disc resting atop a hawk-headed figure. The lean, muscular, broad-shouldered shape stood tall. He raised his arms with a staff in each hand and spoke with a deep, resonating voice, "Welcome to Ra-Atum."

John found himself staring at the sun as it grew brighter. He squinted and then blinked against the glare as it became too much to witness. Paolo, having pulled back the drapes, moved over to John's bed to see if he was awake. John looked up at Paolo but didn't speak. The dream was still clear in his mind and he fought to retain all of it in his memory. John knew that without adequate review, the dream would fade and become nearly impossible to remember.

Paolo saw that John's eyes were open, and was content. He knew to give John ample time to wake before attempting conversation. He, on the other hand, had been up awaiting adequate light to begin preparing for the day. This was likely their only full day on the island and he didn't want to waste it lying in bed.

Over breakfast, everyone asked John how his head felt.

"It's tender to the touch," John told them, "but other than that, I feel no pain."

Paolo, knowing of John's intermittent insomnia, asked how he slept.

"I slept well. This morning, I woke from a dream that seemed to be a continuation of one I had that first night in Athens. Between my visions and these dreams, I am pretty sure I know where I am supposed to go."

"Where is that?" Lorita asked.

"Egypt. I feel like I'm being called to Egypt."

Δ ▲ Δ

The remainder of their time in Santorini, John remained free of visions of doom and destruction. He felt more relaxed. At first he thought it was due to the lack of apparitions, but then realized that he actually missed them and found himself attempting to bring one on.

The real source of ease, as it turned out, was the newfound direction he had gained. Egypt was calling to him, he was sure of that now, and his emotional state confirmed it. He grew increasingly excited, not like when they approached Greece, but in a deeper way. This calling was mixed with purpose, and John felt it. Granted, he had felt driven to find Johannes, and still did, but **this** purpose felt more...significant somehow.

The calm John felt lasted throughout their day in Santorini, all through a restful night's sleep, and into the following morning. It even remained for the short trip between the islands. However, once Crete was within sight, John grew nervous. For months, he had been working his way there to search for Johannes. *What if I find him? Am I prepared for that?*

Felizio, noticing the tension that had taken hold of John, pulled him aside. "My boy, it is hard to believe that here we are arriving in Crete, your destination from when I first met you. Are you nervous about seeing your friend?"

"I am, yet I do not know if he is still here. I cannot sense if he is or not."

"As you know, we only have a few more days that we can remain in Greece; we must return soon so Paolo can get back to the university on time. We are happy to spend that with you here in Crete, if it will help you. But I understand if you prefer to face this on your own."

"I don't want to, but I feel that I will be facing this on my own whether you all are here or not. This trip has been so good for Paolo and Carina, it is probably best that they not see me struggle with this emotion, lest we part with them concerned for me."

"How does this sound?" Felizio proposed. "We will spend the rest of today on the island together and visit some of the areas that Paolo wishes to see. We will stay here over night, and then cast off first thing in the morning."

"That sounds great," John replied. "I **would** like to spend more time with you before you head back to Italy. After this, I do not know when I will be able to visit."

Felizio announced the plan to the rest of the family and followed up with a comment for Paolo, "Son, prioritize what you would like to see here as we'll only have today to explore."

It took no time for Paolo to proclaim his choice to the rest. Knossos was the largest archaeological site on Crete and close to where they had ported.

After securing the boat, they set off to find the dig. Once they arrived, Paolo resumed his role as tour guide. He told the others all that he knew of the Minoan culture.

"The first palace of Knossos was built in 2000 B.C.E. but was destroyed by an earthquake." He paused to look at John to make sure he was OK.

John gave him a look mocking impatience.

"Then the second one was built in 1700 B.C.E. So the Minoans ruled here first. After the Thera eruption, the Minoans fell and the Greeks eventually took over this part of the Mediterranean. That was up until the Romans arrived."

"Now wait a minute, Paolo," John interjected. "Pompeii was a

Roman city, right? When was it destroyed?"

"79 AD."

"And the Temple of Olympian? When was it built?"

"It was finished in 130 AD, but started well before that. The Romans were in Athens by the time it was completed. They started invading the Greek city-states around 150 B.C.E."

"And the Parthenon?"

"The Parthenon was completed in 430 B.C.E., about 20 years after the city-state of Athens reached its prime."

Recalling what Paolo had said earlier, John said, "Hmm, the eruption at Thera was somewhere around 1600 B.C.E. and this place was at its peak before that, right?"

"Yeah, that's right."

"I find it interesting because it is as if we are traveling backward in time. This whole journey from Pompeii to here has taken us to earlier and earlier phases in history. And now I am being called to Egypt. The time of the pyramids was well before the first Palace of Knossos was built, I bet."

"Yes, the Old Kingdom of Egypt started around 2700 B.C.E. The first pyramid was build shortly after that, maybe 50 years later."

"Wow. That can't be a coincidence, not with all of those visions and dreams I have been having."

THREE OF WANDS

Their last day together was full of activity and passed quickly. The looming separation, however, did not dominate John's thoughts. First, he was distracted by his newfound obsession to go to Egypt. It was the last thing on his mind before he went to sleep that night, and the first thing on his mind when he woke in the morning. He had hoped that another dream would further clarify his calling, but none did.

And then, of course, there was Johannes. Laced within his thoughts of Egypt were times when John searched the crowds for that familiar wheat-colored hair and blue eyes. After each fruitless bout, he found himself thinking (or hearing), *He's not here,* and he began to accept it.

When John said goodbye to his Italian family, all had watery eyes save him. He was the one who would be alone, and given everything else swirling within him, he just couldn't let himself feel or express as the others did. He was also a little numb. He assured them that he would be in touch as soon as he figured out what the trip to Egypt was all about.

A short while later, John could no longer see their boat among the others sailing north away from Crete. He lost track of them, because although his eyes were looking north, his mind was far to the south.

He then turned to face the center of the island. He thought about searching for Johannes, but couldn't formulate any sort of plan. He simply could not see himself scanning the island further.

"Am I really going to abandon my quest now, after such a short time in Crete?" he asked himself. But he already knew the answer.

He turned back toward the water and the port. *It is rather convenient that I am standing here with all of my belongings. Maybe I'll just ask around and gather some information.*

Whenever John asked sailors and crewmen about transportation to Egypt, they would respond with, "Where in Egypt would you like to go?" A couple of times he responded with, "Ra-Atum," but no one had heard of it.

Any that were traveling to Egypt were destined for Cairo, the capital city. Since it was the only place in Egypt John had ever heard of, he soon settled on it.

One captain who overheard John asking about Egypt said to him, "I'm heading to Cairo at the top of the hour. My boat is not full. If you come along I'll discount your ticket. That's assuming you're ready to board."

Now John only had minutes to decide: *stay in Crete or leave right now.* He thought about Lorita's story and her words, *Your heart will let you know when enough is enough.* His heart was letting him know; he was just fighting it. He took a deep sigh and accepted the Greek sailor's offer, then looked back towards town and hoped he was doing the right thing.

The course for Egypt had them sailing around the western tip of Crete before heading south. All that while, John looked out over the island that had been his desired destination for so long. He could hardly believe he was leaving after such a short time. *This trip really didn't work out at all the way I had planned*—John thought. He then chuckled, *When in my life has anything **ever** gone as planned?* Most of the time, he didn't have a plan, but even when he did, it rarely worked out as he expected.

As Crete descended over the northern horizon, John turned his gaze and his attention to the south. *This is going to be the farthest south I have ever been.* And then his anticipation grew. The trip to Egypt was relatively short, but upon arriving, John realized that his latest journey was really just beginning. He neither knew where precisely in Egypt he was supposed to go, nor what he was supposed to do when he got there.

He thought back to his dreams and visions of Egypt. There often was either obelisks or pyramids in the locations he had seen. *That's it! I'll visit the pyramids and the other ancient sites and see if I recognize anything.* John was excited by the thought. He then amended it slightly, *Food first. After lunch, I will find my way to the pyramids.*

Δ   ▲   Δ

Johannes was still sore, but after a day and a night of lying around, he was ready to venture out again. He didn't exactly have a plan other than to maybe look for a tour. Many times before, he had told himself he would see the sites of Egypt, but mostly he hadn't. He did know where most of the tour guides loitered, hoping to pick up customers, and so he headed in that direction.

Without warning, a hand reached out of the crowd and grabbed Johannes by the wrist. After what had happened the other night, he was jumpy and quickly tensed up. But he soon realized that the hand that held him belonged to an old gypsy woman and he relaxed.

"Young man with wheat-colored hair and lapis eyes, we do not see the likes of you in these parts much. Yet the Gods of Egypt favor you, my fair child."

"Ha! Woman, you don't know of what you speak. The gods didn't keep me from getting my butt kicked the other night!" he retorted.

"The Gods cannot keep you from your own Karma, but they do walk beside you." She waved her hand along Johannes' side as if she could see a being standing there. She looked him squarely in the eye and said, "Why have you run away from your brother?"

"Brother? I don't have a brother." Johannes was beginning to think the woman was conning him.

"Young man, come to my table and let me read your cards. The Gods have a message for you," she said confidently.

"Why should I believe you, woman? You probably say that to every unsuspecting foreigner."

"Young man, here is my proposal: let me read your cards, and if nothing rings true for you, you owe me nothing, but if I pique your interest, I will convey the message for my standard fee."

"What is your fee?"

"100 Gineih."

"OK." 100 Gineih was not much to Johannes, so he followed the woman over to her table and sat in the rickety chair across from her. He continue to doubt anything would come of it, but allowed things to continue nevertheless.

The woman's cards were large, golden along the edges, and worn from use. She shuffled methodically, the whole time eyeing Johannes in a way he could not identify. "What would you like to know?" she asked him. "Hold a question within your mind and it will be answered."

Johannes thought to himself—*What is this nonsense about the gods and my brother?* He then thought—*What is the meaning of life? Oh, that's a good one. Let's see if she can answer **that**!*

Johannes shook his head and felt silly for actually entertaining a question, let alone such a profound one. He was going along with the reading because it was cheap and an easy way to get the woman off of his back. *Maybe she will say something interesting—* he thought. But he was skeptical.

The woman shuffled the cards some more and then fanned them out asking him to select one.

Johannes picked one toward the middle.

She flipped over the card and placed it in front of him. It depicted a woman, blindfolded, holding two swords in the shape of a 'v', her right hand in front of her left shoulder and her left hand in front of the right. An ominous ocean view lay behind her.

"Young man, you are at the threshold of truth. Your life has been relatively stable, but if you proceed down this path of knowing, there will be no going back. You cannot continue your careless ways and seek truth simultaneously. You cannot return to ignorance once you've come to knowledge. Do you really wish to know the meaning of life?"

Johannes' skin pricked with goose bumps. *How could she know my question?*

She continued, "Divide the deck into three piles, my young friend."

He did as he was told, his hands unsteady, almost perceptively.

"These represent three potentials. I ask you again, do you wish to know truth or do you merely choose to be entertained? Make your choice wisely and with clear intent. Pick the pile that most appeals to you."

The woman's tone made Johannes nervous. He looked at the three piles and found himself drawn to the one in the middle. He pointed to it and shrugged his shoulders.

The woman reassembled the deck with the middle pile on top. She then dealt out five more cards face down. She placed two cards to the left of the first one, a card above and one below it, and then the last one to the right. One by one, she flipped over the cards and read them.

"These two on the left represent your past. In this card, we see a man juggling two coins. There is a ship in the background. This is your livelihood. You are a businessman, one who travels far and wide. You are successful, yet some part of you is unfulfilled. You are balancing two identities…two houses…the house of your father and the house of your mother. Ah, she is not your actual mother, but a…figurehead. You reject her authority and accept only that of your father. This symbolically represents an inner conflict within you. This, in part, is why you ran away from your brother."

Johannes listened, but kept his eyes on the next card. *It's a spooky card for sure*—he thought. A demonic character stood between two humans and held them captive, in chains.

The Gypsy woman saw that Johannes stared at the second card and went on. Pointing at it, she said, "Do not fear the Devil; he is not real. This card merely represents an indulgence in the physical aspects of life. For you, this is a teacher, or, at least, it has been. The rewards of earth are luxurious, but burdensome…and the lessons **are** painful." As she said this, she reached over and touched Johannes' bruised cheek for emphasis. Johannes flinched slightly and then lightly rubbed his sore jaw.

OK, maybe this woman is on to something—he thought.

The card on top showed three people in a boat crossing a river or a lake. The man used a pole to propel the boat forward. Six swords stood upright, having been stabbed into the boat. In the lower card, a knight was shown atop a white horse. He held a chalice in his hand.

Pointing to the top card, the woman explained, "You have been on a journey which has led you here, but your travels continue. You have further to go before you return. You will be heading farther south before heading north toward your home."

Then pointing to the knight she said, "And I again ask you, why do you run from your brother?"

Johannes was growing frustrated. "I don't understand; I don't **have** a brother."

"Young man, 'What's in a name? That which we call a rose by any other name would smell as sweet; So Romeo would, were he not Romeo call'd, Retain that dear perfection which he owes…' A brother is a brother, be him born from the same womb or not. Do not fear the love of your brother. It need not take a specific form that is displeasing to you. He has a love so pure, so genuine; it is unconditional. He merely desires to know his twin once again. Are you aware that your brother arrived at this shore on this very day?"

"John? Are you talking about John? He is **here**?"

"Yes. He is now within the city limits of Cairo. Fear not, and follow your guidance. He judges you not and will accept you with forgiveness. Have forgiveness for him also."

Johannes' mind started to race. The reading was unsettling to him. But if John was actually there, in Egypt, then that was even more upsetting. He was not sure how he felt about running into him right now.

The woman reached over and placed her hand on top of his. "Young man, in time. You will not cross paths for another day or two. Relax."

She then pointed to the last card on the right. "And this card here shows that your journey will bear fruit. The two torches are brought together to light a third. You and your brother must work together. You each hold a piece. When your auras are brought together, an even greater light will shine."

The old woman reached into a bag at her side and pulled out a small statue. The figure was a broad-shouldered man with the head of a falcon. Johannes was sure he had seen this character many times before while in Egypt. As she handed it to him, she said, "May Horus be with you and guide you well."

Johannes reached into his wallet and counted out 100 Egyptian pounds, then added another 20. He handed the woman the money, thanked her for her time, and wandered off—dazed.

A few blocks later, Johannes saw a tour stand that caught his attention. The sign said: "Visit the great pyramids and the Sphinx! Travel to Egypt's oldest temples! Learn the secrets of this ancient culture!"

"Good afternoon, my friend," the tour guide said to Johannes. "Have you been to the pyramids, my friend? Have you seen the beautiful Sphinx up close, my friend? I have many fine tour packages to offer you, my friend."

Johannes was happy to be distracted from the thoughts spawned by the reading. "Tell me about them," he replied.

"My friend, I have one-day tours, four-day tours, and two-week tours. In a day, you can visit the Great Pyramids and the beautiful Sphinx in Giza. In four days, you can travel to Heliopolis by camel and visit the Temple of Ra. In two weeks time, you can sail with us to cities like Luxor, Edfu, and Philae in Upper Egypt and visit the temples there in."

"When is your next four-day tour?"

"It departs in two days, my friend. I highly recommend it. How many are there in your party, my friend?"

"Just me."

"For no cost, we can add one or two more, my friend. We will meet here the morning after next…at sunrise. We will provide food, water, and lodging during the trek. Is this pleasing to you, my friend?"

"Yes, thanks; that's perfect."

FOUR OF WANDS

S eth and Horus sat on the tour guide's left shoulder. Horus gently whispered in the man's ear the same way he had with the Gypsy woman. Meanwhile Seth observed Johannes passively.

When the conversation between Johannes and the tour guide ended, Seth turned to Horus and said, "That was pretty clever, Horus. I especially liked the way you used the card reader. How did you find her?"

"Well, Seth, I just put a message out into the ethers and she was the one who acted on it. Johannes is so free with his spending of Egyptian money; I just knew he would be generous if the reading moved him. So I placed an image of gold with the request. She was amazing! I was quite impressed with her."

"Did you know that Johannes would be so open to it?" Seth asked.

"I sensed that he would be," Horus responded. "Ever since the other day, he has been rather contemplative. That beating released a lot of pent up energy. He had been subconsciously beating himself up for running off. He felt guilty over his actions. He kept playing with fire because he **wanted** to get burned. He believes so strongly in retribution that he had to **pay** for his sins one way or the other. Given his overall belief system, it made perfect sense that he would attract a retaliatory assailant. It is not really his style to punish himself through illness or accident. He generally likes himself too much for that."

"Yes, that is certainly one of his strengths, his self-esteem. As we have seen, John still has so much self-acceptance to work through. He is his own worst enemy. **He is** the one who creates illness and injury; his self-deprecating thoughts attack his body so." Seth suddenly felt strong compassion for John in his heart.

"I agree," Horus added, "but at times, he does like himself and then attracts others who like him. They reflect his light back to him, and then he sees it as well, at least for a while."

"Yeah. He is still working through all of that abuse he experienced as a child. He still thinks that there is something wrong with him. But he has gained so much compassion through that experience. It **is** serving him. Look at how much understanding he has for others who are hurt! He will be able to help so many people as a result of the path he has chosen. And he will get there with the self-esteem; it will just take some more time."

"Well, Seth, shall we call Isis and report the news?"

Isis appeared instantly. "Boys, you summoned?"

"Yes mother. Seth and I have some great news. We have guided John and Johannes to the pyramids. Their rendezvous is imminent. Come look?"

"Ah, yes, I see. You are correct. The Law of Attraction will most assuredly bring them together now. Well done, boys. Ra will be pleased. We have been monitoring all of the greatest potentials and these two are among them. You are aware that a significant planetary alignment approaches, yes? As a result, the veil will become thin for a while and communication between the realms will be much easier as a result. We are most anticipatory."

Seth and Horus beamed with so much pride that they almost became visible.

Isis quickly went on to distract them. "However, for right now, the energy is stable and the veil is strong. You will not be able to reach through it even as easily as before. In this reunion, John and Johannes will be more or less left to their own devices. They, of course can reach out for guidance, but we must not interfere without their asking. So boys, I suggest that you enjoy this short reprieve. Relax, sit back, and watch the show."

FIVE OF WANDS

The excitement John felt among the great pyramids nearly overwhelmed him. The ruins of Greece and Crete were incredible, but due to their size, the pyramids were far more impressive. Each pyramid was immense, but the three together?

John stood towards the center of the complex with the Great Pyramid of Khufu to his right and the Pyramid of Khafre in front of him. The smallest of the pyramids, Menkaure, was off to his left, and the Sphinx was behind him. He felt tiny among the giant structures. The morning sun was behind him, so he knew that the Great Pyramid was to the north. He recalled the vision of the volcanic storm. He tried to figure out from which pyramid it had taken place. He remembered seeing a pyramid in front him as he faced north, so he couldn't have been on the Great Pyramid. Earlier, when he was near Menkaure, he saw that Khafre blocked Khufu, but something inside of him felt that Khafre was the right choice.

He gazed at the top of the pyramid. It looked too steep to climb; yet he could see people nearing its peak. *OK, here we go.* He chose the eastern face to take advantage of the warm morning sun, but as the climb progressed, he questioned his decision. He hadn't yet reached a third of the height and it was already getting warm.

By the time he reached half way, he was damp with sweat. The air was already thinning and he stopped to catch his breath. He looked back towards the Sphinx, then down to where he had started. He experienced a moment of vertigo as the steepness of the steps was far more intimidating looking down than when climbing. *I'll deal with that challenge later.*

He looked to the right and tried to estimate how far the edge of the face was. The stone was now warm enough that he was ready to swing around to the northern side. Since it was winter, that face would not be in direct sunlight, and he hoped the stone would still be cool to the touch.

The shape of the pyramid created an interesting affect. The sun did not shine on the north face itself, yet when standing, one was not in the shade either. It was the perfect combination for climbing; the rock remained cool, yet the sun warmed pleasantly. The Great Pyramid was now behind him and to his left. Every so often, he would look over to it. As he ascended, it felt further and further away.

Few people were above him now. Many who had started ahead of him had reached their limit. They waved to John with encouragement as he passed them. From what he could tell, it was mostly young males who climbed up ahead of him.

He estimated that he was at least two thirds of the way up now. Because the face narrowed as it rose, measuring progress was deceiving. So much more stone lay below him than above.

Surpassing half again the distance to the top, the face was narrow enough that many of the climbers started working their way around the structure. The peak could not accommodate a crowd, so most chose positions further down to rest and enjoy the view. As people rotated faces, John started noticing some he hadn't seen before. Most were dressed in typical Egyptian garb, but some European visitors were among them.

Just as John turned back towards the stone below, he was struck with a feeling of dread. In his peripheral vision, he had caught sight of a fair man with golden hair. The similarity to Johannes was disconcerting. John's breathing grew short as he discretely glanced back toward the peak.

The man couldn't have been more than a dozen steps above him and was looking northeast toward the Great Pyramid. John could not get a clear view of his face, but watched his movements and recognized them straight away.

Panic and fear struck him. John quickly put his face down and held firm to the stone. He felt faint. *How is this possible? Of all places, to encounter him atop a pyramid with no place to hide!*

That morning, John thought the challenge of the day would be the climbing of the pyramid. Little did he know that a greater challenge awaited him at the top.

John's first impulse was to escape, but that was clearly not an option. He looked down and remembered how descending was even more challenging than climbing. One had to use extra care, lest one take the fast way down, a feat no one wished to experience.

I traveled across Europe and the Mediterranean in search of him, and now I find him only after abandoning the whole idea. I guess I have no choice but to face this.

SIX OF WANDS

A s John's mind raced over all that he was feeling and what to do about it, Johannes noticed him for the first time.

"John! Look at this view! Can you believe it?" Johannes climbed down nearly all of the steps that lay between them. "I would say I'm surprised to see you, but I am not. Did you come all this way to find me?"

John still hadn't composed himself and looked at his friend in disbelief. His mouth hung open, but he said nothing.

Johannes continued, "Well, let's not worry about that now. We'll have plenty of time to hash over the last few months. Let's just enjoy the view!"

Johannes' enthusiastic mood brought John relief, but he was still shrouded in disbelief. At least his worst fear, outright rejection, was dispelled. He examined Johannes, refreshing the image of Johannes' handsome face in his memory. It was then that he noticed the bruises.

"What happened to you?" John asked him. "You look as if you fell off of the Sphinx!" He reached out to touch the side of Johannes' face and then caught himself and pulled his hand back.

Johannes touched his jaw where John had intended and said, "Oh, you mean this **little scratch**?" Johannes smiled at the obvious understatement. "Let's just say I had it coming."

"You're OK, though, right?" John couldn't help but show his concern.

"Yeah, I'm fine. I would say my ego was bruised worse, but I don't really believe that either." Johannes grinned even wider. "It's good to see you."

"Really?" John wasn't quite ready to trust that all was fine between them.

"**Yes, really**. OK—I'm sorry I ran off without saying anything to you. That was not fair. I wasn't running away from you, it's… it's just…" Johannes stumbled to find words he was ready and able to say, but they eluded him.

John decided to help him out and changed the subject. "You said you were not surprised to see me. What did you mean by that?"

"Well, you are not going to believe this...oh, wait a minute... look who I'm talking to. **You**, of all people, **will** believe this. I was walking through the streets of Cairo yesterday and this gypsy woman appeared out of nowhere and grabbed my arm. It turns out that she's a card reader. I thought she was scamming me, but she got me when she said I only had to pay her if the reading rang true. So I let her read my cards, and...anyway...she told me that you were here in Egypt. Well, she didn't say your name, she said my 'brother' was here. When I told her I didn't have a brother, she quoted Shakespeare. I guess she was trying to say that you don't have to be blood to be brothers."

"That's funny. Do you remember that day with your sister and her friend, Beth, was it? Isabella said that she thought we were brothers, twins even, in a past life."

"I forgot all about that. Interesting."

"Speaking of psychism, I started having strange visions and dreams when I got to Greece. Oh, that's where I was before I came here. Anyway, one vision I had was from right here, atop this pyramid. I'm sure of it!" John stood looking north and could almost see the dark clouds from his memory. "I went to Crete to try and find you, but by the time I got there, I figured out that I was supposed to come here, well Egypt anyway. I feel like there is a reason for me to be here, I mean, I don't think it was just about finding you."

"Well, if I am to believe the gypsy card reader, which at this point I have no reason not to, then whatever your purpose, I am a part of it. She told me we need to work together. She said something about lighting a torch."

"What? She mentioned a **torch**?"

"Yeah, something about us bringing our torches together to light a third. Why do you ask?"

"Well, in my Egyptian dreams I was always carrying a torch. At first, there was just the one, but later, I was heading towards, and eventually arrived at a second one; it was at a temple. I wonder if the torches mean something."

"Well, I don't claim to understand any of this symbolism," Johannes said. "This stuff is all new to me. Before two days ago, my life was normal."

"Whatever **that** means," John said sarcastically. This got them both laughing.

When they stopped laughing, they remained silent to enjoy the view from the top of the pyramid. A short while later, they made their way back down...**very** carefully.

Each had planned to spend the day in Giza and so by default, they spent it together. John was happy that the reunion was going as well as it was, but he still felt a little cautious. Until they talked about what had happened back in Germany, John wasn't sure if he would be able to fully relax. *There is time enough to worry about that later*—he thought—*I will just go with the flow of the day.*

"The Sphinx is right here. Let's go check it out," Johannes suggested. He had a guidebook of Egyptian artifacts and was flipping through pages. "It says here that the Sphinx is highly symbolic, although its true meaning is still a mystery. Many believe that hidden wisdom is buried beneath her, in secret chambers. Being half lion and half woman, some believe that it symbolizes the cusp between Leo and Virgo, which occurs each year late in August. Others believe it was built during the Age of Leo sometime before 10,000 B.C.E. At that time, it likely had a lion head, which was only much later re-carved into what we see now. It faces due east and would therefore have gazed upon the Constellation of Leo at sunrise on the day of the spring equinox when it was first built."

The boys walked around the Sphinx to enjoy the different perspectives.

"Throughout the year," Johannes went on, "many study the angles the sun makes at sunrise, noon, and sunset looking for clues to unearth her concealed knowledge. In years past, pirates raided the Sphinx in search of her treasures, but no known discoveries were ever reported."

John watched Johannes and couldn't help but think of Paolo. Paolo was, of course, more exuberant in his role as tour guide. Nevertheless, John was happy to have Johannes' company.

By the end of the afternoon, the energy between the boys had returned to those days when they first reached Germany. Johannes told John of the various restaurants he had been to in Cairo and encouraged John to pick one that interested him. They then enjoyed a traditional Egyptian dinner together.

Much to John's surprise, Johannes invited him to stay in his luxury suite. He told John that there were multiple beds, plenty of room, and a fantastic view of Giza. Johannes kept the discussion light, but the thought of them sharing a room seeped into John's subconscious.

Back at the suite, John was reserved and quiet and Johannes noticed. Still not wanting to discuss anything intimate, Johannes said, "I don't know if you have plans tomorrow, but I booked a private tour to Heliopolis. You are welcome to come with me. It will take a full day of travel by camel in each direction—four days in total."

The invitation made John feel a bit better and lessened the weight of what remained unsaid. "I don't have plans for tomorrow," John responded, "or any day for that matter. I would be delighted to go with you. At some point, I have to figure out why I'm here, but since I have no idea where to start, this tour could be fun. Besides, I might learn something that could help."

"Good. Let's get some sleep. It is going to be an early morning and a long day."

PART VI – EGYPT

KING OF WANDS

T he boys made their way through the center of Cairo before the first rays of sunlight appeared. Much to John's surprise, numerous locals had already begun their day. Johannes, however, was more familiar with the early morning activity, having made his way home at that hour on more than one occasion.

In preparation for the journey, the tour guide clothed the boys in local garb. Even in winter, the sun was a formidable adversary when crossing the desert. Four camels were groomed for the trek, the last for carrying all of their supplies.

The tour guide introduced the men to their camels. John, of course, took this more sincerely than most. He circled the animal and stroked him gently. He noticed that his camel was more introverted than the others. Telepathically, he conveyed thoughts of gratitude to the beast.

He recalled that day in the zoo nearly a year and a half earlier and his first experience communicating with animals. He thought back to the trek through France on horseback, which had afforded him much practice in animal-speak.

The tour guide noticed John's acute interest in the camel and took the opportunity to share some knowledge. "My friend, work animals, like these camels, relent to their life of servitude, for the most part. The breeds are less willful than others, which is in part why they are selected. Their strength and endurance are other reasons."

John knew, or at least could feel, how much individual animals appreciated gratitude nevertheless. It may be their nature to please their masters, but he was sure that they experienced additional joy when assured of their worth. *I guess humans aren't that different—* he concluded.

As John considered the perspective of a camel, he questioned other aspects of life that he normally didn't think about. Most people, for example, hardly thought of animals as conscious sentient beings, plants even less so. *And what about other forms of matter? Does the very soil have awareness? Does it feel my presence as I walk upon it? Would thoughts of appreciation affect it as well?*

For just a moment, John felt as if everything had come alive. In response to his question, it was as if a symphony began playing around him. He listened. One voice seemed louder than the rest; it was the sun. Having reached a height completely above the horizon, the sun illuminated the city, serenading all with its song.

John climbed up onto his camel. It felt awkward. Unlike a horse, the camel didn't seem to be designed for riding. As they plodded forward, John noticed that it was easy to fall into a comfortable rhythm with his animal. He thought back to his first day riding a horse and decided that camels were actually a bit easier to ride by comparison.

The men headed north out of the city and continued along the eastern bank of the Nile. John marveled at the lush green that flanked the river. He had never seen such a dense growth of palm trees in his life. All that morning, their route kept them close to the river and within the greenery surrounding it.

"Enjoy the shade while we have it, my friends," the tour guide urged them, "In the afternoon, it will be a different story."

Shortly after midday, the men veered to the east and away from the river. The abundant green abruptly gave way to the desert brown. As they crossed the border between the two, John looked south and then north. As far as the eye could see, the tree line undulated with the river.

The lack of shade kicked the temperature up a notch and just in time for the warmest part of the day. It took little time for John's body to react, emitting rivulets of sweat that ran down his face and torso. He quickly became thirsty. As he drank some water, he thought about his camel.

"Mr. Tour Guide, how do the camels work so hard in this heat without any water?" John asked.

"My friend, that hump that you sit upon in the camel's back is full of water. Camels can store a few days' worth; that is how they evolved to survive this desert climate. That is also why we use them for transportation."

They crossed the relatively flat valley in silence. However, when they began ascending a slight, sandy slope, the tour guide said, "Look, my friends, atop the plateau. Behold the ancient city of Heliopolis! That is our destination, my friends."

This far from the river, the air was calm and the sun's intensity reached its full potential. It was then that John made the connection. "Heliopolis? That sounds Greek."

"Yes, my friend, indeed it is. It literally translates as 'city of the sun'. The Greeks occupied the city for some time, hence the name. Its Egyptian name was Iunu, which means 'place of pillars'. At one time, my friends, there were a number of pillared temples in the city, all dedicated to Ra, but most of them were destroyed."

"Did you say '**Ra**'?" John asked with a raised eyebrow.

"Yes, my friend, Ra, the sun god. In Ancient Egypt, he was considered the one and only God, the God that created himself. He is often pictured with the sun resting atop his golden-feathered hawk head. Many confuse the images of Ra with those of Horus. Horus has the head of a falcon with blue-gray feathers and is the son of Isis. Horus' reign came much later, after Upper and Lower Egypt were united. His crown symbolizes this unification and indicates his rulership of all of Egypt. As the story goes, he competed with Seth and won the right for this reign."

"Hey," Johannes interjected, overhearing the conversation. "I was given a small statue of Horus by the woman who read my cards. I think I have it with me." He pulled the figure out of his bag and handed it to John, "Here."

John examined the figure of Horus and then handed it to the tour guide.

The tour guide said, "My friends, there is a temple dedicated to Horus in Edfu…in Upper Egypt. It can be reached by riverboat in about two days' time. Our Upper Egyptian tours can take you there, my friends."

For the remainder of the afternoon, John thought about the possible connection between Ra, the sun god, and what he heard and saw in his dreams. It took nearly that long for them to reach the city ruins that loomed above them. Although the distance had been short, the sandy climb went slowly.

The men reached the confines of the plateaued city in the long shadows of evening. They dismounted the camels and walked alongside them to the camp. Arriving at the handful of tents, the tour guide again spoke, "My friends, welcome to your home for the next three nights. We will have two days to explore the city before returning to Cairo on the third. I suggest that you relax and enjoy the sunset while dinner is being prepared. The view across the valley is quite nice from here."

A small collection of chairs had been arranged specifically for enjoying the valley view. John and Johannes wandered over to them; Johannes sat while John remained standing. The sun was still yellow but had just begun its transformation towards the orange-red hue it would reach before retiring.

"The river looks wider from here," John observed.

"That's because we are north of the fork," Johannes explained. "When each of us came to Cairo, we traveled up the western fork of the Nile." He pointed into the distance. "This side is the one you would take to travel to the Middle East."

For just a moment, John thought of Sara and the Emperor. His mind then quieted as he observed the shifting beauty of the scene before him.

The sun descended and soon its shadow began crawling across the valley toward them. Just as the sun reached its deepest shade of red, the dinner bell rang.

A table had been set for the evening meal close to where they were already sitting. Neither John or Johannes had noticed it, or the flurry of activity around it, when they headed to the chairs to watch the sunset; they were too enraptured by the scene before them. The tapered candles would soon be the only source of light.

During dinner, the tour guide explained the current state of affairs of the city. "My friends, the Heliopolis of today is being groomed for an increasing volume of tourism. Between the tours and the archeological digs, we now have enough visitors to afford a full time staff on site in charge of food and lodging. All monuments in the northern half of the city are opened to the public. Our first day of touring will be focused within that part of the city.

"Much of the archeological activity has moved to the south half of the city. Situations in that region change daily. I will let you know tomorrow evening if we will be allowed to visit anything there. Don't worry, my friends," he concluded, "There is plenty to see, so you will not be disappointed."

The meal featured *Koshari*, a traditional Egyptian dish consisting primarily of lentils, rice, and pasta. *Baba ghanoush*, fresh vegitables, and bread were served on the side. As John ate, he compared the Egyptian food to the Levantine cuisine he grew up on and the Greek food he had the week before. It intrigued him how similar, and yet subtly different, the various varieties were along the eastern edge of the Mediterranean.

The entire meal, including dessert and wine, lasted two hours. Heliopolis didn't offer anything in the way of nighttime activity, so the evening meal was the highlight for everyone.

Their accommodations were basic, but sufficient. The tent was large enough for a dozen guests. John determined that it would have felt empty with just the three of them, had it not been so lavishly decorated. Beautiful rugs covered the ground, and tapestries decorated much of the walls. Some of the artifacts on display had only been dug up within the preceding months.

In the center of the room, a modest fire burned inside of a wide pit. The light was nearly extinguished, save the red coals that cast just enough warmth to keep them comfortable throughout the night.

The "cots" that lined the room were nothing more than mounds of sand that had been covered with layers of cloth for added comfort. After John climbed onto his, he questioned whether **comfort** was the appropriate word. He figured he would be able to sleep, but not comfortably.

Some unknown number of hours later, John woke. Rustling sounds from outside of the tent drew him out of his sleep. His heart raced. John knew all about desert creatures and had heard many a horror story of one crawling or slithering into someone's bed. The evening breeze tousled the tapestries that formed the doorway, intermittently permitting light from the moon to shine in.

John sat up and took inventory of the room. The others appeared to be asleep. He exited the tent and looked up at the waning gibbous moon. He was able to make out his surrounding in the just past full orb. He looked up to the sky away from the moon and admired the stellar display. He was amazed at how much their color and brightness varied. A particularly bright star caught his attention. It didn't twinkle, so John guessed it was a planet.

John's eyes continued to scan the sky; he locked onto another bright star in the southern part of the sky. This one twinkled within varying hues of blue. *Now that is most certainly a star*. As he stared at it, the star drew him in.

Not now, my son, but soon.

The voice in John's head was his own, but at the same time seemed different. It was soft and gentle. Since the onset of visions, John forgot about the times when he heard voices. With animals, he could perceive their thoughts, but rarely heard them as spoken, except that one time at the zoo. And in his visions, he heard sounds, but only the background noise of the scenes he witnessed.

The times he did hear a voice, it was most clearly heard as words. In fact, the only way he could distinguish a voice from his own thoughts was the words chosen.

John closed his eyes and listened. The nighttime was filled with more sounds than he had first noticed. He could hear the breeze blowing and the flapping of the fabric around the tent. He could hear the torches burning on either side of the entrance. And he could hear sand moving as the wind gave it flight.

Abruptly, the wind picked up and the sounds it created grew louder. In an eerie way, it sounded like someone breathing, or possibly a whisper, "errrraaaaahhhhh." The initial gust passed, but then another followed, "errrraaaaahhhhh."

John took a deep breath and imitated the sound he had just heard, "errrraaaaahhhhh...errrraaaaahhhhh." The third time John imitated the wind, a vibration rose from within his chest as he voiced the sound rather than just whispering it. The sound was deep and reverberated like a hum. It reminded him of the chanting he had done in Asia.

The sound that emanated from him was louder than he expected, certainly louder than he intended. He looked around and moved further away from the tent so as not to wake anyone.

The intermittent gusts continued, as did the eerie sounds. He could hardly keep himself from imitating what he heard, "errrraaaaahhhhh... errrrraaaaahhhhh-tummmm." The gusts turned into a constant wind and John looked out over the valley to face it. He lifted his arms as if to fly across the Nile. He let his self-consciousness go and spoke to the wind, "errrraaaaahhhhh... errrrraaaaahhhhh-tummm."

John chanted the phrase a number of times more until the winds died down and the impetus receded. He looked to the sky and this time felt completion. Sleep pulled at him once more, and he retreated to the tent.

Crawling onto his bed, John felt weariness settle back in and quickly drifted off into a deep, sound sleep.

Δ   ▲   Δ

S hortly after sunrise, Johannes and John woke and staggered out of the tent. Their legs were a bit stiff and unsteady, due to the previous day's ride and the hard beds. Once outside, the boys saw that the dinner table had been prepared for the breakfast meal. The table was set for a larger number of people and soon additional tourists emerged from other tents. Rather than a traditional Egyptian meal, this one was modeled after a simple European breakfast: fruit, assorted breads with butter and jam, and coffee.

At the end of the meal, the guide started into his practiced oration. "My friends, today's itinerary will consist solely of sights within the northern half of the city. That region, our fine archeologists have deduced, was primarily residential. Everything you see there will be secular in nature. You will glimpse the lifestyle of the typical people of Iunu. Most of the buildings were entirely buried in sand over the years that followed the fall of the Heliopolis. Now, many have been completely excavated and some even restored to their assumed original appearance."

The tour guide held up a wand and began walking to the north. The heard of tourists ambled after him. Each stop followed a similar pattern.

The tour was interesting, but progressed at a pace far too slow for Johannes' preference. He decided he would look into a private tour for their second day.

By the end of the afternoon, the tour guide started in on another speech, this time a sales pitch for private tours. "At this very moment, my friends, work continues day and night to unearth what is believed to be **the** Temple of Ra. If this is found to be true, then the long held theory would be verified. It will be determined that Iunu is, in fact, the ancient city dedicated to the worship of Ra and the sun, the lost city once known as Ra-Atum."

The guide went on to say that they had originally been thinking of renaming the city ruins to its previous name of Iunu, but were now debating whether to call it Ra-Atum, awaiting sufficient evidence from the temple dig. John heard none of this.

As soon as he heard the words 'Ra-Atum', he fell deep into thought. The name echoed in his mind, much as it had the morning he woke from that first dream. He thought about the strange interlude in the middle of the previous night and made the connection. John realized that the mantra he had chanted resembled 'Ra-Atum.'

They tour arrived back at the camp just as the guide finished his pitch.

John extracted himself from his thoughts and excitedly pulled Johannes aside. "Johannes, that name, I know it…I know it from my dream!"

"What name?"

"The original name of this city: Ra-Atum. I first heard it in that reoccurring dream. I told you I figured out I needed to come to Egypt. I now think someone wanted me to make the journey to the Temple of Ra! It can't be a coincidence that we are here. We've **got** to go see that temple he spoke of! If it's the temple from my dream, I'll know when I see it."

"OK, I'll talk to the tour guide," Johannes replied, calmly. "He said he could probably get us into some of the sites that are not officially opened to the public. Maybe the temple is among them."

"Oh, and another thing," John added, "we must get there by sunrise. In my dream, it was very important to be at the temple entrance by sunrise. We should be able to see the pyramids from there."

"Well, I'll talk to him, but I am not sure if he'll go for that. I guess we'll see."

"You have to convince him!" John pleaded.

"OK, OK," Johannes responded. "I'll do what I can."

Once Johannes obtained the tour guide's attention, he pulled him aside to discuss the plans for the following day. The guide didn't have a problem with them visiting the temple, but could not guarantee access to the inside. Johannes then asked about being at the temple by sunrise. The guide at first hesitated, but when Johannes offered to pay him extra money, his face lit up, "Of course, my friend. No problem."

Δ   ▲   Δ

T he next morning, the men arrived at the temple after dawn broke, but before sunrise. John was disappointed because the temple did not resemble the one in his dream. The stairway to the main entrance was either non-existent or still buried. The obelisks and statuesque figures were missing as well. "How am I to know if this is the right temple?" he asked himself.

Look south.

John stood at the temple entrance and motioned for Johannes to join him. He looked south and west over the Nile river valley. It was a cool morning and a gentle mist hung over the valley. The sky was light enough to see both horizons, but John could not make out the pyramids, at least not well enough to distinguish them from the hills.

John looked to his left and saw the golden halo rising above the eastern horizon. The few clouds floating over the western sky turned pink, then orange as the sun illuminated them. It would only be a few minutes now before the sunlight raced across the valley. Even before the men could see the sun itself, its light hit the peaks far to the southwest. One peak then another lit up with an orange glow.

"Look!" John shouted, "See that? It's the pyramids!" Just as in his dream, each pyramid became visible as it reflected the light of the rising sun in a way that the neighboring hills did not. John turned to the guide, "Have you ever noticed that you can see the pyramids from here in the morning?"

"No, my friend, I have not. This is so exciting! I will have to include this as part of a new sunrise tour. I am sure many visitors will want to see this as well!"

The men watched the morning display for the few minutes it lasted. Once the sun reached a certain angle, the effect dissipated and the pyramids blended in with the landscape once again.

During the excitement, the three men had been unknowingly joined by a fourth; the guide was the first to notice the archeologist as he turned back towards the temple. "Good day sir. How are you on this fine morning?" he asked the man.

"I am well. I noticed that you were watching the sunrise over the valley. So you saw the pyramids, eh?"

"Yes, sir," the tour guide replied. "We came here for this very reason."

"How did you know about it?" the archeologist inquired.

"Good morning, sir." John greeted the archeologist and the men made their introductions. "I was the one who suggested coming here this morning. I had a dream a few weeks ago. In it, I stood at this very location and watched the pyramids light up at sunrise. This is the reason I came to Egypt. In my dreams, I traveled to the temple via a stone road that led up here from the valley below. It should be down there somewhere." John pointed to where the road had been in his dream.

"This is amazing," the archeologist responded. "Before we found the temple, no one knew about the way the pyramids reflected the morning sun. And until last week, we didn't know about the road either. In the temple, a drawing illustrates both of these. It shows the pyramids glowing in the light of the rising sun and it shows the ancient road that ran up here from the Nile. As you saw for yourself, the sunrise effect on the pyramids is true. After first seeing it, I sent a dig team down the hill to confirm the existence of the road. The sand wasn't that deep, so they found it in less time than I anticipated. It is, in fact, a stone road as you mentioned."

"Do you know what happened to the obelisks that used to be here at the temple entrance?"

"How do you know about **those**?" the archeologist asked, astonished.

"I saw them in my dream. In fact, when I stood at the temple entrance, two stone figures peered down at me from either side. Their backs were against the obelisks and stood as if protecting the temple entrance. Oh, and at the bottom of the staircase there were two lion statues as well."

"This is unbelievable. You've just perfectly described the temple as it originally existed. We only know this because of the drawing. In fact, when we first found the drawing, we did not know it was of **this** temple because of the missing obelisks, statues and the fact that we had not yet dug deep enough to find the staircase. The pyramidal display finally convinced us that this was, in fact, the temple depicted. Discovering the road added to our confidence."

"Would it be possible for us to go inside?" Johannes asked the archeologist.

"We are not yet ready for visitors, but given the circumstances, I would be happy to show you around."

As soon as they entered the temple, John felt blanketed by a tingling sensation. Johannes felt it as well and glanced at John questioningly.

What is this?—John thought.

I don't know—he heard echoed in his mind.

The boys' eyes grew wide as both realized that within the confines of the temple, they could hear each other's thoughts.

This is weird—Johannes thought and John laughed.

The archeologist escorted them from one room to the next. When he reached the innermost chamber, he showed them the drawing he had described earlier.

John looked at the drawing and fell into a slight trance. His eyes started to flutter, and a vision appeared. In it, he was looking at the very same drawing unfinished. It was nighttime and torchlight flickered on the chamber walls. In the vision, he saw a hand reach out and paint additional lines on the drawing. He unconsciously imitated the motion. The vision lasted only a few seconds, but long enough for the others to notice.

John turned to the others and said, "There is another drawing, over there." Of its own accord, his hand pointed towards an adjacent chamber.

"We found **that** drawing just this week! Men were removing sand from the room when it was discovered. The drawing is low on the wall, so we didn't find it until almost all of the sand was cleared. We can go in there now."

The three followed the archeologist into the next room. It was obvious that the room had just been unearthed; large piles of sand were still awaiting removal and the floor was uneven. The only wall that had been dusted clean was the one where the drawing was found. Two torches lit up the drawing from either side of the room.

The boys knelt down to get a closer look. The drawing was simple, as if created by a child. The scene depicted four men sitting in a circle surrounded by torches. The image was drawn as if looking down on the men from above but off to one side. One of the four sat squarely with his eyes closed. The other three faced him.

Floating above the center man was what appeared to be a winged scarab. It held the sun above its head with rays of light shining out from it. In front of the man on the left was a pile of coins. The man on the right held a feathered pen and was writing in a book.

John turned to the archeologist. "What do you think it means?"

"We haven't figured out very much, but what I can tell you is…" he pointed at the winged insect, "…this is the ancient symbol for Ra. Before he was pictured as a hawk-headed man, he was represented by a scarab holding the sun. These hieroglyphs above the picture basically translate to '**The Return**.' And these over here are numbers. We first thought they were a date, the date the painting was made, but they can't be."

"Why is that?" the guide asked.

"Because, based on the old Egyptian calendar, those numbers would represent this very year we just started."

"And look at that. Doesn't that look like a modern pick?" Johannes asked. "Did they have tools like that in ancient Egypt?"

"You know, I never noticed that before," the archeologist

replied. "It is right next to the man with the book. It looks just like archeological tools we use today."

"I know this sounds odd," John said, "but do you think it could be a prophetic drawing? It **is** a bit of a coincidence that you would be unearthing the temple in the same year that is marked on the drawing."

"We can't be sure that the number is a date, but if it is, then yes, it would be **quite** coincidental."

"I didn't tell you this part," John went on, "but in my dreams, Ra spoke to me. He said, 'I am Ra' and 'Ra-Atum.' At the time, I didn't know what either meant."

"Have you ever had premonitions before?" the archeologist asked John.

"No. But when I was in Athens a couple of weeks ago, I started having visions of the past. I saw earthquakes and volcanic eruptions…more vividly than I cared to."

Johannes jumped in, "Last week, I was approached by a card reader in Cairo. I was skeptical when she told me that John was here in Egypt. The next day, lo and behold, there he was. Things have been strange since then, at least for me."

John pointed to a part of the drawing. "These, here in the background, look like the bottom of the obelisks at the front of the temple. Do you suppose that this is showing a ceremony performed there?"

"Yes, I would have to concur," the archeologist said, "and taking place in nighttime. Look, there are stars in the sky."

"I have a funny feeling that we are supposed to do this," John said to the others. "There are four men in the picture and there are four of us here. I think we should come back here at sunset, sit as shown here, and see what happens."

Everyone looked at each other and nodded in agreement.

"In the meantime, my friends," the tour guide said, "I have plenty to show you in this part of town. We'll let our friend get his work done and we'll return after the evening meal."

The tour guide led John and Johannes out of the temple and resumed his normal routine despite the odd feeling that surrounded them. John had a hard time focusing on the tour; his mind drifted with thoughts and memories. He kept trying to sort it all out, assembling a puzzle when too many of the pieces were missing.

The fact that he was distracted did not go unnoticed. Johannes often looked over to him and saw that he was some place far away.

Johannes was a little distracted himself. At times, he too thought about all of the odd things that were happening...*ever since that card reading*. In fact, when he thought about it, he concluded that it was actually since the evening at that nightclub.

The tour guide, meanwhile, continued his spiel. At times, he was sure that neither of the boys heard a word he was saying, yet he continued the tour as usual. After all, he was used to speaking when people weren't exactly listening.

As the day went on, John's behavior got stranger. A couple of times, when nothing was being said, he turned to the others and asked, "What was that?" or "Say that again." Then, at other times, John would react as if he bumped into someone and mouth a, "Pardon me," despite no one being there.

By mid afternoon, the guide finished his planned tour and led the others back to the camp. He figured they had better eat earlier than usual in order to get back to the temple before nightfall.

At dinner, John hardly ate any of the food laid out in front of him. He wasn't sure if he was nervous or just distracted.

The guide noticed, and packed up some food and water for later. He wasn't sure why, but felt it was important for him to do so.

With dinner out of the way, John grew increasingly antsy. He paced around the tent, waiting for the right time to head to the temple. Johannes figured it might be a late night, so he made preparations for their trip back to Cairo in the morning. He knew John was too distracted to help with packing and he didn't want to have to deal with mundane things when they returned later that night.

The men walked to the temple just before dusk. John mumbled to himself unconsciously, but the others remained silent.

The archeologist was waiting for them when they reached the entrance to the temple. He had setup torches, and laid out mats for them to sit on. He imitated the arrangement pictured in the drawing as best he could. He placed his belongings next to the spot he allotted for himself. His journal was among them, handy, in case anything worth noting came up.

The men greeted each other and then moved over to the circle. The archeologist motioned for everyone to sit as he moved in behind the place he reserved for himself. Johannes sat across from him and John sat between them with his back to the temple. The guide setup some cups near his seat and filled them with water from his jug and distributed them to the others.

Once everyone was seated, they all looked at John, awaiting his direction. John closed his eyes and fell quickly into a trance. His head turned to the left and then to the right as if looking around, but his eyes remained closed. His head turned a few more times, then slowed to a stop. He took a couple of deep breaths and then sat so still, the others could not tell if he was breathing.

John's mind was clear. His inner ear strained to listen as if trying to distinguish a distance sound. He focused with increasing intensity and then heard, as if nothing more than his own thoughts, *I am Ra...I am Ra.*

John felt self-conscious. He asked if he was supposed to say what he was hearing, but only heard *I am Ra* again in his mind.

John opened his mouth to speak and his voice cracked. He cleared his throat and tried again.

I am Ra.

John felt odd identifying himself in this way. *Am I making this up?* He spoke, more loudly and with increased confidence.

I am Ra. Greetings, my humble friends, I am Ra. You have done well to have gathered here this evening. You are fulfilling the prophecy of an earlier time. You are completing a contract. You are here as a part of your individual and combined purpose within this lifetime.

This moment is unique, foretold but never to be experienced again. I am Ra and in this way, I have returned.

I am one with **THE ONE** and I am here on behalf of the whole to convey light and thus information to your planet. I do not return in the flesh; it does not serve my path to do so.

I am many, but we are one. We speak with one voice as we hold a singular vibration of shared intent.

I am not gendered, yet we are all genders.

I am, have been before, and will continue to be, in my ever

becoming.

To each of you, I bring a gift. In actuality, this is a gift from your self, your **higher** self.

John turned to his left and addressed the archeologist.

You are a seeker of truth and treasure. Your work is with the past. Your desire is to serve the future by revealing the past. In this manner, you are a scholar and your treasure is knowledge and history.

Tonight, I present to you a map, hints of relics sought. Some time ago, this temple was ravaged by thieves. They pulled down structures and attempted to cart them away. Some did not get far; it was not their fortune to succeed. They did not enable their own success. Their fear brought upon them a storm, which buried them and their loot side-by-side.

Follow the recently discovered ancient road to the south for two days at a camels' pace. There the road runs parallel to the Nile. Look west towards the river; a mound of earth will be visible stretching north and south. Dig carefully into this mound. Use not tools of metal. Buried within, you will find relics of this temple and in a condition well preserved.

You will not find all that you seek there, but will be graced with hints of still further discovery. Look among the human remains for evidence as to their country of origin. Be patient and follow your instincts. These clues will lead you to further treasure and knowledge.

The archeologist had quickly pulled out his journal and wrote feverishly, careful to record precisely as he heard. Ra, through John, then addressed the tour guide.

My friend, you are a kind and gentle man with simple desires. To serve others is the greatest among them.

As of yet, you have not been blessed with family. You were told that your wife is barren. This is not true; it is her diet that prevents her fertility. Indulge in meats, the two of you, to your liking. Allow your individual tastes to guide you. Spare no expense towards quality. Find animals that were honored in life and in death. Thank them for the sustenance they offer.

Follow this advice and within two moons you will imbue her with child. Allow her to continue to indulge her diet for the full term. Trust that your income will increase following the birth.

Discoveries made here will bring more visitors and you will be their escort. Double your rates in six months, then again in a year.

The guide moved into a kneeling position and thanked Ra repeatedly for his bidding. Tears streamed down his face as he anticipated the fulfillment of his greatest desire to father a child.

At this time, I wish to address the one who speaks and you, his companion.

Ra, through John, looked Johannes in the eye.

We first would like to tell you a bit about yourselves. You are what we refer to as 'the Two within One—the One within Two'. Not many chose to serve in this manner; only a select few incarnate as twin flames: two beings, one shared purpose.

You will each come to see your place with the other more, in time. For now, know that you have done well. Together, you have the ability to touch many lives. Through this work, you will experience the greatest wealth, not merely measured in coins, but in contentment.

I am Ra and we are here because we wish to convey to you the teachings of The First Decree, Il Primo Stato, The Prime Essence, THE ONE Being. Words cannot convey its true meaning, but we will work with you to approximate as best we can.

Additional sessions are forthcoming. Through these, you will come to know better who we are, where we come from, why we have come, and for what purpose. The next three sessions will form a series of teachings.

Your journey has led you to us, yet you have always been among us. You have neither drifted away nor returned; yet here you are seemingly for the first time.

You see yourselves as human men and you remember only the past. Yet you are not merely men, and you are not your past.

Do not fret if you do not comprehend fully what you are hearing. Your understanding will grow in time as you remember and become more of who you really are.

It is your path to grow with those you foster, learn with those you teach, walk alongside those you guide.

In the past, men and women came who taught through their example. They reached the full potential of their own enlightenment and their essence was seen and felt by many. However, that form of teaching has created many gods, and that path no longer serves man well enough. Until all are guided primarily from within, some will answer a calling to serve the others, but along side them. You chose and have been chosen. You will guide others by walking a mere few steps ahead of them on the path of ascension.

For the next session, we ask that you travel to Philae, to visit the temple that has been erected there. Leave as soon after your return to the City of Pharaohs as is convenient.

The veil is thin and has facilitated this meeting. You are not the only four who could have been here, but you are the ones who answered the call. Let this be proof of the wellbeing that results when one follows inner guidance. I am Ra and with this, we close.

John opened his eyes and stretched. He felt awake, alive, and full of energy, yet quite hungry. Before he had time to react to the pangs in his stomach, food was placed in front of him. The guide then refilled everyone's cup.

The archeologist intermittently looked up deep in thought, but otherwise focused on his journal. He reviewed what he had written while it was still fresh in his mind, making sure he didn't miss anything.

John, giving in to his cravings, sampled all of what was laid out before him.

Oddly, it was Johannes who remained quiet and contemplative. He wasn't exactly in a panic, but was having a harder time than the others processing the information given. Nothing that came before this experience adequately prepared him for it. And yet, at the same time, some part of him felt peaceful. The urge to run from this overwhelmingly different experience, although consistent with his past, did not emerge within him. In some ways, this unusual reaction, or lack of reaction, struck him more profoundly than the experience itself. He felt different, changed; he didn't recognize the person he observed in himself in that moment. The past few days did not match his life before and now he questioned whether he could go back, whether he could simply stand up and march back into the life he had fully expected to return to.

The archeologist was the first to stand. He had completed his notes and was now brimming with ideas and plans. He thanked the others, wished them well, and encouraged John and Johannes to return to Ra-Atum again, He was confident there would be so much more for them to see in the future. He then excused himself and started moving the various items back into the temple.

The guide, following the archeologist's lead, began packing up the things he had brought. He was glad that they would be returning to Cairo in the morning as he was anxious to share with his wife everything he was told.

John, having satiated his hunger and thirst, stood up and stretched a second time. He still felt energized, but knew intuitively that it would not last long. He tapped his friend on the shoulder and said, "Johannes, are you ready to head back to camp?"

Johannes snapped out of his inner thoughts and replied, "Oh... yeah. I'm ready." He stood up and said nothing more. In fact, the entire trip back to the tent, Johannes remained quiet.

XVII – The Star

As the men traveled back to Cairo, one observing them would almost think that John and Johannes had traded personalities. Johannes, more typically outgoing, remained inwardly focused all day. John, more typically contemplative, made conversation with the guide all day.

John's conversation with the tour guide contained a bit of small talk to pass the time, but primarily had purpose. He was anxious to travel to Philae and asked the guide all about it. "How soon can we leave?" "How long will it take to get there?" "How much does it cost?"

John assumed that Johannes was as interested in the trip as he was. He figured that if Johannes had an issue with any of what was being arranged, he would speak up about it.

Before John expected, they were back in Cairo. In that strange yet typical way, the trip back seemed to take half as much time as the trip out. The shadows in the city were no shorter than the ones in Heliopolis when they'd first arrived there, yet it seemed as if they should have half the day remaining.

As the boys walked through the center of town back to their inn, John spoke to Johannes directly for the first time. At first, John carried on about things they could do for the evening and what they needed to take with them on their trip. He asked questions, but never paused long enough for answers. He suggested that they dine at a restaurant before returning to the inn. Having received no objection, he wandered into the first eatery that looked interesting.

Johannes silently followed John's lead.

The boys sat at a table and looked over the menus. John suggested and then ordered a bottle of wine and then perused the menu to select his entrée. Once he had decided, he put his menu down and eyed Johannes.

"You have been quiet all day," John said to him. "What's going on in there?" He reached over and pulled Johannes' menu down so he could make eye contact with his friend. "In fact, I don't think you've said a word all day."

Johannes turned away. "I've been thinking."

"OK. Do you want to share what's on your mind?"

"I don't know if I am ready to talk about it," Johannes said defensively and then went back to looking at his menu.

John moved Johannes' menu out of the way a second time. "Talk about what?"

"Talk about what happened."

"You mean the channeling?"

"Yeah. And what was said...about us." Johannes looked John in the eye.

"Oh." Now John looked away. The weight of understanding blanketed him and he grew quiet. He opened his mouth to say something, but then hesitated. Months of emotion and fear flashed before his eyes. He was immediately reminded that they had never discussed what had happened back in Germany. Johannes had seemed fine with everything and that was good enough for John. But now that Johannes expressed trepidation, John grew nervous all over again.

The waiter wandered over to take their order. Both welcomed the interruption. It was just enough to ease some of the silent tension that had moved in between them.

After the waiter walked away, Johannes spoke. "John, I don't want to make a big of a deal about this, but I don't know if I am convinced that my life purpose is about this. I don't know **what** I believe. I have a job back in Germany, and all of this woo-woo stuff is just a little strange for me."

John took a deep breath. His initial interpretation gave way to this clearer understanding. "Johannes, I don't know what is ultimately going to happen with all of this either. I can't think about that right now because it's too scary for me too. So I am taking this one day at a time. I am curious and excited. For right now, I am happy to have you here with me in this. You still have some vacation time, right?"

"Yes."

"Well, let's go to Philae and if it helps, just think of it as sightseeing."

Johannes relaxed perceptively. "I guess I can do that. I was going to spend these next two weeks sightseeing anyway."

"Johannes?" John eyed him intensely.

"Yes."

"If this continues to bother you, will you talk to me about it?" John's eyes conveyed more than the words he spoke.

Johannes held the eye contact for a moment and then looked down at his plate. "Yeah, I'll keep you posted."

The boys ate together but spent most of their time deep within their own thoughts. Once their stomachs were full, exhaustion moved in, clearing their minds and neutralizing their emotions. As soon as they reached the inn, both fell asleep quickly and slept soundly throughout the night.

Δ   ▲   Δ

T wo days later, the evening commencing their trip down up the Nile arrived. *Up, right?* John was frustrated; he kept getting the Upper Egypt/Lower Egypt designations confused. They were heading south, but were traveling **up** the Nile, so Upper Egypt was south and Lower Egypt north. *OK, but why is that so confusing? You would think one could just flip the direction in the mind, but for some reason, I can't seem to get it right.* Besides, he was tired of everyone correcting him.

The other aspect of the trip that bothered him was that they were not traveling straight through. The tour guide arranged transportation for them, but that meant joining a previously scheduled tour. There were no other options at such late notice. As a result, they were not sailing directly to Philae, but stopping a number of times along the way. Worst yet, Philae was the last stop, since it was the furthest south for this particular tour. The trip would be far less efficient than John wanted and his impatience challenged him.

The final frustration was they only sailed at night. During each of the intermediate days, the boat docked and the tour group went ashore to explore. John was in no mood to sightsee; he couldn't concentrate and only grew more impatient.

The further south they traveled, the warmer it got, so John decided he would sleep during the day while the others were ashore. This allowed him to spend his nights up on deck, looking out over the land. At first, he was thwarted by this plan because there wasn't enough light to see anything around him. There **was**, however, plenty to see in the sky. Now that they were away from the city, the stars shined brightly and this ameliorated him.

The first couple of nights, Johannes attempted to stay up with John, but got bored and lasted only a couple of hours. He couldn't stay up at night without some form of entertainment. He also didn't want to hang around all day while John slept. He decided to attend the tours with the others.

John didn't mind. He felt that he and Johannes could use a bit of space from each other. They spent a little time together in the evening, when they were both awake, and greeted each other in the early morning.

Each night, John watched the stars and imagined what he saw pictured among them. He remembered a bit of the Astrology he had learned, but couldn't seem to find any of the constellations that were part of the Zodiac. Instead, he just made up his own.

Soon, he grew familiar with the sky. He could tell how late it was by the position of the stars directly ahead. Each morning he watched as the stars faded away into the dawn.

John also took advantage of the quiet to meditate. The first couple of nights, he struggled as he fought the urge to sleep. After that, he was awake enough to meditate effectively. Occasionally, crew-members worked near to where he sat, and although he did sense them, they didn't disturb him. In fact, he was comforted by their presence.

As they neared Philae, John questioned whether to shift his routine back to staying awake during the day and sleeping at night. But then something odd happened, the morning before their arrival, he waited for sleep to call to him, but it never did. Somehow, he lasted the whole day. When he turned in for the night, sleep came without effort. And he had no trouble waking with the sunrise. It was as if his internal clock switched back all on its own.

John wondered how long the hike would be from the shore to the temple once they reached Philae. The day they arrived, he quickly saw that traveling to the temple was not a problem. Philae was a tiny island in the middle of the Nile, and the Temple occupied most of it. "This is one tour I am not going to miss," he said quietly to himself.

John soon learned that they could spend as much time at the temple as they liked. The formal tour was scheduled for the morning, but the boat was not due to leave until evening. The group was free to roam the island as they pleased in the afternoon.

John and Johannes accompanied the tour to learn whatever they could about the island temple. For example, they discovered that the temple was dedicated to the goddess Isis, mother of Horus. It was also one of the best-preserved temples of its time.

After the tour completed and the mid-day meal was consumed, John and Johannes found a spot away from the others to formulate a plan.

"Johannes, what do you think we should do?"

"I was hoping you had a plan. This is **your** thing after all."

"It's **our** thing," John assured him. "Just because I'm the speaker, doesn't mean I can do this without you. I certainly can't do this with a bunch of tourist loitering around. And with the boat docked right here, I doubt we'd have privacy."

"Well," Johannes offered, "I guess we'll have to stay."

"But how will we get back?"

"John, look, I don't want to pretend that I understand any of this, but if this is what we are supposed to do, don't you think Ra will give us instructions…like the last time?"

"I never thought about it that way," John said. "You're a genius! I've been so focused on getting to this point, I never really thought beyond it. You know, something else just occurred to me."

"What's that?"

"If we really are having a conversation with a higher being, why don't we ask him some questions? I mean, if he doesn't give us enough information, we could, I mean, **you** could ask him. I am not sure I can because if I try to talk as myself I think I'll break the connection."

"OK," Johannes concurred. "What should we ask it…I mean him…I mean Ra, whatever he or it is?"

"Let's just say he," John reasoned. "The Egyptians called him a **god** and used 'he', so I doubt he'll be offended."

"Fine. Whatever. But since we're sitting here talking about it, let's think of some questions."

After a short pause, John started thinking out loud, "OK. So we already decided that if he doesn't give us directions; we will ask him about getting back. Um, is there anything else we want to know?"

"I'm curious about where he is from," Johannes mentioned, "but he said that we'll 'come to know that in time.' I am not sure I want to force the issue before he is ready. Besides, I am not sure that will mean anything to us anyway. Would it?"

"No, I suppose not. I mean, if he said he was from the moon, what difference would **that** make?"

"That's pretty funny, John, you speaking for the man-in-the-moon!" Johannes laughed and while John was at first offended, he couldn't help but laugh too.

"I doubt sincerely that he's from the moon," John said, "He is the **sun** god after all. It would just be too ironic for the sun god to live on the moon." John chuckled at the thought.

"Well, we can ask him if there **is** a man-in-the-moon!" Johannes continued the silliness.

Even though John laughed with him, he made every attempt to be serious, "OK, OK, enough. I guess for now we'll just focus on logistics. We'll see what Ra has to say and you're going to have to stay focused. If he doesn't give us enough information as to how we're going to get back to Cairo, ask him."

John rubbed his stomach and added, "And make sure he understands that we need to eat too. There doesn't seem to be anything around here." John looked around. "You know, Johannes, it wouldn't hurt for us to talk to the tour guides, you know, to find out what towns or villages are nearby…just in case."

Johannes smiled. "It's good to hear that I am not the only one who has doubts."

"I never said you were!" John said, his voice rising in pitch. "Last time, I didn't know what was going to happen. But now there is an expectation. I mean, what if nothing happens? We came all this way..."

Johannes interrupted him, "Enough of that. Don't get yourself worked up. It's just you and me this time, and if nothing happens, nothing happens. We'll go on living the way we have before any of this started."

John calmed. "You're so practical! See! That's why I need you around. You're my rock!"

"How exciting," Johannes said sarcastically while rolling his eyes.

"I meant that as a compliment," John assured him. "You're very supportive. It's who you are. I'm just acknowledging you."

"Well thanks," Johannes said, embarrassed. A moment of awkwardness moved in between them, but was quickly dismissed when Johannes changed the subject. "Let's go talk to the guides and see what they have to say."

"OK."

The boys told the tour guides that they would not be leaving with them that evening and were comforted to learn that the next tour would stop at the temple two days later and would be happy to bring them back. It wasn't unusual for individuals or couples to detach from one tour and continue on with a subsequent one. However, it was pointed out that no one ever left the tour **in Philae**.

The boys ate the evening meal with the tour, then unloaded their belongings and watched the boat sail back **down** the Nile. There was still a good hour left of sunlight, so they strolled around the temple. They needed to decide where to sit for the session.

"You know, John, we're not going to have any light," Johannes said.

"I know. There is no moon tonight."

"I didn't even mean that. We don't have any torches, or any way to light it if we had one."

"Yeah, but wait until you see the stars! You have been retiring pretty early so you've missed out on some beautiful starlit nights."

The boys ultimately decided that the best location for the session would be within the structure referred to as Trajan's Kiosk. It was a small hut, which sat within the courtyard of the temple. The lower walls were solid and provided a bit of security, while the colonnade above them, and an open roof, allowed a clear view of the sky. Johannes figured the hut would provide adequate shelter for the night as well, given the beautiful weather they were having.

As Johannes set up the space for their session, John paced. Last time, he could feel Ra's approach hours before the session started. This time, he felt nothing and was nervous. He then decided to watch the sunset from the western side of the temple and that seemed to calm him, albeit not completely.

As John watched the last of the sun, he recalled how it felt when the presence of Ra moved through him. He had never before felt anything that powerful, energetic, and loving. In those moments with Ra, he was no longer a separate being; he was no longer unsure of himself or his purpose.

Yet, despite feeling such confidence within the session, John could not hold onto it afterward. Once Ra receded, John returned to being simply himself, albeit a happier version. Many times since then, he hoped that Ra would return as he had promised. At times, he even trusted that Ra would return. But he was never sure.

After the sun was gone, John stood up and turned to head back to the kiosk. He saw Johannes watching him. Johannes had come around to catch the sunset as well, but stayed back so as not to disturb John. The boys held eye contact for a minute. Long enough for a subtle intimacy to move in between them, but not long enough to be uncomfortable.

John then made his way over to his friend.

Johannes placed a hand on John's shoulder and said, "So, are you ready? Should we make our way over to the kiosk and see what happens?"

"I guess so. I feel calm…**now**. It took a little while, but the sunset helped."

The boys walked over to the hut and entered it. John was pleasantly surprised to find that Johannes had unpacked their things, giving it a homey feel. Between the two makeshift cushions sat the statue of Horus.

Something within John told him that Ra would not return before dark and he expressed this to Johannes. So the two sat comfortably and relaxed. The inside of the kiosk grew dark quickly. The boys passed the time looking up at the sky as it slowly morphed into a deep, dark blue.

John watched individual stars appear, and then whole constellations. It seemed that with each passing minute, the number of stars doubled. Despite the multitude of them, one star in particular held his attention.

He stared at the star and his eyes watered from the prolonged lack of blinking. His sight went blurry. He reached for Ra, but only felt the energy of that one star. He could swear that he actually felt its light shining on him. A tingling touched the center of his forehead and moved back toward his crown. It spread out from the center and opened up. He then felt a spark at the back of his neck.

He opened his mouth and spoke.

Good evening my sons. I am Isis.

Johannes had closed his eyes when he saw John fall into trance, but then opened them questioningly.

Oddly, John was aware of this despite his own eyes being shut. He found that he could see Johannes clearly in his mind. He too questioned why Ra himself was not present, yet having learned about Isis earlier and knowing that this was her temple, he felt comfortable conveying her in Ra's absence.

I know that you were expecting Ra, but know that this is appropriate and as planned. You were versed on the morn of this day that this temple was erected in my honor. It has been imbued with many prayers to me and as such, it is a place that is most in resonance with the essence that I am, that part of me that walked this Earth years ago.

As you sensed, we wished to begin this session in full nightfall. We chose complete darkness because we wanted you to experience our source. I am of Ra and we reside, in your terms, within a system that you see as a star, the very star you found yourself staring at moments ago. From your perspective, it is not a physical place. However, this evening you sensed us travel from where we are to where you are. To us, we are neither transporting nor transmitting. Yes we have to stretch ourselves to reach you, but this is a stretching inward, not outward.

Now please, do not be afraid.

The channeling paused, giving the boys enough time to question what Isis was referring to when she told them to not be afraid. A moment later, they both understood. Movement was all around them. Johannes opened his eyes and noticed flickering light drawing near. He stared at the doorway with wide eyes, awaiting whatever was moving around the kiosk to appear there.

One by one, people entered the kiosk carrying candles. Johannes watched them stream in. The candles cast just enough light for Johannes to see their faces. Each and every one was female. Most were young, up to a decade younger than him, but a few were much older. When the procession finished, the women completely encircled them, shoulder to shoulder.

We intentionally omitted details of this gathering so that you, John, would not be overwhelmed with stage fright. We have observed you for some time and felt that it would be easier for you if you didn't know that you would have an audience. These women, however, have known about the potential of this gathering for a long time. They are, in part, responsible for it. It is their summoning that has fueled this connection and has helped establish this communication.

John's eyes were now open, but they were under Isis' control. She, through him, made eye contact with and bowed to each and every woman within the circle as she spoke.

We now wish to begin the first of three sessions, which all relate one to the other. We wish to convey to you the three states of being, the three beings within each individual. This is known as the 'Sacred Triad'. We call it 'the Three within One—the One within Three.'

In each of these forthcoming sessions, we will discuss one constituent of the Three within One. This night we focus on what you might think of as the middle one. The higher self is not the highest self. It is not hierarchically lower than the highest self, nor is it higher than the lowest self. However, it has less awareness than the one and greater awareness than the other.

The higher self is who you **really** are, in as much as you are any one. Your human self lives a mere blink-of-an-eye incarnation as compared to the higher self. This middle self is not so concerned with the earth plane goals of the lower self. It loves and supports the human personality, but is not attached to the outcomes or achievements of that level.

The higher self is the master creator within you. When you create in the third realm, you are relenting completely to the will of the higher self. You are allowing the higher self to bring to you what is best for your highest good, your greatest growth, and your most efficient evolution. Your higher self is the part of you that **knows** its purpose and thus chooses aspects for each incarnation with intention. It understands that it molds its own existence and thus never blames another for its so-called negative experience.

From your perspective, the higher self is your own personal star: your guiding light. Its light cannot be extinguished. In prayer or meditation, when you feel what you believe to be the presence of God, you are likely sensing your higher self. In your darkest moments, your star shines brightly.

You have more access to the higher self than you realize. Whenever you feel positive emotion, you are connecting to the higher self. Whenever you love someone or something, you are radiating that love from the higher heart.

You will achieve greater success the more you shift into the consciousness of your higher self. Self-awareness facilitates this shift. Mindfulness is the art of shifting your perception from the one doing, saying, and thinking to the one who observes with no judgment.

By raising your attention from the lower self to the higher self, you are executing the first step to enlightenment, a step you will take again and again.

Please recognize that you **can** exist at both levels simultaneously. You are the one that does **and** the one that observes the doing. The one that does is attached; the one that observes is not attached. The one that does feels emotion; the one that observes allows that emotion to flow freely and thus experiences peace within all emotion.

When you are taught to rise above conflict, you are given sound advice. Rising above is the act of moving one's attention from the lower self to the higher self. When you are above a situation, you have access to more information. You do not see from your lower perspective alone, but from many perspectives at once. You see the '**big picture**.' You see the situation from multiple positions in space and from multiple positions in time. In seeing the past, you see how the situation was created. In seeing the future, you gain access to the ultimate benefit and resolution. Rise high enough and you see perfection in everything. Of course, at this point, you approach the highest self, which we will discuss later.

When viewed from the higher self, you see your life as a journey along a path. You are on that path, and that path flows forever from where you are to where you want to be. The higher self sees the entire path and knows precisely where you are along it. It is above linear time and is thus not frustrated by the pace of movement along the path. No point on the path is less significant than any other. No amount of time taken to move from one place to another is inappropriate.

The guidance for this evening is to recognize that you have endless access to your higher self. This part of you knows all that is pertinent to you. You needn't seek outside of yourself for anything, ever.

Your higher self is your piece of Source and your source of peace.

At this point, Isis paused, giving the women time to leave the kiosk. The elders among them knew intuitively that any final words would be meant solely for the boys.

From here, we ask the two of you to travel to the Temple of Horus in Edfu. Arrive by the full of the moon; she has just gone dark and thus begins a new cycle. Tomorrow, she rises with the sun and sets just after. Within each passing day the moon falls back from the sun an additional twelve and one half degrees. You will experience this as a moonrise and moonset nearly one hour later each day as compared to the previous. It is this lagging that causes the phases you witness from your vantage.

You have two full weeks to reach your goal. Travel by foot and only when the moon is above the horizon. In your final approach into Edfu, you will be traveling exclusively by moonlight. She will reach peak fullness as she rises opposite the sunset two weeks from this very night.

Be at the temple in advance of the sunset on that evening. Be well rested and do not eat after mid-day, but do not deprive yourself of water.

Good night my sons and pleasant travels.

The energy of Isis turned off instantly. John felt it as a subtle pop in his ears. It nonetheless took him a moment to return entirely to himself. Once he felt fully present, he stood and exited the kiosk, joining Johannes who by then, was standing just outside.

The women had made their way off the tiny island and could be seen floating across the river. The boys watched as the individual candle lights blended and receded.

When they turned to head back into the kiosk, they realize that it was still lit. A number of candles had been left along the back wall behind where Johannes had been sitting. Neither of the boys had noticed at first.

The boys unraveled their cushions and turned them into makeshift bedding and crawled onto them for the night. Each was thankful for the candles and the warmth they cast.

XVIII – The Moon

T he next morning, the boys rose with the dawn and prepared for their journey. This was their only day to travel solely in the daytime. As they methodically packed up their belongings and moved them outside of the kiosk, Johannes noticed a sack he hadn't seen before. It rested against the outer wall of the kiosk and just around the corner from the entrance. He walked over to it and investigated.

"John! Come here! You've got to see this!" Johannes held the bag open for John to look inside. It contained an assortment of food and canteens of water. "The women left us enough supplies to get us all the way to Edfu!"

"What is this?" John pulled out a scroll that was tucked behind some of the food and unrolled it. "It's a map! And look, the trail from Philae to Edfu is clearly indicated. How did they know about our assigned journey?"

"John, with all that has happened so far, you're asking a

question like that? Why are you surprised?"

John laughed. "I guess you're right; can't be any stranger than what's happened already," he agreed.

The boys crossed from the island to the shore via a small raft left behind for that purpose, and then headed north along the eastern bank of the river. At least once each hour, John pulled out the scroll and scanned it. After the third time, Johannes said, "John, we can only walk so far in an hour."

"I can't help it," John replied. "It indicates a number of landmarks and I don't want us to miss any. Leave me alone; I am enjoying this right now. We are going to be walking for two weeks! Allow me my entertainment!"

John's defensiveness made Johannes laugh.

After sunset, John scanned the western horizon. He calculated, from what Isis had said, that the moon was still six degrees above the horizon. He didn't know what that would look like, however. He searched back from where the sun disappeared, but try as he might, he could not see the moon. *Tomorrow will be the first light of the moon,* he concluded.

The boys set up camp, taking advantage of the remaining light of dusk. "Starting tomorrow, we'll have to do this in the dark," John said to Johannes.

The second evening as they traveled north, John looked to his left to watch the last of the sun dip below the horizon. The sunset was so beautiful that he failed to notice the tiny crescent above it. Once the sun's bright light was extinguished, the sliver of the moon grew in prominence and caught John's attention. He and Johannes both paused to stare at it. Only the tiniest edge of the moon was lit, and yet as the sky grew darker, the rest of the face became minutely visible.

At nearly 19 degrees above the horizon, the moon still had more than an hour's journey to reach the horizon. The light of dusk would not last as long. The boys had to resist the urge to prematurely suspend their travels with the approaching darkness.

"Tomorrow, we'll have to walk longer in darkness," John said to Johannes.

When complete darkness fell, the moon was near enough to the horizon for the boys to stop for the night. After a full day of walking, sleep came quickly.

The following morning, John estimated that the moon would rise a couple of hours after the sun. This gave him time to work out the figures that he had been thinking about the day before. He wondered if they would be able to see the moon rise given its size and the bright morning light.

John thought back. He had noticed the moon in the daylight many times before, but he never remembered seeing any but the latter part of the cycle. He therefore decided to estimate the number of degrees that the moon would lag the sun each morning and evening.

If the moon slows 12.5 degrees each day, then it should lose about six degrees between moonrise and moonset. He also calculated that to cover a full rotation of 360 degrees in a 24-hour day, the sky had to move about 15 degrees each hour. *Tonight, the moon should set 31 degrees behind the sun, almost exactly two hours after sunset. We should be able to test this out to see how accurate my calculations are.*

"Johannes, come look at this."

Johannes walked over to John and peered over his shoulder.

John showed Johannes his journal and said, "I have calculated the number of degrees behind the sun that the moon will rise and set each day. I then translated that into hours. Isis said for us to only travel when the moon is above the horizon, but with it rising in the daylight, it is difficult to see. I figured I had better work it out like this. As long as we have no cloud cover in the evenings, we'll have no trouble seeing where the moon is."

Johannes looked at John with a blank face and said nothing.

Unable to interpret the lack of response, John became self-conscious and looked away. All that day, as they walked, he remained quiet.

Johannes entertained his own thoughts, and therefore didn't notice. Intermittently, he would share what he was thinking, but John never responded with other than a subtle grunt of acknowledgment.

When they stopped for their afternoon meal, Johannes questioned John's silence, "You've been quiet. Have you been doing more calculations?"

"No," John retorted…avoiding eye contact. He assumed Johannes was being sarcastic.

Johannes observed John for a moment. "John, you're acting strange. What's going on? You seem upset. Is something bothering you?"

"It's nothing," John said, unconvincingly.

"John, I don't believe you for a second. Come on, out with it. What's up? Something is clearly bothering you."

John brooded for a bit longer and then said, "Do you think I'm weird?"

The question took Johannes by surprise. "**Weird?** I think this **whole situation** is weird. We are walking through the desert, following the moon, hoping to arrive at some temple by the full moon on advice of a being we can't see or even talk to easily. Yeah, that's weird. But I don't think **you're** weird. What makes you think **that?**"

"Well, I don't know. It's just…you were quiet when I was talking about the calculations…and…you…had a strange look on your face."

"John! I wasn't thinking anything about anything, most certainly not that you were being weird. You read **way too much** into things. Has that been bothering you all day?"

"Yeah, I guess," John admitted as he looked down at his feet.

"Didn't you ask me to talk to you if something was bothering me?" Johannes reminded him. "You need to do the same thing. Talk to me about this stuff. I wasn't thinking anything. You let your imagination get the best of you. Look, I'm sorry I didn't say anything to you, but you shouldn't let yourself get so affected by something as vague as a look on my face, or anyone else's for that matter."

"You're right," John conceded. "I'm sorry. It just seemed as if you thought that I was being weird for taking all of this so seriously."

"Well, I don't think you're weird, OK."

The two men finished their lunch, packed up, and got back to their travels. Within an hour, John returned to his normal self and cheerfully chatted about whatever crossed his mind.

When the sun neared the horizon, John suggested they take

another break. "We have two hours after sunset to travel. Why don't we enjoy the sunset and rest for a bit?"

The moon was far enough from the sun to be easily seen even with the sun above the horizon. Once the sun disappeared completely, but before it got dark, the boys ended their rest and continued their trek.

As the dusk darkened, John marveled at how clearly the dark side of the moon could be seen. He knew that this only happened during the early crescent phases, but didn't understand why. As they walked, he kept thinking about it.

"Hey John, why is it that we can see the dark side of the moon right now?"

"Funny that you ask. I was just thinking about the same thing. Look, you can even see the markings on the dark side."

After a full hour of walking in the dark, the boys decided to stop for the day. John wanted to set up camp with enough time left over to watch the moonset. This was his favorite phase of the moon and he wanted to enjoy it.

With their backs to the erected tent, the boys sat shoulder-to-shoulder gazing at the moon. The moon set across the Nile from them and its light reflected upon it.

John stared past the moonlit river and allowed his imagination to take over. He pictured the sandy desert landscape as if it were the surface of the moon. He wondered what it was like up there, staring back at the earth. The air was cool, but John felt warmth move over him as he fell into a vision.

He sat on the rim of a huge crater. The far side was shrouded in darkness, but the slope below him was lit with earthlight. As John looked around, he could clearly make out the landscape. Everything touched by earthlight was blue; all else was gray.

John looked up into the sky and saw the bright blue globe; it was immense! He reached a hand up to it. Its size was so great, it looked as if it was moving closer and about to collide with the moon.

The blue orb hung low in the sky, but neither rose nor set. It rotated, indicating the flow of time, but did not move across the sky. When John questioned this, he heard a subtle explanation, "The motion of the moon, its synchronous spinning and orbiting relative to the earth, causes the earth to remain fixed in the lunar sky."

John's vision then switched to a spherical map of the moon. One side was labeled Earth-Lit, "the side that always faces the earth," and the other was label Earth-Less. In the middle of Earth-Lit was an area called Earth-Center, "where the earth hovers directly overhead," he heard.

"The earth phases, as viewed from the moon, cycle at the same pace as the lunar phases when viewed from the earth. However, a lunar day is precisely the same length as a lunar month. It takes 30 earth-days for the sun to rise, set, and rise again on the moon, which creates a full cycle of earth phases."

As John heard the explanation, he watched the passing of a complete cycle, a complete lunar day and month, from the rim of the crater. His sight remained focused on the spinning globe.

The cycle started with a waning gibbous earth, just past full. It advanced and the earth darkened to third quarter and then a waning crescent. As the crescent thinned, the lunar dawn grew bright. Then the earth disappeared and the sun rose, passing near to where the earth had been.

Only after the sun reach high enough in the sky did the earth crescent reappear and then grow. The sun continued its trek across the lunar sky, now behind John, and eventually dipped below the horizon. Just as the lunar night began, the globe in front of John reached maximum brightness: a full earth.

As John considered the scene that played out before him, he noticed something. *On this side of the moon, it is never fully dark. There is always either sunlight or earthlight shining. And, of course, there is never a cloud to block either of them out.*

When the earth reached the waning gibbous phase where the cycle had begun, motion stopped and John's vision faded.

Suddenly, John made the connection. The earth phase as viewed from the moon was the very opposite as the lunar phase when viewed from the earth. He and Johannes sat there watching a tiny crescent moon, while in his vision he sat on the moon watching a huge gibbous earth. The near-full earth was so bright that it bathed that entire side of the moon with its brilliant blue light.

"That's it!" John's words of excitement leapt from his mouth.

Johannes turned to him and asked, "That's what?"

"I just figured it out. I figured out why we can see the dark part of the moon. That area of the moon," John pointed as if it would help his explanation, "is lit up by earthlight! I had another vision and in it, I was sitting on the moon looking back at the earth. The earth phase was nearly full and lit up the nighttime. The earth looked huge; there was earthlight everywhere and the whole lunar terrain looked blue!"

Johannes strained to get his head around what John was describing. The more John explained, the more Johannes understood. When he finally got it, he saw that what John said was true.

"That's fascinating," Johannes professed. "What I want to know is where you came up with those names: Earth-Center, Earth-Lit, and Earth-Less?"

"That's a good question. In that part of the vision, I saw the names on a three dimensional map of the moon. In the rest of the vision, it was as if I was looking through the eyes of someone…or something up there. They always say the moon is a cold, barren place, but who really knows? What if there has been life up there all along and we've just never known about it?"

"Maybe there **is** a man in the moon," Johannes joked, referring back to their earlier discussion.

Δ   ▲   Δ

With each passing day, the boys spent one less hour walking in the sunlight and one more walking in the moonlight. It was good that the more they walked at night, the brighter the moon became. They grew to prefer traveling at night, as the nighttime temperatures were ideal for walking. They used the extra hours in the morning to bathe and swim in the river.

Each morning, John pulled out the map to track their progress from the night before. He was sure they were covering less ground now than they had at the start. Not only were they traveling at a slower pace in the dark, but from the accumulated fatigue, they were also spending less time walking. With the way the moon lagged the sun, it was up more than twelve hours each day and there was no way the boys could maintain **that** pace.

At first, John was a little nervous that they would not meet their deadline. However, he relaxed the night of the first quarter. That night marked half way to the full moon, and when John mapped their location, he discovered they were easily two-thirds of the way to Edfu. He then reminded himself that Isis had told them to *only travel when the moon was up*, which did not mean that they had to travel that whole time. *I guess it'll all work out.*

For the second week of travel, John suggested they walk along the west bank of the Nile. The map clearly indicated that the city of Edfu was located on that side, so they had to cross the river at some point. Intuitively, he felt that now was as good a time as any. It was a warm day and a swim across the river was refreshing.

The next few days, the trek on the western bank felt more or less the same, however, with the moon nearing full, they were traveling almost exclusively at night. The penultimate evening was possibly the most difficult. By this point, the greenery surrounding the river grew thick, and with it came the animals.

All throughout that night, the boys heard rustling sounds and frequently thought they saw movement in the bushes. It was disconcerting. Neither was familiar with the animal life of the area, most especially the nocturnal breeds. Their fears got the best of them and they covered more ground that night than many of the previous only because they ran nearly half the time.

Dawn couldn't come soon enough for either of them. In the early light, the city of Edfu was well within sight. After the night they'd both had, the boys were happy to know that they could sleep nearer the city.

The next evening, the boys woke a few hours before sunset. The moon had not risen, so they couldn't begin their trek across the city, but their food supplies were low, so they decided to wander in search of a meal. Luckily, they didn't have far to go before stumbling across an eatery.

"Edfu is a larger city than I expected," Johannes said to John.

"I agree. The map didn't make that very clear. You know, now that we are here, I remember when we sailed by. It was the middle of the night and you were asleep. I was up on deck and could see the buildings and the many torches burning."

"These past few weeks," Johannes observed, "you've spent more time awake in the nighttime than in the daytime."

"And that is unusual for me. I have always been a morning person, early to bed, early to rise," John said proudly.

"I never noticed that about you," Johannes teased. "You always seem to get up late." Johannes smiled as he said this.

John made a face, then said, "OK, I got the early to bed part down, but the early to rise…I'm still working on that."

Johannes laughed. "You didn't seem to have any trouble staying up all night during Oktoberfest."

"That's because with all of the excitement, I quickly caught my second wind," John replied. "Once it kicked in, it was easy to stay up all night long. I guess that's why these past few weeks haven't been so bad. You know, energetically I feel different. Ever since these channelings, I feel like I need less sleep. I like to rest, and I **can** sleep when I try, but I don't feel like I **need** to as much."

The boys ate their first hot meal in nearly two weeks, which they thoroughly enjoyed. Their timing was good. As they walked out of the restaurant, the sun was setting and the moon could be seen just above the opposite horizon.

For a moment, John panicked, thinking he had miscalculated. "The moon looks full already," he said, but then assured himself that it was just an illusion.

As they started their walk, John thought back to the conversation during dinner. *Johannes mentioned Oktoberfest!* John's heart raced a little, with fear and regret. He realized that he missed an opportunity to broach the subject of their last night in Heidelberg. It took nearly half the night for him to let it go.

Johannes, meanwhile, didn't notice. He was distracted and entertained by the city. Edfu was not as lively as Cairo, but **was** active all night long. Locals, tourists, and backpackers milled about everywhere.

Shortly after midnight, with the moon overhead, John broke into the silence and suggested they take a break. It wasn't so much that he needed to rest (although he was tired of his obsessive thoughts); rather, he wanted to look at the scroll. In the dark, John held the map close to his face and said, "The temple appears to be located due west of the center of the town...I think."

"It feels like we are at the center now," Johannes replied. "Let's go over there. It'll be easier to read the map in the torchlight. And I bet that building is an inn."

The boys wandered over and sat against the wall below the torch. They were only a few paces from the door. Traffic was light, but a few still wandered into and out of the inn, even at that hour.

"I tell you what," Johannes said to John, "While you look at the map, I'm going to check out this place. If there is anyone around, I'll ask them how far the temple is from here." Before waiting for a response, Johannes stood up and walked inside.

John watched Johannes until he disappeared through the doorway. *He certainly knows his way around a city. I wish I were as comfortable in strange places as he is.*

Suddenly, John saw the last two years flash before his eyes. He saw himself in Asia, Northern Europe, and the Mediterranean. He saw all of the faces he'd met along the way. The fast paced vision included that very evening's trek across the city and ended abruptly in the present moment.

Then, clear as if spoken out loud, he heard a single word:
Done!

He laughed to himself. "OK, I see your point," he spoke out loud but softly, "I guess I've done pretty well by myself in strange lands, but I've always had help!"

He then heard again clearly:
Well?

He laughed once more. "You're right. Thank you. And thank you for reminding me."

Without actually seeing a face, John felt someone smile and he smiled in return. He couldn't claim to understand how he **felt** the smile, but he was completely confident that someone, somewhere was smiling at him.

No sooner had John's internal conversation ended than Johannes emerged from the inn with a key in hand. "Well, you were right. The temple is not more than a half an hour's walk from here. No reason to make the walk now. I booked us a room for the next two nights. I figure we can come back here after tomorrow's session because no matter what, we won't be traveling tomorrow night. Besides, there is a bar here and they are still serving. We can have a drink before retiring."

"Well don't forget," John said, "we can't eat after noon tomorrow, so we should plan for a good meal late in the morning."

"I thought that only applied to **you**," Johannes teased. It took John a moment, but once John realized this, they both laughed.

The boys walked inside and headed for the bar, which was located in a center courtyard under the stars. It was a very comfortable night to sit within the mix of moonlight and torchlight.

Before ordering, John asked himself if it was appropriate to drink. *I'm not supposed to eat after noon tomorrow, but is it OK if I have a drink now?*

A single glass of wine will not interfere with tomorrow's session. We do not recommend anything stronger.

The barmaid greeted them and asked for their order. Both opted for a glass of red wine. "Whatever is good and local," Johannes added.

John was amazed at how good the first few sips tasted. It immediately relaxed him. He had almost forgotten how much he enjoyed that feeling.

By the time John finished his drink; he was ready to retire. "I'm heading to the room to get some sleep," he said to Johannes. "Are you coming?"

"You go ahead. I'll be up in a bit. I'm not quite ready to go to sleep yet."

John wandered off to the room. A bit later, Johannes headed out to explore the nightlife that Edfu had to offer.

At one point during the night, John woke to find that Johannes had not yet returned. Some part of him burned with jealousy. "He must have gone out. Maybe he met someone," he said to himself. He then thought: *Why do I care? I have no claim on him*.

John got up and looked out the window. He tried to determine how late it was. He couldn't see the moon, but the long shadows told him how low it had gotten.

I have to deal with these feelings I have for Johannes. Someday, he is going to meet a good woman. Oh God, I hope it's a woman... I don't know if I could handle seeing him with another man.

In that moment, John felt completely alone. He crawled back into bed and hugged his pillow, but that offered little comfort. Nearly an hour later, right as he was finally drifting off to sleep, the door creaked and Johannes entered. John stiffened and pretended to be asleep. *Thank God he's alone*—he thought.

Johannes crawled into his own bed and was lightly snoring within minutes.

The sound of Johannes' breathing comforted John, and he too quickly drifted off.

The next morning when John woke, he was surprised to find Johannes already out of bed. "You're up already?" he asked.

"Yeah. I don't sleep well after a few drinks. I'll take a nap later, in the afternoon."

"That's a good idea, actually." John then confessed, "I didn't sleep that well either."

"Was it the wine or are you getting nervous?"

"I don't know." John tried to mask his thoughts from Johannes.

Johannes eyed John for a moment before asking, "What would you like to do today?"

"I would **love** to have a cup of coffee. I haven't had coffee in weeks; I miss it. After that, we can sit down for a meal to tide us over until after the session."

"That sounds good. I saw a café on my way home last night about two blocks from here. Let's go there."

The boys discussed the advantages of urban life while enjoying a thick, strong cup of coffee. Both agreed that they preferred living in the city, but liked getting out of it as often as they could. After lunch, they walked to the temple to scope it out.

"The Temple of Edfu is the most popular tourist attraction in Upper Egypt," Johannes said, echoing what the concierge had told him the night before. "It is also one of the largest."

Yet knowing that the Temple was large did not prepare the boys for what they saw. The façade itself was massive. The temple looked more like a fortress than a shrine. The enormous façade towered over the neighboring buildings. Its apparent size suggested that it was close, yet as they walked further, it simply grew larger.

At the edge of the temple square, John could tell that images were etched into the side of the monolith. They were still too far to make out specific details. The distance across the plaza felt equally as great as the number of city blocks they traversed before entering it. Nothing stood between them and the shrine except for the numerous visitors that milled about, ant-like by comparison.

With each step closer, the feeling of awe within John increased. "Johannes," John said excitedly, "look at the images of Horus!"

"And the female images are of Hathor," Johannes said, remembering something else the concierge had told him.

When they got closer, both noticed the twin statues flanking the entrance simultaneously. John pointed and Johannes nodded. The sleek statues depicted Horus as a falcon with his characteristic double crown. The twin falcons stood proudly and stared straight ahead.

Before entering the temple, Johannes voiced his concern about the mass of tourists, "So, how do you suppose we're going to get any peace around here for the session? There is surely going to be some people wandering around after sunset. Are you sure we should sit then?" Johannes was concerned for John, but more because of how it would look to tourists if they overheard John speaking as Ra. He just wasn't sure how people would react.

"Let's not worry about that now," John replied. "Why don't we take a tour of the temple to get a feel for it? I am sure it will be interesting; this place is amazing! Then, when we come back before sunset, we'll just do whatever feels right. It's worked for us so far."

"That sounds reasonable."

The tour of the temple lasted longer than the boys had expected. They hurried back to the inn to catch an hour of sleep before returning to the temple.

Johannes, once again fell fast asleep as soon as his head hit the pillow. John listened to his friend's breathing and resigned to the fact that he probably would not sleep. He simply relaxed and enjoyed the solace, not forcing it either way.

Although John never felt like he had crossed over into sleep, a knock at the door roused him from someplace other than wakefulness. *Could it be that time already?*

They had asked the clerk to wake them with enough time to get to the temple before sunset. John climbed out of bed to answer the door, but no one was there. He went to the window and saw the long shadows of the early evening sun. *Yup, it's time to get up.*

John shook Johannes to wake him. Johannes, not at all excited about getting up, grunted and rolled over away from him. John decided to get himself ready and would try again in a few minutes if Johannes did not get up on his own. Luckily, Johannes was up when he came back from the washroom.

The boys exited the room, but then Johannes turned and rushed back in. A moment later, he re-emerged displaying the small statue of Horus. "We mustn't forget **him**," Johannes smiled proudly, "especially for **this** session. This is, after all, the Temple of Horus we're going to!"

John laughed to himself thinking: *The skeptic is the one remembering to bring his statue of Horus along. How funny is that?*

As they walked back to the temple, the boys remained quiet. Johannes was still half asleep. John was pensive; he was nervous. *How many sessions will it take before I stop fretting?*—he wondered. *What am I so afraid of?*

When they arrived at the temple square, it was much quieter than they had expected.

"I guess most of the tourists are out having dinner now, or getting ready to," John said to Johannes. "After this afternoon, I thought there would be crowds all through the night!"

"You know, in Europe, we would never get away with visiting ancient sites like this at night." Johannes, in a rare moment, spoke of home. "The sites there are heavily guarded; there's always someone watching to make sure no one touches anything or does something they're not supposed to. And, of course, many of them are locked up for the night."

John typically did not think about it much, but between Johannes' golden hair and fair skin, there was no mistaking him for anything other than European. John's dark hair and olive skin allowed him to blend in almost anywhere along the Mediterranean.

Before entering the temple, John looked east to make sure the full moon had not yet risen. He then looked west estimating how much time was left until sunset. With the temple nearly deserted and enough daylight remaining, John allowed himself to walk around following his inclinations. He played back the tour from earlier that day.

The temple façade, they were told, was called a pylon and stood much taller and wider than the rest of the structure. It faced south and marked the entrance to the temple. The impressive wall, as they had noticed earlier, was visible for many blocks and towered over all other structures in the city.

Behind the pylon, the temple itself was constructed as a series of rooms or halls. The first and largest was the Peristyle Hall. The Court of Offerings, as it was also known, was unroofed except for a perimeter ceiling held up by a colonnade. At this hour, all but the eastern edge of the court was shrouded in the shadow of the western wall.

From the Peristyle Hall, the entrance to the inner chambers was guarded by two statues of Horus depicted as a falcon-headed man. The first room, called the Pronaos, or Hypostyle Hall, stretched the full width of the temple and contained two rows of columns. The columns, in fitting with the scale of the temple, were themselves colossal, both in height and thickness. John felt like a small child crawling among the legs of giants. He felt as if at any moment one of them could unintentionally crush him.

The columns, John guessed, must have had purpose far beyond merely supporting the roof. Like the rest of the structure, images were carved along their entire surface. They were placed closer together than he thought necessary. The room had been dim during the daytime, but was dark now.

Despite his apprehension, John remained among the monoliths for a while. He ran his hands over the cool stone and trace a finger within the etchings. *If they could only speak, what would they say? What scenes have they witnessed?*

Behind the Pronaos was a second Hypostyle Hall called the Festival Hall, or Naos. This room, also of columns, was much smaller than the Pronaos. A number of small chambers branched off of it and lined the outer walls.

John stood in the center of the Festival Hall and looked towards the back of the temple. The Hall of Offerings led to the holy Sanctuary of Horus. At that hour, there was not enough light to see into it. The intimacy of the innermost chamber kept John from going any further. The darkness added an ominous aura. John therefore made his way back through the temple into the Peristyle Hall.

"Johannes, I think this is where we should have the session. I'll sit over here with my back toward the entrance of the Pronaos. You can sit facing the statues of Horus. There is so much energy flowing out of that room and into this one. Can you feel it?"

Johannes shook his head. He looked up at the much larger versions of his statuette and was thankful for not feeling what John spoke of. While John continued walking around, he took inventory of the temple visitors.

Hardly any of the visitors milling about were tourists and this pleased Johannes. He was not concerned about the locals. He figured that if any of them noticed their session, they would probably just assume that they were performing a religious ritual and not think twice about it. It was a temple after all.

The last of the sunlight left the courtyard and John and Johannes walked out to the grand plaza. From there, they had a clear view of the eastern horizon. The few people left in the square all seemed to be heading out.

John tapped Johannes on the shoulder to get his attention. The full moon, not yet glowing, crept up just as the red sun neared the opposite horizon. It was like a changing of the guards, the light source of the day passing a baton to the light source of the night. The two had just a brief moment to greet each other while both were above the horizon.

"Do you think we'll have an audience again tonight?" Johannes asked.

"Gee, I hadn't thought about it," John replied. "I guess I wouldn't be too surprised; there are still a number of people walking around."

The boys watched the moon climb the eastern sky and begin to glow.

John listened for an energetic sign or felling to tell him it was time to begin. Much to his surprise, the sky grew completely dark before he felt anything. He ambled into the Peristyle Hall and Johannes followed. By the time the boys sat in their prescribed positions, the moonlight had already crept into the room.

Within moments, John started speaking.

Good evening my brothers. I am Horus. You were requested to travel to this, the Temple of Horus, and arrive by the full of the moon. You have done well. I am indeed the very same Horus this temple was named for. The attention placed on me by those who visit this temple enables me to reach through the veil more easily here than in any other location.

My dear friend Johannes, I wish to speak specifically to you for a moment. How does this communication feel to you? Does it by chance feel familiar? If it does, it is not by coincidence. I have been with you since your inception into this lifetime, in fact even before. One might say I am your spirit guide as I have been assigned to you by the greater part of you. Suffice it to say, Master Johannes, it is an honor and a pleasure to communicate with you in this manner.

I am here with another. We are two among the many of Ra. One moment...

John paused waiting for the urge to speak again. The energy shifted and he felt it. He almost thought the connection was lost until suddenly he found himself speaking again.

Good evening. I am the one called Seth or sometimes Set. It is now my turn to speak and I wish to first share some words with you, John. You may have noticed that this part of the conversation flows more effortlessly than any other, including that of a few moments ago. That is because I am to you as Horus is to Johannes. I am **your** spirit guide. You have grown to hear me well and this brings me joy.

As your companion, I am well versed on your purpose in this lifetime. Although I do not work with Johannes directly, I do work closely with Horus. As such, I am well informed on his life purpose as well. In fact, our combined purpose forms a collaboration. Prior to your birth and beyond your human awareness, we agreed to work together, the four of us.

The potential of this meeting here in the Temple of Horus has been known for a long time. It was fully within your free will to support or resist this potential. We are grateful that you have chosen to comply.

Isis has made known the success of her discourse with you concerning the oversoul, what she refers to as your higher self. Tonight's topic is the lower self: the combination of soul, ego, and body that is uniquely the man you see when looking in the mirror.

We have been commissioned this discussion based on our own individual paths of expansion. Both Horus and I have incarnated many times in the earth realm. In fact, we have not been long removed from it. In your perception of time, it has been many a year, but not so long from our perspective.

You experience time in a linear flow, moment to moment. This is an illusion. The true nature of time is beyond your ability to comprehend, but do understand that it is not as you experience it.

Some might say we are beings from a different place. Others may even think we are of a different time. In truer reality, we are neither separated from you by time nor space. Yet, we neither live on your planet earth nor swim in your river of time, except perhaps, in situations such as this.

The fact remains that we occupy a **location** outside of your time and space; it is rather a function of vibration. The different realms vibrate within different ranges. It is the **translation** of vibration, the stepping up and the stepping down, which provides for sight, communication, and experience between the realms.

There are beings that are called mid-wayers for they exist within a vibratory range halfway between your reality and ours. They have the ability to manipulate physical matter in ways that Horus and I cannot. They live among you, but go mostly unseen. When you catch the glimpse of a shadow only to find no one there, you have likely peered into their existence for just a moment.

In a similar fashion, we exist halfway between the vibratory range of your lower self and your oversoul. It is for this reason we are commissioned to interface with you. We are better able to communicate through words, thoughts, and images, yet we yield completely to the will of your higher self.

At the moment of your death, understand that you will transcend the gap between your lower self and higher self instantaneously. We will all be reunited and in that moment you will remember us.

Horus and I have birthed and shed human bodies numerous times. We now have complete memory of all of them. You have also birthed many lives; you simply do not remember them.

Although we are the very same Horus and Seth that lived long ago in your past, do not view us as gods. Let it be know that the current mythologies have drifted far from the true events that transpired.

You do not need gods or goddesses. It is better for you to view us as your partners, your associates within the dimensions.

Let us now speak with you about the aspect of self you would call your human self. The human self, in its limited awareness, knows only roughly where it is and vaguely where it wants to go. This is multidimensional. You are many things at once and you desire many things. The human self is more sophisticated than you realize. Nonetheless, you are who you are.

You identify yourself in many ways: by your name, your race, your culture, your family, your place of origin, your profession, etc. You also identify yourself via time and place. For example, one moment you might say, 'I am here,' and later find yourself thinking, 'I am now somewhere else.'

Note, however, that even if you occupy the same location as before, you will be **somewhen** else. You can be in the same **place**, but never the same **time**.

Listen carefully to this phrase we have coined for you this evening: 'somewhen else'. In every moment you are some<u>when</u> else…and thus, in every moment, you are some<u>one</u> else.

In other words, you are ever changing.

Now, let us tell you why the human self, without the higher self, has such difficulty becoming what it desires. In every moment, there is where you are (the here and now) and where you want to be (the sum total of your desires). As we have already stated, you have never before been where you are now because even if you have been in this location, it was in a different time. And you have never been where you hope to be either, not precisely.

So your human self constantly finds that it is in an unfamiliar place seeking to go where it has never been before. If you have never been in either the starting place, or the destination, then how could you expect to know the path in between?

Worse yet, by the time the human self fully realizes the full extent of the present moment; that moment has already passed. Thinking takes time and thus it is impossible for the mind to keep up. So the human self has limited perception of the now, imperfect memory of the past, and nearly no awareness of the future!

Yet the human self, as taught by others, tries to use its past to create a map to what is desired for the future. You are expected to learn from those who came before you. Yet it was different then!

Humankind has invented a field you call science, which constantly tries to create repeatable processes thus identifying supposed laws of the physical Universe. To attain precise repeatability, one has to control the experiment well and not allow aspects to vary. The resulting science is then accepted as religion and applied to the workings of all human behavior.

Yet how do you propose to utilize science within your personal lives? You cannot control all of the variables because one of the most significant is time. You are always **somewhen** else. You are never in the same time twice. You can never control the influences that time has on you, and thus you can never get exactly the same results in the future as you had in the past.

Ah, but there is a solution. You will find the best results when you allow the higher self to be an integral part of your process. You state your desires readily, however, it is your **intention** and **attention** that allows—or not—those aspects to be created in your specific time and space. The art of successful manifestation is the coaxing of desired experience into your dimly lit present.

You each are surrounded by a multitude of unactualized manifestations even in this moment. You think they are separated from you in time or space, yet from our vantage, the probabilities have already been created. Focus on those you desire and your experience will be pleasant. Call forth those you fear, and brace yourself for discomfort.

You were asked to travel only when the moon was high. This was to illustrate an example. As you noticed, the more you traveled at night, the more you fell prey to your fears. That is because your sight became further limited.

In human experience, cycles exist similar to that of the moon and the sun. At times, sunlight will prevail and thus you will see clearly. At other times, you will be encased in fog or trudging through the dim light of the moon.

When blinders obscure your eyes, your inner sight grows. In those times, your imagination paints what is not seen. Color a dim scene with fear or hate and watch the monsters emerge.

Your human self really does stumble around blindly, fearing all that lurks in the shadows. But it doesn't have to. You have access to the power of the higher self. You have more than the five senses you take for granted.

Johannes, please take note of these instructions.

Seth gave Johannes a moment to fetch John's journal.

The two of you are now asked to walk independent paths, to exercise your greater senses, and to follow your own star. A reflected sun shall represent youth to one, and maturity to the other. Seek she who is called by three names and is companion to kings. You will find her where a crescent indicates location and long dark fingers track the flow of time. The mighty sphinx of Giza was indeed erected in the Age of Leo and forever looks to the rising sun, which is the ruling influence of that sign. Allow her kin to be your guides, welcoming you to your destination.

This test allows each of you to set your own true intention. Together, your influence, one to the other, is strong. What will you choose on your own? And what will you create? You have been given tools; will you employ them? Which orb shall be your master?

We say good night to you as this communication draws to a close, but know that we are always with you.

The transmission ended and Horus and Seth watched as John and Johannes considered the information given them.

Horus turned to Seth and said, "So Seth, do you want to make a wager as to who gets there first?"

"Oh boy, do I," Seth responded. "I can taste sweet victory already!"

The two points of light laughed delightfully with each other, vaguely recalling the human selves they once were.

SEVEN OF WANDS

The impact of the channeled message overwhelmed John and he wasn't ready to talk about it. He stood up, grabbed his belongings, and headed out of the Peristyle Hall without saying a word.

Johannes followed. He sensed that John had gone into one of his pensive, possibly emotional states and he knew better than to say anything until John was ready.

John remained mute for the remainder of the evening.

The next morning when Johannes woke, John was already up, but not in the room. Johannes noticed his bag, packed up and lying on the empty bed. Johannes got up and began collecting his belongings, trying to decide where John would have gone. By the time Johannes had all of his items organized, John walked in.

"You were up early today," Johannes said by way of a greeting.

"I had trouble sleeping. For some reason, I am nervous about heading back to Cairo on my own. I don't want to be alone right now."

"Yeah," Johannes agreed. "I've been enjoying the company as well." He quickly followed with, "Do you want to talk about that riddle some before we part? They told us to travel separately, but they didn't say it had to happen right away."

John felt some relief. "You're right! How about we spend another night in the inn and then head north after that?"

"Sure. Shouldn't be a problem. But are you certain we are to go north?" Johannes asked.

"I can't imagine they are sending us south," John reasoned. "And there is nothing but desert east and west. Let's talk about it over breakfast. I'm starved."

The boys left the inn and stopped at the first eatery they encountered. During breakfast, they went over the various parts of the riddle.

John started the discussion. "To start, Let's focus on the part about the sun reflected in the river."

"Wait a minute," Johannes interrupted. "They said, 'A reflected sun...' but didn't say anything about the river."

"Hmm. I just assumed they meant reflected in the river. What else would it be?"

The boys thought for a moment.

Johannes gave up first, "I can't think of any thing else. Let's assume you're right." Reading from the notebook, he added "So, 'A reflected sun shall represent youth to one, maturity to the other.' Hmm. We're pretty much the same age, so what could that mean?"

"I'm guessing they meant youth and maturity symbolically."

"OK. Youth could mean play and maturity seriousness."

"Yeah, but youth could also mean the beginning and maturity the end, as with life."

"That makes sense," Johannes concurred. "So the beginning and end of what?"

John remained quite as he considered the possibilities.

"The sun reflected in the river," Johannes echoed the phrase and looked up. "Hey, wait a minute. It is easiest to see the sun reflected in the river when it is low in the sky, rising or setting, depending on what side of the river you are on. Maybe that's what they meant. If we are being asked to travel on opposite sides of the river, then one of us will see the reflection of the sunrise while the other will see the reflection of the sunset."

John slapped the table lightly. "That has **got** to be it! They talked about walking independent paths, so it would just make sense that they were telling us to be on opposite sides of the river. That would ensure that we don't run into each other."

Having accepted the interpretation of the first line, the boys went on to discuss who would be on which side.

"How about this," Johannes suggested in his practical way, "my home country is to the west, so I'll walk along the west bank and your home country is to the east, so you can walk along the east bank."

"That's fine. So do you want to try figuring out the rest?"

They worked on the next few lines, but had no success. They decided to let it go for a while and headed back to the room.

The rest of the day went by quickly, and although they discussed the riddle frequently, they made no further progress in solving it. Since they only had the one map of the river valley, they decided to draw a copy of it. The hand drawn map was not as detailed as the other, but Johannes was less concerned and let John have the original.

Over dinner, the boys talked about everything except the imminent separation and journey. They savored their time: together and within the confines of a city.

The following morning, the boys parted ways after a hurried goodbye. Neither wanted to show vulnerability in front of the other. Johannes headed north while John made his way east towards the main port.

John quickly regretted agreeing to travel along the east bank.

When John sought transportation, everyone he encountered questioned why he wanted to cross the river. "There's nothing on that side for miles," each one replied. John finally found one man who begrudgingly agreed to drop him off on the eastern shore, but not without trying to talk him out of it the whole time.

On foot heading north, John's regret shifted into anxiety. He couldn't fight the feeling that he had made a mistake. His chest tightened and his breathing strained. Walking felt more like climbing. *What is going on with me?* He tried to put it out of his mind, but found the physical sensation worsening. He could no longer deny that he was scared.

"What am I so afraid of?" he asked. He wondered if traveling alone was his primary concern, but quickly dismissed it. *I've traveled alone so much these past two years; surely that's not it.* Convinced, he then explored other possibilities. *Am I afraid I'll never find Johannes again? This **is** an opportunity for him to run off again!* John knew that if Johannes fled, he'd feel hurt again; *but I couldn't blame him for wanting to leave all of the weirdness behind. I survived the first time; I can survive a second one.* Despite the self-encouragement, his anxiety grew stronger. The weight on his chest felt as if his lungs were collapsing.

John sat down and tried unsuccessfully to breathe more deeply. *Calm down. Focus. Things have been going really well these past few weeks. Better than you expected. It will all work out. You can handle this.* He looked at his situation objectively, but still could not eliminate the fear in his body. *There must be something else going on.*

John again trudged north, but slowly. He continued to search for the cause of his anxiety. The added stress on his body soon exhausted him. By late afternoon, he was ready to setup camp for the night. The sun barely set before he fell fast asleep.

Some hours later, John woke abruptly from a dream. His heart was racing. In the dream, he had encountered a man who had fallen into a large hole in the ground. John heard the man yelling for help. When he peered over the edge to investigate, he saw the man clinging to a tree root that extended out from the inner wall of the hole. The man was just within reach, but only when John lay on his stomach and extended his arm.

John's dream self was not scared, but the man was terrified. He could not see the bottom of the pit, only an abyss of darkness. John grabbed hold of the man's hand and used all of his strength to hoist him up. Little by little, the man, with John's help, inched out of the hole. Once he was high enough, his foot found the root he had been holding onto, and pushed up off of it.

The man's head was now above the edge of the hole. One hand clawed at the dirt while the other clutched John's hand. His one foot pushed harder at the root while his other searched for additional support.

John could feel their hands slipping from the moisture between them. "We have to hurry!" he pleaded.

Crack! John heard the root beneath the man's foot snap. He then felt the man's entire weight pull downward. The sweaty grip between them was no match.

Shrieking and flailing, the man disappeared into the darkness.

The man's screams echoed in John's now fully awakened mind. He was horrified by what happened in the dream. In addition to the fear and anxiety he had been feeling all day, he was now shrouded in grief.

John wrapped his arms around himself and shivered, partly from the dream, partly from the chill of the night. The panic from his dream stayed with him. The images and sounds repeated in his mind. He could still see the man's face and the horrified expression upon it.

John reminded himself that it was only a dream and was thankful that the man wasn't real. *But what does this mean? And why all of the anxiety? Was the dream a manifestation of my anxiety or was it a clue to the cause?* John had learned to trust the wisdom of his dreams, so he believed it meant something.

Δ   ▲   Δ

T he next day, as John plodded onward, the tightness in his chest kept him from breathing normally. He had to take frequent breaks. He felt like a fish out of water, straining to extract oxygen from the thin air. To make matters worse, the afternoon temperature rose unusually high for that time of year.

Given the circumstances, John decided to take an extended

break beneath a grove of palm trees. His body felt weak and although he only intended to wait out the hottest part of the day, he fell asleep.

In John's latest dream, he was standing on a pulpit in front of a congregation; all faces stared at him with anticipation. He looked down at a scroll in his hands, but couldn't make out the words. Everyone was there to hear him speak. In his mind, he called out to Ra, Isis, and Seth, but no one answered. Beads of sweat poured down his forehead.

He closed his eyes and searched for Ra's energy. The pressure of having to speak words of wisdom for a pleading audience weighed heavily on him. *Ra, don't desert me now!*

The anticipating Egyptian audience grew impatient.

Ra's words finally came and John felt himself relax. As usual, he was listening more than speaking. Ra introduced himself and then spoke of his plan. Instead of wise and loving words, he was stern. He reprimanded the crowd for their sins, their misinterpretation of the laws, and their manipulation of history, **his** history.

John saw fear and then anger form in the eyes of all that looked upon him. He tried, but couldn't stop himself from speaking for Ra. The anger in the audience provoked rage in Ra and John found himself bellowing with fire and brimstone. *Ra, why are you doing this? You have angered them and now they are going to come after me!*

No sooner had John expressed his fear than the people rose up out of their seats. Many of them waved fists and clubs. Brusquely, John broke free of Ra's energy and fled the incensed crowd. *I did it now! They are furious. They are going to kill me! Ra, why have you forsaken me?*

John ran away from the village—out into the desert. He soon found himself clambering up a hill of sand in the midday heat. The sand was soft and carried him downward, despite his efforts. He peered over his shoulder and saw the horde advancing, ever closer and ever louder.

He somehow managed to reach the top of the hill and found a staff protruding from the sand. It was the staff of Ra. He pulled it out of the ground and turned to face the throngs that scurried up the hill after him. He didn't see faces, just the sticks and clubs that were swung in his direction.

At first, John held steady against the ambush, but then an especially strong thrust knocked him off balance. He scrambled to regain his footing, but the sand was too soft. As soon as he reached the edge of the mound, he fell backward. He flailed in panic, then struck bottom with a jolt.

John's body shuddered awake. He was lying on the ground in the same position as he landed in the dream. And he was drenched.

The sun had shifted while he slept and was now in his eyes, along with sweat, tears, and sand. He squinted against the light.

EIGHT OF WANDS

S hadowed figures stood over John and encircled him. Each looked down at him and then across to the others.

"What shall we do about this?" one said.

"I don't believe there is anything we can do," another responded. "He has clearly fallen into a vortex of fear. But we mustn't intervene."

"Surely, there must be **something** we can do to help?" pleaded a third. "Is there not someone we can entice to his side to assist him, or possibly distract him?"

"He has had distraction enough from this fear," came an authoritative voice. "That is why it has grown so. It was necessary for the Two within One to be separated lest this fear grew further. It is now up to him to release it and resolve its cause. Unless he asks for assistance, we shall **not** meddle."

"Maybe he is not ready to proceed," reasoned one with a demure voice. "Alas, there is nothing to fear. All is perfect as it is. He will find his way…eventually…and we will be there for him when he calls."

Δ   ▲   Δ

J ohn wiped his eyes to clear his sight. He looked up at the palm trees swaying in the breeze. For a moment, he thought a group had gathered around him. He could swear he heard voices. *Was I still dreaming? Must have been the trees and the wind.*

He stood up and brushed off the sand that had accumulated while he slept. The wetness of his shirt cooled him in the desert breeze. He looked to the sky and tried to determine how long he had slept. He then noticed that his anxiety was gone. He had almost forgotten what it felt like to breathe normally.

He thought about the dream…and the odd impression he had when he first woke. "What was **that** all about? I wish I understood what's going on with me."

In a flash of insight, John found the answer. In the dream, he had enacted an unconscious fear. He now realized that, despite Johannes' participation in the channeled sessions, John felt like one against the world. He felt the weight of responsibility.

What if people are offended by the words I bring through? Will these ideas challenge and anger them? And what if they take it out on me? Will this 'work' bring me pain and suffering at the hands of an angry mob?

Yet knowing the fear did not rid him of it. *If I'm still afraid, why has the anxiety gone?*

Again, in a burst of understanding, John realized that the anxiety was his body's way of communicating with him. It was not that he had to **overcome** the fear for relief, but it was important for him to be fully cognizant of it. The **unconscious nature** of the fear is what caused it to eat away at him, blocking ease and wellbeing.

John's newfound understanding, plus the relief from the anxiety, enabled an energetic excitement to rise up within him. He was ready to continue his journey northward. He pulled out his map to see what lay ahead. He then heard cries overhead and looked up. Eight white ibises flew in formation above him. They were traveling north.

John smiled and admired the birds for their beauty and grace. When he looked back down at his map, he suddenly saw **into** it as if seeing the landscape from the eyes of the ibises above. The trees swayed and the river flowed within the drawing, and the sunlight reflected on the water.

John followed the river northward; it turned east and then gracefully arched back to the west tracing the shape of the crescent moon.

"Oh my God! That's it! That's the crescent that Seth spoke of!" John reiterated line from the riddle, "...where a crescent indicates location..."

John looked up to the ibises, placed his hands together, and bowed slightly, thanking them for their conveyed perspective.

Δ ▲ Δ

Johannes encountered one small village after the next and he traveled north. He quickly discovered that in this part of Upper Egypt, most lived along the more fertile western bank of the Nile. He often thought of John and wondered how he was faring on the eastern side.

Following a routine, whenever Johannes entered a village, he first asked if there were significant temples near by. If it was late in the day, or if he was in the mood for a break, he next asked about inns and taverns.

After a couple of days, Johannes entered a town that had a temple. It was called Esna and had been previously known as Latopolis. The temple was located near the center of town and was dedicated to the god Khnum, not surprisingly, one Johannes had never heard of. Johannes figured it was worth checking out nonetheless.

The temple was in good condition and contained a hypostyle hall of columns similar to the Temple of Horus in Edfu. Unlike the other, this temple was not as well known. Johannes had a hard time finding anyone who could answer his questions.

He ultimately found a man posing as a tour guide, but was suspicious because the man didn't have much information to offer. Johannes thanked him for his time and continued on his away.

Before Johannes got far, the man came running after him, "Sir, I must confess that I do not know much about the temple of Esna. I am, however, knowledgeable of other sites you might find of interest. You say you are heading north, yes? In two days travel, we can reach the Temple of Luxor. It is located on the eastern bank of the Nile. I have friends in the city, which was previously known as Thebes, and can arrange transportation across the river. I can also arrange for luxurious accommodations, if that is pleasing to you."

Johannes, a seasoned negotiator, hesitated, wanting to see what else the man would offer.

"If you prefer, sir, I can also arrange for you a tour. We can visit the tombs in the Valley of the Kings, such as Ramesses VI, Ramesses IX, and Tutankhamen. They are located just beyond the ancient city of Waset, as it was called then."

"Wait a minute," Johannes' mind churned. "Did you say Valley of the **Kings**?"

"Yes sir. It is the most popular section within the Theban Necropolis. There are at least three days worth of sites worth visiting. It is outside of the city and away from the river. I do not recommend traveling there without a knowledgeable guide like myself, as the desert can be very harsh and dangerous."

"And did you say that the city of Luxor had **two** other names?"

"Yes sir. It was known as Waset before the Greeks renamed it Thebes."

Johannes thought back to the riddle, *Seek she who is called by three names and is companion to kings.* "You've sold me. I will stay here in Esna tonight and then in the morning we can head to Luxor. I will pay you for your time, but as of yet, I am unsure what sites I will visit."

NINE OF WANDS

John's newfound ambition from having solved the clue about the crescent propelled him through the next few days before dissipating. His progress was slower than he had hoped and he did not acquire any new information about that area. From the map, there appeared to be a city toward the bottom of the sweeping arc of the river, but it wasn't labeled. The women who created the map must have only known of their trip to Edfu and nothing more.

John was frustrated. He hoped to obtain some information in the next town along the river, but went two more days before encountering one. All of the small villages shown on his map were on the opposite side of the river. The few people he did encounter on the east bank didn't speak any of his languages.

In a typical encounter, John showed them the map and pointed to the city he wanted to know about. In each case, he received a nod and a response he didn't understand. He thought he would at least learn a name, but after a few encounters, he couldn't pull out any words in common. He was just going to have to wait until he reached the next substantial village. There appeared to be a good-sized town coming up on the other side of the river, so he hoped that there would also be a settlement on his side at least substantial enough to find someone he could speak with.

The next day, John saw structures up ahead. Across the way was indeed a good-sized town. The river banked slightly to the east, but not enough to indicate that he had reached the crescent. He looked at the map and guessed that he had arrived at the last post before reaching the city. At the very least, he was able to find some food there.

After filling his stomach, John asked around for information. The first thing he learned explained some of the difficulty he had encountered earlier. The city nearby, now called Luxor, had only been recently renamed from its previous, Thebes. He recognized both of those names from earlier conversations.

He was also happy to know that Luxor was a large city and was located on the eastern bank of the river. *Finally, something on **my** side!* Now that he thought about it, he roughly remembered passing through Luxor on the way south. He wished that he had not been so anti-social then. *If I attended the tours, I might have figured out more of the riddle by now.*

Although he obtained good information on the city, no one he spoke with could tell him about the sites. All assured him that Luxor had plenty to offer the foreign traveler, but none gave details that resembled anything from the riddle. John was happy to know that the city could be reached in a single day's travel, if he left first thing in the morning. *I just want this part of the trip to be done.*

John rented a room for the night in a modest inn. He slept soundly and was completely refreshed by sunrise.

While John walked, he used the position of the sun to determine the direction of the river. This enabled him to gage his progress. Up ahead, the river was still bending slightly to the west.

By noon, with the sun overhead, John wondered whether he would notice if the river banked back to the east. When it did, he was happy to see that it was not a subtle shift. The river took a sharp right turn and headed directly east. He studied the map and estimated he was half way to Luxor with plenty of sunlight remaining to complete the journey.

John was thankful to be walking east. That put the sun behind him. He now entertained himself by monitoring his shadow, which, for the time being, pointed the way to Luxor.

At the outermost edge of the city, the river banked slightly to the north. John noticed this mostly from the change in direction of his shadow. As the day went on, the length of his shadow grew longer.

"Whoa, I think I just figured out part of the riddle," he muttered to himself. "'You will find her where a crescent indicates location and long dark fingers track the flow of time.' That's it! The length of my shadow indicates how late in the day it is. My shadow doesn't look like a finger, but the shadow of an obelisk does!"

John was excited, but couldn't help but think—*With all of the dream images of obelisks, I should have thought of this earlier. Then again*—he reasoned—*my dreams always took place at night, so I never saw the obelisks' shadows.* Furthermore, he hadn't visited to a temple that had obelisks intact and standing upright. *That's got to be it. We must be looking for a temple that has at least one obelisk that's still standing!*

John was tired and hungry, but neither of these sensations could compare to the desire to discuss his ideas with someone. *I have to find out if there are obelisks nearby.* Rather than search for lodging or food when he entered Luxor, John sought anyone who knew about the local temples and sites.

Toward the center of town, John was excited to find signs of tourism. A number of booths selling tours clustered together in one area reminded him of Cairo. He picked the first one he came to, but after waiting impatiently behind a group of inquisitive tourists, he decided on another.

"Good evening sir. Can I help you?" the merchant asked him.

"Yes you can! I would like to know if there are obelisks in town?"

"Are you an archeologist, sir?"

"No, I am just interested in obelisks. I have been to a number of temples in Egypt, but have yet to see an obelisk that is still standing. Are there any here or nearby?"

"Well, sir, you will be happy to know that indeed, three have survived here in our great city of Luxor. The Greeks and Romans carted away so many of them. They decorate **their** foreign cities with **our** history." The merchant's voice rose in pitch and volume, indicating his anger with the ancient invaders. He then composed himself and continued, "The first one is located at the Temple of Luxor, just north of here. The other two are located at the Temple of Karnak also in the northern part of the city. The Temple of Karnak is still within the city limits these days, but in the past, Karnak was a village in its own right. These are the three tallest obelisks that remain standing in all of Egypt."

"Hmm, I wonder which temple I am supposed to go to," John mumbled out loud, but to himself.

"Excuse me sir?"

"Oh, nothing. I would like to take a tour of the temples. Is there time enough this evening?" John looked up and saw that it was dusk. "Oh, I guess not."

"No sir, I am sorry, but there are tours available all day tomorrow."

"How early do you start?"

John booked the first available tour that included both temples.

"They are fairly close to each other," the merchant said to him. "A single road connects the two temples. It has been recently restored to its full and original glory!"

John wandered pensively, resisting the urge to head straight over to the temples. *I guess I can wait one more day. Besides, I still haven't eaten.* Now that he had satisfied his hunger for information, his stomach complained loudly.

Δ ▲ Δ

J ohannes made his way back to the inn. He had spent two full days in Luxor and had toured both temples…**twice**! Somehow, he had neglected to retain any memory of the place from his first visit during the trip south to Philae. *That seems like such a long time ago.*

As soon as he arrived at the temple in Luxor the first day, he realized that he had already been there. *No harm done*—he thought because he had only seen the one temple. *This time I get to visit and learn all about the Karnak temple as well.*

Two full days of touring helped Johannes interpret only one additional clue from the riddle, the part regarding the mighty sphinx of Giza. *Allow her kin to be your guides, welcoming you to your destination.* That line became immediately obvious since running between the two temples was nothing less than the *Avenue of the Sphinxes!* Miniature versions of the original lined the entire length of the street on both sides.

I guess I'm where I'm supposed to be. I can't imagine there are other sphinx-lined avenues like this in Egypt! Now where is that John? I'm even on his side of the river; he should have been here by now!

XIX – THE SUN

T hey sure are lax around here. In Cairo, tours start at sunrise! John laughed at his impatience.

The air was cool and the sun was shining; it was a beautiful day. The tour guide showed up shortly after a number of other tourists had gathered around John. They walked the short distance to the Luxor temple.

As soon as John saw them, he laughed out loud. *Well, I guess that's obvious.*

The others tourists looked at him questioningly.

John pointed to the sphinxes that lined the avenue, as if that would clear up their confusion.

The others shook their heads, then turned their attention to the pylon, which marked the entrance to the temple.

John looked at the single obelisk where there should have been two. He then glanced down at its shadow. Sure enough, the long slender finger pointed more or less west indicating early morning.

John soon learned that the Temple of Luxor was also called the Temple of Amon Ra. This intrigued and confused him.

The tour guide explained that Amon was not only the name of an Egyptian god, but it was used by more than one pharaoh as well. He didn't, however, explain the 'Ra' part. John thought to ask about it, but decided against it.

John was sure that the Temple of Luxor was the right temple… until they arrived at the Temple of Karnak. He learned that the Temple of Karnak was the largest temple supported by columns and was home to the tallest obelisk in Egypt.

Although John could not decide which temple was the correct one, he was sure it was one of them.

Now where is that Johannes? I hope he didn't pass right by Luxor? I can't imagine it took him longer to get here than me, unless he decided to spend a few nights out on the town somewhere!

John, excited with his discovery, didn't even consider the possibility that Johannes wouldn't show up…eventually.

Δ   ▲   Δ

J ohannes spent the morning walking from one café to the next, but did not find John. He thought about asking if anyone had seen him, but then decided against it. *A man with dark hair, olive skin, and green eyes doesn't stand out enough here.*

The day was cool and comfortable, so Johannes decided to take one last stroll along the Avenue of the Sphinxes hoping for some inspiration as to what to do next. His walk from the Temple of Luxor to the Temple of Karnak and back took just about all of the remaining afternoon. By the time he approached the Temple of Luxor a second time, he noticed the sun reaching a deep orange color. *If John is here in Luxor, he will surely be at the entrance to one of these temples at sunset. How could he resist? But which one? It's too late for me to make it back up to Karnak. I guess I'll hang out here until the sun goes down.*

Δ   ▲   Δ

J ohn's tour ended and rather than walk back to town with the group, he decided to wander on his own. The afternoon was interesting, but explained none of the unsolved riddle clues. He was still unsure which temple was the desired location.

John's mind churned as he marched down the Avenue of the Sphinxes on his way to his hotel. He glanced up at the sun and realized that he would not likely make it back to the inn before sunset. *When was the last time I ate?*

Clear as a friend standing next to him, John heard:

Since when do you think about food when the sun is setting?

"You have a point there. I am usually more interested in the sunset than food, but I'm hungry today."

Never mind food for the body, you ought to be focusing on food for the **soul!**

"Very funny, Seth." John was sure it was Seth communicating with him. *It's kind of nice that I can put a name to the voice.*

Don't be so sure it's me. I may be the one talking to you the most, but I am not the only one…

"OK, but getting back to the soul thing, do you have a recommendation?"

I thought you would never ask. Why don't you look down there, to the end of the avenue?

John saw the Temple of Luxor with its single off-centered obelisk. He also saw someone loitering around it.

"Is that who I think it is?"

Since you asked, I am obliged answer. Yes, it is. He has been here for three days now. I think he was about to give up on you.

"**He** give up on **me**?"

Now, now—be nice.

John hurried his pace some but didn't exactly have the energy to run. However, he didn't need to. Once Johannes caught sight of him, he knew it was John by his walk.

Upon meeting, Johannes hugged John firmly and said, "Welcome to Luxor!" with a tone as if John had just arrived.

"Thanks, but I got here yesterday."

"Good, so you got to visit the temples?"

"Yeah, Luxor this morning and Karnak this afternoon. So, I guess this is where they wanted us to be. But I am not sure which temple is **the one**."

"Me neither," Johannes admitted. "I haven't figured out half of the riddle either."

"Well I figured out the crescent and long dark fingers," John offered.

"You did?"

John pointed down to the long shadow that extended out from the base of the obelisk. "That's the long dark finger that tracks the flow of time. The crescent refers to the shape the river makes here."

"I didn't notice, but then again, you had the better map. Did you figure out the line before that?"

John shook his head. "Uh-uh."

"Good, cause I did. Luxor was previously called Thebes and before that Waset, so this is 'she who is called by three names.' Also, the Valley of Kings is nearby, just across the river and out into the desert, so she is also, 'companion to kings'."

"Amazing! We each figured out half of the remaining riddle; the

Avenue of the Sphinxes **was** pretty obvious. Do you think we missed anything? Don't you think they would have told us which temple?"

Did it ever occur to you to ask?

John started laughing and Johannes looked at him inquisitively. John then explained, "That's Seth. He started talking to me a few minutes ago. He was the one who pointed you out when I was down there. Anyway, he just asked me if it had ever occurred to me to ask them which temple was the right one. I guess it's pretty silly that I never thought to ask."

"Do you think he would have told you the whole meaning of the riddle if you asked him?"

"I just heard a 'yes'."

"Somehow, I think there is a lesson in that." Johannes said with a grin.

For Johannes' benefit, John continued his dialog with Seth out loud. "OK Seth, which temple are we supposed to have the next session and when?"

John then conveyed to Johannes what he heard. "He said that the temple doesn't matter, but he likes Luxor better because it is smaller. Oh, and he said tomorrow at noon. Noon? Seth, did you really mean noon? OK, I guess noon it is."

After a short pause, John said in a serious tone, "So, Johannes..."

"Yes?"

"Are you hungry?" John grinned widely.

"Yes. Let's go eat."

A bit later, as they walked with no specific direction in mind, Johannes added, "You know, I spent all morning looking for you among the cafés that are nearby. I thought I might catch you getting a coffee."

"Don't remind me," John replied. "I haven't had coffee since we parted. Would you believe that there was only one town on the east bank between Edfu and here?"

"I wondered about that," Johannes said thoughtfully.

"Yeah, and the morning I was there, I was so focused on getting here that I didn't spend the time to look for a café."

"Life is rough sometimes," Johannes said seriously; then they both burst into laughter.

Δ   ▲   Δ

T he next morning, after John had his coffee and they both ate, the boys wandered over to the temple.

"Where do you think we should do the session?" John asked Johannes.

"I don't know. Is Seth around? Ask him?"

"Seth?" John paused. "I am not getting an answer. You know, I can't hear him all of the time."

"Sounds like something to work on." Johannes paused, and then continued hesitantly, "Well, either I am talking to myself or Horus just told me that I might want to work on that myself."

John laughed. "Sounds like something Horus would say, not that I know him that well, but I have a feeling..."

The boys looked around for someplace away from the crowds, but the only place that felt right was in full sun. Each placed a cloth over his head, which had them looking like some of the locals, at least from a distance.

John entered into a trance more quickly than expected.

Good day my friends. We are Ra. You may question why this session is taking place at midday in the full of the sun, but you will soon see why.

First, I would like to congratulate you on your accomplishments. Not only did you arrive at the desired location in a timely manner, but you, John, worked through your fears. You are not through with the likes of them, but **you** are now **their** master, and that pleases us greatly.

For a moment, let us play with some of your words. As you have been told, Ra was known as the Sun God by the ancient Egyptian people. but why would Ra be associated with the sun?

In English, the words sun (s-u-n) and son (s-o-n) are homonyms, spoken the same with different meanings. You are a son of the Universe much as the sun is.

Now let us look at another language; the Italian word for sun (s-u-n) is *sole* (s-o-l-e). This word, as you know, is pronounced in two syllables, *sol-e*.

Now these same four letters, s-o-l-e, in English spell the word sole, meaning only. The Italian word for only is *solo* (s-o-l-o). Thus, only one letter differs between the Italian words *sole* and *solo*. The difference is 'e', which happens to be the Italian word è, meaning 'is.' From *sole*, sun, we get *'sol è'* or *'solo è'*—meaning 'it only is.'

Il sole solo è: the sun only is; the sun is only in a state of being. Throughout all of the day, the sun of your solar system shines its light, guiding all beings of earth toward a state of being. Think of all of those times when you take a break and sit in the sun, 'soaking it all in,' as you say.

Let's get back to the English word sole (s-o-l-e), which itself has a homonym, soul (s-o-u-l). The sole task of your soul is to be. Your soul is no different than the sun. Both are sons of the Universe, individual pieces of source and in a constant state of being, *solo è*.

Let's follow this through another exercise.

The Prime Decree is also known as THE ONE Being. In English, the phrase: 'THE ONE Being,' describes a thing, a single entity, the one and only being. However, 'THE ONE being,' is also a complete sentence, THE ONE being as opposed to THE ONE doing.

These exercises are meant to help you see that the highest you or your highest self, is **THE ONE** and the only one.

THE ONE has no worry. It has no need. It has no goal. The human you desires, and cannot help but to desire. The higher you creates, and thus becomes what it creates. The highest you is.

We have described to you the higher self and the lower self. When you move up, you move from the lower self into the higher self. But where is this highest self, the god self? It is within! The highest self is the space **in between**. It is in between the thoughts, in between the atoms, in between the smallest measure of time. It is the no thing in between the every thing, the nothing within everything.

The highest self contains no movement. Movement is an illusion. In ultimate reality, there is no space, and thus there is nowhere to go. The highest self **is**—always and forever. In every moment, it is and yet, it is something different in every moment.

It does not move out of one state of being and into another. It just is...then is...then is: now...now...now. The change does not occur in time, as time is also an illusion. The highest self does not evolve; it does not become. It just is.

When you attain God consciousness, you are everything all at once; you are every **thing** within THE ONE. You are every **one**. You are **THE ONE**, the **only** one.

It is very difficult to attain this state of oneness from your human consciousness. That is because you not only have to let go of your lower self consciousness, you must also let go of your higher self consciousness. You must let go of **self**-consciousness completely.

Nevertheless, you can still benefit from your god self by simply knowing that it exists. Even if you never gain access to it directly, you can allow the knowing of it to influence your life. Know that you simply are and always will be, that you need not become what you want to be, merely **be** it. It takes zero time to shift into being-ness.

The more you allow yourself to accept that the highest self exists, the more you allow all other selves to exist, not just your lower and higher selves, but the lower and higher selves of all others. The highest self of you and the highest self of me are one and the same. There is only one highest self and we are all a part of it.

Many within your realm view God as the supreme father/mother, an omnipotent being at the top of a hierarchy. In this way, man views God as **Source**. You came from your mother and father in the same way that all of creation comes from God, from Source.

However, in seeing God as a sentient being like one's mother or father, man has given God the same traits as his mother and father. Therefore, God is seen as loving and kind, but also punishing and vengeful. Many have, on occasion, feared their parents and have thus become God-fearing.

Man prays to God, asking for all he desires and protection from all he fears. In this way, man gives up his power to God and thus suffers.

For eons, man has searched for God, for the one true God. In the process, he has created many gods and goddesses and then argues with others as to which god or goddess is the true God/Goddess. It is time for man to stop looking for God in this way.

Some on your earth have advanced into a broader view of God, God as **All-That-Is**, the alpha and the omega, neither male nor female, but both. They see God as the creator **and** the creation. Your English word for God reflects this view.

Take a look: G-o-d. Position it vertically:

G

o

d

Above is 'g' meaning god, goddess, or good: the higher aspect of God. Below is 'd', meaning the devil (evil) or destruction: the lower aspect of God. Thus God as All-That-Is is the sum total of everything. This view has served man by helping him let go of limiting beliefs about God. Man thus begins to open up to the infinity that is God.

However, problems arise when man observes and experiences what he dislikes. If God is All-That-Is, how can God be pain and suffering, war and starvation? Man still wants God to be only the aspects of creation that are desired. Man wants God to be only the good and can't understand the presence of that which is not good.

It was from this that man adopted the concept of Karma to explain the existence of that which is not desired. Here the devil is hidden within. 'It is your sins that attract to you that which is unpleasant,' they say.

XX – JUDGMENT

May we suggest a new way to view God; a way to set you free from the Wheel of Karma; a way that can serve you through this next phase of growth?

Rather than viewing God as everything and everyone, view God as nothing: the no thing, the no one. See God as that which is in between, the 'o' in between the 'g' and the 'd': the zero.

Zero existed before time and space, before the first second, before the first atom. At zero, there is no separation, no beginning and no end. As soon as there was an observer, there was the observed, and from the zero came the one and the two.

This is a great secret. The God consciousness exists **in between** the good and the evil.

When meditating, you use the sacred word 'om', known as the sound of life or creation. From the 'o', the zero comes the ongoing vibration of the 'm', matter and man. From the nothing is cast forth the everything. Every utterance of om is a remembrance; it is a celebration of the ever flowing creation of the everything from the nothing.

The pieces of everything are not God. They are merely the reflections of one's **thoughts**. If you observe something you dislike, change your thoughts about it. God is not that which you dislike. God is not that which you like. That which you like or dislike is only a part of God created by you enabling you to observe and experience your thoughts. In seeing that which is, you know that which was thought. But God existed before thought and outside of thought. No thought can hold all of what God is.

The beauty of life is in the choosing. By choosing that which you think, you create that which you observe and experience. The infinite allowing of God enables all to create their own experience without bound. If God were to limit your creating, its own creating would be limited.

God is not outside of you. God is not outside of anyone or anything. God is within.

God is the 'am' within every statement of being.

When you say, 'I **am** John,' or 'I **am** Johannes,' God is in between you and your identity.

When you say, 'I **am** tired,' or 'I **am** sad,' God is in between you and your experience.

When you say, 'I **am** working,' or 'I **am** playing,' God is in between you and your action.

When you say, '*Io **sono** venuto,*' or, '*Je **suis** allé,*' God is in between you and your past.

To see the **bigger** picture, rise above to the perspective of your higher self. To see the **complete** picture, go within, into the nothingness, in between time and space, to the everlasting state of being. Here, there is no I or you; there is no here or there, there is no past or future, there is no doing, becoming or experiencing, there only is, like the sun—*solo è, come il sole*.

What, you may ask, separates your daily experience from the experience of Oneness? Ego. Ego is the giver of individuated experience. The ego, like your body, is a creation of your higher self and is a vehicle for experiencing separation.

Yet, it is within your choice to view the illusion of separation as a prison of isolation. Many, in search of salvation, have decided that the battle of duality is to cast out the ego and to lay aside the body.

These are not your **prisons**. They are your **children**. Yes, you can cast them aside or lose yourself within them, but the greatest glory comes from neither and both.

It is not by waking up or falling asleep that we come to know who we really are. Rather, it is the two working together: the repetition of submerging into one and then emerging out to the other. The point of life is not death, nor death rebirth, yet one will forever lead to the other.

It is in this way that the one separated can experience its piece while THE ONE united experiences its peace.

Through raising and nurturing your children: mind, body, and ego, you gain proficiency in your creating. You thus increase your power and your yield. THE ONE grants each piece as much energy as it can wield, for in obtaining power and transmitting energy, that individual portion better comes to know more of the whole.

Do not fear or condemn the misuse of power; neither fear nor condemnation will save you from it. It is only the recognition and acceptance of one's **own** power that will set you free of the illusion of lack and suffering. You alone create your experience. All paths lead to Source and all choices are valid.

TEN OF WANDS

In numerology, the one through nine lead up to the ten, yet ten is merely the one of another cycle. In this way, you have completed a journey, a journey that has led you here, into your purpose and into your gifts. From here, a new journey unfolds.

To consider the journey's entirety before taking the first step is to see only the burden of the task. Joy and bliss can only be found when taking each step in the moment.

XXI – THE WORLD

Before we complete this communication, we wish to convey to you one final aspect; it is called the Cycle of Creation. It is the same as the Wheel of Life or Wheel of Fortune, rather viewed from a higher perspective. We wish to teach this to you, to remind you of what you already know, so that you may teach and remind the others.

In the beginning, there was only THE ONE. THE ONE existed within a continual state of everlasting being, liken to an eternal flame.

Through eons of time, THE ONE became aware of itself and this sparked thought. Fire gave birth to air.

THE ONE wished to know itself, observe itself, and study itself. Through observation, THE ONE saw that it was giving birth to thoughts, and these thoughts were alive. Focus on thought gave rise to more thought and through the Law of Attraction, these thoughts sought like to like.

Over more eons of time, the swirling bodies of thought coalesced and became dense. Soon, matter was born. Air gave birth to earth.

Through thought, the entire physical Universe was created.

THE ONE, experiencing itself as Creator, was pleased with its creating. Yet **pleasure** was, in and of itself, something new. The Creator, looking back on Creation, felt. Thus earth gave birth to water.

Feeling is the **reaction** to **creation**. Notice that they are the same word, nothing added; nothing removed. Reaction, emotion, is nothing more than creation transformed into experience. It is this experience that excited the Creator and inspired anew. And look at that word: **inspire**. THE ONE, the everlasting fire, was inspired, **in-fired**, by its own creation. Through water, fire was reborn.

So THE ONE thought, in thinking created, in creating experienced, and through experiencing was inspired anew. This is the Cycle of Creation.

The Journey of the Fool is from where you are to where you want to be. You have all of the time in the world, yet there is no reason for you to wait. The entire Universe conspires to help you travel. You, nevertheless, have to make the journey. Every step along the way prepares you for a place further down the road. If you were to jump to the end, you would find yourself unable to handle, accept, and be where you are.

Accept or not what is offered. The choice is yours and all choices are valid. There are times when you will fail to see the Perfection that is. Within your displeasure, you will ask, 'Why is it this way?' The answer is that you simply have not yet created it the way you wish it to be.

When one journey ends, another begins. Walk this beautiful earth knowing that she loves you, supports you, and feeds you. You are blessed beings, every single one of you. You are the glory of God and an ever-significant piece of All-That-Is. You are never alone. You are never less than. You are never separate. You are loved beyond words.

Walk the Cycle of Creation: follow your individual star, your guiding light. Create your life experience as is pleasing to you. Be what you wish to be in this illusion of separation. Know that your service of others is simultaneously your service of self.

And never forget that you are loved beyond words.

#   #   #

EPILOGUE

J ohn and Johannes left the Temple of Luxor and trudged back to the inn…dazed, partly from the intense, midday sun, but mostly from the session. They felt overwhelmed by the message John had channeled.

Are we being asked to deliver these teachings to mankind?— John wondered. *How are we supposed to do that? Ra, you didn't give us further instruction? Seth, where do we go from here?*

Ra told them that they are never alone, and yet each felt completely alone, albeit together.

How am I supposed to go back to any semblance of a normal life after that?—Johannes thought. *I am not a teacher; I am a businessman.*

One journey had indeed ended. That much was well understood. The next journey, however, was just beginning…

ABOUT THE AUTHOR

David P. Tangredi is an intuitive guide. He employs archetypal tools such as Tarot, Astrology, and Numerology to bolster, assist, and inspire. Foundationally, he utilizes healing energies and the Akashic Records within all of his work.

David first achieved success as a Software Engineer and Architect. In 2005, he began the transition from technology to philosophy, from physics to metaphysics. Instead of writing code and technical specs, he now writes a blog and books. His core goals remain the same. He continues to combine logical, problem solving skills with creativity, intuition, and intention to help individuals accomplish their ambitions.

In recent years, David founded **A Fool's Inclination**. We are all fools on this journey called life. Guidance is always available, but often appears as subtle inclinations. The archetypal Fool teaches through his example. He shows us the joy and bliss that can be experienced by living in the present moment. He reminds us that the courageous are not fearless and that through increased awareness everything becomes easier.

David divides his time between writing and working with clients in private sessions, group workshops, and seminars. He is based in Austin, Texas, where the city slogan is "Keep Austin Weird." Can you think of a better place for a Fool?

Visit afoolsinclination.com to learn more.

Scribe
to the
Pantheon
of Rome

0 – *Zero* – **Nihil**

Zéro – Zero – Cero – Null

Zero existed before time and space, before the first second, before the first atom. At zero, there is no separation: no beginning and no end. As soon as there was an observer, there was the observed, and from the zero came the one and the two...

0 – 0 – 0

J ohn carefully ran his index finger under the flap, breaking the wax seal. He pulled out the contents: a letter, as expected, but he also immediately discovered what provided the additional bulk. He placed the Egyptian currency aside and read the letter...

1 – *One* – I

Un – Uno – Uno – Eins

R a? Seth? Is anyone here with me?" John looked around, but didn't recognize anything he was seeing. "Where am I?" he wondered. Something felt odd, but he didn't know why.

Up ahead, a small cabin piqued John's interest. Actually, it looked like a miniature castle, or maybe a part of one. It was the **size** of a small cabin, but the façade was topped with a crenelated roofline, characteristic of a medieval fortress.

As John got closer, he saw the deep moat that surrounded the structure. He then asked himself, "How do I know it is deep? The water is dark and murky." The moat was too wide to jump over, and too ominous to swim in, so he decided to walk around it to see if there was a way across.

As he circled the building, each face came into view: the second, the third, and then the fourth. They all looked identical. He counted as he went along, but was never quite sure how many sides there were. Not a window or a door was found in any of them, and never a bridge across the moat.

Why does this fortress feel so familiar?

He continued a bit further until he faced the next side squarely. From that angle, he could only see the one wall. He examined it intently and could almost feel the texture of the stone as if touching it with his hands.

Where have I seen stone like that before?

John began searching his memory for clues, but was interrupted by a screech. He looked up and saw a golden hawk circling overhead. It screeched a second time and then soared toward the horizon.

John watched the bird until he could no longer make out its shape. It simply became a black dot barely visible against the dusky sky. His eyes moved down to the horizon—to the silhouette of three pyramids that separated the dimly lit sky from the dark sandy land.

"I have to get back to Cairo! What have I done?"

Urgency took hold of him and he began running towards the pyramids, following the hawk's lead.

"Is there enough time?" John said aloud. "Please tell me there's enough time."

"You have all the time in the world; there is no reason for you to hurry."

John stopped in his tracks and spun around to see who had spoken to him. He saw nothing but sand in all directions.

"Who's there?" he called out to the emptiness.

"Do you not recognize my voice?" came the reply.

"Ra, is that you?"

"Yes my son. I am Ra."

"Ra, what is happening? I need to get back to Cairo…right now! Can you take me?" There was worry and panic in John's voice.

"I can guide you, yes, but what is your concern?" Ra said calmly.

"I don't know. I just have to get there before…before I don't know **what** happens!"

"John, do you remember what we told you about the Journey of the Fool?"

"You told me a lot about it," John said, a bit annoyed.

"The most important part is this: the Journey of the Fool is always from where you are to where you want to be."

"Yes, I remember now."

"So, you are clear where you want to be, yes?" Ra asked.

"Yes!" John said impatiently. "I need to get to Cairo and soon!"

Ra's patience was unending. "I understand, my son, but do you know where you are?"

"Well…no. I thought you could help me with that." John looked around, but saw no landmarks, no road signs.

"My son, the greater part of most journeys is figuring out where one is. That is the point—or rather the **starting** point. Ha!"

"So, does this mean you aren't going to tell me?" John lowered his head, feeling defeated.

"Dear **one**, did I not give you **two** eyes with which to see? Behold your here and now. You look, but you do not **three**!"

"**Three**!? What does **that** mean?" John voiced the question, but he somehow knew that Ra had already departed. He fell to the ground, sobbing. He covered his eyes with his hands and the world went dark. When he removed his hands, however, he still could not see.

"Ra? Ra! Where are you?" John screamed, and his voice echoed. He was no longer out in the middle of the desert. It was now dark and cold and he was inside...

Is this a cave?

The ground was no longer the soft, warm sand of the desert; rather, it was a cold, hard, stone floor. He stood and walked slowly, his hands scanning the darkness in front of him. The sound of his footsteps echoed, causing him to shiver with fright. The air around his hands was somehow cooler than the air around his face, and then he felt the cold wall in front of him. He traced his fingers along the mortar around the stone; the shape was a rectangle.

A stone wall. Am I in a prison cell?

And then John understood. He put his ear to the stone and could hear the faint sound of water flowing in the moat just beyond the wall.

"How did I get in here? More importantly, how do I get out? Ra, help! I'm trapped!"

"Look first...then see. Know where you are...and know where you want to be. Then take the first step."

www.ingramcontent.com/pod-product-compliance
Lightning Source LLC
Chambersburg PA
CBHW030919260626
47169CB00002B/329